**Charity swiped angrily at a tear.
She'd run away, if she had anyone to run to.
It wasn't right they were all dead.**

On impulse, she jumped to the ground. "I'll go anyway," she muttered. "Eat nuts and berries and live in the woods."

"Will you go alone?" a low voice asked.

Sucking in her breath, she whirled around. Less than twenty feet away, grasping his musket, stood a tall young brave. Stripes of red and black paint blurred his striking features. His dark brown eyes riveted her in place. This warrior was like no other and the most savagely handsome man she'd ever seen.

God help her. She should flee now, but could only stare, open-mouthed. She swept her disbelieving gaze over the loose black hair brushing an open buckskin vest that revealed his bronzed chest and shoulders molded into contours of muscle. An elkskin breechclout left a great deal of his hard thighs exposed. Despite the dread hammering in her chest, a fiery blush burned her cheeks. But it was the sheathed knife hanging on his left side and the lethal tomahawk slung on his right that snapped Charity from her near-trance.

In a rush of memories, she recalled the stories of her father's death under the scalping knife and neighbors who'd suffered the same violent fate. No Indians had been spotted in their settlement since the Shawnee grew hostile and war had erupted nine years ago, but the warfare had ended. Hadn't it?

Clenching ice-cold fingers, she dug her nails into her palms. "What in God's name are you doing here?" she forced past the dry lump in her throat.

"Watching you."

Praise for Beth Trissel

"I love historical romances. They are one of my favorites and anymore when I think of an historical I think of Beth Trissel. She is an author who has proved herself over time...a beautiful storyteller."
~Bella Wolfe, Reviewer for You Gotta Read

"Ms. Trissel's alluring style of writing invites the reader into a world of fantasy and makes it so believable it is spellbinding."
~Camellia, The Long and Short Of It Reviews

"With characters so perfectly created, like intricate works of art, you feel each and every emotion that they possess."
~Angela Simmons, Reviewer for Book-Views.com

"Ms. Trissel has captured the time period wonderfully. As I read I am transported back to the mid-1700's on the American frontier...I felt I was there through Ms. Trissel's descriptions and settings. I look forward to reading more of Beth Trissel."
~Shelia, Reviewer for Two Lips

"In addition to creating memorable characters, Ms. Trissel makes wonderful use of descriptive language."
~J. Thomas, The Long and Short Of It Reviews

Red Bird's Song

by

Beth Trissel

This is a work of fiction. Names, characters, places, and incidents either are the product of the author's imagination or are used fictitiously, and any resemblance to actual persons living or dead, business establishments, events, or locales, is entirely coincidental.

Red Bird's Song

Cover Art by *Rae Monet*

The Wild Rose Press
PO Box 708
Adams Basin, NY 14410-0706
Visit us at www.thewildrosepress.com

Publishing History
First American Rose Edition, 2010
Print ISBN 1-60154-812-5

Published in the United States of America

Dedication

To my dearest sister Catherine
whose unwavering support has encouraged me in
my writing over these many years.
Back in the 1990's, she cautioned me that getting
Red Bird's Song published
might take more than a few months.
But she stayed the course and so did I.

Chapter One

*Autumn 1764, Middle River in
the Shenandoah Valley of Virginia*

With the wariness of a hunted fox, Wicomechee crept along the hazy river to scout out any danger from Long Knives in the Scots' settlement. Damp leaves muffled his soft tread. Farther behind him, the war party stole through the early morning mist. Smokey-white hills rose on either side of the swift water and beyond these spread the veiled Alleghenies.

The day before, he'd looked out over this fair valley from a lofty mountain ridge. All that his eyes beheld had been Indian hunting ground time out of mind until British settlers came and claimed it in the name of the Crown. For nearly as long as he remembered, his people had fought against the scorn of English policies. Like lightning, war parties struck all along the frontier. Bitter defeat seemed their lot. Today these intruders would receive a scorching reminder that the Shawnee hadn't forgotten whose land this once was.

And yet, beneath Wicomechee's anger a sense of anticipation tugged at the corners of his mind. Hadn't his grandfather predicted he would find a priceless treasure in the valley? 'Seek for your treasure by the river. Once you have found it, do not let go,' the farsighted man had said.

What could these people possess of such value...ample goods, yes, but wealth? He was baffled, as was his adopted brother, although the

1

wanted Englishman had his own reason for accompanying him on this raid—a woman.

Stopping in his tracks, Wicomechee sniffed the tang of wood smoke from a settler's hearth. The homestead they sought lay just ahead, as his English brother had said. Ears attuned to the snap of every twig, eyes scouring the hazy foliage, he glided forward. At the first sign of trouble, he'd sound the warning cry of a jay. If they were fortunate, no one would see them coming.

****

"I'm turning twenty on my next birthday, not thirty." Gripping the edge of the trestle table, Charity Edmondson breathed in the pungent herbs hanging from the blackened rafters overhead and braced for a response. It came in the twitch of a cat's tail.

"Humph." Aunt Mary turned from the crackling hearth and wiped her hands on a striped apron as if readying for battle. Her plump face, still fair for her years, creased beneath the fiery-red tendrils that strayed from her linen cap. "I was a bride at sixteen. Emma wed by your age."

Charity flung up her hands in a vain attempt to ward off her tenacious aunt. "That doesn't make me an old maid."

"Near enough," the disgruntled woman said.

Charity glanced at her cousin, Emma, seated on the bench along one side of the oak table. Surely Emma, of all people, wouldn't have her marry where she had no desire to. Wasn't it enough that this domineering matron had bullied one of them into a loveless union? But Charity couldn't quite see the young woman's expression. Emma bent near her trencher of corn mush, dark lashes swept over delicate pink cheeks.

Aunt Mary gave a sniff. "Enough dilly dallying, lass. I'll see you wed afore snow flies. Your uncle's given his blessing to Rob Buchanan and there's an end to it."

"We're childhood friends," Charity argued. "That's all."

"Oh, aye? You know right well Rob's keen on the match."

"Mightn't I be allowed to choose whom I'll wed?"

"If only you would," her aunt snorted. "As you seem bent on remaining a maid, we must do the choosing or have yer keeping 'til the end of our days. And then what, lass?"

Charity faced an indomitable force, one she'd not overcome, today, at least. "May we speak of this later? I'm off nut-gathering now."

Emma laid down her spoon. "I'll come with you."

Like a busy wren checking her brood, Aunt Mary darted sharp eyes at her daughter. "You mustn't tire yourself, my girl. Your time's drawing near." She flicked a glance at Charity. "See yer back by mid-day. Rob's calling."

Heaven preserve her. She was as good as betrothed—and trapped. Charity fled out the door of the log house to the stoop and snatched up a woven basket. Hickory smoke from the massive stone chimney tinged the foggy air. The thunk of an ax rang out, likely Emma's husband, Edward, splitting wood. He was a hardworking man, yet Emma bore him scant affection. Another had a claim on her heart but he'd mysteriously vanished—as Charity should do before Aunt Mary had her way.

Wild geese called from the river, mingling their high-pitched cries with the rushing water in a primal summons. *There*! Charity made for the tapestry of red-gold trees.

She skidded down the dewy hill, scattering black-faced sheep. Her burgundy cloak was wet to the knees by the time she'd reached the split-rail fence that enclosed the meadow. She unlatched the slatted gate, darted through and swung it shut, then raced into the brilliant oaks. A branch snagged her cap, freeing her riotous spill of auburn hair.

That's better, more like she used to be before Aunt Mary's dictates. She'd fetch the cap later. Catching up her green skirts, she scrambled down the rocky bank. Startled geese flapped up from the water at her arrival. Rapid wings circled above her, disappearing into the whiteness, and the honks faded. How glorious it would be to fly up into the sky far away from the demands of her relations.

As flying wasn't a possibility, Charity climbed onto the wide flat stone at the water's edge. Her troubled thoughts tumbled with the current. Surely one accustomed to running free as she'd once been under her indulgent father and then her older brother's care shouldn't be so restrained—forever. Charity swiped angrily at a tear. She'd run away if she had anyone to run to. It wasn't right they were all dead.

On impulse, she jumped to the ground. "I'll go anyway," she muttered. "Eat nuts and berries and live in the woods."

"Will you go alone?" a low voice asked.

Sucking in her breath, she whirled around. Less than twenty feet away, grasping his musket, stood a tall young brave. Stripes of red and black paint blurred his striking features. His dark brown eyes riveted her in place. This warrior was like no other and the most savagely handsome man she'd ever seen.

God help her. She should flee now, but could only stare, open-mouthed. She swept her disbelieving gaze over the loose black hair brushing an open buckskin vest that revealed his bronzed chest and shoulders molded into contours of muscle. An elkskin breechclout left a great deal of his hard thighs exposed. Despite the dread hammering in her chest, a fiery blush burned her cheeks. But it was the sheathed knife hanging on his left side and the lethal tomahawk slung on his right that snapped Charity from her near-trance.

In a rush of memories, she recalled the stories of her father's death under the scalping knife and neighbors who'd suffered the same violent fate. No Indians had been spotted in their settlement since the Shawnee grew hostile and war had erupted nine years ago, but the warfare had ended. Hadn't it?

Clenching ice-cold fingers, she dug her nails into her palms. "What in God's name are you doing here?" she forced past the dry lump in her throat.

"Watching you."

He stepped closer to her in deerskin moccasins that fitted well up his sinewy legs. Feet adept at stealing through the woods made no sound on the layer of fallen leaves.

Paralyzed, she gaped at him. His English was fluent, as smooth as his approaching steps, uttered with a voice as warm as his eyes...him...like the man in her dream...the one who'd kissed her. But that was insane.

He slid the musket over his shoulder by a woven strap. A faint smile curved his lips. "You wish to go live among the trees? Come with me."

Instinctively, she shied back.

He closed the distance between them and extended a corded arm circled with twin bands of silver. His voice went from butter to grit. "Now."

Musket shots cracked above the rapid water. War whoops rang through the trees. Charity scrambled back with a shriek.

He lunged at her. Jerked fully to life, she flung the basket at his chest and spun around. Catching up her skirts, she raced over the uneven ground along the river.

She had only the hair of a head start, but by

heaven she could run. Hadn't her brother, Craig, said as much?

Clinging to his praise, she tore through grass heavy with seed heads. The slap of her shoes and swish of her petticoats sounded alongside the rapid water. She sensed but didn't hear the warrior's stealthy pursuit. Dodging rocks masked by the haze, she hurtled across downed branches, risking a nasty fall. But what did that matter with the hound of hell snapping at her heels?

Faster! Heart pounding in her ears, she leapt over a moss-encrusted log and stumbled. Grabbing a bent sapling for support, she righted herself and sprang away through a blur of color. Her chest thudded. She could scarcely get her breath and shot a glance over her shoulder.

Lord, no! Her pursuer's glove-like moccasins had the advantage over her square-toed shoes, as did his ground-covering strides. He rapidly narrowed the gap between them. God save her or she'd be killed and scalped like her father.

Summoning every ounce of speed, she spurted ahead, sides heaving, pain stabbing her chest. She flew around a bend in the river and stopped short. A prickly tangle of burdock and brambles blocked the path. She looked wildly around. No way through. Shooting to the side, she clamored up the bank.

Down she went, sliding over loose stones, lurching forward with outstretched hands and scraping her palms. She ignored the sting and scrambled up to pelt through tall grass and spikes of mullein. If she hid among the stand of cedars just ahead, he might not find—too late. He'd come.

A scream ripped from her throat. She grabbed up a stout stick and spun around. Shaking the loose mane from her eyes, she brandished her makeshift weapon. "Stay back!"

He arched one black brow. "You think to strike

me with that?"

Before she heaved another ragged breath, he snatched it away. "What now?" he challenged.

She lunged, pushing against his rock-hard chest—like trying to dislodge an anvil. She dug in her heels and struggled to knock him off balance and down the slope. Not a prudent move. She'd unwittingly placed herself in his hands.

He snapped unyielding arms around her. "I have you."

She twisted, shrieking, in his steely grasp, kicking at his rooted legs and grinding her feet into the earth. The fragrance of spearmint charged the air. How ironic to die surrounded by such sweet scent.

Gripping her tightly, he forced her down to the leafy ground in a press of hard muscle and heated skin. His gleaming black hair spilled over her face as he pinned her thrashing arms. "Stop fighting me."

"I'll fight to the end!"

He straddled her and stilled her pummeling legs. "For your life? Have I tomahawk or knife in my hand?"

She gaped up at him, her breath rasping in her throat. Whether he spoke in bemusement or annoyance, she couldn't tell from his controlled expression, but the weapons remained at his side. And he wouldn't waste gunpowder and a lead ball on her when he could so easily kill her with a single blow.

"You'll let me live?" she gulped in short bursts.

"Did I not say you will come with me?"

She searched his eyes for signs of malice and saw none, only a keen watchfulness. Her stomach churned as he clasped her wrists with one hand and reached toward his waist.

A spasm shuddered through her. Had he only been tormenting her? Was he—even now—drawing his knife?

She squeezed her eyes shut, moaning, against the cruel blade. But no fatal kiss of steel met her throat. Instead, firm, warm fingers lightly stroked her cheek.

"I have no wish to do you harm. You are my captive."

She opened her eyes in breathless tension. There it was again, that piercing gaze. If she hadn't already been winded, one glance from him would have robbed her of air. She inhaled his scent, both intimidating and strangely compelling. Her panting eased. "What will you do?" she asked hoarsely.

"Slow you. You run like *peshikthe*, the deer."

He drew buckskin cord from the fringed, beaded pouch at his waist and bound her wrists. "Tell me your name."

"Charity Edmondson."

"Charity," he said with a pensive edge to his strangely accented baritone. "I do not know this English name."

"You know others?"

"Many." He shifted to her side and stood, pulling her up with him. "I am called Wicomechee."

In her distress, she echoed only the last two syllables. "Mechee?"

He took her arm. "This will serve. Come."

"Where?"

"Where you wish. The woods," he said with a hint of amusement.

"I never really meant to go," she stammered.

"Have care what you wish for."

She had prayed too and it certainly wasn't for this.

He forced her back past the trees along the river. In dread of what she'd find, Charity looked ahead to their log home on the hill. The clearing mist revealed several dozen warriors carrying away

Aunt Mary's prized woven blankets, cherished cooking pots, and sacks of cornmeal. Others bore cured hams, kegs of apple brandy and whiskey, to load the plunder on Uncle John's sturdy horses.

The gray mare, chestnut gelding, and black and white piebald tossed their heads and whinnied. Warriors grabbed at their reins while the speckled red-combed chickens cackled, flapping, in the yard. Squealing pigs loosed from their pen bolted through the garden, trampling orange pumpkins. The placid cow galloped into the woods behind the log barn.

Charity's burning thought was the fate of the others. "Aunt Mary! Uncle John! Emma! James—" she choked on her young cousin's name.

No one replied. She sought their familiar figures in mounting desperation. "What's become of them?"

"I cannot say," Wicomechee replied.

One answer came in the form of a woman's screams. Across the meadow, Emma struggled in the grasp of a fearsome warrior. The hair from the back and sides of his head had been plucked, leaving a glistening scalp lock on top. His powerful painted form eclipsed the petite young woman.

"No! Let her go!" Charity wrenched away from Wicomechee and bounded toward her cousin.

He sprang after her. Seizing her shoulders, he jerked her to a halt. "You wish to fight Chaka?"

"Help Emma, Mechee. Please."

Chaka snatched off Emma's cap to tug at the knot of hair on her fair head. Sunlit lengths cascaded to her waist. "That woman is the golden-haired one," Wicomechee said, as though this were of great significance. "Come."

Charity hastened with him. How did he know about Emma?

"Chaka!" Wicomechee shouted.

Chaka turned toward them with a menacing grin and combed his fingers suggestively through

9

Emma's blond curls.

Wicomechee spoke in his native tongue, but his anger needed no translation.

Chaka's taunting smile faded. Defiance glinting in his eyes, he grunted out a reply.

Wicomechee stopped a few yards away from them and hissed a command.

Chaka jerked the weeping woman around. "Waupee's?" he sneered, sweeping one hand at her swollen abdomen.

Charity stared in confusion. "What's happening?"

Wicomechee answered gruffly. "Chaka says this woman is not my brother's wife. She carries the child of another."

"Of course she's not. Emma is wed to Edward Estell."

"No longer. Waupee will want her back."

Charity couldn't fathom what claim this Waupee had to Emma. Only one matter was vital now and she shouted at the menacing brave who grasped her cousin. "Let Emma go!"

Chaka fastened black eyes on Charity. "*Metchi scoote.* You have much fire." He restrained the sobbing woman with one hand and gestured at Charity with his other. "Trade me for your red-haired woman, Wicomechee."

Charity shrank from Chaka's probing stare to press against Wicomechee who'd terrified her only minutes ago. Ironic, but he was her and Emma's best chance of survival.

He shook his head. "No trade."

Chaka returned his chilling grin to Charity. "I like your captive."

"Do not touch her."

"She is the daughter of an English dog." Chaka raked Emma with his contemptuous stare. "This one also."

"Release the wife of Waupee," Wicomechee demanded.

Chaka drew a wicked knife. "I'll have her scalp first."

Wicomechee sprang with the speed of a striking snake and clamped his fingers around Chaka's muscular arm. Chaka flung Emma to the grass and grappled with Wicomechee. Emma crawled out of their way and collapsed, shaking violently.

Charity ran to her cousin. Dropping to her knees, she bent over her protectively, unable to do more with bound wrists. "I pray the ruthless warrior doesn't win this, Emma."

The knife loosed from Chaka's grip, Wicomechee heaved his adversary onto his side. Wicomechee's chest rose and fell as he threaded Chaka's arm through his own legs, seizing it from behind and grasping his other. Charity was so engrossed in their combat she scarcely noticed the approaching rider until he was almost upon them.

She lurched from the battling warriors at the drum of hooves. "Who—"

****

Chest heaving from his all out struggle with Chaka, Wicomechee glanced around to see his English brother rein in his horse. The wind whipped the loose chestnut hair hanging around his shoulders and over his blue hunting shirt.

Charity sucked in her breath. "Good heavens. Colin Dickson?"

Wicomechee knew that English name, though he called the adopted warrior Waupee. Glancing to the side, he observed the golden haired woman huddled on the grass beside Charity. Tearful eyes the color of a brooding sky were fixed on the former Englishman as if he'd returned from the grave; so he might as well have done. He was dead to the white world.

Waupee rushed past the women to where

Wicomechee and Chaka clashed like two great elk. "Do we lack sufficient enemies that you two must battle—again?"

Wicomechee fought to keep the upper hand over the brave bucking in his hold. "Chaka would take your woman's scalp."

"By heaven, I'll have yours, Chaka!" Waupee hurled back, and drew the silver-mounted dagger from the sash at his waist.

"No," Wicomechee grunted, "I'll finish this." In a surge of power, like a mighty wind, he flung Chaka onto his back. Breathing hard, he bent over him, "Surrender the woman now."

"Take her," Chaka bit out. "I go."

Wicomechee rolled aside. The sullen brave stood, blood trickling from his mouth, and picked up his knife.

Waupee turned toward the golden haired one. "Are you all right, Emma?"

"Colin—" she sobbed.

"My poor darling." Fury replaced the fleeting tenderness in Waupee's blue eyes and he rounded on Chaka. "Bastard! If you ever come near her again I'll—" he caught himself, hissing the rest of his threat, one Wicomechee didn't doubt his ability to carry out. He had taught his brother well.

Chaka gave a grudging nod and turned away. Wicomechee might have forced him to relinquish Waupee's woman, but the look he shot at Charity in passing held vindictive promise. Her face whitened as he strode off across the meadow. Anger hazed Wicomechee's mind. Always, Chaka wanted what was his.

"I owe you, Wicomechee, for coming to Emma's aid."

Waupee's gratitude returned his focus to his white brother. "You owe me nothing. Now you have what you want?"

"Oh, yes." Waupee reached Emma in three strides and knelt beside her. He gathered her against him and she clung to him, weeping as though she'd never stop. He pressed his lips to her head. "Hush...no one will harm you now."

Charity seemed astonished at the attachment between the distraught woman and this former gentleman. Did none know?

With visions of furious Scotsmen on their heels, Wicomechee grasped her arm and pulled her up. "Come with me."

"Wait—please." Eyes searching, Charity swiveled her head at the smoky homestead. "What of the others?"

Wicomechee paused. "What of the family, *NiSawsawh?*"

Waupee looked up, remorse in his face. "I'm terribly sorry I didn't reach you sooner, Emma. I was securing the life of your little brother."

"James is safe? Thank God," she choked out against him.

Charity heaved an enormous sigh. "And Aunt Mary?"

"I expect she escaped."

Her lips trembled. "Uncle John?"

Waupee's jaw tightened; plainly, he'd rather not answer. "I tried to persuade John McLeod to surrender. He refused."

The woman called Emma cried, "What are you saying?"

"One brave grew impatient and fired. I deeply regret I was unable to prevent your father's death."

Charity crumpled like an injured bird tumbling to the ground. She staggered in Wicomechee's grasp and he steadied her with his hand on her shoulder. Her eyes flashed to his in surprise, as though she expected no kindness from a warrior. Then tears welled in her green gaze.

Emma seized Waupee's upper arms and shook him; his solid form yielded little under her frenzied assault. "I don't understand! You make it sound as if you're in charge!"

He grasped her wrists. "In a way, I am."

"How? Why? Your being here makes no sense—"

"Wicomechee and his grandfather found me in the frontier two years ago. I've lived with the Shawnee ever since."

"Couldn't you escape, Mister Dickson?" Charity asked.

Wicomechee cast her a disdainful look. "Where would Waupee go? The English seek his life."

Charity gulped. "*This* is Waupee? What kind of trouble drove you to the Indians, Mister Dickson?"

"A duel—"

Emma's strangled cry drowned him out. "I thought you were never coming back. Why have you returned now?"

"For your sake. When I learned war parties were headed to the valley, I agreed to lead one of the groups."

Emma's liquid gaze grew molten. "Colin—how could you?"

"To assure I was with the men coming here. Warriors are raiding settlements along this stretch of river. Was I simply to hope yours was overlooked? It's a prominent homestead."

Emma writhed to escape him and her blond hair flew about them both. "Traitor—"

"Stop this at once, Emma," Waupee said sternly, but failed to stem her mounting hysteria.

"Think of the baby," Charity pleaded, to no avail.

They could delay no longer. "Enough," Wicomechee said, and knelt beside the struggling woman. Clasping her face between his palms, he forced her to meet his flinty stare. "My brother is no traitor. We would find you. Shawnee take captives or leave bodies. Which do you prefer?"

Emma swallowed and grew still. Wicomechee dropped his hands and stood while she slumped, weeping, against Waupee.

Wicomechee waved at the trees. "We must go, *NiSawsawh*. The militia will chase us like a she-bear after her cubs."

Waupee stood, drawing the shaken women up with him. He glanced at Charity. "Is it necessary to bind that poor girl?"

"She runs like the deer. Perhaps I will bind her legs."

Charity reeled, stopped short by the tightening of Wicomechee's fingers on her arm. She eyed him uncertainly.

He returned her study with the inscrutability of a wolf. Better she not know his full intent.

Waupee shook his head at him. "You're frightening her."

"Good. She must not escape me."

"Give my brother no trouble, Miss Edmondson, and you will be well," Waupee said, and whistled for his horse.

"Don't leave me, Mister Dickson," she pleaded.

"We will meet often, Miss Edmondson. It's a long journey to the Ohio Country."

Not one Charity seemed persuaded she would survive. She stared after the retreating rider, auburn brows drawn beneath a smooth forehead. Her finely arched nose sniffed and lips the hue of the rosy dawn quivered.

A twinge of jealousy shot through Wicomechee. Shrugging off the volatile stab, he pulled his knife from the beaded skin sheath at his side. "Stay still," he said tersely, put out with himself.

Charity's shaky trust evaporated at the sight of the blade and she bolted. He sprang after her.

Circling his arm around her waist, he jerked her to a halt. "Do you not know the meaning of still?"

"And wait while you do what—slit my throat?"

"Your skirts, to pass more easily through the trees."

She stood as if poised for flight while he knelt and slashed through her petticoats. Wielding the knife like an old friend, he shortened the layers to just below her knees. Her cream-colored stockings and shapely legs were visible now. He must find some leggings to shield her skin from briars. Meanwhile, he savored the appealing sight.

Forcing his attention back to the task at hand, he stuffed some of the linen into his pouch. He retook her arm. "We are behind," he said, and sped her through the meadow so quickly she had to run to keep up with his strides.

Acrid smoke stained the blue sky. She slanted tearful eyes at the flames consuming the log house and outbuildings. Pity touched him at the pain in her face, but he would have another bout of hysteria on his hands if he didn't keep moving. He hurried her past the flaming homestead and field where her guardian lay beside the plow he'd never use again.

Charity jerked against him as if to run to her kinsman. "Uncle John was a good man! He wasn't even armed!"

Wicomechee pulled her up. "Hush."

She only reached midway up his chest and tilted her head to shout at him. "You are cowards to strike him down!"

He clapped his hand over her lips, imprisoning her in his arms. Enticing curves tempted him from beneath her cloak. She smelled of hickory smoke and the scent of soap clung to her hair. As his grandfather predicted, this enraged woman was the find of a lifetime and he must work fast to keep her.

Hot tears spilled over his hand. "I did not kill

your uncle," he said, easing his grip on her supple lips.

"Only because another killed him first."

"No. *NiSawsawh*, my brother, did not wish his death."

"You may be his friend, but you're my enemy and always—"

"Be still." He clamped his palm back down and sensed her defiance, as if she wanted to wrestle him to the ground as he had Chaka. "Or I will bind your mouth."

Charity gave a short nod and he slid his hand from her lips. She wiped her damp face on her cloak, smoldering rebellion in her eyes. Most women were easily suppressed. This one would bear close watching.

He steered her forward and they overtook the war party. The men's stony faces were set on swift retreat. He joined the single-file formation and positioned her in front of him. She hiked the trail in tearful silence, each step taking them farther away from the fenced-in meadows and plowed fields so beloved by settlers. As they ventured into the woods, the earthy musk of plants and crumbling leaves enveloped them. Here lay the realm of warriors and frontiersmen—his realm.

Shafts of light poured through the dark forest where the boughs had been torn away and storm-felled trees lay toppled like slain giants. The burnished leaves shone. Birdcalls echoed from high branches. A doe flashed her white tail, an elk bugled, sights and sounds that stirred Wicomechee's blood.

On they journeyed, and the sun heated the air even under the leafy cover. Charity's feet dragged. Wicomechee took her cloak. She wore no jacket, only a skirted-bodice laced up over her shift. The nut-brown top molded her rounded breasts, triggering a more rapid heartbeat in him than the march alone. As for her hair, he both admired and resented the coppery-red mantle. Like a scent long ago remembered, her hair lured him back into a past he'd shoved deep inside him, and yet, he yearned to run his fingers through the glowing spill.

Sweat trickled down over Charity's face, her chest heaved, and her shoulders sagged. She gazed longingly through the leaves at the stream. He would willingly let her stop to drink, but if he did they would fall far behind his party.

A root snagged her unsteady foot and she lurched onto the trail, striking her knee on a stone. She lay clutching her leg, shaking with sobs. If he didn't tend to her, some impatient brave might put a permanent end to her suffering.

Motioning the others past, he knelt beside her. "Charity, let me see." She made no objection as he turned her over and lightly pressed his fingers around her gashed knee.

She peered through pain-glazed eyes at the blood running down her torn stocking and gasped, "I've lamed myself."

"No." He slid his arms beneath her and lifted her.

She slumped in his hold.

Relishing the feel of his burden, he carried her past yellow chestnuts covered with scarlet vines, through drifts of tawny fern, to the stream. He laid her on a bed of moss beside the water. She sank down and was still as he cupped the cold water in his hands and poured it over her knee again and again to numb her injury.

"The cut is not deep. Very bruised."

She watched him take fluff from his pouch and pack the wound. "Buzzard down," he said. Retrieving a strip of linen, he bound the dressing in place. "Is the pain less?"

She gazed at him with wide eyes, her dark fringe of lashes beaded with tears, and nodded. "Thank you."

"You will not run from me now, I think." The late day sun touched his blade as he drew his knife and cut her cords.

She rubbed her wrists and bent near the stream to cup long mouthfuls of water. Lengths of her hair trailed in the clear ripples, mirroring the russet leaves swirling by. She was like a fair spirit of the woods. Her coloring blended with the autumn hues perfectly.

"I could drink forever," she said between gulps.

He knelt beside her to drink. "You would burst."

She splashed her face then flopped down onto her side at the stream's edge. "I should like to climb in there."

He tore his gaze from her bodice that had slipped down to reveal the tops of mounded breasts. Leaves colored like glass beads rustled overhead, but the shadows lengthened among the trees. "You would shake with cold. The day is far gone."

She closed her eyes. "If I had something to eat I would ask nothing more than to sleep for a while."

"What of the nuts and berries you will eat?"

She looked up at him in drowsy bewilderment.

"You spoke of this," he reminded her.

"Oh. I'm not able to seek anything now."

As he thought, she was ignorant of survival out here. Taking strips of dried venison from the pouch at his waist, he gave them to her. She devoured each scrap and ran the tip of her pink tongue over her lips.

"You eat like the wolf," he said, determined not to let her inviting mouth distract him from their urgent journey.

"Often I'm scolded for eating too little. Aunt Mary says I'm skinny, like a boy."

"You are nothing like a boy." He couldn't resist smoothing a tendril at her forehead. A responsive shiver ran through her. Fear alone, or something more? He looked at her for a moment then lowered his hand and stood. "We must go."

She remained as she was. "Let me rest a bit longer."

A doe couldn't have blended with the woodland any better. But they would not long have it to themselves. "I have no wish to face the Long Knives alone."

"Who?" she asked, pushing up on her elbows.

"The men you call militia. Come."

She sank back down onto the green moss. "Not yet."

Wicomechee narrowed his eyes at her. "Do not refuse me."

"But I'm too weary to move," she groaned.

"You will move, if you fear I will beat you."

Her mouth flew open. "You said you wouldn't harm me!"

"Nor do I wish to. If I am kind, you will not obey me."

"If you are cruel, I will hate you."

He set his jaw. She would not intimidate him.

She blinked and loosed one last arrow. "I'll tell Mister Dickson. He will punish you."

That shaft struck home. Wicomechee had never resented his adopted brother, and it especially annoyed him that she threatened to come between them like a blade wedged between two stones. "Get up, Charity," he growled.

She dragged herself to her feet, staggering with a cry. "I can't bear weight on it."

He reached into the brush and pulled out a stout stick. "Use this to walk with, not to strike me."

Her expressive face told him she'd rather the latter use. "How far have I to go?" she asked.

"We will journey until the stars are bright."

"I'll never make it, Mechee."

"You will. The deer is not only fast, she is strong."

Chapter Two

Like a deep well, the sleep Charity had fallen into lay far beneath the realm of consciousness. Her exhausted mind and body wanted to remain in that distant place, but an insistent snuffling on her cheek nudged her back to wakefulness. She rolled onto her side, only to have the moist assault commence on her other cheek.

Brushing at the offender, she discovered a wet nose and tongue. Had some wild animal pushed open the door and entered their log home? If so, he was extremely friendly.

She opened her eyes to find a dog licking her face. The McLeod's didn't have a dog, although many of their neighbors did. "Where did you come from?" she asked drowsily.

Stroking his floppy ears, she explored the surrounding darkness—too much darkness. Not only that, but a damp cold permeated the room and she was chilled through. Orange coals should glow in the hearth. Aunt Mary would never allow the fire to die out.

"Sit," she commanded the exuberant hound.

He settled obediently at Charity's feet allowing her a better look around. Faint gray light emanated from what appeared to be an opening, not a doorway, and she heard breathing. Far more breathing than she was used to. The sudden realization came to her that she wasn't in the McLeod's log house. Where in the world was she?

She sprang up, crying out as the pain in her knee jolted her to horrific awareness. Fiery images rushed back—the burning homestead, their animals gone mad, Uncle John lying dead. Wherever she was, unseen warriors surrounded her.

"Charity—"

"Mechee?" She stumbled over his rising figure.

He caught her as she fell. "What the—" he broke off, colliding with the scrambling animal. He pulled her down with him and landed on his back. Dry leaves crunched beneath them.

Her chest made sudden impact against his. Gasping, she sprawled atop him, closer than she'd ever been to any man—a startling sensation.

"The wee dog found me," she said breathlessly. "Don't harm him."

"No." Wicomechee held her a moment longer than necessary before shifting her to one side. The worried dog licked at her hand. "Stay," he said in low tones, and relocated her newly found friend. "Come, Charity. Lie on the blanket."

She couldn't even see it in their tomb-like surroundings. "Where are we?"

"A cave in the mountains."

A smothering sensation enveloped her, emphasized ten-fold by the inky blackness. Bears and mounds of rattlesnakes were known to den up in caves. Worse, she shared this confined space with an unseen human enemy.

Heart racing, she bolted upright. "Get me out of here!"

Men stirred on every side of her. Sleepy voices grunted.

"Hush. You will wake all." Grasping her shoulders, Wicomechee pushed her down onto the woolen blanket.

She struggled to rise, choking back the scream begging her throat for release. "Please. I beseech you."

He forced her to remain where she was. "Calm

23

down."

"I can't. If I don't get out—"

"Shhhh…" He bent over her and spoke in her ear. "Hear me, Charity. I will take you from here if I must."

Her panic eased slightly. "You will? You promise?"

"Have I not said? You see the way, just there." He pointed to the ghostly opening then wrapped the edges of the blanket around her. "You shake like a leaf in the wind."

It whistled beyond the cave and the cold air blew inside. Despite the chill, she'd far rather bolt out into the teeth of the bluster and lie beneath the stars than remain in here. "It's so dark, Mechee," she said in a small voice.

He lay down beside her so that his shoulder pressed against hers. "You fear the dark?"

Denial was pointless. "And those it holds."

"None seek to harm you."

She was acutely aware of men slumbering all around her. "Chaka could kill me before I even knew."

"No. I will keep you safe," Wicomechee reassured her.

She relaxed a little more. "How long have we been here? I don't remember coming."

"Night is far gone. I brought you."

Memory returned of him forcing her to trudge on and on through the dark woods until she'd slumped onto the ground weeping uncontrollably. She must have fallen asleep the instant he'd lifted her. A sharp twinge of resentment ran through her. "You were cruel—"

"For bringing you?"

"For making me go on."

"That was cruel? You do not know the meaning of this word," he said gruffly.

"I fear you will teach me."

He turned onto his side facing her. Even in the blackness she felt the force of his personality. "Because I made you walk? Has no one made you walk, made you work?"

"Not like you did," she said through chattering teeth.

"I tended your knee, fed you, carried you. Was I to leave you along the trail?"

"Someone would have found me."

"Or another war party. If hunger and cold did not kill you first. You would perish out here."

"Maybe so,". she argued. "But you were still harsh."

He made an impatient sound under his breath. "If I warm you, will you say I am harsh?"

A startled gasp escaped her as he pulled her against his chest, molding her to him. She had the sense of his hard thighs and long legs pressed along hers. His scent enveloped her, a blend of earth, trees, and wind mingled with his own unique essence.

"Do you suffer now?" he whispered.

All protest died on her lips. She was too stunned to speak. The heat from his solid warmth penetrated the cloth between them, easing her chill. Yet this new awareness of his strong body lying next to hers was stirring in a way she'd never experienced. Only her father and brother had ever held her, and never like this. Nor had their embrace evoked any of the odd quivers fluttering inside her now.

What on earth was wrong with her? She should beg him to let her go, insist, if he would heed her, but the feel of him was so unexpectedly inviting...the masculine scent emanating from him oddly comforting, and she was sorely in need. Berating her weakness, she remained as she was.

He settled onto his back and nestled her in the

crook of his arm. "You can bear my punishment?"

Refusing to concede any gratification, she said nothing.

"Sleep, stubborn one."

Charity's last sensation as she drifted into oblivion was of Wicomechee lightly stroking her hair...like the man in her dream, but he couldn't possibly be him. She must have struck her head as well as her knee.

****

The second time Charity opened her eyes, sunlight filtered through the rock walls of the spacious cave. Golden rays slanted across Wicomechee and Colin Dickson seated on one side of her speaking quietly together. Chestnut hair fell below the Englishman's shoulders, not tied back as he'd worn it two years ago, and the fine clothes were gone. His high top moccasins and leggings were like Wicomechee's, though his blue hunting shirt covered his thighs.

Lying perfectly motionless, she shifted her drowsy focus to Wicomechee and lingered there. This was her first opportunity to study him without being observed in return.

Streaks of paint smudged his face, but *savage*, the term she was used to hearing, did not apply to him. There were characteristics in his mannerism that reminded her of Colin, the way he tilted his head, gesturing with long tapered fingers, his earnest expression and fluency, as though he were a mix of Shawnee and English.

Perhaps Colin had transferred some of his finer qualities to his adopted brother. Wicomechee was undeniably attractive. She'd never expected that in a warrior. His eyes reminded her of dark pools where the deep-woods fern grow. His nose, neither too large nor too small, complimented his smooth brow, high cheekbones and strong chin. Nor could she fault his gleaming hair, or muscular chest partly revealed beneath the cream-colored hunting shirt open at the neck. But his intimacy in the night left her bewildered, as did her disquieting response.

Colin's presence was reassuring. He was about the same age her brother, Craig, would have been if he'd lived, eight and twenty. In a comforting way Colin seemed like an older brother and he had some control over these warriors, although the close bond between him and Wicomechee perplexed her.

The Englishman held a sleeping little girl in his arms. Brown ringlets concealed her face and a striped blanket wrapped her. Charity hadn't seen any other captives taken. "Mister Dickson, whom have you got there?"

Colin shifted his gaze to Charity. Sadness hazed the blue depths. "Lily McCue."

Charity cringed. "What of Lily's family?" she asked, dreading his reply.

Grim lines edged Colin's mouth. "Dead."

Her stomach twisted in a sick knot. She envisioned Mister McCue lying in the field and his young wife crumpled by the hearth. "No," she cried softly. "I liked the McCues."

Colin blew out his cheeks in a heavy sigh. "So did I. One of the other war parties attacked them. I could in no way intervene for their lives."

Charity sat up, feeling her aches from yesterday's ordeal. Helpless to alter the McCue's grisly fate, she fixed accusing eyes on Wicomechee. How could she, for one single moment, forget who—or what—he was?

****

The fire in Charity's jewel-like eyes and the tremor at her pretty mouth told Wicomechee she sought a target to strike. He could stare endlessly at this English beauty, but had the distinct impression he was about to be attacked.

27

She loosed the first volley. "How can your people be so heartless?"

He bristled. Here was this glorious girl in all her ignorance daring to berate him. "You speak to me of caring, daughter of the Long Knives? Your people cause us much suffering, also to Shawnee women and children."

"That doesn't make it right to attack ours, or unarmed men," she flung back.

"Would you have our warriors wait until your men stare at us down a musket barrel? And leave your women to birth an army of sons to grow up to fight us and steal our land?"

She sputtered. "That's not what I meant."

"Yet this is what I know. You have no understanding."

"No. But I have," his adopted brother, Waupee, interceded. "Man to man. That's how war should be conducted, if it must be. What chance have these helpless ones?" he asked, looking from the child he cradled to his woman still asleep beneath a dark blue blanket.

Wicomechee's conscience chided him, but the hardship his people endured ate at him like a festering wound. "Shawnee anger is great, *NiSawsawh*."

"And you know I despise British rule in America."

"The English will not allow us to trade for what we need. Without powder, shot, muskets, how are we to hunt, to eat? They must pay for the suffering they bring," Wicomechee insisted. "Perhaps then they will hear us."

Waupee shook his head glumly. "I despair of them ever hearing. Men in power are far removed from the harsh reality of life in the frontier." Lily whimpered restlessly and he patted her back. "Hush, little darling," he soothed, and spoke again to

Wicomechee. "It is not they who suffer from the rage their scornful policies create, but these."

"Many helpless ones are also stung when the hornets fly in anger. This, I too, regret," Wicomechee conceded.

Charity's baffled gaze slid between them, settling on Wicomechee. "What will happen to Lily?"

He pointed across the cave to the warriors clustered in sunbeams and shadowed corners. The mood of the group was relaxed, partly due to the strong drink taken from homesteads. The casks had been tapped. Braves poured the brew into wooden and stoneware cups, sharing the stash between them. He singled out one man with the sinewy look of a lean wolf.

"Wacuchathi took her captive to adopt in place of the daughter he lost to white man's sickness."

Charity glared at the unaware brave. "That's wrong."

"Is it better she dies?" Wicomechee asked.

"That warrior took part in the murder of Lily's family." Charity turned to Waupee. "Can you do nothing for her, Mister Dickson?"

He eyed Charity in sorrowful resignation. "It is Wacuchathi's right to keep Lily, but he doesn't object if I care for her until we reach the village."

"Why did all of the McCue's have to die?"

Wicomechee answered simply. "No warrior wanted them."

"Captives are taken for different reasons," Waupee said. "Lily was the only one they felt inclined to trouble with."

."Aren't some captives later tortured, Mister Dickson?" Charity asked with a hitch in her voice.

"Sometimes in revenge for braves lost in battle. Not you, Miss Edmondson," he hastened to add. "None of you are destined for torture."

She shifted uneasily. "And if we were?"

"I would do all in my power to aid you. Far more captives are adopted into the tribe and treated well than those tortured. Some are also sold or traded."

The tremble in her lower lip belied the proud tilt of her chin. "You make us sound like slaves."

"For all intents you are," Waupee said.

She started to speak to Wicomechee. The question seemed to falter at the tip of her tongue and she returned again to Waupee. "What will become of me?"

"You are my brother's captive. Why not ask him?"

Her gaze averted, she asked, "What if I don't like what Mechee intends?"

Waupee smiled at her variation of his name. "*Mechee*? You are fast becoming familiar with him, are you not?"

A pink blush colored her cheeks and crept down her throat. "Even so."

Wicomechee almost smiled at the telltale flush, but he knew she'd never admit to feeling anything for him beyond loathing. "Fear not. I will not be harsh."

She refused to meet his eyes. "You were yesterday."

Annoyance thrust through him. The stubborn, ungrateful—

Waupee cocked his head at Wicomechee. "What did you do to this fair lady, brother?"

"Let her speak. She wishes your pity," he muttered.

Her eyes flashed. "Why should I speak, Mechee? You will only deny your treatment."

He lifted his hands, palms up. "What treatment?"

"I said you'd deny it," she shot back.

Wicomechee grasped her smooth cheek and turned her face for Waupee's inspection. "Show

NiSawsawh your swollen cheeks, your bloodied mouth. Have you still all your teeth?"

"My face did not suffer."

"No? Shall I remove your clothes to show him the bloodied bruises on your back and legs where I beat you?"

Her auburn brows arched and she stared at him open-mouthed. "Don't you dare."

"Do not call me cruel with no mark on you. I only made you discover the use of your legs. Endurance will come."

Wicomechee doubted Charity was appeased, but she said nothing more with him threatening to strip her. If he hadn't been so irritated, he might have chuckled at her shock. He wished they could speak of something besides the strife between them. When she wasn't irate, her soft voice and musical accent was pleasing to his ears.

Waupee's woman roused from sleep with a moan. She shifted onto her back and circled a hand over her swollen middle. "I might as well have fallen off your horse as sore as I am."

"I was afraid of that as unaccustomed as you are to riding," Waupee said gently.

Even blinking sleepily in the muted light, Emma's gray eyes reproached him. "I never expected the need to keep in form, as though in readiness for riding to hounds. That is an occupation for the idle gentry and rakes."

Wicomechee pondered the strange reference.

Waupee smiled faintly. "You'll get no argument from me. What of breakfast? Does that meet with your approval?"

She sat up with a frown and pushed back tumbled lengths of pale gold hair. "I could do with a wash first. Will you allow me this, sir, or will I swiftly find myself thrust back upon your mount?"

"We're in no hurry at present. A spring lies not

far from the cave. I'll just settle Lily and take you," he said, and rested the little girl among the leaves.

Emma considered him. "How is it a reckless adventurer is cradling a child?"

"The poor lass rushed at me the instant she saw me."

Pity softened the antagonism in Emma's face. "Perhaps you remind Lily of her father. You're the same height and both handsome—similar in appearance," she hurriedly amended.

"I'm also the only white man here. No matter. Children may be just the thing to settle me." He gave Emma a crooked smile and reached down to take her hand. "Let's have you up."

She groaned as he pulled her to her feet, and rubbed her lower back. "I might have fared better walking."

"Never," Charity said. "Your mother feared you would tire yourself out nut gathering."

Emma winced and her rounded figure sagged under the weight of emotion.

Remorse crossed Charity's expressive face. "I'm sorry. I shouldn't have spoken of Aunt Mary."

Waupee enfolded Emma and held her to him. "She got away, darling. Likely she'll seek refuge with your brother Robin and his family."

Emma blinked at tears. "Are you certain they weren't also attacked?"

"Their homestead lies beyond the targeted area. Your mother is a tough woman, Emma. She will survive this."

"I pray so," she whispered.

"As for James, the boy will stay with us. Wake up, lad. Breakfast," Waupee said, summoning the sleepy child.

James hopped up from the leaves, having wriggled off his blanket in the night. Awareness drove all drowsiness from his green-gray eyes.

Plucking leaves from his blond curls, he ran his widening gaze over the cave. His small lips puckered and he turned to Waupee. "I don't got a Papa no more."

Waupee closed one arm around the boy's slight shoulders. "I'm sorrier than I can say, lad. How about helping me with your sister? Take her hand." James clutched Emma's fingers and Waupee tucked her other arm through his.

"You have another child to settle you," she sniffed.

"And one yet unborn."

"What of its father? Will I ever know Edward's fate?"

Waupee's chin jutted at an unbending angle. "All I know is that a young man fitting Edward's description was injured, but whether he lives or dies, I'll never surrender you."

Emma lifted glistening eyes. "You may have to, sir. Captain Buchanan may leave you no choice."

"Much as I admire Captain Buchanan, he has me to reckon with before he can take you back." With that, Waupee led them from the cave.

Wicomechee wondered about this formidable militia leader and the Long Knives under his command. Just let these Scotsmen try to reclaim Charity. They'd rue the day, he determined, getting to his feet. In imitation of Waupee's civility, he bent down and reached out his hand to her.

"I will help you to the spring."

She eyed him coldly. "No thank you. I can manage."

Her icy refusal drove a shaft of indignation through him. She'd been compliant enough when addressing his brother. "Go to Waupee. You will accept his aid, I think."

He swiveled on his moccasins and stalked from the cave.

33

Chapter Three

Wicomechee had scarcely disappeared from sight before Charity repented of her rash outburst. His abrupt departure had left her in the cave with warriors and no guardian at hand. Thankfully, the rowdy assembly didn't seem to be taking any notice of her. Some who'd imbibed too freely reeled outside. She must hasten past them to reach Colin and Emma.

She rose stiffly and took a tentative step. Despite the soreness in her knee, she quickly limped toward the opening.

"Where you going?" a husky voice asked from behind her, his words slightly slurred.

She froze, almost too paralyzed to speak. "To Mister Dickson—I mean, Waupee," she squeezed from her throat.

Chaka seized her shoulders and spun her toward him. Everything about him seemed larger than life, nightmarishly so. His black eyes swept her with a hungry gleam in his broad face. "Why such haste? Eat. Drink."

She recoiled from the thought of food in her knotted stomach. Whiskey would never mix with her quaking fear.

The taunting smile played at his lips. "Stay with me."

Her heart drummed in her ears. "No."

Nostrils flared in a prominent nose. "Who are you to refuse me? Do you know who I am?"

The significance of his identity was lost on her.

"Where is Wicomechee?" he demanded.

"Nearby."

Chaka smiled at her attempt, apparently gleaning the truth from her face. As though in a bad dream, she could summon no resistance as he pulled her farther back into a dark recess. An inner voice urged her to struggle but her body wouldn't respond except to tremble. She shook as he trapped her against a stone wall. The gloom swallowed his overpowering features, but not the fiery miasma of whiskey and the scent of bear grease used as a base for the war paint.

"You're drunk," she argued breathlessly.

"Not so much."

"What do you want?" she panted.

"You."

Her stomach gave a sick lurch. Was he simply toying with her, enjoying her terror, or would he act?

He ran large hands down the loose hair cascading to her waist. "So beautiful, your hair."

Was he truly admiring her auburn lengths, or would he scalp her? He could swiftly accomplish that bloody deed in the dark. A shudder convulsed her. "Let me go."

"Shhhh. I will not harm you, pretty English girl." Whiskey permeated every word.

His fingers, seemingly unaffected by alcohol, smoothed her cheeks and drifted to the curve of her neck without a tremor. He could easily draw his knife and slit her throat, but if this was his aim, why was he stroking her skin? His fingers roamed lower, over her bodice.

She jerked in a new sort of alarm. "Stop—"

Disregarding her plea, he tugged at the lacing and the drawstring of her shift.

Coming violently back into control of her body, Charity fought to push him away as he jerked down the freed cloth and pawed her exposed breast. Rough fingers scraped her nipple and she slapped his hand.

Then he closed his arms around her and she caught her breath, feeling herself being crushed against his scratchy shirt. His burning lips covered hers, pressing down, forcing her mouth apart. Horror consumed her as she felt his tongue thrust inside her shuddering mouth. Her first kiss from a man was anything but tender.

She kicked wildly at his muscular legs and twisted in his vise-like grasp. But he held her so tightly she couldn't move while his lips enforced her silence. Not that anyone could readily hear her over the boisterousness in the cave, even if they were willing to aid her. Never had she felt so helpless, not even when Wicomechee had taken her captive the day before. She desperately wished him back.

Growling erupted near their feet. What animal could be causing the commotion? Her frantic thoughts touched on the dog that had adopted her in the night. He must have burrowed down into the leaves until, in that peculiar way animals have of connecting, he'd sensed her panic and come to life.

Men's upraised voices neared their blackened nook in response to the irate dog.

Chaka clamped his hand over her mouth. "Hush."

"Chaka! *Naga!*" the men called.

Above the barking, several braves spoke to him, but she couldn't see them in the dim light. Wrenching her head to the side, she sank her teeth into Chaka's hand. He freed her mouth. She shrieked, gaining their immediate attention.

"Wicomechee's *tamsah*. *Wehpeteh*, Chaka," one man scolded.

The name 'Wicomechee' caught her ears in the heated exchange that followed, while she prayed the newcomers would interfere on his behalf if not hers.

Chaka tersely relinquished his hold. "You will not escape me," he hissed in a voice only she could hear.

His ominous threat echoed in her mind as he left and her legs shook so badly she couldn't stand. She sank down onto the cave floor, clutching her sagging bodice with shaky fingers. "Take me to Emma," she cried.

"I take," a warrior rumbled in his deep bass.

She sensed his enormous size as he lifted her. Like a gentle giant, he carried her from the cave out into the brilliant sunshine. The dog, revealed to be a brown and white beagle, trotted beside them as he bore her toward the small group seated in the rippling grass and fern near the spring.

"Waupee!" he beckoned.

Colin turned his head and sprang to his feet. "Muga? Good heavens. What's happened?"

Emma clambered up. "Are you all right, dearest?"

Any response Charity intended strangled in her throat.

Colin's brow furrowed. Taking her from her rescuer, he said, "*Megwich*, Muga. Posetha," he added, with a distracted nod at the second brave who'd accompanied them from the cave. He laid Charity on the navy blanket spread under a red maple tree. "I thought you were with my brother, Miss Edmondson."

"He thought I was with you, but Chaka—" Tears overwhelmed Charity and it was all she could do not to sob.

Colin dropped his anxious gaze to her disordered bodice and turned explosively to the two warriors. The confusing sounds of Shawnee broke forth while Emma tied the neckline of her shift and redid the lacing at her chest with fingers that shook nearly as much as Charity's. Then she adjusted the bodice, ordered her petticoats, and rewrapped her cloak.

"They're not certain what Chaka did," Colin

said, kneeling beside Charity. "But have their suspicions." He took her chilled hand in his warm fingers. "I hate to press you, dear heart, but must ask, did he violate you?"

She felt violated to her depths. "What do you mean?"

Colin's eyes softened. "Poor girl. So like my sister Rachel."

Emma nodded as though she knew the connection, and Colin continued. "It strikes me as especially vile when such innocence is robbed. Did Chaka harm you, Miss Edmondson, other than groping you disgracefully? Please tell me."

"He terrified me. But no, he did not cause me pain."

Breath rushed from Emma. "Thank God."

Dismay overshadowed Charity's sense of relief. "He's not finished with me yet."

Colin's brows arched sharply. "What do you mean?"

"Chaka said, unless he's too drunk to know what he said."

Colin gritted his teeth in an effort to contain the rage she sensed boiling just beneath the surface. "Whether he was or wasn't, rest assured his attentions to you are at an end."

She clung to Colin's nearly fierce assertion and to his hand. "What does he want from me, Mister Dickson?"

"Something precious he has no right to. I'll let Emma explain, or your husband when the time comes."

Charity felt left on the perimeter of some vital secret with no hope of Emma enlightening her. Something else Colin had said caught her attention. "How am I like your sister?"

He lowered questioning eyes to Emma. She gave a nod. He exchanged glances with the two warriors

38

and they took James in hand, disappearing into the trees. Colin had the air of a man revisiting a place he'd far rather leave behind.

"Rachel was your age when a man took cruel advantage of her. The difference between you is that you got away before it was too late."

Charity pitied this unknown girl. "What happened?"

"Rachel was one of the young ladies preyed upon by Lawrence Montgomery, an arrogant dandy. His father, Lord Montgomery, is a thoroughly unprincipled man and Lawrence was no better. I was out and our father in bed recovering from illness when Lawrence paid Rachel a call and persuaded her to go for a drive in his carriage—his closed carriage. The driver was instructed to ignore female cries from within. I expect you have some idea now of what followed."

Charity shrank from the repugnant image he painted.

Colin fingered his dagger. "After I'd seen to Rachel, I sought Lawrence out. He trusted his reputation as a swordsman would dissuade me from challenging him. He thought wrong."

"Did you run Mister Montgomery through?"

"Not entirely, but the wound I gave him in my fury was mortal. He died soon after, never to torment a woman again."

Charity shivered with satisfaction. "A just punishment."

"Not to his father. Lord Montgomery's trumped-up charges of murder are responsible for my flight from England. Damnable liar. Sorry. You don't need to hear all of this."

"I don't mind, really. Go on, please."

"He sent word to his powerful brother in Philadelphia, a discovery I made soon after my ship docked. It seems Oliver Montgomery also intends my arrest on the same false charge and had his cronies watching my uncle's home for my arrival."

"Is that when you came to the Shenandoah Valley?"

"Yes, after dashing off a letter to my uncle to inform him of my whereabouts. It must have been intercepted. How else could Oliver Montgomery have discovered my refuge?"

"He must be terribly vindictive to risk coming into the frontier to seek you."

Colin's sun-browned features creased in contempt. "Oliver is a base coward. He sent his men. I fled deep into the mountains to escape them where Wicomechee found me."

"And now you're with the Shawnee, all because of Rachel?"

"Not only am I with them, I'm one of them. And I must deal with Chaka. What he did defies their code of honor."

"I didn't know they had one."

"Oh yes. Forcing any woman, even a captive, is strongly frowned upon. Chaka has no shame."

Charity considered uneasily. "What will you do?"

"Challenge him." Colin's eyes promised retribution.

Emma flinched. "No. What if he kills you?"

"I'll give him a good fight, darling."

She grasped his sleeve. "If you kill him, what then? Will you not anger many warriors?"

Colin shrugged. "He's well liked. So am I."

"Don't take the risk," she pleaded.

Charity blotted her damp face with her sleeve and sat up. "Won't Mechee protect me? He said he would in the night."

"I thought I heard some talk between you in the wee hours. You were sleeping mighty close together when I awoke."

Her cheeks warmed at his observation. Emma

swiveled her head at her, fair brows drawn together above gaping eyes.

"I was cold—" Charity faltered, and appealed to Colin. "Please, sir, could you not allow Mechee to deal with Chaka?"

"That's not a great deal better than my intervening. Those two have been rivals from the start."

"With your temper, you're sure to be in deep," Emma said, eyeing Charity as though she had some peculiar ailment.

"Very well. I'll let Wicomechee handle this," Colin agreed, still weighing Charity. "It's odd he left you so suddenly. Did he say where he was going?"

"No. Though I might have vexed him," she admitted.

"Ah. I'll speak to him. Now, you really must eat."

"I only want to wash away Chaka's touch."

"Certainly. But you must keep up your strength or you'll never make this journey."

"Mechee will see to it that I do."

Colin's lips twitched. "Ah, Miss Edmondson. The stars are calling to you. Mars is aligning with Venus."

His mysterious allusion sent a frightening yet strangely exciting tingle through Charity.

****

The beagle begged for the scraps James tossed him while Charity sat eating slices of ham and wild grapes and listened to the unintelligible exchange between Colin and her rescuers. Whatever they discussed seemed to be a matter of disquiet.

As they spoke, she grew increasingly aware of the young brave sitting beside her. Like Wicomechee and Colin, he wore his shoulder-length hair loose. His chiseled features set off black eyes shining with intelligence. She glanced his way, caught his warm gaze on her, and averted her eyes.

41

He spoke rapidly to Colin, who gave a nod. "Posetha wishes to be introduced." He laid his hand on Emma's shoulder. "This fair lady is Emma, my wife, *niwah*," he said and gestured at Charity. "This beauty is called Charity. We will stick with Christian names to simplify," he explained. "James they know. I entrusted him to their care yesterday."

The big warrior nudged Colin. "Ah yes, Muga. His name means bear. Posetha and Muga are my good friends, *gitchee niNeeakahs*. They, Wicomechee and I are a band of brothers."

Both men seemed pleased, and if they had any reservations about the condition of Colin's newly recovered *wife* they concealed it well. "Do they speak English?" Charity asked.

Posetha smiled. "I speak. Muga speaks little." He pointed at her knee. "You are injured. Let me see."

She watched cautiously as he knelt and pushed her cloak aside. Yesterday's bandage was stained and a dismal sight.

He beckoned. "Come to the water."

"Might I borrow your comb, Mister Dickson?"

Colin withdrew a comb carved of bone from the beaded elk skin pouch hanging over his shoulder. The item in hand, she limped to the small spring bubbling up from between gray rocks and flowing into the trees at the base of a wooded slope. Inhaling the earthy scent, she sat on a sun-warmed stone.

Where was Wicomechee, and why did she care? Only for protection, she reasoned, glad of Posetha's friendliness.

Though not as tall as Wicomechee, he stood a handspan above her. He motioned her knee nearer the water to wet the bandage then carefully unbound the linen. The cut was closing well, though badly discolored with a purpling bruise.

"Wait." Posetha darted into the trees, returning

with a handful of mitten-shaped leaves. "This kind brings healing."

The spicy scent of sassafras rose around her as he pressed the crushed leaves to her wound and bound the poultice in place with a strip of linen taken from the pouch at his waist.

"Thank you," she offered.

"*Megwich*."

Was he teaching her Shawnee? "*Megwich, Posetha*."

He watched appreciatively as she combed out tangles. "Your hair is colored like a red leaf. *Pocoon sisqui*. Your eyes are *skipaki*, the color of leaves in the planting moon."

Colin stepped beside them. "Very poetic, Posetha."

The earnest brave stood, plucked a fluffy milkweed pod, and bent to touch her cheek. "Like this, your skin."

"Enough," Colin chuckled. "Does Wicomechee want you to speak honeyed words to his captive?"

Posetha shrugged. "I speak the words I like."

"Until he puts a stop to it."

Charity looked up at Colin. "Would Mechee really mind?"

"Quite possibly. He took you captive for a reason."

"What?" she asked guardedly, with that curious tingle.

"He will tell you in his own way." Colin leaned down and held out his hand. "Let's have you up."

Puzzled and a little alarmed, she took his hand and got to her feet, walking with him to where Emma lay curled in her cloak like a slumbering cat. The wine-colored hood hid much of her face, but her cheek and long, closed lashes peeked out.

"Poor darling." Colin knelt and gently shook her. She parted rosy lips in a yawn as he slid his arm beneath her and lifted her from the blanket. "We must return to the cave and see to Lily. You and Charity can rest while we await the third war party. I can't imagine what's keeping them."

Charity shook her head. "I'm not setting foot in that cave with Chaka there, Mister Dickson."

"Fine. I'll toss him out."

Emma blinked in alarm. "No, Colin. You mustn't."

Charity hadn't meant to distress her. Neither could she possibly go back there. "Would Posetha guide me to Mechee?"

Colin seemed surprised. "You really want to go to him?"

Strangely, she found that she did. "Yes, please."

"Perhaps you'd be better off with my brother just now, if he can be found." His lips twitched. "Keep an eye on the stars, Miss Edmondson."

Chapter Four

Charity followed Posetha toward the overlook where he thought Wicomechee kept watch somewhere further up the tree-shrouded ridge. A woof sounded behind her and the beagle brushed against her legs. She stopped to stroke his ears. "May he come with us?"

Posetha paused ahead of her and gave a shrug. "Yes."

"*Megwich*. He ought to have a name."

"*Weshe* is dog in Shawnee." Taking a wrinkled brown root from his pouch, Posetha sliced two aromatic pieces and handed one to her. "*Gensang*. Good for the stomach. For more also."

She chewed, savoring the sweet taste. He popped a piece into his mouth and proceeded at a pace her knee could tolerate, seeming more like an amiable escort than her enemy.

A woodpecker hammered overhead as the first men in a line of warriors appeared in front of them. The drum of the bird had muffled their stealthy approach, and a bend in the trail hid the emerging figures. Even without the distraction, she wouldn't have detected their coming, like silent owls winging across the sky.

Posetha stepped to one side of the trail and pulled her with him. "It is all right. They are Shawnee."

These tidings weren't equally reassuring to Charity. The men's forbidding expressions spurred her apprehension. More braves walked by, fifteen so far. This must be the third war party Colin had mentioned, their mood entirely unlike the other two bands. "What's wrong?" she whispered to Posetha.

"Bad fight." He pointed to a warrior with an ugly leg wound leaning on the support of a friend and hobbling along. Another man's bloody shoulder bore witness to a musket blast.

A young warrior hailed Posetha. "Stay here, Charity," he said, and headed toward his friend.

She watched the sullen procession file past. Her stomach lurched at the sight of two braves dragging a young man by a thong around his neck, his wrists bound, torn shirt bloodied. He was a strapping man, but the beatings had laid him low.

Dear God. That swollen bleeding face belonged to Rob Buchanan, the man her guardians wanted her to marry.

One of the warriors dragging Rob gave him a vicious kick. The other brave plunged a fist into his stomach. Rob doubled over, groaning. Two other warriors ahead of him turned around and joined in the assault. Rob fell down onto his knees, struggling vainly to rise under the blows raining down on him. The first warrior kicked him to the ground and the others pounded at him with their fists. He lay face down, moaning.

"For God's sake—stop!" Hurtling past the startled warriors, Charity shouldered one brave aside and threw herself over Rob's barely conscious form. "Leave him be! Leave him be!" The loyal dog punctuated her screams with ear-bending barks.

The staring warriors paused in their attack and stood like statues carved of flesh and blood. Posetha rushed to her side and closed his arms around her waist. "Come away."

Digging her toes into the earth, she clung to Rob's bloody back. "I won't leave him to die. Make them stop!"

"I cannot." Posetha tore her from Rob.

The moment of stunned stillness ended. Grumbling angrily, the warriors closed in on her like wolves for the kill. Posetha, alone, didn't seem enough of a barrier to the snarling pack. "Mechee! Mechee! Help me!" *God let him hear.*

"Be still, girl," a low voice hissed from behind.

She turned her head. The clustered men allowed a powerful warrior through the circle—surely the most menacing brave yet. He glared down at her with slitted eyes.

"Your cries wake even the trees. If Long Knives are near, they will hear you. Silence *weshe*, Posetha."

Posetha released Charity and grabbed the outraged dog, muzzling him with his hand. "*Okema*, Chief Outhowwa," he said. His quiet voice held fear.

Black terror constricted her stomach and her legs grew weak. Even if Posetha hadn't told her this was the chief, she would have guessed. Everything about Outhowwa spoke of crushing strength and the knowledge that comes with hard experience. Sunlight touched his gleaming scalp lock and the silver pendants hanging from his split wire-wrapped earlobes.

Bear claws dangled from the necklace around his thick neck and rested on his chest. Four parallel scars ran from just below his right eye to the iron set of his jaw in testimony to the price he'd paid for this gruesome prize.

She clenched her teeth against another desperate cry. One blow from the club in his fist would splinter her skull.

Outhowwa dismissed her with a contemptuous glance and addressed the warriors in Shawnee. Her dread intensified with each alien word he spat out. He was passing a harsh sentence.

Posetha inserted himself between Charity and Outhowwa and pleaded with the incensed chief.

That much was evident in his impassioned tone and face. Unspeakably grateful for his presence, she strained to discern the impact he'd had.

Outhowwa's scornful gaze raked him, and her heart sank.

Again, Posetha appealed to the menacing figure.

Some of the surrounding heads nodded, but Outhowwa eyed Posetha as he might a squashed toad. He hissed a reply.

Posetha colored and opened his mouth.

"*Puckechey!*" Outhowwa barked, and pointed at the trail.

With agony in his face, Posetha firmed up his grip on the dog and ran with him back toward the cave. Charity watched his retreating figure in dismay. He couldn't possibly bring Colin in time to appease such fury. She was as good as dead.

Slumping to her knees, she pressed her cheek against Rob's bloodied shirt. His back was warm beneath her, but he didn't move. She could barely speak. "God help us, Rob, or we shall perish together." It seemed the height of irony to die for the suitor she'd badly wanted to evade.

"Charity?" he murmured, and drifted away again.

She envied Rob his unconscious state. Her senses prickled with the awareness of glowering warriors and the chief poised behind her ready to strike. She clutched Rob's limp hand, but found no comfort. She must face Outhowwa alone and lifted her eyes to his narrow gaze. "Have mercy."

Outhowwa's grim features made it clear he would grant none. "You did what is not done." He lifted his club.

She squeezed her eyes against the death blow. She'd soon be reunited with her brother and father, she told herself, and uttered a final petition. "Have mercy on my soul, O Lord."

"Outhowwa! *Naga!*"

Her eyes flew open at Wicomechee's voice. Hope rose in her like a bird fleeing the hunter's snare. "Mechee!"

****

Wicomechee's chest pounded beneath his shirt from his race down the ridge. Charity's anguished shrieks had sent cold dread knifing through his heart, unlike anything he'd ever imagined. She must be in dire peril to call out to him. Her name for him swelled in his ears. She still lived.

He glimpsed her crouched over a fallen figure. Her wealth of red hair covered them both, but he didn't dare look into her face. Rather, he kept his eyes on the irate chief. "This woman belongs to me, Outhowwa," he said in English so Charity could follow the exchange.

Outhowwa regarded him coldly, but lowered his arm. "You? Posetha is her captor—"

"Posetha?" Where had Outhowwa gotten that idea? "No. I took her captive."

Outhowwa considered this new twist, his lips pressed together in a hard line. He pointed at Charity. "Look how she holds to my captive."

Wicomechee swiveled his head to see her clinging to the Long Knife. Jealousy and annoyance assailed him. Outhowwa wouldn't tolerate such willfulness for an instant, never mind that she was young and beautiful. The mature warrior despised redheads. "Charity, take your hands from this man now."

She panted so hard she could scarcely speak, but did not peel back her fingers. "Wait—what will happen to Rob?"

Outhowwa rounded on her. "This is not for you to say. You do not interfere with his punishment."

Her pleading eyes passed between them. "Don't kill him."

"He is dead to you. You must learn respect," Outhowwa growled, and raised his arm over her head once more.

She ducked with a shudder.

Wicomechee sprang forward and seized Outhowwa's wrist. "Let me discipline her."

"Your eyes hold softness for this woman," he scorned.

Wicomechee locked him in an unyielding stare. He was equal to Outhowwa if it came to that, although he hoped it wouldn't. Nor did he know if any of the braves looking on in tight-lipped scrutiny would back him up.

"I will do as I must, Outhowwa."

He snorted at his reply, but made no move one way or the other.

"May I speak with her?" Wicomechee asked.

Outhowwa gave a short nod. Wicomechee dropped his gaze to the Long Knife lying face-down beside her. "Who is he?"

"Rob Buchanan," Charity said shakily. "The youngest son of Captain Buchanan."

Waupee had spoken the militia leader's name. Wicomechee wondered if Charity were promised to this son she'd risked her life to defend. A fresh shaft of resentment pierced him as he addressed the exasperated chief. "Your captive is the son of the leader of the Long Knives."

Outhowwa waved Wicomechee on. "Speak more of him."

Wicomechee knelt beside Charity and met her tearful eyes with a stern look. Keeping his voice low, he asked, "Must you infuriate Outhowwa?"

"I was just trying to help Rob."

"You should trouble more about yourself."

"I'm sorry," she offered, too little, too late.

He waved aside her reasoning. "Tell me of Rob Buchanan," he said, hating the very name.

"Rob's father will do anything to recover him. He's the youngest son, the favorite, and the Buchanan's have more wealth than most."

"Is he an able hunter?"

"One of the best shots in the valley. Can you aid him?"

"Perhaps. Be still."

"But—"

Wicomechee shot her a hard glance. "Not one word."

Lips pursed, she nodded.

Finally. What a stubborn girl.

Wicomechee patted the Long Knife's shoulder and raised his voice. "Outhowwa, Captain Buchanan will pay you well for his son's return. Or, if you prefer, adopt him. Rob Buchanan is a skilled hunter. Think of the meat and skins he could provide your family. His death brings you nothing."

Never one to allow possible reward to slip through his grasp, Outhowwa considered Wicomechee's argument. "I will think on your words." But it seemed Charity wasn't to be excused so easily. He regarded her with all the warmth of a baited bear. "Foolish woman. She flies without thought." He shifted his shrewd gaze to Wicomechee. "She must learn."

Wicomechee didn't waver. "I will teach her," he said, getting to his feet.

Challenge glinted in Outhowwa's eyes. He said nothing more and the tight circle of braves leaned in expectantly.

Now it was up to Wicomechee, and he'd rather do almost anything else than punish this most desirable of all women. She would surely despise him after this.

She lifted eyes awash with fear, like water churning before a storm. Wicomechee seized her arm and jerked her up. She cried out at the accompanying stab in her knee.

Hating himself nearly as much as she must, he shook his head at her and drew back his hand. How vulnerable her face looked...her soft woman's body.

Rob Buchanan roused from his stupor. "No! Don't harm her! Punish me!"

Noble words. Any more punishment and he would lie dead.

Charity fixed her beseeching gaze on Wicomechee. "Mechee—don't—"

Weak from his beating, the Long Knife thrashed vainly.

Despite the surly chief and intent onlookers, Wicomechee could not strike her. He dropped his hand. "I will discipline her, Outhowwa." Without a moment's hesitation, he pulled her roughly away from the gathering. Once out of sight and sound of the others, he lifted her sobbing in his arms. She sagged in his hold as he bore her over the path.

Wicomechee cursed himself and the cruel fate that now likely awaited him and Charity.

****

Orange leaves brushed by Charity in a blur. Shaking, crying, she was scarcely aware of the direction Wicomechee carried her. Nor did she care, and only knew that saffron leaves blew overhead in the place where he laid her.

What would he do? Fearing abuse, she turned onto her chest and buried her face in her arms. The gurgle of water and birds calling through the trees mingled with her muffled weeping.

She sensed Wicomechee crouched beside her like a panther lying in wait. Still he said nothing. Did nothing. Yet he had promised the infuriated chief he would punish her.

They remained like this for long minutes, together, yet acutely apart. Gradually her sobs faded into an occasional sniffle and her rigid muscles relaxed. Little by little, she unwound from her tight ball, and dared to lift her head.

She wiped away the last tears from her nose on her sleeve. "You will not strike me?"

Wicomechee regarded her with immovable eyes. "Outhowwa would say I should."

Gone, the kindness and solace she'd known in the night, gone, the man in her dream. Shrinking from this intimidating warrior, she returned to the shelter of her arms. If she could, she would run from him. Better yet, fly.

Wicomechee clasped her shoulder with his strong hand. "Do not hide from me, Charity. We will speak."

She remained huddled on her chest, hugging the leaf-strewn earth. She gasped, feeling him tighten his hold—crying out as he suddenly forced her onto her back. Fresh alarm coursed through her. "Don't!"

He pinned her arms at her sides and bent over her. "Look at me."

He needn't have said it. His eyes compelled hers. Heart drumming, she stared up into his intent gaze.

"The Long Knife pleaded for you and cursed me. He risked death. This Rob Buchanan cares much for you?"

"Yes," she gulped, "since childhood."

"You also risked death. Do you love him?"

Wicomechee's grim face blurred through her tears. "No. Uncle John and Aunt Mary want—wanted—me to wed Rob," she stuttered, terrified he would let his hand fly.

"Do you desire this man for your husband?"

"I never did."

He seemed perplexed. "Yet you held to him like a lover."

"That was never my intention. 'Tis only Christian to aid someone in distress."

"Christian?" he echoed, as though the word

offended him. "You speak of your English God?"

She answered in bewilderment, never expecting to witness in this way. "God's son, Christ Jesus, desires mercy."

His lips curled. "Shawnee find little mercy from the English."

"I'm sure it must appear that way at times—"

"At times? Do you know what you speak? English ears do not hear the voice of the son of their God."

She was at a loss to reply and waited, trembling in his grip. Long moments passed under his scrutiny. What was his searching gaze telling him about her? Did she detect a slight softening in his face? His lips weren't drawn so severely.

"So, you possess mercy," he said at last.

She blinked wet lashes. "Do you?"

He freed her arms and sat back on his heels. "For you, much."

It certainly hadn't seemed that way, but she seized the opportunity and reached an entreating hand to him. "Do not punish me harshly. I beg you."

Regret tinged his eyes as he clasped her outstretched fingers. "Charity, I do not want to."

"You don't?"

He shook his head. "Only to keep you from Outhowwa's wrath. You would not long survive his punishment."

She pulled her fingers away and pushed up on her elbows.

"Rob Buchanan would cut off his hand before ever using it against me."

The steely look returned to Wicomechee's face. "Then he would have no hand and you would lie dead by Outhowwa's."

"I thought you could keep me from harm."

"No. Only make the harm less. When we return, he will look to see if I spoke the truth."

Understanding dawned, and with it came an upswell of fear. "I do not appear punished."

Wicomechee shook his head.

A low wail escaped her. "Dear God. What will you do?"

The flint in his eyes softened. "Shhhh...I will not lash out at you. I despise to make my hand fly against you."

The strong emotion in his admission was beyond anything she'd ever expected. "Do you care for me as much as that?"

"Yes." He took a swathe of linen from his pouch and handed it to her. "Now you will hate me as you promised."

She blotted her face with the cloth and considered. Slowly, she said, "I don't hate you."

His keen eyes followed her every move. "No?"

She'd never been observed so closely, as if he read her thoughts as well. She regarded him hesitantly. "If Outhowwa is still angry?"

"He can strike me."

She stared at him. "Why would you risk this?"

He smoothed her cheeks and cupped her face in his palm. How was it the hand that had jerked her up so rudely now offered a caress?

"You are *paca*, beautiful." Closing his arms around her, he drew her gently against him. He combed his fingers through her hair. "Like fire, your hair, and your eyes...never have I seen such a color. You are the sun, the trees, come to life."

Again he was the man in the night, only more so. The man in her dream had spoken tenderly to her, though she couldn't recall his exact words, only the feel of them. Dazed, she held herself still, her breath in her throat.

Wicomechee pressed his lips to the side of her face. "For you, I would risk much."

She listened in deepening uncertainty. Was he

simply telling her how he felt, or did something else, something unsavory, lie behind his sweet words and gentleness? Doubt thickened. Did he want what Chaka wanted?

"No—" she whimpered. "Not again."

Wicomechee stiffened and pulled back to look at her. "Why such fear? I said I will not harm you."

"Chaka said the same at first, too. Before he—" she faltered, and then blurted out the rest. "I thought I could trust you, Mechee. But you're like Chaka. Let me go," she pleaded, struggling to escape his arms. "Let me go."

He restrained her so that she couldn't move. "Go where?"

"Where you will not molest me."

"Calm down, Charity. You make no sense. What troubles you?"

"Don't you know? I was afraid you would—" she stopped, unsure how to explain.

Wicomechee's eyes were like a darkening sky. "Force you? No warrior will—should. Did Chaka do this?"

"I'm not certain what you mean."

He arched one black brow, a raven's wing circling the tempest. "What do you not understand?"

"Exactly what happens when I'm forced. No one ever said."

He exhaled slowly. "If Chaka did this to you, you would know. I need not say."

"Then I wasn't. But it was bad enough."

"Tell me."

She recoiled from describing such an unspeakable act. "He pulled me away from the others, tore my bodice, and pawed my—" she faltered, and finished in a gulp. "Breasts. And kissed me hard—with his tongue."

Wicomechee drove his fist against his knee. "Bastard! I'll—" he caught himself, hissing his unintelligible threat.

She jerked at his vehemence. "Chaka was rather drunk."

"This I also believe." He glared past her as if at the unseen transgressor. "How did you escape him?"

"The dog barked. Muga and Posetha took me to Waupee."

Wicomechee raked his fingers through loose black hair. "I never should have left you alone in the cave."

"When Chaka seized me, I hoped you would come. He says I will not escape him," she confided tremulously.

"It is he who will not escape my wrath."

"Don't get yourself into any more trouble on my account."

"I am already. Outhowwa has little liking for me."

Charity had assumed the warriors were as thick as thieves. "Why?"

"Before my birth he very much wished to wed my mother."

She had difficulty imagining Outhowwa as a love-struck youth. "Outhowwa holds her refusal against you?"

"That, and Chaka is his son."

She gaped at him. "Is this why Chaka went after Emma, to punish Colin for leading the war party into the Valley?"

"Chaka was angry Outhowwa did not choose him. He hates that I am a scout." With that, Wicomechee broke off. Apparently he felt he'd divulged enough. "Come to the stream."

He rose, lifting her with him, and stood her on her feet almost with reluctance. Circling his arm around her shoulder, he guided her past wine-red dogwood, to the stream. She knelt awkwardly to splash her face and drink.

When she glanced around, he was gone. "Mechee?"

Nothing.

Rising a little giddily, she limped over the mossy stones. A bend in the stream revealed him prying a root from a tall leafy plant. He beckoned her near. "This is good medicine." He mashed the tuber against a stone and licorice scented the air. "Lie down. Rest."

She sank onto the carpet of leaves beneath a golden sassafras tree. He squatted beside her and reached to her rebound knee then stopped. "Who tended this injury?"

"Posetha. Earlier today. He was very kind." A wave of fatigue engulfed her as the severe tension of the day faded and she felt herself collapsing under its weight. Her eyes would not stay open. "He was bringing me to you. I need—your help." A huge yawn interrupted her.

"My aid you have. I will care for you."

Reassured, she began to drift. "Like a brother?"

"No. Not like a brother."

Wicomechee's throaty chuckle followed her down into the blessed oblivion of sleep.

Chapter Five

Charity pushed up on her palms on a bed of evergreen needles and gazed around at the boughs tossing overhead and on every side of her. Hadn't she fallen asleep beneath a bower of yellow leaves with the stream gurgling close by? The spill of water reached her from a distance now and an orange sun hung low over the trees.

Not a soul was in sight; she had no idea where Emma and Colin were, or even where she was...only that she was alone, and it would soon be dark. Did she dare call out to Wicomechee? What if Chaka lurked close by? Her chest tightened.

"Mechee," she called softly, unable to keep the quaver from her voice.

"You fear I am gone?"

Sucking in her breath, she twisted toward his voice.

With a slight smile, he stepped out from behind a heavily branched spruce. She hated to admit the depth of her relief at his coming. Not only that, but for some reason, he looked different now, and it took her a moment to reply.

"How did I get here?"

He knelt beside her. "I brought you."

She vaguely remembered the comforting sensation of being in his arms. "I thought that was a dream."

His undeniably handsome face creased in a grimace. "You are too heavy for a dream, like carrying a bear."

She sat up straighter. "A bear? Never."

He leaned in closer until the tip of his nose nearly touched hers. "You are certain?"

She detected a teasing spark in the depths of his eyes, and smiled hesitantly.

He lightly touched her lips with the tip of his index finger. "I like this mouth."

"Is that why you teased, to make me smile?"

"How do you know I tease?"

"I am not that heavy."

He slid his arms beneath her, scooped her up, and sprang to his feet. "You will break my back," he said, staggering as though he could barely support her.

"Mechee—" Giggling, she threw her arms around his neck.

"I even made you laugh. I like this sound."

He stood still, and she broke the circle of her arms to tilt back and look at him again. The fierce stripes of red and black paint were gone, fully revealing his smooth light brown skin. "You washed your face."

His small smile faded, and he cocked his head a little. "The paint frightened you."

"Yes." How could she begin to understand this warrior who'd helped attack the McLeod's homestead and carried her away? He could be stern and harsh, yet also gentle, even funny. And now, he was trying to ease her fear of him.

He remained as he was and made no move to return her to her feet. "There is much you do not know of me, Charity."

"How do you guess my thoughts? You've done this before."

"A warrior must see in the face what lies in the heart. This is why we are careful to guard our thoughts."

"Why don't you want others to know?"

A hawk shrilled overhead as he answered.

"Much danger lies in this."

"I don't know how to hide mine."

"No. Like clouds making shadows over the earth, your face changes to show what you think."

"It's just as well I haven't any secrets, then."

His eyes looked deeply into hers. "None?"

"Perhaps I've a few." Suddenly self-conscious, she squirmed under his forceful gaze. "Would you put me down?"

"One moment." He drew her into a more intimate embrace, and nuzzled her hair. "So soft you are."

His tenderness took her completely by surprise. She hardly knew what to say. "How do you mean?"

"Your face, your hair, your body...everywhere you are soft." His lips drifted over her cheek toward her mouth.

She tensed. Was Wicomechee about to kiss her?

"Posetha," he groaned, and nodded toward the spruce.

The young brave was just visible among the evergreens with a bedroll tucked under one arm. He stepped into their sheltered space and considered them, dark brows arched.

What must he think, catching them like this? It was pure madness. "Mechee's just seeing how heavy I am," she blurted out, immediately wishing she'd bitten her tongue.

He surveyed them with a skeptical air. "She is heavy?"

Wicomechee lowered her to her feet. "Like the bear."

Posetha's lips twitched. "Waupee told me to seek you out. He wants to know how I find Charity."

She smoothed stray needles from her skirts self-consciously. "Please, just tell him I do not suffer."

"I say you suffer little in Wicomechee's arms."

Charity felt herself flush.

Posetha touched her shoulder. "I will not speak this. I have gift for you." He held out a wooden comb and pointed to the maple leaves he'd carved along the side. "Red leaves, for your hair. See?"

She smiled. "*Megwich.* It's a good gift. *Gitchee.*"

Wicomechee considered his friend with narrowing eyes. "How much were you with her today?"

Posetha lifted both hands as if to show his innocence. "Little. She learns Shawnee fast."

"She also runs fast. Why did you not keep her from the Long Knife?"

Posetha glanced away from him. "I did not know she would run to this captive."

"I have known Rob Buchanan since childhood. Was I to stand by and watch him beaten to death?" Charity reasoned.

Wicomechee shifted his disapproval to her. "You must not go to him again. Not go to any captive."

"But what if I can help someone?"

"No. Do you learn nothing?"

She lifted her chin and angled her head at Posetha. "Does Rob Buchanan, the Long Knife, still live?"

"Yes. Outhowwa says he will adopt this captive."

She glowed with vindication. "See, Mechee, I saved him."

He grasped her shoulders and swiveled her to face him. "You did not save him. I persuaded Outhowwa."

"If I hadn't gone to Rob, he would have been dead before you got there."

Wicomechee tightened his grip on her upper arms. "If I had come any later, you also would be dead. Never interfere again. Give me your word you will not."

"How can I promise never?"

His demeanor was severe. "You must. I will not

lose you to Outhowwa's anger. If you do not obey me, I will bind you."

"No. Please. I hated that, and the awful way Rob's neck was tied."

"I would never rope your fair neck," he promised. "But I will do what I must to keep you safe. Will you heed me?"

She nodded, unwilling to test her boundaries any farther.

"Charity has courage," Posetha said. His youthful features drew together in an expression of self-disgust. "I left her to Outhowwa's anger."

"You did all you could for me. I am grateful."

"I failed you." He kicked at the thick carpet of needles. "Outhowwa called me a boy before all."

"You must prove yourself to him," Wicomechee said.

Posetha lifted his shoulders. "I will find a way." Laying his bundle down on the forest floor, he added, "I brought a blanket, food. Waupee speaks with Outhowwa for you, says you must stay far from Outhowwa tonight. Perhaps tomorrow his anger will cool."

A fresh tide of dread flooded Charity. "Why is he still so angry with me?"

Wicomechee slid his hands over her cloak, down her arms. "Because of you, three warriors challenged Outhowwa. He cannot do as he likes. You must not increase his anger."

"Colin isn't a real warrior, is he?"

"You think not? He fought with us at Bushy Run against British forces led by Colonel Henry Bouquet."

She'd heard of this battle in western Pennsylvania and tried to imagine Colin firing from the trees, fighting alongside Wicomechee. Beyond shocked, she sputtered, "Colin—Waupee—is kind to us."

"You have not seen him in battle," Wicomechee snorted. "He is not kind then."

Posetha gave a nod. "I have no wish to fight him."

"But to war against Englishmen? How could he do this?"

"They are our bitter enemy," Wicomechee said bluntly.

She sighed, wearied to death of the endless hostilities. "Will Shawnee and the English never be friends?"

Wicomechee looked at her as though she'd suggested they make a pact with the devil. "How are we to befriend men who do not speak the truth? Foxes have more honor."

"Not all English are bad, Mechee."

The hard edges at his mouth softened like the earth after a rain. "Not all. The one who calls me by this name is not."

She faltered in the face of his sudden tenderness. "I'm not entirely English. Papa was, but Mama was Scottish. The Scots have fought many bloody wars with England."

"Virginia Long Knives fight for the English," he pointed out.

"Even so, we are not content under British rule."

He shrugged. "English, Scot, all are glad to kill us."

A pang of sorrow knifed through her. "I wish it were otherwise. What's the use in all of this death?"

Wonder diminished the skepticism in his eyes. "You have much mercy. You would be a good Quaker woman."

"I could never be *that* forgiving."

His lips curved in a wider smile that flowed into his eyes and made him, in that moment, the most amazingly attractive man she'd ever seen. She realized, just as quickly, that her traitorous heart was in grave danger.

"Only for you am I forgiving," he said.

Posetha smiled. "Wicomechee is not kind in battle."

"Nor you, *niNeeakah*, my friend."

She could well imagine. Though not as tall or broad as Wicomechee, Posetha was muscular and agile. She'd felt his strength when he wrenched her from Rob. And Wicomechee was like a sleek, swift panther with head-snapping power.

Teasing touched his eyes. "Will you teach us to be gentle in battle?"

She answered in a somber tone. "I've never seen a battle. Nor do I wish to."

The hint of mischief faded from his expression. "It is not for your fair eyes to see."

With appalling fury, a dark dread seized her with the violence of a sudden storm. And like the memory of a vile scent never forgotten, she knew this dire sense of foreboding. She'd sensed her father's passing on that distant battlefield and felt the approach of something terrible just days before her brother Craig had died. Her thoughts swirled back to his final moments as he lay tossing with fever.

Craig's pale face disappeared and the rapport of musket fire resounded in her mind. The smoky gunpowder clouded warriors, their upraised hands wielding bloody knives and tomahawks. Agonizing screams tore from the frontiersmen twisting in the grass. Too shaken to speak, she sucked in shallow pants of air.

"Charity?" Wicomechee's voice came to her as if from a distance.

Weak-kneed, she instinctively reached out and closed her arms around his chest. Rather than trying to escape him as she'd done hours ago, she clung to him like a drowning woman.

He enfolded her in turn. "Are you taken ill?"

As swiftly as the horrific images had come, they departed. She shook her head and pressed her face against his shirt, stained with her blood. She felt his warmth, heard the steady beat of his heart.

"I go now, tell Waupee two trees could not grow more close than Charity stands to Wicomechee," Posetha said.

She no longer cared what tale he carried to the others, and sensed the puzzled warrior departing.

"Why do you hold to me in fear?" Wicomechee asked.

"I had the strongest feeling, like a warning, come over me when we spoke of battle. Then I saw men fighting, dying."

"Never will I take you to war, sweet one. Our women and little ones remain in the village."

She fought to steady herself. "This battle may come upon us suddenly."

"Long Knives?"

"Perhaps. I saw militia and warriors fighting."

"Have you the sight?" he asked.

"What is this?"

"The knowing of what will be. Of what is to come."

She lifted her eyes to his perceptive gaze. "Sometimes."

"Only evil things?"

She started to nod and hesitated, flushing at the memory of her dream. "Not only bad. Good, also."

He searched her face. "What else did you see?"

"Just a dream...of a man."

"You know him?"

Her cheeks grew increasingly heated. "I might."

Amusement crept into Wicomechee's expression. "What did he do?"

"Nothing—much."

A slow smile turned up the corners of his mouth.

"You are a bad liar."

She fervently wished she were better and looked away.

"Do not fear battle. I will keep you safe. Come with me now." Wicomechee's arms slacked and he eased his support.

Weighted with conflicting emotions, she lowered her arms with a little reluctance, also unsettling. "Where?"

"Not far." He grabbed up his musket, slipped its woven strap over his shoulder, and stepped ahead.

She limped behind him through the evergreens, emerging from their shelter to the full force of the wind. Stiff breezes tore at her cloak and petticoats, billowing the cloth around her. She beat at her skirts, but the wind exposed her thighs with every gust.

Wicomechee turned, and grinned.

"You brought me here on purpose!"

He chuckled. "Not for this, though I like it much."

"Don't look at me," she protested, and spun away.

"Stay." He caught her around the waist and swept her up off the ground, keeping one arm over the flapping cloth. "Why such shame? You are *paca*, beautiful."

Mortified at what he'd seen, she said, "Not *there*."

A smile spread over his face. "You know little of men."

Surefooted as a deer, he picked his way over the rocky path and between the stones littering the trail. Here and there, clumps of grass bent in the constant wind and stunted pines struggled to grow, but plants thinned out and the stones became more prominent. He rounded the boulder blocking her sight and she saw he was carrying her near the edge of a cliff.

"Mechee!" she screeched, her embarrassment forgotten at the yawning chasm rushing up at her. She threw her arms around his neck and held onto him for dear life. But even his strength wasn't equal to this. "We'll tumble over the edge!"

"No," he said, projecting his voice above the wind. He stopped on the massive ledge jutting out over the vast expanse like a rocky fortress. "Look. The hawk circles below."

"Dear God." She'd never been above a hawk.

Pushing back the hair whipping across her face, she gazed out over the mountains in awe. Blue-green ridges flowed beneath her in an undulating sea that seemed to go on and on forever. Shafts of late day sun shone on the nearest crests and burnished the splashes of red and gold leaves. Beyond these gilded rises, the dark blue swells were swallowed in purple shadows.

The distant ridges seemed to beckon her on to a mysterious realm, an untamed world. "'Tis a wondrous sight."

"Yes. This is where I kept watch today."

"You heard me call to you from all the way up here? It must be miles."

"I ran very fast."

He truly must have. She owed him at least a grudging appreciation. "Thank you for saving my life."

He returned his gaze to her, hair blowing around his face, and nodded then pointed to a place where the trail snaked up the side of the ridge among the rocks. Trees were sparse. "If the Long Knives come, I will see them there."

Her trepidation rushed back with the accompanying stab of disloyalty. "Will they come today?"

"It would be foolish to seek us now. Darkness will soon be upon us."

"Captain Buchanan will come, though, and bring as many men with him as he can muster. Rob is dear to him."

"The captain will also fight for your return, will he not? You are the woman his son desires."

"Yes," she said, without any spark of enthusiasm.

"You do not wish to be recovered?"

She kept her eyes from Wicomechee's and focused on a ridge flaming in the last rays of the sun. "Of course. Only…"

"You do not want to wed Rob Buchanan," he concluded. "Are you promised to him?"

"Uncle John gave his consent. If Captain Buchanan takes us back I will be expected to wed Rob."

"Have you no other family to aid you?"

His question touched a raw chord. "No. The McLeod's took me in after my older brother Craig died. I adored him," she added, unsure why she was confiding in Wicomechee.

"This is the reason you want me for your brother?"

"I suppose so."

"I have no wish to be your brother."

"I would feel so much easier with you if you did."

"Can you not feel easy with a man who is not your kin?"

She shivered in the wind. "You are not just a man."

"No. I am the man in your dream, but you will not say." Without waiting for her stammered reply, he continued. "You grow cold. I will take you from here."

"Wait. Before you do, where is my home?"

He pointed to the east. "There."

She searched the rippling ocean of ridges for a final glimpse of the lush green valley called

Shenandoah, Daughter of the Stars. "Will I ever see the valley again?"

A sweep of his arm encompassed the western sky. Lavender and rose streaked the golden rim of the ruggedly beautiful Alleghenies. "Your home lies that way, beyond the mountains. You belong to Shawnee now."

Chapter Six

Wicomechee sought shelter in the fast-descending darkness. These ridges would be cold tonight and Charity was especially vulnerable to the chill. A wolf loosed a long thin howl above the wind crying through the trees.

She jostled against him. "Mechee—a wolf."

"Brother Wolf will not harm you."

"How can you call that beast your brother?"

"He is clever. Shawnee respect him." Wicomechee guided her through the dusky light to the cluster of evergreens. A rocky mound on the windward side of the trees offered additional cover. He paused before the dim outline of the thickly branched evergreen. "Go under."

She crawled beneath the sweeping boughs and hunched on the layer of needles. He slid in beside her. The force of the wind instantly lessened and he kept her in the innermost recess of their hideaway. He laid his musket down and slipped the shot pouch and powder horn from his shoulder, barely discerning their shapes in the gloom. His tomahawk joined the others at arm's length. The knife remained at his waist. Like trusted friends, he kept his weapons close.

The lone wolf inspired others and their chorus swelled in the wind-tossed night. Charity burrowed against him. "The whole pack's coming for us!"

"*Petweowas* will not come," he assured her.

How quickly she'd gone from regarding him as her greatest threat to her protector. Though he doubted she realized it.

"I wish we could have a fire to keep them at bay."

"We would burn all the trees in this wind. If Long Knives are near they will see the flames." He wrapped the wool blanket around them both then took slices of the ham from the pouch at his waist. "Here is food, eat. Gain strength. Tomorrow we will leave with the sun."

"Just now, I'm more concerned about surviving the night."

Breaks in the tossing boughs revealed the round white moon rising above the trees and the first stars glittered. "The moon is bright this night. If I must I will fire by its light. If a wolf comes near, he will die."

"A second one may attack before you have time to reload."

"I have other weapons. *Sedikoni*, eat."

She stayed as she was, her soft warmth pressed against his side, her face tucked in his shoulder. "Charity, have I been eaten by the wolf? Lost an arm or leg to his hunger?"

"No. But he may prefer me," she reasoned, her voice muffled against him.

Wicomechee smiled. "You will taste better?"

"Women might."

He chuckled. "You are foolish."

"Maybe so. But I'm not used to sleeping with wolves."

"I am. Eat, and I will give you a gift," he bargained.

She lifted her head. "What?"

He'd captured her attention. "First eat." He handed her a slice of the smoked meat. She chewed that while he ate six times as much and was still hungry. "Do you want more?"

"No. Give me what you promised."

He withdrew a handful of tiny berries from his

pouch, poured his find into her open palm and popped a few berries into her waiting mouth. She chewed with enthusiasm.

"I love these. Craig used to gather partridgeberries for me when he was hunting. They taste of wintergreen. He brought me hard candy once that tasted very much like them."

Wicomechee crunched several berries and the taste she'd declared wintergreen flavored his mouth. "Tell me of your brother."

"Oh, Craig was the best of brothers and far cleverer than the wolf you claim kin with."

Wicomechee smiled. "Who cared for you before Craig?"

"Papa. Mama died when I was three. I don't remember her, but Craig said she was nothing like Aunt Mary, and Papa told me I looked like my mother."

"Beautiful, then."

"If you say so."

She seemed embarrassed by his praise, yet pleased, which only charmed him all the more. "Why did your father not find a woman to care for you?"

"He did, after a bit. Aunt Mary wanted to take me, but Papa took on an indentured servant from England to tend me."

"Did your father never marry again?"

"No. He was too grieved and said he would be with Mama again in heaven. But he loved me. Aunt Mary vows he and Craig spoiled me entirely."

Wicomechee weighed Charity's disclosures. "You are not accustomed to doing as another says."

"Is it wrong to run free? To fly?" she asked, with more than a trace of wistfulness.

He popped the last berries in her mouth. "You would be snatched by a hawk. You must learn caution and obedience."

"And you think to be the one to teach me, I

suppose?"

He had no doubt.

"I may try your patience. I gave Aunt Mary fits."

"Do you think to frighten me? I possess more determination than you."

"More strength anyway. I don't expect you to indulge me as Craig did, but in some small way you remind me of him."

Her concession touched him, though it wasn't at all what he wanted. "This does not make me your brother."

"You would make a good big brother," she attempted.

"No."

"Why?"

It was as much of a plea as a question. Rather than another futile reply, he pushed back her hood and cupped his fingers around her chilled cheeks. Without a word, he tilted her face toward him.

"Mechee—" she balked, suddenly wary.

"Shhhh..." Mindful of her timidity, he lowered his head and gently covered her uncertain lips with his. From the first light touch, a wealth of sensations flowed into him like the headiest brew he'd ever tasted. The dewiest berry in the forest couldn't compare to the deliciousness of her lips...as though he'd truly captured an elusive spirit of the trees and held her now, claiming her mouth.

All else faded from his mind, the incessant warfare between their people, her deep-seated fear...there was only Charity and her melting sweetness. Desire surged through him with startling force, but he guarded this powerful urge.

She didn't try to pull back as he'd expected after her initial shock faded. If she had, he would have released her as he was resolved to do. Rather than fright, she relaxed against him...breathless, unresisting.

Manito had smiled upon him. He slid one hand to her smooth throat and felt her heart pulse beneath his fingers. As though unaware of what she did, she circled her arm around his neck and her lips parted. In that moment, he knew.

His own heart pounded like the beating of many drums. He'd never felt this inflamed when he'd kissed any other woman. Not even when—but no, he wouldn't think of her now. Charity was seductive without the least intention of being so, or the faintest knowledge of how to go about rendering a man speechless, witless, wanting only her. His loins throbbed with need, but he could never abuse such purity. With a will hammered from the fires of rigorous training, he restrained himself and slowly released her mouth.

She sighed near his ear, her warm breath intoxicating. The quiver running through her drew him like a fox scenting a hare. "Is this the kiss of a brother?" he whispered. "Your lips did not answer mine as a sister's."

"I didn't mean to answer you at all."

"Yet you did."

"I don't understand. I never even kissed Rob. He tried, but I ran away."

Her bewilderment amused Wicomechee. "No kiss for the great hunter."

"Nor for any man."

"None? What of the man in your dream?"

She hesitated. "Only him, until now. But you can't be that man, Mechee. You just can't."

"No?" He covered her protesting mouth with his and poured all the tender passion he possessed into a wondrous washing wave that engulfed them both. Almost as breathless as she, he pulled back slightly. "Tell me why I am not him?"

She sank, panting, against his shoulder. "That's not fair. You know I can't answer. But I can't stay with you."

He trailed his fingers through her glorious hair and felt her tremble at his touch. "Charity, when I first saw you at the river, you were sad, angry. You wished to run away."

"So you carried me off? What if I'd been happy?"

"I would have taken you anyway. I knew I would make you *newah*, my wife."

She jerked up her head. "Of a warrior? I couldn't possibly."

"It's simple. I choose you, you agree. We give each other our pledge."

"I can't believe you're saying this."

"You wish me to say I hate you? We are enemies?"

"No. But we are." She seemed to come to an abrupt awareness. "How can I wed someone who killed my father?"

"When did I do this?"

"Not you, exactly. Papa was killed by the Shawnee and their Indian allies at the defeat of General Braddock during the battle over Fort Duquesne. Fort Pitt now."

He thought back, her nearness distracting to the extreme. "Ah yes, I heard of this battle from returning warriors. I was fourteen years old, too young to fight."

"I was ten. Not too young to remember. Terror struck every settler's heart."

"That was a great victory for us. We had much feasting and dancing after."

"It was terrible. Hundreds of men died."

How different her memory was from his. "British Redcoats fought poorly. Many did not fight at all. They ran from our warriors in fear. Yet I am told the Virginia Long Knives fought with much courage.".

"I don't doubt Papa fought bravely, but he never

came home. Oh—you don't understand. You live to fight."

"No. I must fight to live."

She said nothing more and he grew still, their silence broken by the wind and the distant wolves. Finally, he spoke. "I know what it is to lose both mother and father. When I was a child, I lost them both."

"What happened?" she asked, sympathy warming her voice.

"My mother died after giving birth, her baby girl also."

"How sad. What of your father?"

He'd known she would ask, and the mere mention of that man sent painful venom coursing through him. "I cannot say."

"Why not?"

"I do not wish to speak his name, or anything regarding him," he said, fighting to conceal his virulent emotion.

She seemed mystified, but let it pass. "Who raised you?"

"My Grandfather. His English name is easier for you to speak. He is called Eyes of the Wolf."

"What a unique name. Is he the same grandfather who adopted Colin—I mean, Waupee?"

Wicomechee spoke with admiration and affection, so unlike his poisoned feelings for his father. "Yes. Eyes of the Wolf has much wisdom. I will take you to his *wickon*, his lodge, as my wife. Through me you will be adopted into the tribe."

She sucked in her breath. "No, Mechee. I'm frightened to death of Shawnee. I don't want to be one."

"You will come to accept us as Waupee did. He saved my life at the battle of Bushy Run, struck down the Long Knife who ran at me as I lay wounded. Because of him, I live. We both bear the scar from joining our blood. Here." Wicomechee placed her fingers on his wrist to feel the small scar.

She traced the raised line. "No wonder you are such good friends. Did Colin teach you to speak English?"

"More, yes. Some I already knew. I taught him our tongue and to become a great warrior."

"But how can he forget his own people?"

"Waupee has some regret, but he cannot return. Now that he has recovered his woman he will be content. He will never surrender her. And I will not let the Long Knives take you. When Captain Buchanan and his men come, we will be ready."

"I don't want you to kill them."

"I will kill who I must," he said gruffly.

"What if they kill you?" she asked with a new fearfulness in her tone.

"Have you had another of your warnings?"

"Not exactly."

He slid his fingers beneath her cloak and up under her sleeve. Goosebumps flushed over her arm. "The thought of my death troubles you?"

"A bit," she conceded with a hitch in her voice.

He untied her cloak and pressed his lips over the curve of her neck...like swans' down. "You feel some fondness for me? Before, you said I am only your enemy."

"You are. I'm just—having difficulty remembering."

He laughed. "You said your father was English, your mother Scottish. This made them enemies when they wed, yes?"

"No. That was entirely different."

"How?" he breathed out.

"It just is—I can't think when you do that."

He chuckled. Dragging his mouth from her smooth neck, he pulled her down onto the forest floor. The cloak cushioned her beneath and he covered them with the blanket. Stars glittered through openings in the boughs and the moon silvered the trees. He lay on his side, tucking her in his arms. "You belong to me. *Manito* gave you to me."

"Who on earth is *Manito*?"

"The Great Spirit of the Shawnee."

"For pity's sake, how can you expect me to become the wife of a man who isn't even Christian?"

"This Christian you speak of, I think many Englishmen are not."

"That's beside the point. You certainly aren't."

"Still, you shall be *newah*, my wife," he said, and buried his lips in the vulnerable crevice behind her ear.

"Wait," she stammered. "You said I must first agree. And that I never will."

"And I say you will call me husband, *wyshetche*."

"*Wyshetche*? Not unless you force me."

"Ah, Charity. I will have no need for force."

Chapter Seven

Straining to see beyond the braves ahead of her, Charity sought Wicomechee's familiar figure at every bend in the trail. Tiny chickadees darted into cedar boughs, white-tailed deer sprang away on slender legs and she spied a stately elk, but saw nothing of her captor. She should have remained with Emma on Stuart, instead of asking Colin to lift her from the big gelding. Now she'd fallen behind the couple and her search for Wicomechee was proving futile.

It doesn't matter, she told herself, and tried diligently to send her thoughts elsewhere. But they sailed back to the handsome warrior as if borne on the breeze.

Ashamed of how willing he'd found her lips when they took shelter beneath the evergreen, she'd resolved not to be alone with him again. Grudgingly forgiven by Outhowwa, she'd rejoined the larger party for yesterday's journey and ridden behind Emma on Stuart, collapsing beside her at the day's end. She'd seen Wicomechee only briefly at breakfast before the group had set off once more. He had no excuse for keeping her to himself tonight. If only she didn't wish he did.

A root caught her toe and she lurched forward, jerked back to reality. The warrior behind her grabbed her arm, preventing a fall, but he offered no other assistance. None of the men she journeyed between were particularly helpful. Wicomechee had given her far more aid than she'd realized on that initial trek. How distant her valley seemed, like the eagle wheeling high above her on the currents. Rugged mountains with their endless ups and downs were her world now.

Surely the warriors would stop soon. They'd hiked all day, pausing only for short breaks. The hasty lunch Colin had given her was long gone and an empty stomach gnawed at her along with her knee. Her breath in her throat, a stitch in her side, she clambered over yet another fallen limb.

Finally, the braves ahead of her angled to the left and she followed them into a clearing. Butterflies fluttering among white milkweed and purple asters scattered as the men passed into the trees. The sound of rushing water beckoned to her from beyond the brilliant leaves. Would the men just let her go there? She nervously scanned dozens of strange faces.

Strong fingers grasped her shoulder and spun her around. "Why did you not stay with Waupee?"

Relief displaced her momentary alarm and a quiver ran through her middle. "Mechee. I looked everywhere for you."

The annoyance in his face softened a little. "You would see me sooner if you stayed where I left you."

"I grew tired of riding."

"What of your knee?"

"Sore. May I go to the stream?"

"Go. Your friend waits there with the little ones. Waupee and Posetha tend the horses. I will get food."

She left the clearing and descended into the shade of hemlocks. The rasp of breathing was just audible above the gurgling water. She sought the source. The bloody homespun she glimpsed through the trees resolved into the shape of Rob Buchanan slumped at the base of a trunk, his wrists bound.

How she pitied him. A kind word from her might lighten his spirits, but she didn't dare approach the prostrate man. Outhowwa and Wicomechee had forbidden contact between them.

She crept past her would-be suitor and neared the roaring tumble. A small waterfall collected into a wide pool. Red cardinal flowers sank their roots into the moist shade, while purplish Joe-Pye weed grew in the sunny spaces.

James, Lily and the beagle played in the shallow end; Emma sat on a stone trailing her fingers in the clear water. Warriors knelt at the edge to drink and several waded near the fall. Chaka's broad bare shoulders stood out among these, but she refused to hang back on his account. He wouldn't dare molest her with so many gathered around. The scent of moist earth rose around her as she descended the fern-covered bank. She stopped beside Emma and reached down to take off her shoes.

Emma smiled wanly. "No chance of keeping you out?"

"None." Charity tossed her shoes beside the children's discarded pairs. She peeled off her stockings and dropped them and her cloak on the pile. Reveling in her bare toes, she stepped over the mossy stones and bent to drink.

Clusters of grapes dangled from the vines climbing throughout the trees on the other side of the pool. She pointed at the fat bunches partially concealed by yellow heart-shaped leaves. "Emma, look. I could fetch some."

"Better wait. The pool might be deep in the middle."

"Nonsense. I can swim if need be." Snatching up her skirts, Charity waded in past the children and collected warriors. She couldn't choke back a gasp, though, as the icy water climbed to her knees. She tugged the layers of her skirts higher and picked her way over the stones and grit on the streambed. The water now lapped well up her legs. Gritting her teeth against the chill, she waded farther in. As the water rose, so did her skirts, nearly to her thighs. "Good heavens, Charity! Have you cast all modesty to the wind?"

"I'm hungry! Aren't you?" she tossed over her shoulder.

"Yes," Emma admitted.

"Me too!" James and Lily chimed in.

Charity reached the pool's center. "Not so deep here—" she ventured, and promptly lost her footing on a slick stone.

Plunged backwards, she squealed as the icy water closed over her head. She floundered in her petticoats and surfaced, spluttering, to the amusement of the men. Chaka seemed especially entertained by her display.

"Come on back," Emma urged.

"Why? I can't get any wetter."

In spite of Chaka's mirth, or perhaps because of it, Charity waded doggedly to the other bank and struggled up the rocky incline. Her dripping skirts clung to her legs as she claimed her reward and sucked out the grape's tart sweetness. After harvesting handfuls of clusters, she waded back.

Emma eyed her in concern. "You'll take some drying out."

Charity thrust the fruit into her hands. "I'm fine. Take these. I'll harvest some more."

James and Lily pounced on their share and stuffed the fruit messily into their mouths. Emma hesitantly accepted her portion. "Thank you, dearest."

"For me, you also get, dearest?" Chaka mimicked. Surrounding warriors roared with laughter.

Tight-lipped, Charity waded past him, her skirts floating around her. She crossed to the pool's center forgetting the slippery spot in her anger. Again, she was thrown backwards, more forcefully this time. She scrabbled for her footing, choking on the water she'd gulped. One foot slipped between two large stones at the bottom. She fought to jerk it out, but was trapped and thrashed in a panic.

Powerful arms pulled her, strangling, to her feet.

Emma called out, "Charity! Are you all right?"

Chaka kept one hand on her shoulder as she coughed. It took several moments before she'd recovered her breath enough to sputter, "Yes!"

That infuriating smile played around his lips. "Pretty English girl cannot stand. I help you over."

She could imagine what kind of *help* he might offer if he got her on the other side, alone. "Leave me be."

He fingered her dripping hair. "I saved you from the water. I will not harm you."

At least he was sober, but the glint in his eyes wasn't reassuring. She pulled from him and backed away.

Weshe growled from the water's edge as Chaka stepped toward her, hand outstretched. "You are a frightened rabbit. Come, *petakinethi*. Will you hop from me?"

His taunt elicited more laughter from spectators.

An overpowering urge welled in Charity to see this arrogant warrior fall as she had done. With all the speed she could muster in sodden skirts, she hurled herself at him and shoved his solid bulk.

"Charity! No!" Emma shrieked.

Chaka staggered under the sudden impact, but held his ground. All trace of humor vanished from his face. "You attack me?"

No one laughed now. Multiple pairs of eyes watched, silent and expectant. Charity raked tendrils of wet hair away from her face. "I only tried to knock you down."

He drew thunderous brows together. "That is attack."

James grabbed the frantic beagle. "Charity didn't mean nothing! And she ain't no damn rabbit!"

Emma hushed him. "Apologize to Chaka at once, Charity."

She lifted her chin. "He provoked me."

Chaka's narrow gaze was unrepentant. "You provoke me."

He snagged her, shrieking, around the middle and lifted her up into the air then flung her into the icy pool. She landed on her back. Shaking with cold and fury, she staggered to her feet amid hoots from onlookers. She saw at a glance that Emma had gone, taking the furious dog with her.

"You lout!" Charity shouted up at Chaka.

"You will learn respect." Digging his fingers into her shoulders, he forced her back under the water.

She twisted to escape his grip, pushed against his legs, clawed at his hands, but he didn't budge. The cold water imprisoned her and her tortured lungs spasmed for air. Was he holding her under to teach her a lesson or something far more insidious?

If she took that desperately needed gulp, she'd drown. But she couldn't deny her body's reflexive need to breathe much longer. Her struggles grew more and more feeble.

Suddenly she was yanked to the surface and her chest filled again and again with great gasps of air. Chaka pulled her upright, and she swayed in his grasp. James and Lily crouched on the stone beside the pool, thin arms wrapped around each other, eyes wide, while the gathering looked on.

"Wicomechee will punish you," Charity choked out.

That maddening smile curved his lips. "I did nothing."

"You did plenty." He knew where and when. Drawing back her hand, she struck him across the cheek hard enough to leave her palm stinging.

"Charity! What are you doing?"

Wicomechee's shout rang out across the frozen tableau. All eyes followed his rush to the water.

Chaka jabbed his finger at her. "She attacked me."

"Why?" Wicomechee shot back.

He shrugged. "This English woman has much temper."

James jumped off the rock and ran to Wicomechee's side. "Chaka threw Charity in the water, two times!"

Wicomechee slid the musket, powderhorn, and shot pouch from his shoulders and laid them on the bank. He loosed the knotted sash at his waist and dropped the pouch and sheathed knife hanging from it onto the pile. "Wait here small one," he instructed James. Leaving his tomahawk behind, he waded into the pool wearing his shirt and buckskin vest. "Do you want to fight her or me?"

Chaka sneered. "Fighting is not what I want from her."

Like an incensed elk, Wicomechee flung himself at Chaka. He hurtled backwards, yanking Wicomechee down with him. Charity dodged the clashing men. Splashing through waist-high water, she headed to the bank where she'd gathered grapes and huddled beneath the vines.

More warriors joined the excited crowd.

Wicomechee smashed his fist into Chaka's jaw with a bone-cracking uppercut. Chaka reeled backwards, flailed to recover his balance, and stood unsteadily. Blood ran from his lip as he lunged at Wicomechee with a hoarse cry. Both men went down in a fury of churning water.

"*Howay, NiSawsawh!*" Colin burst from the

trees and shoved several braves aside to reach the water. He stripped the musket and powder horn from his shoulders. Flinging them on the bank, he charged into the stream between the battling men. "You want Outhowwa to know Charity's the cause of this?"

A punch intended for Wicomechee caught Colin on the cheek. He staggered back, eyes flashing. "Back off, Chaka."

"*Puckechey*! It's not your fight, Waupee."

The Englishman clenched his fists. "You leave that sweet girl alone, or I'll make it my fight."

Chaka's lip curled. "Sweet? She attacked me—"

"And didn't inflict nearly enough damage!" Colin swung hard and his knuckles opened a gash on Chaka's chin.

Chaka recovered and struck out, getting off a crack to Colin's jaw. He hurtled back—a momentary retreat—then tore into the warrior. His fists were a blur as he pummeled Chaka's face. The waterfall muffled onlookers' enthusiasm.

A visibly winded Emma staggered through the gold leaves. "Colin! Stop!" she cried, but he was beyond heeding her plea.

"*NiSawsawh!*" Wicomechee grasped Colin's arm, but his friend pulled free and plunged his fist into Chaka's stomach.

He doubled over, gasping like a stranded fish.

"Enough!" Wicomechee seized Colin's shoulders from behind, struggling to force him away.

Colin lunged. "Just one more good—"

"*Naga*," Wicomechee panted. "As you said, Outhowwa may be angry."

Chest heaving beneath his wet shirt, Colin wiped at the blood running down his cheek. "I'll stop, if Chaka will."

Chaka slowly straightened and regarded him through a rapidly swelling eye. Breathing hard, he gave a nod.

Wicomechee released Colin and gingerly fingered his jaw. "Keep away from my captive, Chaka."

"She attacked me first," he grunted, and turned away.

Charity chewed her lip as he left the pool. His sour expression made a sharp contrast with the other warriors, their spirits boosted by the entertainment. Now that the brawl was over, they followed him into the trees. She shivered from the chill and sobering awareness of her rash actions. Would Chaka complain about her to his father?

Colin waded back to his shaken flock and gathered Emma and Lily in a damp embrace. "It's over now," he said, tousling James's head.

Charity didn't dwell on this touching scene. Wicomechee was making his way through the water toward her. Any relief she'd felt at being rescued evaporated at the rigidity in his bruised face. She shrank back under the vines, feeling far more subdued than the woman who'd dared to defy Chaka.

In one lithe movement, Wicomechee was out of the water. With three short strides he stood over her, his black hair streaming. "You attacked Chaka first?"

She stared up at him, shivering in her wet clothes. "He provoked me," she faltered. " I only tried to knock him down,"

Disbelief mixed with the potent censure in Wicomechee's eyes. "Is this a fight you thought to win?"

"I didn't mean for it to be a fight."

"It is well Chaka has much desire for you, or I would find my fair captive with her throat cut."

"He made me so angry. I didn't think."

"No. You did not. Come, Charity. We will speak."

He appeared on the verge of a great deal more than that.

She waded behind him back across the pool. Emma and the children pressed around Colin. Emma clasped trembling fingers to her mouth. "Oh, Charity, whatever possessed you?"

"I can guess that easily enough." Colin reached his hand to Wicomechee's shoulder. "Let me handle matters if there's any trouble with Outhowwa."

He arched one brow. "You are the calm one?"

"Not so much where Chaka's concerned. But better than you with his father."

Wicomechee shrugged. "You speak."

The men caught up their weapons and supplies. Charity pulled on her stockings and shoes. Colin headed up the trail with Emma and the children. Wicomechee fell in behind him, his displeasure with Charity evident in the set of his shoulders. She grabbed her cloak and followed. The wrap did little to ease her chill or trepidation.

Camp lay above the falls in the grove of hemlocks. Their boughs rocked with the evening breeze. Thin high clouds like soft white fish scales laced the sky. A change was coming in the weather, though there was no sign of impending rain beyond the swirls overhead. She sensed a change coming for her too.

As their subdued group approached, they found warriors eating chestnuts, cornmeal and the last of the ham carried off on their raid. Some sharpened knives or cleaned muskets. One animated group was playing a game of cards before the light faded. Campfires were still taboo for fear of detection.

Outhowwa sat, flanked by warriors, his back against a large stone. Some men recently come from the stream walked between them, but the eagle-eyed chief took in Colin and Wicomechee's damp, battered state and shifted his study to Charity. His mouth tightened at the sight of his son.

"*Umbe* Chaka," he said, motioning to him with his fingers.

Charity waited in an agony of suspense. Would Chaka rush to Outhowwa with accusation? To her surprise, he approached his father with evident reluctance. Arms crossed over his chest, he stood in rigid silence as Outhowwa questioned him.

Chaka strained each short syllable through his teeth.

Clearly dissatisfied, Outhowwa pressed him for more.

"*Naga*," Chaka bit out, and strode away.

Colin and Wicomechee exchanged glances. Colin left his little band with Muga and walked to the exasperated chief. Charity slipped behind Wicomechee and peered around him.

Earnest words passed between the two men. Then humor hinted unexpectedly in Colin's face and a slight smile curved Outhowwa's hard mouth. Colin sat beside him. Their conversation flowed more easily, the mood lighter.

"Come, Charity." Carrying his blue-black blanket, Wicomechee stole from the camp. She followed at his heels through the hemlocks, past rhododendrons. He stopped on the other side of a thick white cedar. "Here. Speak softly."

They were only yards from the others. "Are we hiding?"

"No. Just keeping away for a time."

Her skirts dripped steadily onto the carpet of needles. "What of Outhowwa? What did Colin say to make him smile?"

Wicomechee slipped off his musket and laid it on the ground with his blanket. "He said you wish to be a warrior."

She couldn't be certain if he were serious. "Really?"

Wicomechee's supplies joined the musket, and he took off his vest. "Waupee said you are a foolish woman who thinks to fight his son. Warriors laugh at you both."

She clutched trembling arms around herself. "Is that why Chaka is so angry?"

"You caused him shame."

"What of Outhowwa? Is he still angry with me?"

"Not so much." Wicomechee stripped his shirt over his head, exposing the chiseled planes of his chest.

Apprehension undercut her sense of relief. "Are you?"

He spread the fabric over a green bough and draped his vest. "Speak later. Clothes must dry. We can make no fire."

"I can't undress with you here."

"You prefer to freeze? I will share my blanket."

"At least turn your head."

****

Wicomechee looked away, watching from the corners of his eyes as Charity dropped her cloak beside his pile. She tugged at her bodice, fumbling the ties with grape-stained fingers.

"Blast these laces." She shook all over.

"Let me help you," he offered.

"Oh, all right. I grow more chilled by the moment."

He freed the sodden cords, peeled the bodice from her, and tossed it to the fragrant tree. He undid the drawstring at her waist and pulled the saturated petticoats to her knees. She shivered out of the bedraggled heap. Her shift clung to each rounded breast and puckered nipple. The pleasing sight nearly took his breath away.

"You're enjoying this," she protested through chattering teeth.

He smiled and swept his admiring gaze over her.

Despite her slender build, her breasts would spill over his hands if he cupped them, and her hips curved enticingly. He fingered the drawstring at her neck. "You would be warmer without this."

She crossed her arms over her chest in an attempt at modesty. "You are not removing anymore. I'll be naked."

"Yes."

"You are not supposed to be looking at me," she chided, and grabbed up her cloak to wrap in.

"How can I stop my eyes from such beauty?"

She settled, shaking, beneath the cedar. "Do you truly find me beautiful, stained from grapes, my hair a tangle?"

He knelt beside her and ran his fingers through the damp spill covering her like a second mantle. "Truly, I do."

"Perhaps purple becomes me," she said with a half-smile.

"Any color." He sat at her side and closed the blanket around his shoulders then drew her beneath the cover. "I will warm you, feed you. Then we will speak."

She shook against him. "I hoped you'd forget that."

"No. Though you give me other thoughts."

"Good ones?"

What a guileless girl. He was acutely aware of her body pressed hip to hip against his. She kindled a fire in him that shot a scorching signal to his loins. If he weren't careful, all rational thought would flee.

"Very good." Taking slices of jerky from his pouch, he handed them to her.

She bit into the meat, darting glances at him. A pink blush stained her cheeks and she looked away.

What had triggered the flush and averted eyes? Did her feelings flow as his, like a swift stream?

She ate in silence, seemingly doing her best to

conceal her emotions.

He took hickory nuts already separated from their shells out from under the blanket and gave them to her. She devoured her share and he crunched his, enjoying the nutty flavor. "Would you like these?" he asked, dipping his hand back into his pouch and opening his fist to reveal the tiny red berries.

She looked wonderingly from his offering back up to him. "When did you gather them?"

"While you warred with Chaka."

"Oh." She lowered her guilty gaze. Scooping up some of the berries, she poured them into her mouth and slowly chewed.

He chewed the remaining portion.

She seemed to come to a decision. "I'm sorry...for most of what I did, anyway."

"Only most?"

"Surely, you can't expect me to regret everything? Not after what Chaka did to me."

"You risked much. Who taught you to behave this way?"

"Craig said never to let any man get the best of me."

Wicomechee doubted she had any real idea what he meant. "If I had not come, Chaka would have gotten more than this."

"He taunts me. He's infuriating."

"Can you not hold your tongue, pretend not to hear?"

"He called me a scared rabbit."

Wicomechee considered her in bemusement. "For this, you struck him?"

"No. That's why I tried to knock him down."

"You are like a small dog who attacks the wolf. Must I tie you to a tree?"

"Why won't Chaka leave me be?"

"Has no one told you anything of men?"

"Not really. I asked Colin. He said to ask Emma, only she won't tell me. Or my husband, when I have one."

Wicomechee's chuckle interrupted her.

"I was being serious," she reproached him.

"I see this. Also see something more. You asked me to tell you what Chaka wishes."

Charity weighed him with a cautious look. "So?"

"My brother told you to learn from your husband. Do you want me for your husband?"

Her mouth fell open. "I—just thought you might say."

"I prefer to show you."

She blinked at him.

He closed his arms around her and pulled her inviting softness against him. To his delight, she sank into his embrace. Her smooth back was firm beneath his hands. "Be my wife, Charity. I will teach you what you ask, give you much pleasure."

She stiffened as if catching herself. "I can't. You ask the impossible, Mechee."

He pressed his lips to her damp hair. "Why do you continue to speak this name? I think you can say Wicomechee."

"I hardly know. It's more of a feeling really."

"Tell me," he invited.

"Wicomechee is a warrior I fear. Mechee is…my friend."

He blew lightly into her ear. "I would be far more."

A tremor ran through her. "I mustn't let you."

Not only her wonderfully responsive body, but her words betrayed her. He pounced on them like a sharp-eared cat. "Now you say mustn't. Before, you say can't."

"Can't, mustn't, shouldn't—what's the difference?"

"Shouldn't is weaker still," he pointed out.

She buried her face in his shoulder. "I wish you didn't speak English so well."

He chuckled. Not once had she said she didn't want him. He smoothed her hair aside and pressed his lips down the curve of her neck. "Do not hide from me, sweet one."

Goosebumps flushed over her. "I'm afraid to do anything else."

"Why? Am I harming you?"

"No—"

"What of this?" he asked, untying her cloak at her neck.

"I'll grow cold if you take that from me."

"Not in my arms." He spread the cloak beneath them and coaxed her down onto the earth, covering them both with his blanket. Turning onto his side, he held her to him. Only her shift lay between them and her breasts swelled against his chest. He took care to shield her from his pulsing loins. "Are you still frightened?"

"Some."

Yet, he felt her pressing nearer. "Do you like my touch?" he asked, loosening the drawstring of her shift and sliding his fingers over her smooth shoulder.

"Yes," she admitted with a shiver.

"Why such fear to wed me?"

She sighed. "How can I betray my father and all the others who died at Shawnee hands? Your people are brutal."

"I do not ask you to wed my people. Only me. Am I brutal?"

"Not just now."

"Never to you. Tell me again why you cannot care for me."

She struggled to reply as though his nearness muddled her mind. "It's not that I don't care. I can't wed my enemy."

Beth Trissel

She gasped as he slid his hand lower and rested it just above her left breast. Her heart pounded beneath his fingers and it was all he could do not to let them stray. "Your heart agrees not with your words. Why not do as your heart wishes?"

Her chest rose and fell under his palm. "My heart forgets you are Shawnee."

"Let us see if your lips remember," he coaxed, and curled his fingers around her cheek.

"Don't kiss me. Please."

He halted a whisper away from her lips. "I will not, if you do not wish it. Tell me you do not."

"It's not that I don't wish it. I mustn't."

"Again you speak this. Can you not do better?"

Settling his lips over hers, he silenced her faint refusal. Her mouth parted beneath his and all his feelings for her swelled inside him. She pressed his lips in return...the elusive spirit of the trees bending under his persuasion and giving back to him. What bliss it would be to join himself to this fairest of women. And if she conceived with his seed, what a strong beautiful infant she would bear. These imaginings charged him with even greater desire, as though he'd swallowed the most powerful love potion.

Twice he released her mouth only to surge back, covering her lips again. A small whimper escaped her but she did not try to break away. And he couldn't possibly get enough of her lips. Her kiss was honeyed torment, her scent heated his blood. Whether she understood what she did or not, she called to him and he longed to drink great draughts of her nectar.

"Enough—no more—" she pleaded, flushed against him.

"Ah, Charity. I could make you my wife now, so easily."

"How? We haven't even exchanged vows."

Even in the deepening dusk he saw her perplexity. Groaning at her ignorance, he forced himself to stay his hand. "So tempted I am to take you."

"But you will not?"

"Not without your consent to wed. I give you my word."

"I cannot give you mine."

She would drive him mad. There was only one immediate solution. "I will return you to your cousin."

Still, she held to him in all her alluring sweetness. "Must I go from you?"

Despite being nearly wild with frustration, he smiled. "You will not agree to wed me, yet you wish to remain in my arms?"

"What will happen if I stay?"

"Do you really want to know?" he whispered.

"Better take me to Emma."

"Hide by her while you may."

Chapter Eight

Charity gazed around her in amazement. How had she come to be in this grand room? Never had she beheld such luxury.

Candelabras on the blue walls shone over an immense sideboard that held sprigged-floral platters heaped with pastries, steamed puddings, fish in sauce, roast beef, and a whole cooked goose. Red and yellow apples and nuts of all sorts spilled from the polished silver bowls. A magnificent table ran the length of the room, laden with china plates, soup bowls, silver spoons, forks, pearl-handled knives and sparkling goblets filled with red wine. Ornate chairs carved of fine wood with seats of gold cloth lined the table.

Servants waited to serve the merry party of ladies and gentlemen entering through the double doors. The elegant assembly was dressed as she'd always imagined the wealthy would be. Men wore tailored coats and breeches of rich fabric. Ruffled shirts showed above their waistcoats.

What a contrast the ladies' glowing gowns made to her plain homespun. Flowered fabric or stunning solids in blue and crimson draped their shapely figures. Conserving precious cloth wasn't a concern given the abundance used, and they displayed a great deal more bosom than she was accustomed to.

Powdered wigs covered many heads, though some men wore their own hair pulled back and tied at the neck with black ribbons as Colin had when Charity first met him. Ladies piled their tresses high on their heads, tendrils at their cheeks. Jewels winked at their white throats. Rings shone on the men's fingers as they assisted the women to their seats.

An impressive figure stood at the head of the table, his muscular build evident beneath his stylish clothes. A smile creased his weathered features and crinkled the corners of his blue eyes. Still in his prime, he would be about the same age as her father if he'd lived and bore some resemblance to him, including red hair. But so many years had passed since her father's death that she couldn't be certain of his appearance.

"A toast!" the man called out.

The glad assembly raised their glasses.

She sidled nearer the jovial host, but he continued as if he hadn't seen her. No one at the table took any more notice of her than if she were a ghost. She lifted a pastry from the sideboard and bit into the meat filling. Savoring the delicacy, she eyed the fir boughs and holly decorating the wide mantle. Was it Christmas? Their servant, Hannah, had spoken of lavish parties given in the great homes at Yuletide.

Lilting music summoned Charity from the fireside. She glimpsed a spacious hall through the open doorway. Musicians seated in a candle-lit corner plied bows to their fiddles. Others blew flutes. One man sat before what she guessed was a harpsichord. They played while the merry company ate.

Then the music changed in tempo and swelled to a jig. Laughing couples rose from the table. Arm in arm, they entered the hall and formed two columns, gentlemen on one side and ladies on the other. Partners joined hands, circling and promenading up and down. The couples separated to step and turn with others in the figure, yet always finding each other again. Some of the steps Charity knew, while others were far more complex. Her tapping feet longed to join in.

"Dance with me," a low voice invited.

She turned to see a tall young man behind her. When had he arrived? She hadn't noticed him among the company.

He held out his hand. "Come."

She reached out hesitantly. "I don't know the steps."

"I will teach you."

She looked closely. His handsome face was familiar, but he was dressed as she'd never thought to see him. "Mechee?"

****

Charity awoke to cold gray light. Divergent emotions churned inside her, leaving more questions than answers in the bewildering flood. Her heart behaved like an unruly child who must be restrained. She was at a loss to face Wicomechee, or the day. Maybe she could escape into oblivion a bit longer—

"Wake up!" James bounded at her like an exuberant dog.

She sat up, gripping the wool wrap. "Give me a minute."

"I did. Lots." He pounced on Lily, asleep beside her.

"Easy." Charity would like to give him a sound shake.

He ignored her and heaved the bleary-eyed child to her feet. "Get a move on, Charity!" he called over his shoulder, and propelled Lily in the direction of the stream.

"Who put you in charge of me?"

"I sent him to wake you," Wicomechee said from behind her and slipped his fingers over her disheveled hair.

A host of sensations swelled in her that she didn't begin to know what to do with. "I'm weary,

Mechee."

He stepped around her and held out grapes, nuts, and cornmeal. "This will give you strength."

"*Megwich.*" She'd have preferred corn mush, sizzling bacon and hot tea, but her empty stomach wouldn't complain.

He sat beside her as she wolfed down his offering.

"I dreamed I ate a delicious pastry. You were there too in a great house and dressed as a gentleman."

His brow furrowed. "Are you making me English?"

"I don't understand the meaning of the dream. But you asked me to dance."

"I know some English dancing."

She almost choked on her grapes. "How?"

He smiled. "Waupee taught me. He drank too much rum and sang very loud. We danced in my grandfather's *wickon.*"

She tried to imagine the two men dancing around an Indian lodge and smiled despite herself. "Did you also drink rum?"

"A little." He slid his fingers over her cheek with enticing ease. "You tremble."

Every time he touched her. "I'm cold."

"Were you chilled in the night?"

"Yes." She refused to concede any more than that.

"Stay by my side tonight. I will warm you well."

"I cannot."

"Or will not?" he pressed.

"Both. I don't intend to be alone with you again."

He shrugged, but she sensed a reserve in his manner not present before. "We shall see."

"No. Please. Let me stay with Emma and Colin."

He frowned at her. "You are my captive, Charity."

"Couldn't I be his?"

"You wish to belong to Waupee?"

"I feel safe with him."

"Not with me?"

Dropping her eyes from the chill in Wicomechee's, she shook her head.

"Go then. Journey with my brother. Sleep by his side."

****

Charity twisted to ease the crick in her back. Her fingers were numb and chafed from picking through burs for those still containing nuts. Animals and warriors had scoured the chestnuts closest to camp. "I can't find anymore here."

"Me either," James grunted. Droplets beaded the blanket wrapping him from head to foot. His cheeks were rosy from the wind and the damp cold reddened the tip of his freckled nose.

"Oh, for a warm blaze and a fat goose roasting over it."

He brightened. "Wicomechee and Posetha promised to take me hunting when we have a fire."

She stood, using her cloak as a basket for their find. "Likely those two are off together now." Posetha had avoided her since his humiliation by Outhowwa and Wicomechee disappeared after their curt exchange this morning.

James straightened. "I dunno where they are."

Charity swiveled her head at the foggy trees, her spirits as bleak as the gray clouds cloaking the ridges. "If Mechee doesn't want to be found, he won't be," she said with a sigh.

"Are you sad?"

"Just tired and hungry. Come on. It'll be dark soon."

They tracked back along the soggy path. His liveliness dampened by the long day, James lagged behind and Weshe followed, tail drooping. Emma and Lily were as they'd left them, slumped together against the silvery trunk of a yellow maple. Emma's hood covered most of her face and her cloak also enclosed the child. Fatigue was plain in the way they slouched together, but they needed to eat. Charity ducked under the branches and emptied her nuts into Emma's lap.

She roused. "Thank you. Sorry I'm so useless."

"James and I can manage."

"Yep." He opened the skin of a chestnut with a sharp rock and handed the peeled nut to Emma, then plopped down beside his sister and set to work on the rest of the pile.

Lily woke and took the nutmeat he offered. Emma chewed hers without enthusiasm. "Chestnuts are far better roasted."

Charity blew on her cold fingers. "I'll go and see what else I can find."

"You've already been. Colin and Wicomechee will have something."

"Colin will be a while yet." Charity glimpsed him through the hazy foliage, rubbing down Stuart's flanks.

Emma's lips pursed. "Sometimes, I think he cares more for that horse than he does for me."

"Nonsense. You and Lily would never manage on foot. Besides, when Colin looks at you, his eyes are so tender."

"I suppose so," Emma said, her demeanor mellowing. "Wait on Wicomechee, then. He should be along soon."

"Heaven knows where he is. I haven't seen him all day."

"That's strange. Won't he be joining us with food?"

"He might not, after what I said this morning."

Creases lined Emma's smooth brow. "Oh my. It won't be easy to manage without him. Colin can only do so much."

"I know, but what am I to do? Marriage is out of the question."

Emma's expression grew thoughtful. "Wicomechee is attractive and clever, and he speaks well for—"

"Not you, too," Charity broke in.

"We're stuck out here, Charity. Each day takes us farther and farther away from the life we knew. Besides, you care for him."

"Not so much."

"More than a little," Emma countered.

Charity evaded her scrutiny and watched a brown rabbit hop past the tree. "That doesn't mean I want to be his wife."

"Who are you going to wed then, Posetha, Chaka?"

Charity recoiled. "How can you even suggest Chaka?"

"I wasn't being serious about him, but captive women who don't wed within the tribe can end up as some sort of slaves. And women in the village will treat you badly if you haven't got a husband. Colin told me."

"Would she be like Jenna?" James asked in a shocked whisper, referring to the Negro purchased by a valley family. "She got whipped real bad."

Lily looked around in drowsy confusion. "Who's Jenna?"

"Never mind. I'm not going to be anyone's slave," Charity said. "Colin won't let that happen. Or Mechee."

"But if you've offended him, who can say what he'll do for you?" Emma asked.

"I didn't mean to offend him. Oh, Emma, he asks too much."

"Calm down. No one's forcing you to marry him. But consider carefully. Some captives are sold to the

French."

"Dear God." Charity stood and did what she normally did whenever life became too overwhelming—walked, or ran, away. "I'll go and see what else I can find to eat."

"Don't stray. The warriors won't approve," Emma warned.

"I won't." Charity left the trio in a shower of yellow leaves, Weshe at her heels. If nut trees weren't at hand, she'd peel black birch bark and strip the inner layer. It was nourishing and tasted of wintergreen. Wicomechee showed her.

She stepped across knobby roots and rocks, wet branches brushing her shoulders. A likely tree emerged in the haze. Remembering his caution, she snapped a twig and sniffed the disappointing whiff of bitter almond. Wild cherry was poisonous.

A trace scent of wintergreen wafted up from beneath her feet. She looked down. A few partridgeberries clung to the waxy green leaves creeping across the trail. Weshe nosed in the undergrowth as Charity sank down onto the fragrant mat and plucked every berry, devouring her find like a famished deer.

Fat raindrops spattered her cheek. Slipping cold hands inside her cloak, she got to her feet. "Come on, Weshe."

The beagle stood as if rooted to the trail, staring into the foggy pine boughs. Tiny chipmunks scurried over the leaf-strewn earth. Nothing appeared amiss. Yet the dog growled from deep in his throat, and the fur on his back bristled.

"Weshe," she summoned, turning away. Whatever it was, they'd leave it behind—

A snuffling sounded behind her and she spun back around. The lower boughs of a massive evergreen whipped about like the last leaves of autumn in a late-season storm. Needles sprayed down as two large branches spread with the wet crack of living wood. A black nose nearly as big as her fist pushed between the broken limbs. Another rough snort and the broad snout and huge hairy head forced through the opening. Then an enormous brown bear heaved its thickly pelted bulk out of the trees right in front of her.

Charity staggered backwards with a gasp. Beady black eyes inspected her coldly without any evidence of surprise. She stood frozen in place, but her mind raced; run, don't run, play possum, climb a tree—wait—couldn't bears climb?

Weshe charged forward barking madly. The bear snarled and struck out at him with a big claw-studded paw. "Weshe!" Darting back and forth, the little dog kept just out of reach.

The annoyed bear swiped again at Weshe, then reared up on his hind legs and roared, exposing a great mouthful of wicked-looking teeth. Charity's paralysis broke. Bolting past the ferocious creature, she raced off the trail into the trees. Branches snagged her skirts and her hair as her hood flew back, but she tore free and ran on.

Trunks loomed out of the mist ahead of her and just as quickly disappeared behind. She had no idea in what direction her desperate flight carried her. The wet leaves threw her off balance and she latched onto a sapling for support. Without pausing to catch her breath, she sprang away again.

Weshe's baying faded as she rushed headlong through the woods. She thought she heard a musket fire from somewhere behind her, but couldn't be certain. Her chest drummed and her ears pounded.

Not slacking her speed, she shot out from the trees into a rocky clearing. She skidded to a halt, sliding on the loose pebbles underfoot. The ground fell away before her into a deep unexpected ravine. A few scraggly trees and undersized brush grew among the large gray boulders that led up to the brink. Sides heaving, she picked her way to the edge.

Cold rain stung her cheeks and the wind thrashed her skirts as she peered down into the yawning chasm. Clouds shrouded the lofty swells on the other side. Only a bird could bridge the gulf between them. Rivulets of water ran down the sides of the ravine and into the misty hollow below.

Unlike the overlook Wicomechee had shown her, this drop wasn't immediate. Rocky outcroppings interspersed the sparse trees for a hundred yards before the stony grade dropped off into a tremendous slide. Not a plunge she cared to take, but which was worse, her fear of heights or of bears? Yellowed fangs and enormous claws glinted in her mind's eye.

Grasping a twisted branch, she scrambled over the side, buffeted by the wind. She clung to the slippery bark with one hand and strained toward the next branch, scrabbling at the rocky ground with her shoes. Just a bit farther and she could wedge herself in among the stones. With any luck, the bear wouldn't see her or risk searching down here.

She stretched a little farther, reaching. Her foot slid out from beneath her, the limb slipped out of her grasp and she spilled down the slope, slamming onto the ledge. She bit back a shriek at the pain knifing through her ankle and pulled herself into the narrow space between two jutting stones. Tortured moments passed. No ominous growls carried over the constant wind. Weshe had grown silent.

Shielding her face with her hand, she looked up. No snarling mouth greeted her fearful gaze. Had she fought shy of the bear? Had Weshe? Heart in her throat she waited, every overtaxed muscle in her body shaking.

Even if she'd successfully escaped its jaws, she'd freeze to death wedged among these rocks. No one knew she was here and she couldn't make it back up the side of the gorge unaided. Teeth chattering, she wriggled further into her crevice to break some of the wind's force. More raindrops spattered. The heavens might open up at any moment and drench her to the skin. Groaning, she buried her face in her arms.

A whimper overhead snapped her back to wide-eyed alertness. Bears didn't whine, but distressed dogs did. Squinting against the rain, she looked up.

Her heart leapt in her throat. Wicomechee stood at the edge of the drop off with Weshe in his arms. She couldn't clearly see his expression but he didn't seem equally pleased to see her.

"Mechee! Thank God!"

He set the beagle down. "Stay, Weshe."

Grasping the same slim limb she had, he swung over the side. He seized the next branch and dropped nearer, his moccasins finding toeholds in the rocky grade.

"I was afraid no one would find me."

"The trees have eyes, Charity."

****

Wicomechee climbed down the rocks and caught hold of the tree limb above Charity. There she sat, huddled among the stones like a forlorn dove. Why could she not remain where she was told for once? It was well he'd kept a furtive watch over her. One this impulsive needed continual guarding and his brother had let her slip from his sight.

Resentment at the hold Waupee seemed to have on Charity gnawed at Wicomechee. The gladness in her face upon sighting him stirred fresh hope, but that might just be relief at her rescue. She might have been just as glad to see Posetha or Muga; no doubt particularly overjoyed had he been Waupee.

Annoyed again, he braced himself with his feet and bent toward her. The hazy ground lay far below. He stretched his free hand out to her.

She reached toward him. Misting rain wet their fingers—mustn't let her slip. He clasped her chilled hand. "Come."

Secure in his hold, she scooted from her nook and started up the cliff. "Have care," he cautioned. "The stones are slick."

"That's how I came—" she broke off as her foot slid. She dug in her toes and her ankle buckled. "Oooh—"

He braced himself to prevent them both from falling and held on. She sucked in her breath and glanced down. "Mechee!"

"I have you."

She turned her face toward him. Tears filled her eyes.

"What have you injured?"

"My ankle," she gulped.

He hoped she hadn't broken it. "Look only at me."

Gripping her hand, he climbed to the next branch and pulled her up onto the stone slightly beneath him. He grasped the next limb and hoisted her into the crevice at his side.

"Almost there." He saw her try not to look down as he towed her along step by step.

One of the stones slid beneath his moccasin. Another gasp sounded from Charity. But he quickly recovered his balance and worked his way to the limb nearest the top.

Breathing hard, he heaved her over the side, muddied shirts and all. She crawled shakily away from the edge and collapsed on the hard, wet ground. Weshe licked at her face.

Wicomechee pushed the dog out of the way and knelt beside her. "Let me see." He ran his fingers over her stocking-clad leg and gently felt along her ankle.

She winced as he carefully rotated her foot. He

hadn't meant to cause her pain. "I think you have only turned your ankle. A poultice will take the swelling down."

He stood and drew Charity to her feet. "Lean on me. I will help you to camp."

She lifted her face, uncertainty in the wash of emotions in her eyes. Again, he saw that mixture of wanting and wariness, of reaching out and pushing him away just as he had this morning. Would she ever fully accept him?

The branches ahead of them parted and Waupee appeared. His brows arched in marked surprise. "Charity, what on earth?"

She left Wicomechee and staggered toward him. "I twisted my ankle going over the side."

"Why in God's name did you do that?"

Giving a short cry, she went down on one knee.

Waupee sprang to her side and drew her up, closing ready arms around her. Shoulders shaking, she burrowed into his embrace. "There, there, dear heart. You'll be all right."

Anger roiled through Wicomechee like storm clouds and red haze colored the gray mist.

Waupee regarded him with a puzzled squint. "What happened, *NiSawsawh*?"

"Let her speak. She prefers your ears, your arms," he ground out.

For once, Waupee seemed at a loss to reply.

Without another word, Wicomechee strode into the trees.

****

The stone ledge protruding from the side of a less hostile ridge kept the rain from Charity as she huddled in the blanket, but cold breezes found their way beneath her skirts. And this was only the beginning of foul weather. Plenty more lay ahead as the autumn days shortened and frigid nights grew longer. Beyond that, winter storms lurked like thieves lying in wait.

Such morose thoughts did nothing to lift her spirits, nor was she cheered by the pleasant company. Careful not to arouse further suspicion, she sat well back from Colin and consequently Emma. James and Lily also snuggled near their Uncle Papa, as the children affectionately called him. Muga and an amiable warrior called Hoskasa enjoyed the Englishman's wit and cast appreciative glances at his wife. Even Weshe left her to go sleep by James. No one had seen Wicomechee since their terse encounter at the cliff.

Laughter rose from the circle, the merriment lost on Charity. Only snatches of the conversation reached her as Colin translated portions to Emma. She spied Rob beyond their rocky shelter, squinting at her through the rain. Outhowwa came up behind him. Seeing where Rob's attention lay, the chief seized his arm and sped him toward another outcropping.

Chaka stepped from the mist, pausing outside her overhang. "Waupee," he grunted. "Muga, Hoskasa."

The three men nodded a greeting. Chaka's eyes swept past them and fixed on Charity. After an unnerving moment, he proceeded in his father's direction. Posetha ducked inside her ledge, his glum manner so unlike the friendly brave she'd first met. He picked up a blanket left on the dry leaves beneath the stone and sat beside Muga.

"Posetha, will Mechee come?" she asked.

He shrugged. "Hard rain may bring him."

"Are you pining for my brother?" Colin asked.

She swiped at a tear. "I just wondered. That's all."

"Then why are you weeping?"

"My ankle." It still ached despite the poultice, though that wasn't what really troubled her; she had no idea how to ease the throbbing pain in her heart.

****

Wicomechee stooped under the overhang where the others sheltered. Rain ran down his face and his shirt clung to him beneath his vest. He could take the wet and the cold. This burning anger and sting of betrayal was far worse.

"*NiSawsawh*, you decided to join us," Waupee said by way of greeting. "I suppose you prefer our company to Chaka's."

"To Chaka? Yes." Barely glancing at his English brother, or Charity, just visible in the murky light, Wicomechee laid his musket down and settled near Posetha.

He detected a sniffle from behind him, but was determined to ignore Charity's tears. Likely they had to do with that thieving Waupee who clearly wanted both women. And why not? His golden haired wife was great with child. Charity would do well to slake his lust until Emma was fit for his ardor.

If she wanted Waupee so be it. Wicomechee had done with her, he vowed, angling a glance in her direction. He slipped his powderhorn and shot pouch from his shoulder, untied the bedroll at his back and draped the blanket around his shoulders. She could huddle in her corner for all he cared.

She turned her face to the stone as if to hide her weeping from him, but stifling sobs seemed no easy matter. Bent on release, they escaped her as jarring hiccups.

"You sound like a sow with a bellyache," Waupee told her.

The children giggled and even Posetha chuckled, but Wicomechee kept his stony silence.

"Here, gal. I was saving this, but you need it more." Waupee held out a pewter flask.

She turned toward him. "Mustn't take your last

drop. I'll get a drink from the stream."

"Now?" Waupee asked, voicing Wicomechee's disbelief.

Rising unsteadily, she cracked her head against the low ceiling. With a cry, she stumbled and sprawled across Muga.

"You beat all, girl. For heaven's sake, *NiSawsawh*, help her," Waupee said.

Wicomechee stayed as he was. "She does not want my help."

Colin threw his hands up. "Oh, don't be so bullheaded."

Muga gently righted her. Posetha made room and the big warrior tucked her in between the two of them. Again, Waupee extended the open flask. This time she took it.

"Wicomechee, I swear, you're as stubborn a fellow as I ever saw, sitting there brooding while Charity goes to pieces," Waupee chided him.

He bit back, "She is yours to trouble with now."

Charity tilted the flask and gulped, choking, on the potent brew. "Sip, don't gulp," Waupee cautioned her then bent toward Wicomechee. "You don't mean that."

"You want two women. I give you mine."

"That is the most ridiculous thing I've ever heard."

Heat flared in Wicomechee's gut. "I saw you hold her."

"For pity's sake. Was I to offer the girl no comfort?"

Wicomechee crossed both arms over his chest. "Offer her all you like. I care not."

"I do not mind to comfort her," Posetha said.

"*Naga*," Wicomechee growled at him.

"If you do not want her—"

Charity convulsed into a coughing fit.

"Posetha, enough," Waupee admonished.

113

"*NiSawsawh*, your heart is full for this girl and you know it."

"Her desire is for you."

"I'm not the one she's weeping her eyes out for."

"I'm not—weeping," Charity argued in a strangled voice.

"You're every bit as stubborn as he is, little sister."

Wicomechee sat bolt upright. "She is your sister?"

"Not an official adoption. It doesn't make her yours. It's just how I feel about her."

The fury drained from Wicomechee like water from a damned up creek and he turned his attention to Charity. "Always you seek a brother. Is this what you want from Waupee?"

She nodded and managed a quavering, "Yes."

He reached across Posetha and touched her damp cheek, tracing her tears with his fingers. "Why do you weep?"

"You wouldn't come. Wouldn't speak to me."

"We speak now?"

Waupee waved him on. "Go. Give the rest of us a moment's peace."

Wicomechee got to his feet. Keeping his head low, he reached down and helped Charity up. She staggered, clutching his arm, and leaned on him as she hobbled to her former solitary corner. "It's all the fault of that bear, chasing me toward the ravine," she got out between winces.

"If you stayed by my side I would shoot the bear before he gave chase."

"I thought you no longer cared for me."

If that were true his life would be far easier but cheerless as gray coals. "My caring is all for you."

She sank onto the leaves and didn't seem to know what to say or do. Lifting the flask, she took another pull.

"Will you drink until the whiskey is gone?"

"'Tis warm and soothing. How do you abide the chill?"

He sat beside her. "Shawnee dip their children in the river each day, even little ones, to make them strong."

"No wonder you aren't shaking. I hate being cold."

"I do not prefer it." He peeled off his shirt and closed his dry blanket around them both. "This is much better. Yes?"

"Yes," she agreed, and held the flask to his mouth.

He drank and wiped his lips. Reaching into his pouch, he took out a handful of shelled nuts. "You like these?"

"Hickory? How did you find them?" She scooped some into her mouth, crunching the nutmeat.

"The same way I found you at the cliff. Searched."

"I wish you had found me sooner."

"I am here now. Are you glad?"

She leaned against his shoulder. "Very glad." The whiskey must have loosened her tongue.

"When I am away from you, how is your heart?" he pressed.

"Like this stone," she conceded.

"Still, you fear to wed me?"

"There are other reasons besides fear. Good ones."

"Charity, I will force you to nothing. Only give me your word you will consider my request. I shall not make another."

She swallowed hard. "I will give you an answer."

But would it be the one he desperately wanted to hear?

Chapter Nine

What a difference a few days made. Clad only in her shift, Charity leaned back in the soothing water to rinse the suds from her hair. Tiny green dragonflies skimmed over the pond-sized spring and hardy katydids droned from the trees. Calls of "Bob White!" rose from the grassy clearing that spread beyond the heated pool.

She straightened and shook back dripping lengths. "This weather is like summer and the spring better than any tonic."

Emma washed the soap from Lily's ringlets. "Certainly better than Mama's. Slippery elm, dock roots, and God knows what else, to 'let out the bad.'"

Water glistened on Colin's torso as he lathered James' head. He smiled appreciatively at Emma. "That brew must possess wondrous power. You're in fine form."

Her wet shift accentuated every curve and the sun glinted from highlights in the damp mane falling around her shoulders and down her back. "You shouldn't be watching me bathe, sir."

James wriggled in Colin's grasp, spitting at the bubbles sliding down his face. "Why'd you have to go and find soap?"

"Keep your mouth shut, lad, and you'll not suffer," he said, and pushed him underwater to rinse.

James reappeared, his soapy curls dripping. "All done."

"Not quite." Colin dunked him again.

James shot to the surface. "Enough! I want to

play."

"Water's tolerable for play, but not bathing, eh?" Colin chuckled, and gave him an affectionate pat.

Emma freed the squirmy little girl. "Go on then, the pair of you. Stay where it's shallow."

Colin pointed to the red sourwood at the side of the spring. "The bottom falls away just past that tree."

Like cubs, the children splashed to the end of the spring farthest from the clearing. Charity lay on her back in the balmy water and drifted beneath an endless blue sky.

"I wish I could float like that," Emma said.

"Nothing could be easier."

"For you. Craig taught you how to swim."

"Had to, he couldn't keep me out of the river."

"I remember. He said you should have been a boy."

Charity smiled with the familiar wistful pang. "The water is only waist high at this end. I'll help you float."

Emma rubbed one small hand over her swollen middle. "I'm far too large for you—" Colin clasped her from behind and lifted her from the water to hold her, dripping, in his arms.

"Put me down!"

Deaf to Emma's protest, he bent and suspended her over the surface. "I'll teach you to float."

"No!"

He bent lower. She was only inches above the water. "Stretch out."

She clung to his neck as though a fathomless loch lay beneath her. "I'll go straight to the bottom."

"Trust me. I'll not let you go."

She looked up at him and slowly gave a nod. He held her on the surface as she leaned back, still clinging to him. "The water's not above your chin, darling."

Her tense posture gradually relaxed. "You're still breathing. Not lost in the depths," he teased, and swirled her lightly through the water, then brought her to a halt.

She smiled slightly. "'Tisn't so bad."

"Pleasant, even?" he asked, coaxing another nod. "Good. Time for the next step. Let go of me."

Her mouth flew open. "I can't!"

"It's not deep. Besides, I've got you."

"Very well. I'll try." Eyes glued on him, she slid curled fingers from his neck.

"Move your arms gently," he said.

Emma fluttered her arms like a newly emerged butterfly trying its wings. "Wonderful. You're nearly there," he encouraged.

"But I couldn't float alone."

"You could."

A wordless agreement passed between them and Colin slipped his arms from beneath her. Late day sunshine poured over Emma suspended on the surface, her hair swaying about her like golden grasses.

Triumph shone in her face. "I'm floating."

Charity clapped her hands. "I knew you could."

Colin held Emma to him in tender reward then drifted with her to the far side of the spring. Their low conversation faded. Sunlight spilled through the leaves, dappling her blonde head and his reddish brown hair. They were partly hidden by branches, but Charity saw his lips cover Emma's unresisting mouth.

James half-waded, half-ran to Charity, craning his neck at the couple. "Why is Uncle Papa kissing Emma?"

"Because he loves her."

"Does she love him back?"

"Oh, yes."

Lily leapt at James like a little frog, her shift

slipping over one shoulder. "Me too."

"Me first!" he yelled. "Is kissing a sin, Charity?" She surely hoped not. "Never mind. See who can dress the fastest."

James scrambled from the spring. Lily's short legs worked hard to overtake him. Weshe leapt up, tail wagging.

Charity climbed from the water and took one of the towels Colin had liberated from the plunder to wrap around her streaming shift. The cloth was too small to cover her below her knees, or higher than her chest. Clean and warm, at last, she sat on a stone to pull on her stockings and shoes.

James dashed to her side. "Done." He'd donned breeches over his tiny breechclout. His shirt clung to him.

Lily darted beside him, her short blue gown pulled on over her dripping shift, petticoat askew. "Me too."

He radiated superiority. "Your shoes aren't on."

Lily looked downcast.

"You can race another time," Charity told her as she turned away.

"I'll win then too," James bragged. "She's only a girl."

"I can beat you every time and I'm a girl."

"A big girl. Aren't you going to dress?"

Charity pointed to the yellow spicebush where she'd spread her freshly-washed clothes to dry. "I can't yet."

He shook his head. "I can see more of you than usual."

"Stop looking then."

His small chin jutted at a stubborn angle. "That towel don't cover enough."

"Leave me be."

Colin chuckled. "The lad's only guarding your honor." He swam from the drop off back toward them with Emma. "In all honesty, you aren't entirely proper."

"He's right. You can't go about like that," Emma agreed.

"I'm not fighting my way back into those wet clothes. I'll soon have my cloak."

"Wicomechee will have something to say about your attire, or lack of it," Colin warned, shading his eyes with his hand. "Is that him?"

Muga emerged through the leaves at the edge of the spring. Disappointment welled in Charity. Wicomechee had been away hunting for hours. Not that it mattered, she reminded herself. She was fine with the others, and shouldn't always look for him.

James and Lily bounded over to the big warrior. "Take us to camp. We're hungry." The congenial brave nodded.

Charity walked to him. She'd accompany them and recover her cloak before Wicomechee knew the difference. Muga stared at her as though he wanted to say something. Instead, he set off with a child on either side of him and Weshe at his heels.

His disapproval on top of everyone else's was too much; Charity followed further back. The grassy scent in the clearing reminded her of their settlement in the valley...the meadow enclosed by split-rail with sheep and the log house, hickory smoke curling up from its stone chimney. Homesickness tugged at her. Reluctant to leave the sunny space, she trailed behind Muga into the trees.

Something hard bit into her heel. "Ouch!"

She stopped to slip off her shoe and shook out a pebble. Rubbing her bruised foot, she looked around. The others were out of sight. Apparently unaware of her difficulty, they'd gone on and been swallowed among the leaves.

She slid on her shoe and started to follow, then stopped. She was all alone. Or was she?

Her heart quickened. Someone or something was near. Was it only the light slanting through the forest making patterns among the leaves or did she spy a figure up ahead?

Dear God. Prickles swarmed down her spine like scattering ants. Was that Craig?

Impossible. It couldn't be.

And yet...a year ago by the riverbank, she'd caught sight of him. She was almost certain. Had he come to her now? The woods were a meld of light and shadows. Seeing Craig might have been an illusion, or maybe he was here.

She couldn't be sure. As quickly as he'd appeared he disappeared, but she supposed he could go where he liked if he were a spirit. Perhaps he watched over her as a sort of guardian angel and wanted her to follow him.

Paying scant attention where her feet led her, she left the path and tracked over the spongy ground between the branches toward the place where she thought she'd seen him. Just beyond the undergrowth, the gurgling stream reflected the rays from the lowering sun.

A doe drinking at the edge of the water lifted its head and studied her for a moment before springing away over the stones upstream. The stream flowed east and would lead Charity in that direction if she followed the waterway. Was that what Craig intended?

What would he have her do? Deny her people, or her heart? Wrenching pain tore through her. How could she possibly leave Emma or the children or Colin? She'd grown deeply fond of him. And what of Wicomechee? Her chest fluttered wildly at the mere mention of his name.

What a coward he must think her, staying close to Emma these past few nights while thoughts of him consumed her. She couldn't give into these volatile emotions, though. She'd agreed to consider his request to wed him, but she'd been intoxicated then. She was painfully sober now.

If only they could be together with no talk of marriage, or anything more. Just them. But a warrior and a white woman wedding...how could such a union ever be honored?

Perhaps leaving Wicomechee was the only way to break the irresistible hold he had over her. But wouldn't that also break her heart? And how would she survive out here? She'd never find the settlement alone.

Craig had always known what was best. His insight must be a hundredfold better now. Steeling herself, she petitioned her brother. "If I'm to go back, you must lead me."

After that whispered petition, she waited.

The vibrant colors faded with the coming twilight, and the wind picked up as the sun dipped lower behind the ridges. The woods grew darker now and a chill touched the air so recently blessed with summery balm. Something was different than when she'd first come to the stream.

Unease gripped her. She was no longer alone. But who was with her, friend or foe?

She looked guardedly through the trees. Upstream, an indistinct masculine figure watched her from purplish shadows. He beckoned and the chill that traveled her before doubled in strength and charged down her spine to her knees.

"My God." Was it truly Craig?

Had he returned now to direct her path? Like a sleepwalker, she stepped toward him, but again he disappeared.

No. She couldn't follow a vanishing ghost.

Fierce fingers dug into her shoulder from behind. "Where are you going, English girl?"

She jumped in almost unbearable alarm and

stammered, "Back to camp."

Chaka spun her around to face him. He pointed west. "Camp lies that way."

"I must be lost."

Accusation glinted in his eyes. "You think to escape."

"No! I just—"

He ripped her towel away. "This will not warm you." Casting the cloth aside, he seized a handful of her damp hair and jerked her head back. "Where is your blanket? You will freeze in the night."

She winced. "Don't."

"How do you think to eat? You will die in these mountains." His dark gaze drank her in. "So fair to die."

The hunger in his face alarmed her as much as his anger. "Take me to Wicomechee."

Chaka's mouth hardened and she saw the ghost of Outhowwa in his forbidding features. "Wicomechee will beat you. Teach you not to run."

"I didn't."

Chaka snorted. "Shall I give you punishment?"

He would surely kill her. She clasped her hands together as if in prayer. "No. I beg you."

"Why should I not?"

"Have mercy."

"Mercy? Perhaps...for you." He closed his arm around her waist, pulling her against his hard chest.

Was he expecting something in return? Something she had no intention of surrendering? "Let me go! Wicomechee will—"

Chaka clamped his hand over her mouth. "I do not fear Wicomechee." He caught her up, struggling, in his arms. She aimed a kick at his thigh, but he only held her more tightly.

"Be still."

Her pointless resistance gave way and she went limp in his grasp. He swiftly put the stream behind

123

them. She didn't know where he was taking her, but not back to camp. Branches slapped against her as he charged over the path, then angled to the side and ducked into a secluded nook. Evergreens hid the dusky space as he knelt and laid her on the needles.

"Quiet," he warned, his hand still covering her mouth.

She lay too frightened to scream even if he'd given her the chance. The paint was gone from his face, but the lines in his features were like granite. She had to reach him. Her very soul entreated him through the haze of her tears.

He bent nearer until his face was a hand span away from hers, and stopped. His harsh expression softened and he drew back slightly. The brimming moisture in her eyes spilled over his fingers.

"I will not harm you. I give you my word."

She nodded, and he freed her mouth. "Release me," she begged him in a panting whisper.

"Do not fear. I have no wish to give you pain."

"Then why did you bring me here? Please—" she shuddered. "Take me to camp."

"Shhhh," he whispered. "Speak with me. Only this."

She weighed his request in profound mistrust.

"Why so wet?" he asked, running his hand over her sleeve. "You try to flee, fall in the stream? Remove your clothes?"

"I swam in the spring," she said, forcing each word from her dry mouth.

"English women cannot swim."

"I can. Ask Waupee."

He trailed his hand through her hair. "You are different from other captive women. With you, I would be gentle."

"How is that possible? You tried to drown me."

"No. Only frighten you. I regret—" he broke off, and began again. "I no longer wish you to fear me."

He slipped his fingers lightly over her cheek in an unmistakable caress. "I like your face, your hair...all of you."

She listened in amazement. His tone was gentle, but would he suddenly turn on her like a mad dog?

"Do not run again. You will suffer much punishment."

"I wasn't running."

He touched her lips, and his fingers lingered at her face. "I saw you. Speak the truth to me, Charity."

She was almost too shocked to reply. "You said my name."

"Any name you like. I will cover you with furs. Trade for cloth you can sew. Feed you. Protect you. Be my wife."

This unwarranted tenderness was even more intimidating than his usual menace. "I can't. I belong to Wicomechee."

"Forget Wicomechee," he whispered, lifting her and crushing her against his brawn. He was like an impassioned bear, and she cried out in his fierce hold.

He lightened his grip. "I will be a good husband. Hear me, Charity."

How on earth could she make him let her go? "You don't understand. Wicomechee is my husband."

His eyes were cynical. "No."

She desperately sought to remember the Shawnee word for 'my husband' Wicomechee had spoken the night they'd sheltered under the hemlock. *"Wyshetche!* Wicomechee is *Wyshetche!"*

Chaka laid her back on the needles, staring at her. Before she contrived another lie, an unforgettable voice hailed them.

"Outhowwa heard you," Chaka muttered.

She clutched his arm in dread. "Don't let him kill me."

"He will not kill you." With clear annoyance, Chaka closed his hand around her wrist and pulled her up with him. Looking as though he'd rather be headed anyplace else, he propelled her through orange-tipped fern back to the trail.

A small group of warriors stepped aside to allow them passage through to Outhowwa. The chief's cold predatory gaze pierced her before he tore into Chaka, in Shawnee.

Chaka answered gruffly. She caught something about 'the Englishwoman,' then he bent close to his father and uttered the rest of his reply in such a low voice that Charity couldn't hear, even if she'd understood the words.

Outhowwa's annoyance was less marked as he turned the force of his regard to her. "Wicomechee is your husband?"

She didn't dare repeat her falsehood to him. "Wicomechee asked to be my husband. Chaka has no right to me."

"Yet he desires to make you his wife. In this, there is honor." Outhowwa lifted her tangled hair and let it fall. He wrinkled his nose as though at a noxious scent, then he shrugged. "Chaka likes you much. He has one wife to keep. Still, he is good hunter, takes enough game to feed two."

"Two?" she echoed, beyond shocked.

"He will care for you," Outhowwa emphasized. "For the little ones you bear him."

Dear God. Would Outhowwa hand her over to Chaka, despite his antipathy to her? "Do not make me wed him. Please."

He studied her scornfully. "I do not force any woman to wed. You may choose."

If she didn't wed, Shawnee women would make her life harsh and break her back with hard work. Hardly able to believe her response, she gave a faint nod.

Outhowwa continued. "Chaka, Wicomechee are strong warriors. Speak your wish."

Numb, Charity said, "I choose Wicomechee for my husband."

Chaka scowled, but had no choice other than to abide by her decision with his father witnessing every word.

Outhowwa took her arm as though he sensed the urge to flee welling inside her. "Come girl. Wicomechee will keep you." He sounded glad that his family wouldn't be afflicted with such a troublesome wife.

The other warriors fell in behind them as he pulled her along. They rounded a bend in the trail and nearly collided with Wicomechee's rapid approach. He stepped back, not fully concealing his amazement upon seeing her in the chief's grasp.

"Charity? Muga said he lost you on the trail."

Outhowwa brought her to a halt. Most of his words were lost on her, but she recognized *memequilah* 'run' and saw the responsive anger in Wicomechee's face. Nor did the exchange between them lessen his cold fury.

Then Outhowwa held up his hand. "Will you take this woman to wife?"

Wicomechee gave a terse nod as though he would wed her, and then kill her.

"She will have you for her husband. Is this not so, girl?" Outhowwa prompted with vise-like pressure on her arm.

Charity bit her lip. "Yes."

Wicomechee watched her as he might a wild horse that might spring away at any moment, and this was how she felt.

"She needs Shawnee name," the chief said.

Wicomechee replied without hesitation. "*Penashe Pocoun,*"

A faint smile crossed Outhowwa's mouth and he

took her chin in his hand commanding her attention. "You are English no longer, *Penashe Pocoun*. Be an obedient wife to Wicomechee. Bear him many sons to grow into warriors, fight for Shawnee." He placed her chilled fingers into Wicomechee's warm grasp. "Care for this woman, Wicomechee. Teach her our ways."

With that, Outhowwa turned on his heel and headed back down the trail toward camp. The rest of the assembly drifted off in his wake. Chaka stood unmoving for a few beats, and his face might have been carved from stone, then he spun away.

Charity stared after them. What on earth had she done?

Chapter Ten

Wicomechee lowered his stare from the departing chief to Charity's dazed eyes. Damp hair spilled to her waist and the shift concealed little of her feminine form. She'd never looked more inviting, and it infuriated him all the more to think of Chaka ogling her, if that were the worst of it. He didn't seem averse to breaking every moral code they had.

Releasing her cold fingers, Wicomechee swept his hand at her. "Where are your clothes? Did Chaka tear them from you?"

A jumble of words tumbled out, almost as if English were her second language. Her explanation so astonished him, it took a moment to sink in. "So you go about like this?"

"I had a towel—Chaka took it," she stammered.

Anger flared in Wicomechee. "You made it easy for him to take all. Your breasts show beneath this cloth. More."

With sudden self-awareness, she wrapped one arm over her chest. "Now you hide from your husband?"

Abandoning her attempt at modesty, she reached unsteadily to him for reassurance, but he wasn't inclined to offer any.

She dropped her arms. "Chaka only asked me to wed him."

"Outhowwa said. He also told me you tried to run away."

"I didn't. Will you listen to me or to him?"

The sting of betrayal sharpened Wicomechee's ire. "Why should I hear you?"

"Because I don't lie."

"You lie now. Chaka found you going away from camp."

"I had good reason—"

Wicomechee cut her off. "Enough."

He'd said all he intended to and propped his musket against a tree. She watched in marked uneasiness as he grasped her wrists in one hand and pulled a buckskin cord from the pouch at his waist with the other.

"What are you doing?" she gulped.

"Teaching you not to run."

"Don't!" she cried, trying to wrench away from him.

He whipped the cord around her wrists and knotted it.

"Dear God. Would you bind your wife?"

He frowned down at her. "I have none if she runs."

"I wasn't. Only thinking what I should do."

"You did more than think."

She pressed her cheek against his sleeve and the warmth of her body along one side, all he'd allow her to reach of him. "Don't be harsh. I beg you. Chaka stayed his hand."

A river of want flowed hotly through Wicomechee, but he was determined to resist her appeal. "I am fortunate not to find you claimed by him already."

"It wasn't like that. He was gentler this time."

"Chaka, gentle?" Those two words did not fit together and Wicomechee scrutinized her. Why must she be so fair, so frightened, confused? He badly wanted to gather her in his arms. And yet, this captivating girl had betrayed him as surely as though she'd twisted a knife in his back.

"Mechee, please. I'll not wander again."

"No. You will not," he said, his voice harsh with

hurt. "I will never trust you again."

Tears filled her eyes. "Give me a chance to explain."

He pulled her along the trail. "What will you speak? It is still in your head to run back to the English."

"'Tisn't my wish."

She seemed so sincere, but Outhowwa's revelation still burned in his mind. "You said you cared for me."

"I do."

"How do you show this? By running? I was a fool to believe you."

"No. Stop. You must hear me."

"There is nothing you can say."

"There is," she choked out. "But you'll think me mad."

"I think you a traitor."

"Mechee—listen. I saw Craig."

He stopped in his tracks, eyes riveted on her. "What?"

Tears spilled down her earnest face. "If you'd let me, I could point to the spot."

He shook his head as if to clear it and to be certain he'd heard her right. "You told me your brother was dead."

"For two years."

"You saw his spirit?"

She inhaled shakily. "Only a glimpse, but Craig summoned me. I was seeking him when Chaka came. Do you believe me?"

Wicomechee didn't answer at once. He imagined her sighting someone, possibly Chaka, in the forest gloom. Given her longing for this lost brother, she'd mistaken him for her beloved relation. It wouldn't be the first time the shadows had misled someone. "I believe you think you saw Craig."

Her brow puckered. "I did. Will you punish me

131

for this?"

He softened his tone. "I despise to bind you, but you were straying already. Why were you here, alone?"

"I was troubled and asking Craig what to do when he appeared. I saw him last year, by the river."

"If you see him again, will you follow?"

"I didn't mean to. Craig wanted me to come."

She said it so simply. Maybe she really had seen this spirit. Sometimes when loved ones were lost, those left behind sought them until they achieved that union, in the beyond. A warning, like a chilled hand, wrapped icy fingers around Wicomechee's heart. "Does Craig wish you to join him in death? You cannot live long in these mountains alone."

She startled. "Craig would never wish me harm."

"So badly you want this brother. I will not lose you to a spirit, real or imagined." Wicomechee caught her up in his arms, crushing her to him.

She gasped in his near fierce embrace. He eased his hold, but possessiveness still raged in him like a wolf claiming its mate. "Promise me never again to follow Craig."

Her voice quavered as she asked, "How will I know for certain if he's there, if I do not?"

Everything in Wicomechee warned him not to back down. He refused to relent. "Give me your word, Charity. Now."

"You ask a great deal."

He fought for control. He mustn't frighten her away. "I know. For me, will you do this?"

"For you," she agreed in a small voice.

"I will care for you, sweet one. You do not need Craig."

Still they stood as they were. She sagged against his chest. "Are you no longer angry?"

"You try me sorely, but my anger is flown." He

buried his face in her hair and inhaled the fresh scent. "You said you will have me for your husband. Did you mean your words?"

The apprehension he sensed in her swelled and she whispered, "Yes."

"So fearful you are. Did I force you to wed me? Did Outhowwa?"

"No. But he urged me to choose between you and Chaka."

Wicomechee smiled faintly. The old fox had trapped her.

"I know nothing of being wed, and I scarcely know you."

"Would you like to learn more?" he coaxed.

"Yes...but not too much. Papa and Craig wouldn't approve of my marrying you. They would never forgive me."

"What of your merciful God? Do you pray to him?"

"I prayed for God's aid the morning you took me captive."

"Perhaps he gave you into my care," Wicomechee suggested.

She lifted her head and looked hard at him. "Surely Papa and Craig would not dispute God?"

"You are meant to be mine, Penashe Pocoun."

"What does that strange name mean?"

"Red Bird. I know not where you will fly, what song you will sing. We shall see if you fly from me."

"I don't want to." She tried ineffectually to close her arms around his neck. "I'm still bound."

"Yes."

"Surely you do not intend leaving me like this?"

He couldn't resist teasing her a little. "It is easier for me to keep you."

"But I'm your wife."

He weighed her tremulous declaration. "Are you?"

"I gave you my consent."

"Will you give me your pledge?"

She took a steadying breath. "As God is my witness, you have my pledge, Wicomechee. Is that your whole name?"

"Enough of it. You also have my pledge, Penashe Pocoun."

"That sounds so odd. Could you speak it in English?"

"If you wish." He unknotted the cord at her wrists. "Shawnee warriors do not bind their wives."

She swallowed in evident relief then stiffened again. "What do they do?"

"I will teach you. More than words are needed for you to be mine. I will take you to myself."

Her eyes opened wide. "Now?"

He dropped the cord in his pouch. "No. We must return to camp. The others watch for us."

She regarded him as one awaiting torture. "Tonight?"

"Calm down. Do not distress yourself. My love is not punishment."

The word seemed to catch her. "Do you really love me?"

"My heart, *kitehi*, is yours."

She was silent, searching, her eyes wistful, yet guarded.

"Have you no love to speak?"

"Telling you what is in my heart is difficult," she faltered. "You are a warrior."

Again, that sharp sting bit at him. "Charity, if you deny my heart, you deny your own."

****

Raw silence hung between them like a wound as Charity trudged behind Wicomechee along the darkening trail toward camp. He'd lent her his shirt and his bare back was just visible in the last of the light. His unique scent enveloped her and the garment swallowed her down to her knees.

Ahead through the trees a series of campfires lit the dusky sky. Breezes carried the comforting fragrance of wood smoke and the mouth-watering aroma of roasting venison.

"Do you no longer fear smoke will attract the militia?" she asked.

"All food taken on the raid is gone. We must eat."

"Did you shoot the deer?"

"I killed *peshikthe*, returned to find you gone."

Remorse kindled in her. She quickened her step to match his and walked at his side. "I won't go from you again."

"Like the child you run. I fear to let you from my sight."

She held out her hand to him. "I'm sorry."

His warm fingers enfolded hers and sent little prickles up her arm. Why did he inflame her the way he did, she wondered, baffled by her opposing emotions.

Hand in hand, they walked to the fire where Colin and James sat in a circle of warriors. The little boy leapt up and dashed over to them, Weshe darting just behind. "Like this, you run," Wicomechee said. "The dog also."

James interrupted any further comparisons. "Charity! Did you run off? Chaka said you did." Not awaiting a reply, he squinted up at Wicomechee. "Did you punish her?"

"No, small one."

"Good," James said, with touching relief. "She's wearing your shirt. I told her she weren't decent."

Wicomechee smiled at the boy. "Go find her cloak."

James and the dog scampered off and Colin waved them over. He patted the empty spot beside him, evidently reserved for her. The usual humor was absent from his demeanor. "Sit, dear heart. I have a bit to say. You've caused quite a stir."

Seated braves eyed her over their pipes and talk buzzed through the gathering as she settled beside him. Sympathy softened Colin's firm expression. "Poor girl. My brother's brought you in like a lost puppy. Still, you don't appear to have suffered any. Chaka was certain he would beat you."

Wicomechee glared at the sullen warrior sitting at a distance from the others. "It is him I should punish. He tried to make her his wife."

"Best leave him to lick his wounds," Colin advised.

Wicomechee shrugged, apparently willing to bide his time.

"I will get meat." He strode to where the spitted venison roasted over glowing coals. His amiable comrades hailed him, some plying him with what seemed to be questions.

Colin tossed a stick into the fire and a shower of sparks sizzled up against the night sky. "What on earth have you been up to? I hear you've a husband now and a Shawnee name."

Her head swimming, Charity stared into the flames and tried to grasp her altered state. "I'm not certain. It all happened so quickly."

"So I gather. You've had quite an evening."

"And it's not over. What am I to do with a husband?"

"Don't fret. Wicomechee will guide you."

"But I don't feel ready for whatever it is husbands do."

James swooped down on them, her cloak flapping in his hands. "Charity's got a husband?"

"She has," Colin said matter-of-factly. "Wicomechee."

"Is that 'cause she ran off?"

Colin wrapped the cloak around her. "No, lad.

She needed him anyway."

"Ain't it a sin to wed a warrior?"

Charity groaned, and buried her face in her hands.

"No. It's not. Stop pestering her and go tell Emma she's safely returned."

Charity peered through her fingers as James ran toward Emma's blanketed shape lying on the far side of their campfire. Lily was tucked by her side. "How is she?"

"Resting, or trying to. She's been fretting over you."

"I didn't mean to worry her, or any of you."

"It can't be helped with your knack for trouble. Chin up, little sister. You'll adjust to life among the Shawnee and being wed. Wicomechee's a fine fellow."

"But he's not English."

"Even so, I'd trust him with my life, and there are many Englishmen who would gladly put me in my grave."

"I suppose I trust him, too, at least when he's not furious with me. It's just—he's a man."

Colin chuckled. "Husbands normally are."

Answering laughter resounded behind them and she turned to find Wicomechee, a blanket over his shoulders, holding a trencher of streaming meat. His eyes danced with mirth. "You must give her more pity than this, Waupee."

"Your turn now. I must rescue Emma from James."

"Won't you eat with us first?" Charity invited.

Colin stood. "I already have, thanks to Wicomechee. He alone was successful in the hunt. Best shot I know. He can fire from a greater distance than anyone and strike his mark."

She swiveled her head to gaze admiringly at Wicomechee. "Craig was good with a musket, but not that good."

The firelight reflected his pleasure in her praise. "I have greater skill than your brother?"

"Yes. You're full of secrets."

"Perhaps a few." He took Colin's place beside her.

He'd quoted her own words, she realized.

"More than that, I'll wager."

He shrugged and stuck his knife into a slice of venison then held it out to her. She took the buckskin-wrapped wooden handle and bit into the smoky meat, chewing hungrily. "This is good. I've missed venison."

He nodded. They ate in silence, but men's voices hummed around them. The same word repeated in their conversation.

"What does *wanisaka* mean?" she asked in between bites.

Wicomechee's lips twitched. "Crazy, foolish."

She flushed. "They're talking about me, aren't they?"

He set his empty trencher aside. "You listen well. They also say you are beautiful."

He circled his arm around her and warmth washed through her in a pulsing wave. His lips hovered at her ear, and he spoke in a voice only she could hear. "Do not be frightened. You fear what you do not understand."

"Why is it everyone seems to know of love making except me?" she whispered. "Were you born knowing this?"

"All must learn."

"How did you?"

"How else? From a woman."

An unfamiliar emotion swelled in Charity that could only be defined as jealousy. "Who was she?"

"My wife."

She reeled in shock as that newly sprung

sensation ripped through her. "You never spoke of a wife."

"No. I did not have Mequana for long," he said, a sad note in his low voice.

Chastened, Charity asked, "Did you love her, very much?"

"For her, my heart was full."

"But I thought—" she broke off. How could she tell him that she'd believed herself to be his first and only love, and earnestly desired his undying devotion to belong to her alone? "What happened?" she asked instead.

"She died of white man's sickness. Many die from this." He pointed at the sky. "See that long white path?"

The cloudy luminescence arched across the vast black vault of the sky among glittering stars. "The Milky Way."

"That is the road to heaven. Mequana has traveled this."

"You believe in heaven?"

"Manito guides us there if we do good. If not, we go with Matchimanitoh, the evil one, to punishment."

"Forever?"

"No punishment lasts forever. That is not just," he said, speaking her unvoiced sentiment.

"We also pray for forgiveness, so there's a way out."

"Have you a truth-bearer to carry your prayers?"

"I've never heard of this."

"When Shawnee pray, we burn tobacco, sacred to us. This carries our prayers to Manito. If we have none, we use another truth-bearer, the wind, fire, feathers of the Eagle."

"That makes no sense. Why not just pray?"

"How can you expect to be heard?" he asked in return.

"I just do. Will you insist that I believe as you?"

"No. Believe as you like."

She absorbed his acceptance with gratitude. This was more than anyone except Craig had allowed her. "Thank you."

"For this, you thank me?"

A blazing light streaked across the sky and captured her attention. "Look. A falling star. Quick—make a wish."

"You wish upon *alagwa*, the stars?"

He could hardly have sounded more incredulous if she'd declared that she could fly. "Craig said I might."

Closing her eyes, she offered a tentative but fervent wish that somehow, someway, she and this most unlikely of husbands would be happy together. It seemed impossible.

"For what did you wish?" he asked as she looked up.

"It won't come true if I tell. Did you make a wish?"

"No need. I have all I desire in you."

"Do you really wish for nothing more than me?"

"From you, I will have all I want. Look closely upon the road to heaven. See the small stars? This is where little ones wait to be born."

"Ours?" she blurted, evoking glances from curious onlookers. "Yours and mine?"

"Who else's? You will give me strong children of much beauty."

"I'm very afraid to."

"Charity, you told me you are alone, without family. I, too, have lost all of my blood, save for *Nimesoomtha*, my grandfather. Together, we will have much."

"Perhaps, if I survive."

"You are strong like the deer."

"And frightened like the rabbit. Chaka was

right."

He chuckled. "Do not fear anymore this night. I will not take you to myself now," he whispered.

She listened in an odd meld of relief and disappointment. When would he?

Chapter Eleven

Gray, pre-dawn light filtered through the woods. The rich hues of autumn awaited the sun's golden touch to bring them to life. Her hand in Wicomechee's, his shirt beneath her cloak, Charity walked at his side, her troubled thoughts circling around the fact that, at least to his people, she was wed to a Shawnee warrior. And she'd given him her pledge before God. Her yearning for him clashed with everything she'd been taught and transcended all she knew. How could she reconcile herself to the bitter enmity between their people?

It seemed to her that truly loving anyone incurred a great deal of risk to one's heart. And if she were parted from him now, the memory of him would go with her all of her days...a painful ghost.

Wicomechee bent back the branch of the large sourwood and gestured ahead to where mist rose over the spring. Slowly, he released her fingers. "I will wait for you. Make haste."

She watched his bare back disappear into the leaves then knelt by the pool to drink and refresh herself. Only the clear whistle of a song sparrow broke the serenity. Her petticoats and bodice were draped over the spice bush where she'd left them and nearly invisible in the subdued light. Dew had saturated the cloth. Nothing in her wanted to feel that wetness against her skin. Leaving her clothes to the coming sun, she twisted off a fragrant twig from the bush and chewed the spicy bark as she walked back through the trees.

The clustered trunks gave way to grass and the

grayness brightened in the clearing. Her shoes, stockings, and the edges of her cloak were soon soaked. Even at this hour, though, the balmy air felt more like August than October. She'd expected Wicomechee to wait nearby, but didn't see him.

There. He waved to her from the other side of the meadow, his muscular shoulders silvered in the light. An impulse to be near him sent her running in his direction.

He did the same. His long legs carried him toward her in smooth ground-covering strides, and the race was on to arrive at mid-field first. Milkweed pods released fluffy white seeds, like tiny sails, on the barely-there breeze. Just as they were about to come together, she skidded on the grass. Her feet slid from beneath her and she thudded onto her back. Her surprised gasp dissolved into muffled giggles.

Wicomechee put on a burst of speed and reached her in moments. Panting from laughter, as much as exertion, she smiled up at him. "Was that fast enough?"

He smiled back. "Like the wind. Yet you lie at my feet." He pulled her up, and held her against him. "Ah, Red Bird. I never thought to hunt with one so fair."

"Or so clumsy. Craig never took me. He said I'd only be a nuisance."

"You are no nuisance." Wicomechee pressed his lips over her cheek and lightly kissed her mouth, his first kiss since the evening she'd begged him to stop.

A potpourri of sensations, like contrasting scents, flowed through her as he lingered tenderly at her lips, releasing her with the same reluctant restraint he had before.

"Are you certain 'tis only hunting you want me for?"

"Why do you ask this?" Humor tinged his voice.

He led her across the meadow and into the trees bordering it on the other side. They followed the path their party had taken yesterday to ascend this ridge.

"Is the hunting good back this way?"

"Very good," he said.

The path dipped sharply and grew rough, like a dry creek bed. Grooves scarred the earth where the soil had been washed away by countless rains. Stones of all sizes littered the ruts. She stumbled on a loose stone, lurching forward. Only his grip kept her upright.

"Must I carry you, Red Bird?"

"No—I'm—"

She startled as he scooped her up and leapt across a wide furrow in the trail. His moccasins landed noiselessly in a patch of fern at the edge. Cradling her to him, he spun her around in a circle.

She clung to his neck as misty leaves whirled by. "Mechee!"

"Shhhh—you will frighten my game," he chided, laughing under his breath.

"Behave yourself, then."

He stopped twirling and buried his face in her neck, eliciting exquisite tremors. "With you, I am always gentle."

"Yesterday you almost weren't," she reminded him.

"You gave me much cause for anger."

"Am I truly forgiven?"

His warm lips hovered at her ear. "How can you not be?"

Her heart pounded like the little wren's she'd once held in her hand. "Will you put me down now?"

He set her upright in the fern. Squeezing her fingers, he sprang back onto the path and led the way while she followed more slowly down over the uneven ground. The trail leveled off a bit. The ruts smoothed out as waxy mountain laurel leaves closed in around them, blocking their view of the forest and preventing any route other than the close path.

After about twenty minutes of a brisk downhill trot, she saw the laurel thicket give way to a rocky outcropping scattered among the trees and a tangle of grapevines. He motioned to her and ducked behind the rocks.

She darted where he'd gone, but found no trace of him among the brown stones. "Mechee?"

"You seek me?" he asked quietly from behind her.

She spun around. "You move like a ghost."

"Do I feel like a spirit?" he whispered, and pulled her down into a leaf-strewn crevice just wide enough for two.

She pressed against his bare chest in a heady rush and felt his hard thighs beneath the breechclout. "Not at all."

He pointed through a gap in the rocks down to the shadowed hollow veiled in light haze below their vantage. "*Peshikthe,* the deer, feed there. *Wabete,* the elk, also."

The narrow valley was empty now, but an elk bellowed off in the hazy distance. Wicomechee lifted the beaded flap of his hunting pouch and took out a wooden whistle. "This will bring Brother Elk." Putting it to his lips, he blew in a skilled imitation of the elk's high-pitched bugle.

"You sound very like, but 'tis quite a way to fire from here," she whispered.

His musket lay on the leafy ground within arms-reach. "I do not miss."

"Truly you have amazing skill."

He slid the whistle back into his pouch and fixed his eyes on her. "Firing is not difficult. It is you who are difficult. I fear to let you from my sight."

She glimpsed the yearning in the depths of his

dark gaze. "Do you truly care so very much for me?"

"What more must I do to prove my love? I cannot show you with words only."

"Words alone will not content me," she admitted.

He pulled back to look fully into her eyes. "Do I dream?"

The silver light and solitude lent a sense of unreality to the moment. She slipped her fingers through the black hair falling across his shoulders. Wanting grew in her, though she couldn't have said for what, only more. "You are so handsome, *Wyshetche*, your face, your hair…all of you."

"Now I know I dream."

"Not unless we both do. Oh, I wish you were English," she sighed.

"That is not my wish."

She nuzzled her cheek against the smooth skin in the hollow of his cheek. "Everything would be so much simpler."

"Charity, forget I am a warrior, think only that I am your husband, friend. Am I not also this?"

"You are, but—"

He touched his fingers to his lips. "Do not speak. Show me your love."

"Me? I haven't your skill."

"Try. You are doing very well."

Streaks of pale rose and gold tinged the eastern sky as she inched her face nearer to his, until her mouth was only a breath away from his lips. Like a hunter mindful of frightening a deer, he held himself still, waiting.

"Won't you help me, Mechee?"

"Come to me first."

Shutting her eyes, she closed the remaining distance and slowly pressed her uncertain lips to his welcoming mouth.

"You are all that is sweet," he said huskily, deepening their kiss and enveloping her in his arms.

Desire flared up in her and she felt as if she were melting into him. "What about your elk?"

"What elk?" he asked, his breath warming her cheek.

"The one you would shoot."

"Later."

Reclaiming her lips, he drew her down with him onto the leaves. The stone walls of their hideaway left little room to move. He lay on his side and she on hers, pressed to his chest, her heartbeat drumming in her ears. A mockingbird let fly its first song of the morning and squirrels chattered. The forest was coming to life, and so was she.

"Let me make you my wife." he invited. "Completely."

Every shivery part of her wanted him, but an inner voice urged caution. "Will it hurt?"

"Perhaps a little."

"How much is a little?"

"Charity, I heard you tell *NiSawsawh* you trust me."

"I do."

"Then let me love you."

She wanted to, oh how she did. She craved his devotion, affection, his all...even more than he'd felt for Mequana, his late wife.

A horse whinnied in the hollow below, shattering their dreamy idyll. Wicomechee clapped his hand over her mouth and sat upright to peer through the stones. His rigid back told her what she already knew—the militia had come.

****

Still covering her mouth, Wicomechee returned his scrutiny to Charity. In her widened eyes he saw fear, also devotion, but what was the depth of her loyalty? He couldn't make her slip away with him. If she resisted, any thrashing or muffled outcry might alert the horsemen to their presence.

"Come with me?" he mouthed.

She nodded without a waver.

Despite the imminent danger, he grinned as he grabbed up his musket. Keeping low, he stole from the stones and headed up the trail. A glance over his shoulder revealed her creeping close to the ground just behind him.

He straightened when they reached the laurel thicket. Musket in hand, he sped away, alert to her quiet presence. She ran with the speed he'd admired and kept pace with his long-legged strides. The laurel swished past in a green blur as they climbed higher up the ridge. The rutted ground they'd crossed before came into view. Here she might stumble. He grasped her arm with his free hand and they leapt over the washed out grooves together.

Again he took the lead and they raced through dew-beaded leaves sparkling where golden shafts streamed though the branches. They burst into the clearing without slowing.

"How many men?" she gasped out.

"More than twenty. Well-armed."

On they ran back across the meadow. She panted behind him, but pushed on through the trees toward camp. They rushed in among the men.

"Long Knives," Wicomechee hissed.

Word of the militia's approach flashed through the band. Warriors prone in bedrolls were on their feet, snatching up weapons, blankets, pots, anything of value.

Wicomechee stopped and clasped Charity to him. Her chest heaved against the rise and fall of his. "You flew like a bird," he praised her.

She looked up at him, pride warming her eyes, but only for an instant. "What will happen?"

"We pull back. And watch."

****

The hour Charity had feared was at hand. The

militia would be ambushed. Still winded, she gulped out, "Mechee—please."

Sympathy touched his eyes like momentary sunshine, but steely resolve lay behind it. "Shhhh. I will do as I must. Wait here."

He let go of her and ran to Outhowwa. Their heads bent together in rapid conversation while the rest of the party disappeared into the cover of pines and hemlocks. Chaka dragged Rob Buchanan off. The cloth tied across Rob's mouth would prevent him from crying any warning to his father.

Muga whisked the sleeping children up into his arms, blankets and all, the dog at his heels. "Wicomechee."

Outhowwa and Wicomechee glanced around at his low summons. Muga nodded at Emma, wrapped in a blue blanket, writhing and moaning beside the dying embers of the campfire.

Charity rushed to her cousin. "Emma—the militia's come. We must away."

Emma lifted frightened gray eyes and clutched at her swollen abdomen. "I can't. The baby's coming."

Charity nearly staggered back. "Does Colin realize?"

"No. The pains were mild in the night, so I didn't wake him—" she caught her breath. "I was dozing when he left to tend the horses. My water broke. Pains are fast—hard now."

The news struck Charity like a blow to the head and she dropped onto her knees. "You'll be all right."

Emma closed icy fingers over her hand. "Stay with me."

Wicomechee ran to them. He took in the situation at a glance. "Her little one's coming."

Charity looked up at him in desperation. "Do you know what to do for her?"

He gave a nod and bent to slide his arms

beneath Emma. She cried out as he lifted her, twisting with the onset of another contraction. He lowered her gently to the ground.

"I dare not take her. Her cries will draw the Long Knives."

The weight of realization came, and with it a lump in Charity's throat. "I can't leave her, Mechee. The men will force me from you."

He set his jaw. "Never."

As fraught with anxiety as she was, she hated to think of his deadly skill being directed at Captain Buchanan and the others. "Go, then. Before they arrive."

"Colin!" Emma's ragged shout tore across the empty camp.

"Do not fear. I will find my brother." Wicomechee slipped his fingers across Charity's cheek in a parting caress. "Do not forget. You are mine now, Red Bird."

Tears blurred her sight of him vanishing into the trees. How could she bear it if their time together was at an end?

There was no opportunity to dwell on her troubles, though. Emma needed her. Charity had witnessed a birth once. The details were sketchy in her memory, but she hadn't forgotten the screams. What had Mrs. Buchanan done?

She had a vague recollection of a tea brewed from the roots of slippery elm given to the mother, and its sap used to ease the birth. There were no elm trees at hand, no pot, nor any fresh water or cloth to sponge Emma. The blanket beneath her was soiled with birth water, as were her skirts. How was Charity to find dry linens, fetch water and medicinal herbs, let alone tend to the birth, ignorant and unaided?

She winced as Emma's nails dug into her palm. Sharp cries punctuated her moans and she rolled from side to side.

"God help me. I didn't think it would be this bad."

"You'll be all right," Charity repeated over and over without any real sense of assurance.

At last Emma relaxed her fierce hold. But she'd scarcely drawn breath before she tossed again in the grips of another spasm. "I'm gonna die!"

"No. You'll be fine." Charity shakily smoothed the damp curls from Emma's forehead. "'Tis easing now. Try to rest between pains."

"I can't. There's so little time."

"Calm down, dearest. Please."

"I want Mama. I can't do this without Mama."

"You can." Charity heaved a grateful sigh at the sight of Colin shooting out behind the nearest hemlock."

"Sorry I'm late. We were moving the horses." He crouched over Emma and tenderly gathered her against him. "Poor darling. I thought you were with Muga."

"I was afraid you wouldn't come."

"Promised you I'd be here, didn't I?" He eased her back down to the blanket and gripped her fingers.

For a moment Emma was calmer. Then another onslaught seized her and she loosed a piercing cry. "Colin!"

"I'm here, Sweetheart. Hold on."

She thrashed like an animal trying to escape a trap. "Hurts—it hurts." Tears spilled down her flushed cheeks, leaving shining trails. "How long until the baby's born?"

Colin glanced at Charity, and she could almost see him thinking this wasn't anything like delivering a foal. But he kept any doubts to himself. "Anytime now, I'm sure."

She thumped the back of her head on the ground

as if trying to knock herself out. "Too hard. Can't wait."

Neither could Charity. "Shall I see if I can fetch any supplies for her? Maybe I can find Mechee. Ask him what—"

"No!" Emma wailed. "Don't go. It feels like a great serpent has me in its coils—crushing me."

Colin wiped her beaded brow with his sleeve. "He'll not crush the life from you. You'll get through this."

She clutched at his shirt. "If I don't, save the baby."

"Hush," Charity pleaded. "Your mama lived. You'll live."

Her eyes were wild. "Colin—cut the child from me if you must." She flailed her hand at Charity. "You take it."

Colin grasped Emma's chin, forcing her to meet his eyes. "Charity has no milk to give. This baby needs a mother. Fight, Emma. For the baby. For me."

Her vision cleared and she seemed more herself. "I'll try."

"Emma Estell!" a kindhearted voice called out. "Are you birthing the babe now? What a time for the wee one to come."

Captain Buchanan's brawn filled Charity's view, his broad felt hat perched atop graying, sandy-brown hair. A group of frontiersmen strode behind him. She spotted his oldest son, Jeb, with a short reddish beard and built like his father. The company Captain Buchanan headed was made up of settlers who farmed their holdings, except for two trappers, often away checking their lines. Bear skins wrapped the trapper's hats and they wore moccasins in place of shoes or boots.

Charity recognized all these men. She counted twelve. Where were the others? Wicomechee had reported more than twice that number.

"Captain! Help me!" Emma cried.

"Aye. In just a shake." His keen eyes took in the three of them as he neared. "Colin Dickson? I never expected to find you out here. Glad to see Miss Edmondson's well."

Colin nodded a quick greeting. "The captives are safe, Captain. Even your son, Rob."

Captain Buchanan's weathered face creased in relief. "Thank God," he said, making visible effort to stem his emotions. He looked warily at the trees, as did eleven other pairs of eyes. "Where have those savages gotten to?"

"Your questions will be answered as soon as I'm able, Captain," Colin answered. "Meanwhile, I strongly advise all of you to remain near us. It's your best hope of survival."

Captain Buchanan ran callused fingers over his graying beard. "This makes no sense. You wouldn't sell us out to Indians, would you?"

"No. I count you as my friend."

"What say you to this, Miss Edmondson?"

"I trust Mister Dickson with my life, sir."

"Good enough. Do as he says, men."

Emma's cry rose above the captain's orders. Her flushed face scrunched together with the force of her convulsed body.

He laid his musket on the ground. "This birth is damn close. I've helped my wife with a few and I can tell you when a woman sounds like this, it's coming, or—" he broke off, his expression sober. "Have either of you checked her yet?"

It hadn't occurred to Charity to do this.

Colin shook his head. "Haven't had the chance yet."

Captain Buchanan knelt beside Emma. "Mind if I look?"

"Make the baby come out. Please!"

The rugged company turned their heads while their leader pushed up her skirts and spread her legs apart. "What do you know, I can see the head— a patch as wide as two shillings. Shouldn't be long now. Get behind her, Dickson, and support her back. It's best she not birth the babe lying flat."

Colin scooted behind Emma and lifted her onto her haunches. She grasped his hands and braced herself against him as Captain Buchanan urged her on.

"Knees up, gal. That's the way. Now push hard!"

"I'm tearing apart!" she shrieked.

"No. You're faring right well. Keep at it."

Her face colored to a deep red and she collapsed back trembling against Colin. "I can't."

He kissed the top of her head. "Yes you can, darling."

The captain's sandy brows shot up. Charity could imagine what he must think, seeing Emma consoled in this loving manner by a man not her husband. But her cousin's immediate need seemed far more crucial right now than propriety.

"What the devil's going on?" a coarse voice demanded.

Startled by the intrusion, Charity looked beyond Captain Buchanan to the brown unkempt hair and bushy beard of Neville Paxton. Hard on his heels were ten men. That made twenty-one all told. One or two may have been left in the hollow with the horses. Wicomechee had counted right.

Captain Buchanan pursed his lips, a glint of annoyance in his eyes. "I'll let you work out the obvious for yourself, Paxton. And allow this poor woman some privacy."

"Certainly, Captain." With an ingratiating smile, the unsavory newcomer shifted his bulk a few steps backwards. He wasn't as tall as the captain, but he was wider. "Give the little lady some air, boys."

Jeb glared at them. "We thought you boys lost your way, or were waiting to see if we survived before joining us."

Still smiling, Paxton merely shrugged.

His insolence goaded Charity. Craig and Uncle John had held an extremely low opinion of this man. Like most, they suspected Neville Paxton and his men of using the Paxton homestead in the foothills of the Alleghenies as more of a hideout than working it as a respectable holding, and that their forays were for something other than trapping. Though there was no proof, folks had linked Paxton to a string of robberies in the valley and beyond, but he kept so many vicious dogs that no one went near his place.

Paxton's pale blue gaze passed over Charity and Emma with scant interest and settled on Colin with the predatory intensity of a fox studying a chicken house. Colin briefly returned the newcomer's scrutiny. Contempt narrowed his vivid eyes, while Paxton's washed-out stare held pure cunning.

Emma pushed violently with the next contraction. "Oh God! Ohhhh—help me!" Panting, she twisted against Colin, her cries interrupted only by huge tattered breaths.

Captain Buchanan's face lit up. "The head's crowning. Come on, gal. Have another go."

"Colin!"

"Once more."

"Too hard—can't!"

"Fight for this, Emma, like you've never fought before."

She clung to his hands, straining until Charity feared she'd lose consciousness.

"The wee one's coming! Anyone got some cloth I can wrap this babe in?" Captain Buchanan asked.

Charity flung down her cloak. Heedless of male

onlookers, she pulled Wicomechee's shirt over her head and stood in her shift. If he were watching, he'd just have to understand. "Here." She thrust it at the captain.

"Good heavens, gal. Did warriors steal your clothes?"

"No, sir." Snatching up her cloak, she wrapped in it.

Clearly he was baffled, as were a great many others, no doubt, but this wasn't the time to dwell on the mystery.

He reached thickened hands between Emma's legs. "Hold on. Don't push yet." She blew out hard while he carefully turned the baby's head. "All right. Now give it your all."

Emma gave one tremendous heave and the tiny body slid into his waiting hands. The wails of new life filled the air.

"You've a bonnie wee lass, Emma." Smiles eased the drawn tension on the faces of the watching men.

"Thank God," she cried, leaning back against Colin, her face red and glowing. Tears of joy and relief wet her cheeks.

"You did it," he said.

With a grin, the unlikely midwife swaddled the crying infant in Wicomechee's shirt, and laid her on Emma's deflated stomach. "I'll see to the afterbirth and cut the cord."

Charity stroked the baby's downy head and moist curls. "She's beautiful, Emma."

Colin slid one finger over her tiny cheek. "She is that. I've never seen a babe so new and small."

Emma cradled her protesting infant in her arms. "Thank you for staying with me. Both of you."

"Where else would I be?" he asked.

Her liquid gaze anxiously scanned the gathering. "What about all these men?"

"I must speak with them and see what's to be

done."

"What if they—"

"Don't fret. Lie quiet," he said under his breath.

"How? I'm so afraid for you. For us all."

"We are not alone. Trust my brother. You too, Charity."

Charity knew Wicomechee was out there watching them. She shuddered to think of a fight between the warriors and Captain Buchanan's militia, but she couldn't concern herself with that now. Emma and the baby were sorely in want of attention. "Colin, I need water and fresh linens."

"I know. I detest leaving her untended. All shall be done as quickly as may be." He slid out from behind Emma and laid her down. "See to the baby, darling. Try to calm her."

Emma stared at him dazedly.

"Feed her," he prompted.

"Oh." She began unlacing her bodice with trembling fingers and stopped. "There are so many to see."

Colin unbelted his sash, stripped off his shirt, and handed it to her. "Cover with this." He retied his belt around his waist. His sheathed dagger hung from the sash, but he must have left his other weapons behind. "Now you have both our shirts," he added quietly.

Captain Buchanan wiped bloodstained fingers on his homespun breeches. "Right then, Mister Dickson. What's happening here? Have the savages gone on without you?"

"No, Captain. They're not far removed."

He nervously eyed the dense evergreens, as did every other man present except Colin. "Is this some sort of trap?"

"Not of my making. You were seen entering the hollow."

The captain took off his hat and swatted its brim

against his leg. "So they're out there now, watching?"

"Our every move," Colin assured him.

An uneasy murmur ran through the gathering.

Captain Buchanan combed his fingers over hair loosely tied back at his neck. "How many braves are there?"

"Sixty."

"Bloody hell. Why haven't they attacked?"

"Because you cluster near to us."

He eyed Colin skeptically. "Come now. Since when are captives so precious to them?"

"I'm no longer a captive, but an adopted son and blood brother. And I've told them that Emma is my wife."

Captain Buchanan's disbelief was mirrored in his oldest son's face and nearly two dozen others. "I reckon this explains the affection between you two." He motioned Colin aside, and Charity sidled after them. "Maybe that will help ease the blow. I hate to tell her about Edward's passing now."

"Don't say anything yet," Colin advised.

He gave a nod and scratched his head then restored his hat. "I always thought you a decent sort, Dickson, a cut above most, you being a gentleman and all. But it must be true what Mary McLeod said. There was a white man with the party that attacked them. That fellow was you, wasn't it?"

Colin made no denial. The men, especially those who'd known him from his days in the valley, gaped at him.

"Hear me out," he entreated. "The area targeted for attack was already laid out. I accompanied the warriors to lessen the damage inflicted on the McLeod's. I've won much respect among the Shawnee, allowing me some influence."

Captain Buchanan squinted at him, his astonishment giving way to scorn. "Why stay on?

You're clever enough to escape."

"I'm in dire need of the sanctuary they provide."

"Whatever for?"

Neville Paxton stepped up. "I can answer that. This fine gentleman's got a price on his head, Captain."

Captain Buchanan's jaw dropped even farther. "What on earth have you done, man?"

"Nothing to warrant a bounty for my arrest. I'm unjustly accused of murder by a vengeful lord for the death of his lecherous son."

"Says you," Paxton sneered.

Colin eyed him as if he would gladly wring the life from this loathsome man. "It was a fair fight, damn you. A duel."

"The dead man's uncle don't see it that way. Mister Montgomery's men were out scouting for you. He's mighty eager for the recovery of the gentleman what murdered his nephew."

"A duel isn't murder. Lawrence Montgomery was a skilled swordsman. The death could just as easily have been mine."

"But it weren't. Poor young Montgomery, done in for a bit of sporting."

Colin's eyes glittered dangerously. "Lawrence Montgomery raped my sweet sister."

A rumble of disapproval rose from Buchanan's men.

"This puts the matter in a whole different light," the captain growled. "There's nothing lower than a man preying on an innocent lass. I don't care how rich and mighty he is."

Paxton waved Colin's assertion aside. "Pay no mind to Dickson, a renegade hiding out with bloodthirsty savages. Mister Oliver Montgomery, a proper Philadelphia gentleman, declares the young lady was little harmed in the affair."

Colin fired a scorching look at Paxton and

fingered the silver hilt of his dagger. "Oliver Montgomery is as devoid of decency as his English brother. I held Rachel sobbing in my arms, her gown torn, her lovely face bleeding. She had a stabbing pain between her thighs, and there was nothing I could do but fetch a physician and draw my sword."

Pulling his hand away from the blade, Colin charged forward and smashed his fist under Paxton's jaw. "Anyone who calls my sister a liar is a damn scoundrel!" he shouted, following through with a second punishing blow.

The hefty man reeled back, wiping at the blood running down his chin. "You bastard. If I didn't need you alive to collect that bounty, I'd cut your guts out now."

"Alone, coward? Or with the help of your boys?"

"Get the son of a bitch! Just don't kill him entirely!"

Emma shrieked and Charity's heart caught in her throat as his men rushed Colin. "No! Stop them, Captain!"

The militia leapt forward in Colin's defense. Jeb Buchanan pulled a knife from his belt. "Not fair odds, twelve to one. You boys want to fight? We'll give you better than we get."

Captain Buchanan grasped Colin's upper arms from behind and wrenched him back. "Have you all gone mad? Fighting among ourselves with savages lying in wait?"

Paxton's lips curled. "You only have Dickson's word for that. Likely they've abandoned these three."

"Take a stroll through the trees," Colin invited. "The wolves will feast heartily tonight. They like a fresh kill."

Captain Buchanan hauled him farther back from his antagonist. "I'm well aware of Shawnee loyalty to one they consider their own. Nor am I without sympathy for your plight." He glared at Paxton. "I see now why you accompanied us so eagerly."

"Paxton's a snake," Jeb hissed, brandishing his knife at Paxton's head. "And what do we do with snakes?"

Captain Buchanan rounded on him. "Put that blade away, son. Our predicament's bad enough." His furious gaze flashed back to Paxton. "Does your word signify nothing? You agreed to help recover all the captives. Not just this one."

Paxton shrugged. "I would hold to that agreement, Captain, but me and the boys are dog-tired."

"You were holding up well enough until you found Mister Dickson."

"Aye, well, we're right worn out now."

The captain looked on the verge of attacking Paxton himself. "Need I remind you my son remains a captive? No man's going anywhere without my say so."

"Just how do you think to prevent us?"

"With a musket ball through your ugly head, if need be. Now keep still while I question Mister Dickson." Paxton gave a curt nod and waited in grudging silence.

Captain Buchanan released his grip on Colin. "Tell me all you know of my boy."

"Rob has mended from his beating. I persuaded Chief Outhowwa to spare his life. He plans to adopt him."

Paxton snorted. "Make yourself out to be the hero."

"He did," Charity interjected. "I was there."

"Anything you say, young Miss."

Her palms itched to slap his insolent face. If she sprang as Colin had, and struck out fast—

Colin gave her a sharp look. "Miss Edmondson

also aided your son, Captain. If she hadn't intervened, my assistance would have come too late."

"I'm indebted to you both. We're mighty fond of that boy." Captain Buchanan's voice cracked with emotion.

"Thanks," Jeb added gruffly.

Colin nodded. "You've every right to be proud. But you endanger his life if you attack. The chief may kill him in revenge for any warriors lost."

The rugged captain swiped a tear from his grizzled cheek. "It's damn foolish to march right into an ambush. What do you suggest we do? We've all the captives to consider."

"Rest assured they are being treated with kindness."

"For now."

"No one intends any harm to these captives. You may be able to purchase their freedom later. The village lies along the Scioto."

The captain passed work-worn fingers over his brow. "It might be I can look to Colonel Bouquet and his advancing army for aid in their recovery."

Colin's eyes held no joy at this prospect. "Perhaps so."

This was the first Charity had heard of an army.

"Even if you claim us as friends, surely the warriors won't simply let us walk away?" the captain pressed.

"I'm willing to go and plead for your lives."

Paxton sneered. "That's the last we'll see of you."

Captain Buchanan balled his fingers into a fist. "Let the man finish. This situation is highly unusual. So is Mister Dickson. I'll hear him out."

"Wise decision, Captain. In addition to my plea, you hold the women. Both are greatly valued. It may be Chief Outhowwa will agree to an exchange."

The captain was incredulous. "Are you suggesting we sacrifice these defenseless women to save our own scalps?"

"Never. Ask them if they are willing to remain at least until they can be recovered later."

Captain Buchanan appraised Emma lying on the ground, clutching her newborn. "Surely you don't wish to stay behind with these savages?"

Her eyes were gray pools in her now pale face. "I'll not be taken from Mister Dickson, sir."

He turned disbelieving eyes to Charity. "What of you?"

"I'll stay, too."

"Must be for Rob's sake," he muttered, shaking his head. He threw his hands up. "I know not what else to do. Go then, Dickson, see what Outhowwa says. We'll wait with the women."

"I've a better plan," Paxton intruded. At a nod from him, his men aimed their muskets at the captain and militia. "We're through taking orders. Dickson's going with us, now."

"Are you mad?" Captain Buchanan barked. "If the Shawnee don't kill you, I'll report any survivors on my return."

"Who's to say we're the ones the savages will go for? Bind Dickson, Runyon." A large man with greasy blond hair and stained buckskins emerged from the pack. Unwinding a length of leather cord, he walked toward Colin.

"No!" Choking sobs shook Emma.

Charity raced to Colin and threw her arms around his chest. Breathless with emotion, she said, "I'll not let you take him."

"Have you an army hidden beneath your shift? None that I saw, though I don't mind the curves," Paxton guffawed.

His coarse laughter grated on her ears. For a moment she was torn between clinging to Colin and clawing Paxton. "You slimy toad-faced weasel. The Shawnee will fell you."

"Hush, little sister. We don't want a fight *here*," Colin said pointedly. "Don't weep, Emma. Have courage."

Runyon yanked Charity from Colin and shoved her aside. Pleasure gleamed in his sweaty face as he bound Colin's wrists, giving a cruel tug to the cord. "That'll hold you."

"Bully!" she cried, helpless with fury.

Paxton seized her shoulders. "Never fear, Miss. This ain't the last you'll see of him. You're coming with us."

She kicked at his legs. "Let go of me!"

He spun her around, ensnaring her from behind with his arm. "Can't oblige you, gal. You may prove real useful."

"Charity!" Emma rose up on one elbow, then her eyes rolled back to the whites and she slumped to the ground. The tiny baby slipped, wailing, to her side.

Colin surged toward Paxton. "You'll pay dearly for this," he snarled. Runyon jerked him back.

"Are you an utter heathen, man?" Captain Buchanan fought to reach Charity, but the leveled muskets kept him and the others at bay. "How dare you."

"Oh, I dare more than this." Paxton drew the wide knife affixed to a handle made from an antler, and held it to Charity's throat. "Hey!" he yelled, dragging her away from the evergreens out into full view. "Any of you bastards give us trouble and I cut her throat! Translate, Dickson."

"No need. They understood you perfectly," Colin said with menacing calm. "I advise you to let her go, Paxton. The warriors are excellent shots, especially the one that fancies her. You'll be his first target."

"They can't fire at me without putting her at risk," Paxton scoffed. "Stay close, boys. If we catch any of you following us, Captain, she's wolf fodder."

Chapter Twelve

Seething with more anger than he thought possible, Wicomechee watched the traitorous Long Knives from leafy shadows. Despite their leader's bravado before Captain Buchanan, the man he'd heard called Paxton used Charity to hide behind, both arms pinned to her sides, the menacing blade poised beneath her chin. Keeping to the center of his men, he forced her back over the trail toward the spring. Beyond that, the path wound down the ridge to their waiting mounts.

Whether intentional or not, an ill-placed nick from that sharp blade could open an artery in her throat. He suspected as soon as Paxton had no more use for her, it would be intentional. A man who had defied his own leader would stop at nothing to silence witnesses.

And Wicomechee couldn't come to her aid. Not yet. He dared not take a shot at her captor with the risk of striking her. Not only that, the man who jerked his brother along was positioned closely to Waupee. If Wicomechee fired into the party and struck a man further back, Charity or Waupee could be killed in vengeance before he fought them free. And Waupee was the one they most wanted.

He imagined his brother's anguish at leaving his wife and the tiny baby lying in blood and birth water. The fresh scent would attract predators. With the militia still by her side, she would be protected. What was to become of those men afterwards, Wicomechee didn't know or care. If the militia escaped Shawnee wrath, Paxton and his band would likely pick them off, but only if they survived.

Wicomechee focused his narrow gaze on the vile Long Knife. The attack must be timed just right or Charity or Waupee might fall with them. Lurking braves waited further back for his signal, as did Outhowwa. The life of his precious wife and beloved brother rested on his skill to be unseen and unheard.

He didn't need to see Paxton and his men to know where they were. The noxious scent told him.

"You're squeezing me too hard!" Charity gasped out, sending red-hot fire scorching through Wicomechee.

"Don't want you squirming away," Paxton growled at her.

"I can scarcely breathe."

"You've breath enough to yap at me," he grunted, and thrust her roughly over a fallen bough blocking the path.

She banged her shin against the furrowed bark. Burning with fury and frustration, Wicomechee held himself back in the hope that this impulsive girl would do the same.

The sudden pain must have unraveled any last self-preserving rein on her voice. "You great hulking coward!" she yelled up at her captor.

Paxton crushed his meaty arm across her chest. "Keep a civil tongue in your head, Miss. Or I'll cut it out."

Wicomechee wanted to cut off his offending limb.

"Calm down, Charity. It'll be all right," Waupee urged from behind her.

Listen to him, Red Bird, Wicomechee silently pleaded. If she kept still awhile longer, he'd find an opportunity to strike.

"Lord. No," she gasped out.

"*Ouishi catoui!*" Waupee called out, as if to her, the Shawnee phrase for *be strong.*

Wicomechee hadn't yet taught this phrase to Charity but it was the verbal signal he and Waupee had agreed to use when either of them were in trouble and scheming a way out.

"Shut up! No more damn Injun talk!" Paxton snapped.

No more was needed.

****

Colin's strange encouragement was lost on Charity. She only prayed it reached knowing ears, though she couldn't imagine what Wicomechee could do to free her from Paxton.

She despised everything about the lout, from the bush of a beard scratching the back of her head to his all-pervasive stench, as pungent as a polecat's, or worse. The sunlight pouring through the breaks in the forest canopy only magnified his stink and her thirst. She was sweltering in her cloak and his sweaty bulk further cooked her like a mutton stew boiled over the coals.

A wave of queasiness washed over her in a swelling tide. God help her. If she were to be sick, she'd find scant patience from this appalling excuse for a man.

Of a sudden, it seemed to her that the trees bending high overhead were closing in on her. The morning was calm, yet the branches tossed in a circle. The red and gold whirling leaves melded together and faded into shadows, then...nothing.

A rude hand yanked her head back. "Don't swoon on me."

For a confused moment she couldn't remember why this brute grasped her. Then she felt a sting across the skin of her throat and cried out in a rush of awareness. Paxton must have slashed her with his knife.

"For Christ's sake! If you kill her, she'll be of no use to you!" Colin shouted from behind them.

"Only a scratch. Stupid chit slumped against the blade."

A warm trail ran down Charity's neck—blood. Despite the heat, she shook all over.

"Lower that knife! She's likely to go down a second time!" Colin yelled. When Paxton pulled the blade a scant inch from her throat, he shouted, "More, you idiot!"

"Will someone kindly shut Dickson up?"

She cringed as Runyon's obliging fist smacked into what must be Colin's face.

"Knock me out, Paxton, and the warriors will think we're both dead and blow your fool heads off."

"Ohhhh—I feel giddy." Taking the hint from Colin, she let her eyes roll back into her head and went limp, pretending a deep faint. She didn't need to fake the twitching of her muscles; she trembled from head to toe, but if Paxton feared losing both prisoners, it might give them a much-needed edge.

"Leave Dickson be," he ordered. "One down is enough. Damn chit. Now I'll have to haul her."

"What do you expect? You've frightened the poor girl senseless," Colin tossed back.

"Blasted nuisance," Paxton muttered, lifting her.

Charity fluttered her fingers at Colin as the big man shifted her in his arms like an unwieldy sack.

"She looks in quite a swoon," Colin observed.

Paxton jabbed a finger at her shoulder. "Wake up, gal."

Charity ignored his prodding and lay like the dead.

"No use, Paxton. She's out cold," Colin said.

He spat. "What a weakling. How in blazes has she survived a trek in the mountains with bloodthirsty savages?"

"They never cut her throat. Fancy this beauty alive, you see. Particularly the warrior I mentioned."

"That bastard better not give me any trouble if

he wants her to stay that way."

"I don't know if he can tell she lives now."

"Balls. She's breathing right enough," Paxton argued.

"Not discernable from a distance. I wouldn't wonder if he thinks her lost to him. Excellent shot, that one. Never misses his mark," Colin added.

"Quiet, damn you, Dickson. I'll have you gagged."

"Try it, and you'll be hauling me too. I'll look so dead the warriors won't hesitate to fire. Miss Edmondson and I are all that's holding them back."

"Only if your stinking friends are out there. I'm not certain of that."

"No? The trees have eyes and ears."

"And teeth, I suppose," Paxton mocked, but Charity sensed the hesitation behind his ridicule.

"She really does look gone," Colin said. "How far did that blade go in?"

"Not far." Paxton dug his fingers into Charity's shoulder then gave her a teeth-rattling shake. "Wake up."

Eyes closed, she allowed a low moan to escape her.

"Girl's starting to come round. See?"

"Only just," Colin countered. "She ought to have a drink. Water revives women wondrously well."

"Thought they needed some sort of salts for that."

"Water will serve. The spring's across this meadow."

"A quick drink," Paxton agreed grudgingly. "Stay close, boys. Runyon, bring Dickson."

Charity badly needed a drink, but she suspected Colin had something more in mind than that. She felt the sun fully on her face as Paxton carried her out from beneath the trees and strode into the field. Scattering bobwhite called and the scent of grass

169

rose around her. Just a few happy hours ago, she and Wicomechee had raced to each other across this meadow. It seemed far longer now. How she yearned for that silver light and his arms around her again.

Paxton stood her upright at the end of the spring they'd arrived at first, the deep end. "Make it quick."

"I can barely stand." She stepped unsteadily between the stones and knelt on a grassy patch beside the water.

He hovered over her, gripping her shoulder. "Watch yourself. I can't pull you out if you fall in."

Runyon and Colin stood behind them. "Quite deep, Charity," Colin agreed. "I wouldn't want you to tumble in."

Why was he cautioning her? He knew she could swim.

Cupping water to her mouth, she glanced up at him. 'Jump,' he mouthed.

It took her dizzied senses a moment to understand his reason. Giving a slight nod, she bent back to the water.

Paxton nudged her. "We ain't got all day."

"I'll just splash my face first. I'm so weak."

"A lot of good this did, Dickson," he said gruffly.

"It takes a bit. Say, is that the gleam of metal?"

Paxton swiveled his head. "Where?"

"Over there. By that chestnut. I thought I saw the sun reflecting off a musket barrel."

An uneasy murmur ran through the men and all eyes riveted on the great tree. Paxton raked at the tangled mass of hair falling past his shoulders. "You're just trying to spook me."

"No. I think it's some sort of signal."

"Aw—"

Snatching up a stone large enough to make an impact, Charity smashed it down onto Paxton's boot.

Bellowing like a bull, he released her and

grabbed at his injured foot while hopping around on the other. She seized that instant to jump out into the spring.

"Damn bitch!" rang in her ears.

The mineralized water stung the cut on her neck and her heavy cloak and shoes dragged her down, but she had to remain in the deep. Struggling to stay afloat, she paddled around to face the shore. Paxton ceased gyrating and sat like a petulant oversized boy on the grassy patch near the water, cradling his foot in his hands, narrowed eyes boring into her.

"What in hell are you playing at?" he ground out.

She scrabbled at her shoes and kicked them off. "You want me back? Come here," she challenged, and untied the sodden cloak. It sank into the greenish depths.

He waved at Runyon. "Get in after her!"

The big man shrugged massive shoulders. "I can't swim."

Paxton clambered to his feet, looking wildly around. "Who can bloody well swim?"

"I can." Colin slammed bound fists up under Paxton's chin.

His teeth snapped together with a crack and he staggered back, blood running from his mouth. Then Colin kicked out and caught Runyon hard in his ample stomach, knocking the wind out of the bounty hunter. He reeled into Paxton. The force of their collision toppled them both to the ground. Runyon gashed his cheek on a stone as he fell. Scarlet ran into his lank blond hair and dripped onto his much stained buckskins.

"Get up, you big ox," Paxton grunted, shoving Runyon off.

The other men stood staring like stunned sheep while Paxton surged to his feet and lunged at Colin. He ducked his outstretched arms. Dropping to the ground, he rolled between large rocks and leapt up. He whirled around. Dashing back, he kicked out at Paxton and hurled him into a boulder.

"What are you lot gaping at?" he roared. "Get the bastard!"

Runyon scrambled back up. Jerked from their shock, the men charged at Colin. He dodged their punches and spun away.

Doggedly treading water, Charity watched in amazement. Where had he learned to fight like that, from Wicomechee?

Colin burst ahead of his pursuers and ran into the trees. All the men, except Paxton, galloped after him, stampeding through the trunks and leafy brush. They shoved aside any branches in their path, snapping weaker limbs in half.

Charity glimpsed Colin out in front. He tore into the meadow. If Paxton went too, she could climb from the spring and bolt for cover. Likely that was Colin's plan.

Paxton remained stubbornly behind. "Are you boys bloody useless? Teach the fine gentleman some manners!" he bawled, and dashed to the edge of the spring. "Come to me, gal."

"No!" Charity wished the deep end were wider, but the pond narrowed as the bottom fell away. Paddling more slowly now, her arms and legs weary, she fought against a strong southerly wind that had blown up seemingly out of nowhere. The relentless breeze pushed her toward Paxton.

He dropped onto his knees, beckoning to her with grimy fingers. Perspiration oiled his bruised, bloodied features. "I can see you're tiring. I'll turn you loose once I'm away."

"I'd rather drown!"

"Come now. That'd be a shame." He flopped down onto his belly and reached to her.

Musket fire checked his wheedling. He clapped a

hand to his shoulder with a howl. Crimson spouted between his fingers, and he half-dove, half-fell behind the boulder Colin had shoved him into.

More explosions erupted.

Charity swam toward the side, straining to see through the leaves. Fallen men were strewn across the grassy clearing. Some lay unmoving. Others writhed, their tortured cries rising with the hopelessness of the doomed. She covered her mouth at the sight of the nearest man sprawled beneath a tree at the edge of the meadow. He twisted like an eel on a line while those still able to run scattered for cover.

Two figures threw themselves behind jutting rocks in the field. Another fled to the charred remains of a trunk, little more than a scorched stump. Long barrels protruded from the stones and stump. Musket reports rang out as they fired back at their foe. But how could they hit what they couldn't see?

Then she spotted Runyon obstinately chasing after Colin. Why was he still pursuing him with Indians attacking?

Shrill whoops rent the air above the screams of the wounded. As if heedless of the danger, Runyon overtook the Englishman and bore him to the ground. He swung his fist again and again, punching Colin once, twice in the face.

Colin bucked the bigger man off and rolled away, but Runyon pulled his knife and came at him. Had thirst for revenge made him mad?

"Colin!" Charity cried, and climbed from the water. Hair and shift dripping over the stones, she ran. Her stocking-clad feet slipped. She fell forward, scraping her palms on the small rocks underfoot. "Help Waupee!" she sobbed out to the warriors pouring through the trees.

"Who's gonna help you, girl?"

Paxton! In her terror for Colin she'd forgotten the menace still crouched behind the stone.

He peered around the boulder, ashen-faced, but very much alive. In his hands, he held a musket. The barrel was aimed at her. "Get over here or I'll blow your fool head off."

She struggled to stand. "Go ahead. Shoot."

"Stupid chit." He slid the musket strap over his sound shoulder.

Moving far faster than she'd expected for an injured man, he sprang at her and snagged her around the waist. She shrieked. "Are you crazy? Warriors are all around!"

He jerked her close to his bloody shirt and drew his knife with a debilitated arm. A strip of stained linen torn from the ragged hem bound the oozing wound. "If they shoot at me, maybe they'll hit you."

"Where are you taking me?"

"To the horses and beyond."

****

Wicomechee drew on his rigorous training to keep a clear head as he crept through the undergrowth and dodged from trunk to trunk. His well-aimed shot had only winged Paxton who'd suddenly dropped onto his belly. Now he clutched Charity again. And Wicomechee spotted his English brother, still bound, in a desperate fight for his life. Much as he wanted to hack Waupee's tormentor to pieces, he couldn't leave Charity for a moment. Posetha and Muga must do the deed.

She dug her stocking feet into the grassy earth between the stones near the water. "Fight like a man!" she shouted at Paxton. "I'm not going with you!"

"Like hell." He dragged her away from the spring. Even wounded, his grasp was unyielding. But his labored breathing betrayed the cost as he forced her on through the trees.

Her resourcefulness in escaping Paxton at the spring had astonished Wicomechee, particularly as he didn't know she could swim. But she was out of her element now. Once more, Paxton held her so closely Wicomechee didn't dare fire, and if he rushed him, Paxton would cut her throat, maybe just enough to further weaken her, then drag her off again—the coward.

Wicomechee had closed the gap between them to twenty yards, when the Long Knife forced Charity into the clearing.

"Mechee!" she cried, raking at his heart.

Paxton gave her a back-handed crack across the mouth. "No Injun talk!"

Wicomechee thought rage would consume him when he saw Chaka. While other warriors streaked past to visit punishment on the stragglers in the field, Chaka slipped behind a broad tree in front of Paxton. With quick work of his blade, he took the scalp of the man fallen near the trunk then stood eyeing the hated Long Knife. Chaka's stance told Wicomechee he was angling for a kill—Paxton, his target.

Maybe Chaka did care enough about Charity to help get her back, or maybe it just goaded him that Paxton had taken her. Alone, Chaka couldn't free her without endangering her anymore than Wicomechee could. Perhaps together, they'd find a way.

Paxton dragged her into the grassy opening, his back to Wicomechee, his near panicked focus on the mayhem in the field. Wicomechee stole behind the two and signaled Chaka with his tomahawk. He pointed to himself and Paxton, gesturing at Chaka to approach the Long Knife from the front.

****

Charity never thought she'd be glad to see Chaka, but when he stepped out from the tree, she felt a desperate rush of hope. He stood before Paxton, blocking his way.

The shaken man held the blade closer to her throat. "Let me pass or I'll kill her."

She winced as the edge grazed her raw wound. "Chaka! Stop him!"

Chaka waved a freshly-taken scalp. "This belongs to your man. English girl belongs to Shawnee. Let her go."

Fingers shaking, Paxton pressed the blade deeper. "Stay back."

Screaming in pain, she tore her arm free from him and closed her hand around his grip on the knife handle. With a violent tug, she pulled his weakened hand away.

He dealt her a blow in the stomach, and knocked her arm down. She dangled, wheezing, in his grip.

"You bastards will never take her alive!" Paxton yelled.

Scorn curved Chaka's lips. "No?"

A strangled breath gargling in Paxton's throat was his only reply, and a violent shudder shook him like a seizure. His arms spasmed out and his fingers flexed, spilling the knife to the ground.

Triumph shone in Chaka's face. "Foolish man."

Charity staggered back, gulping in air. She hardly recognized her loving companion of early morning in Wicomechee's slitted eyes. Wrenching his tomahawk from Paxton's shoulder, he threw him to the ground. The sprawled man stared up in helpless terror as he bent over him and seized his knife.

He grasped Paxton's greasy hair, forcing his head back. "You took my woman, put your blade to her throat. Her fear cried out to me and I could do nothing. Your men bound my brother, struck him. For this, you will die. All die."

In one swift slice Wicomechee opened Paxton's throat.

"Oh God." Charity's shaky legs failed her.

She collapsed on the grass, but oblivion didn't come and steal her from the grisly scene. She knew where she lay and who lay near her. The anguished screams of men sharing Paxton's fate rang in her ears and the stench of death filled her nose. Her ominous premonition had become a reality.

Wicomechee shifted his gaze to her. In that instant, she knew he remembered.

Never will I take you into battle, he'd said. What else could he not prevent from happening to her?

Chapter Thirteen

Five Days Later

Lashing rain scattered the swirling leaves to the four winds, and thunder boomed. Lightning flashed through blackened trunks awash with the deluge. Ordinarily Charity disliked blustery weather, but she was grateful for the respite it had provided from the relentless journey.

Those warriors not out hunting were clustered along the fortress-like stone beneath overhanging rocks. Protected from the worst of the storm, they sat near campfires to mend worn moccasins, clean muskets, and smoke pipes. The tempest drowned out much of their conversation. A strong musk from the press of men added to the earthiness of saturated humus and aromatic wood smoke. The gunpowder scent, reawakened by cleaning, mixed with the pungent tobacco.

Hugging the tiny infant to her shoulder, Charity hovered as near the blaze as she dared without setting herself afire. With her free hand, she lifted the wooden ladle lying across two of the stones that surrounded the firepit and stirred the broth simmering in a large black kettle. The pot was suspended over the flames by a sturdy pole passing between two forked sticks. Boiling stock from scraps and bones had been her idea. The meaty aroma wafting through the tang of wood smoke brought a small measure of comfort to the cheerless day.

Colin sat cross-legged by the fire, Lily tucked in his lap and James by his side, intent on a card game with Muga. The children were engrossed in the play of red and black colored cards and apparently oblivious of the tumult descending just beyond their rocky shelter. Charity would gladly learn the game, but little Mary Elizabeth was fretful. Bouncing on her toes, she patted the restless newborn.

Colin threw down his cards and glanced up as Muga spread a winning hand on the ground with a grin. "You can't stall that wee lass much longer, gal."

"I'll try for a bit more. Emma's so tired."

He looked past Charity to where Emma lay as snugly bedded against the stone wall as he could make her. "Poor lady. What a grueling ordeal this has been for her. Only two days to regain her strength before Outhowwa insisted we go on." His troubled gaze met Charity's. "I'm thinking of falling behind the larger party to travel more slowly with the warriors who would agree to go with us."

"You mean, linger here awhile?"

"Yes. But few men will tarry. Most are in a hurry to reach the village and hunt for their families. The women grow corn, squash, and beans but supplies dwindle as winter nears."

A gust of wind sent cold fingers beneath Charity's skirts. "That can't be long in coming. I fear for Emma if we continue at this pace, though, and the little one suffers."

"I know. Still, it's risky to travel in such a small party," Colin said. "There's far greater safety in numbers and danger takes many forms in the frontier."

Muga finished dealing out a new hand of cards and removed the pipe from his mouth. "I go with you. Posetha go."

Colin squeezed his shoulder.

Charity shifted the squirming baby onto her other shoulder. "Mechee will."

Colin flipped over an eight of spades. "That's a

given. Though I doubt Outhowwa will thank me for depriving his party of their most skilled hunter."

"Outhowwa knows you two are inseparable."

A fleeting thoughtfulness softened Colin's somber expression. "I sometimes feel there's a kinship between us that goes beyond adoption, even beyond being blood brothers."

"You're about the same height."

He smiled faintly. "Our coloring's a bit different."

"True, but you're both well-favored."

"So are you. Does that make us relations?"

"I could do with a few more." She peered vainly into the haze and rain for Wicomechee, longing to be with him and equally uncertain. How fierce he'd been when he felled Paxton, his face so grim...every bit the warrior she feared. Could she ever truly feel at ease with him?

Mary Elizabeth wailed, and Colin laid down his cards. "Perhaps you can distract her long enough for me to bring Emma a bowl of broth. Take my place, James." The little boy nodded absently, his focus on the game. "I see we've found the way to keep you still. Lily, you'll have to move, sweetheart," he said, and lifted her from his lap.

She reached small arms around the dozing beagle's neck. "Weshe can play."

Colin's lips twitched. "As soon as he learns the cards."

"I will teach him."

"You do that, little darling." Colin smoothed her golden-brown curls then stood. Taking a wooden bowl from the stack near the fire, he ladled steaming broth to the brim and sipped. "Delicious, Charity. Hits the spot."

Mary Elizabeth renewed her lusty protest. "Hand her here. I'll take the babe and broth together." Holding the bowl aloft, Colin curved his other arm around the wriggling bundle. She fixed her blue eyes on him and quieted. Her puckered mouth curved in an unmistakable smile.

He smiled back, seemingly entranced. "You're a real little charmer when you want to be, aren't you?"

Charity stroked the fuzz on the baby's crown peeking out from the swaddling. She looked from her minute features to his masculine face, still mottled with the fading bruises. "Mary Elizabeth favors you enough to be your true daughter."

He smiled crookedly. "You're giving me relations left and right, dear heart. Come, little bird," he said to the baby. "Let's find your mama."

Charity turned back to the fire. Ladling a bowl of broth, she sipped the hot liquid and gazed at the rain drumming the leaves piled on the ground. How could Wicomechee find his way in this fog, let alone hunt?

"Charity," a low voice called softly from behind her.

She spun around to see Rob Buchanan half-hidden in the shadows back against the rock wall. When had he made his way there? She'd glimpsed him earlier with a different gathering.

"Will you bring me some broth?" he asked.

She hesitated. Outhowwa and Wicomechee had been quite clear about there being no contact between them.

"Please. The others haven't come yet."

"I suppose it couldn't hurt." Dipping the ladle into the kettle, she refilled her own bowl and carried it to him.

He smiled and reached for it with unbound wrists. "I thank you most kindly."

"You are most kindly welcome. I best go now."

"Wait. Bide awhile and speak with me."

She darted a glance around the encampment. Muga had his back turned to her and Colin was preoccupied with Emma.

"No one's paying us any mind just now," Rob said.

"Very well. For a bit."

He brightened and patted a spot near him. "Sit here."

She lowered herself uneasily onto the layer of dry leaves.

"I'm supping in grand style with you by my side." Lifting the bowl to his lips, he swallowed hungrily. He gulped a final swallow and wiped his mouth on his sleeve. "By heaven, I needed that. You had a hand in the soup making?"

She nodded. Little physical evidence of the beating remained on Rob's face. He was the youthful image of his good-hearted father, attractive in a rugged way and intelligent, but his ordeal was fresh in her mind.

"You're not tied. Does Outhowwa leave you unbound now?"

"During the day. I'm trussed up again at night."

"I'm glad you have some freedom."

"He usually sees to it I'm guarded. I reckon no one thinks me fool enough to run out into this storm." He smiled. "I would, only I've a far more pleasant occupation just now." he smiled.

Her cheeks warmed at the open appreciation in his hazel eyes. "Do you still think to escape?" she whispered.

"First chance I get."

"Don't take the risk. Your punishment would be severe if you're retaken."

"Afraid you might have to come to my rescue again?"

"I doubt I would be successful. Outhowwa has scant fondness for me, though he seems to like you well enough."

Rob shrugged his wide shoulders. "He doesn't

abuse me."

"You are fortunate he wants to adopt you."

Two warriors ducked under the generous overhang beyond Muga. She recognized the white deer tail decorating Hoskasa's scalp lock. Limp rabbit ears protruded from the bulging haversack he'd taken from a fallen Highlander in battle.

"The hunters are returning. I better go."

Rob closed his hand over her arm. "Wait. Wicomechee's not among them, nor Outhowwa. I haven't had the chance to thank you for what you did. I owe you my life."

She hovered nervously beside him. "I was grateful to be of service, but Mister Dickson really made the difference."

"Those few minutes you bought me before his arrival were vital. 'Twas very brave of you, Charity. I feel terrible you were punished."

"My suffering was little in comparison to yours."

He set the bowl down and clasped her hand. "I would spare you all manner of suffering, were it in my power. If we hadn't been taken captive, you might well be my betrothed."

She tried to pull back without drawing attention. "Rob, you mustn't. If Mechee sees us—"

"Mechee? Is that what you call him?"

"Easier to say. He'll be furious."

Rob kept tenacious hold of her. "Hear me out. I've been longing to speak with you."

She couldn't escape him without creating a scene. "Be quick. Please."

He reached out his other hand and tucked a tendril behind her ear. The familiarity of his touch only increased her discomfort. "I adore you, Charity, and have for ages. You must know the strength of my regard."

"Yes." She prayed no one else would notice.

"You fled the last time I came calling,

remember?"

"How can I forget? You tried to kiss me."

His lips curved in a wry smile. "And off you went like a startled doe. Still, I was willing to be patient and win you. Even now, I've not lost hope. Promise you will wait for me."

His ardent regard heaped on her like hot coals. "Oh, Rob. I can't promise."

"Listen, our recovery may be more possible than you think. An army under the command of Colonel Bouquet is marching on the Shawnee and their Delaware allies."

Not long ago she would have rejoiced at these tidings. Now, a weight sank in her middle. "Your father spoke of it."

Rob nodded eagerly. "The Indians are beaten down from years of war. Without French aid it's likely they'll be forced to seek terms of peace, the Colonel's terms. If this happens, I'm confident he will demand the return of captives."

Her throat tightened. "All?"

Rob's sandy brows drew together. "Yes."

"Even if they don't want to go back?" she forced out.

"What in God's name are you talking about? Oh, you mean your cousin, Emma Estelle?"

"Not only her."

"Who, then? Does James want to play at being an Indian?"

There was nothing for it other than to speak plainly. "I couldn't bear to leave Mechee."

Rob looked at her in the same manner his shocked father had. "Good Lord. You truly care for this warrior?"

She nodded.

He blew out his breath. "I saw Wicomechee with his arm around you. Made me madder than a baited bull, but I thought you were feigning affection to appease him."

Her constricted throat made speech difficult. "Mechee is unlike anyone, and any other warrior."

Rob ran agitated fingers through his hair. "It's unexpected, yet understandable, I suppose. Wicomechee's not bad for a warrior, and you are dependent on him for your very survival. But he's Shawnee, Charity. You belong with your own kind. Don't you want to go home?"

His wounded question pierced the ache way down in her heart. "I fear I shall never see the valley again."

"*Our* valley. We grew up there together. I know I could make you happy if I had the chance."

She lowered her eyes from the appeal in his. "Perhaps you could have, once. I was afraid to give you that chance."

"It's not too late."

"It is. I'm promised to Mechee."

"How so?"

"As his wife, with Outhowwa's blessing."

"Hell. Has Wicomechee consummated this union?"

She glanced up and answered haltingly. "Not if that means what I think it does. But he will."

A red flush colored the fading bruises on Rob's cheeks. "And there's little I can do to prevent him, damn him," he muttered. "That thieving son of a bitch."

She'd rarely heard such coarse language in her life and never from Rob. She shrank back.

"Sorry." He reined in his tongue and cupped one hand to her cheek. "Even if Wicomechee has claimed you, I swear I'll find a way to get you back. If Colonel Bouquet doesn't succeed in his quest, I know my father will go to any length to gain our freedom. In time, you'll forget this warrior. The regard you bear him is only a fleeting infatuation."

"How can you say that? You don't know how I feel."

"I've known you since we were children." He circled an arm around her waist, further entrapping her. "You're just confused, not thinking clearly. I'll teach you to love me."

"Please, Rob. You're endangering us both. Let me go."

"I haven't so much as spoken to you in weeks. I am not turning you loose to run back to him."

Her stomach churned. "I'll find a way to speak with you again."

"They'll keep us apart."

"Release me. I beg you."

"So sweetly you plead. Have you pleaded with him?"

"I've asked Mechee not to consummate our union yet, as you called it," she said, stumbling over the unfamiliar term.

"At least that's a step in the right direction. If he's as noble as you say he is, he will respect your wishes."

"It's not that I don't care for him. I'm frightened."

Rob clinched her tightly. "You bloody well should be. Keep the savage at bay, Charity. Give me a chance."

She didn't dare struggle and arouse suspicion. "We're going to be in so much trouble. Especially you. Let me go."

"Kiss me first."

She couldn't believe her ears. "Are you mad?"

"With love."

"Shhhh. Don't speak so."

"Can't be helped. Allow me the kiss I was denied before, and you are as free as a captive can be."

"Do you promise?"

He smiled. "Of course."

Apprehension pounded in her chest and nearly choked her. "All right. On the cheek, mind."

"Oh, no." Gripping her chin in one hand, he brought her lips forcefully to his.

****

Wicomechee ducked under the stone, wet through and discouraged, but the broth smelled savory and his spirits lifted a little as he slid his hunting pouch to the leaf-covered earth; it held only three small rabbits.

James bounded up from beside the fire and caught his sodden sleeve. "Play cards with us."

"Not now, small one." Wicomechee ladled the hot liquid into a bowl, grateful for the sustenance awaiting him.

He swallowed and glanced around for Charity. Usually he found her eyes seeking his and then she came up to him with that wary yet wanting look in her face. Even though she'd been hesitant ever since he'd killed Paxton and frightened her half to death, he hoped maybe this evening he could take her aside and speak with her alone, maybe even—

He halted in mid-sip and almost dropped the bowl. She sat back in the shadows caught in Rob Buchanan's embrace, his greedy mouth pressing hers. What in blazes was going on, as Waupee would say? And for how long?

The panther inside Wicomechee rose up on all fours, its fur bristling. He fastened his furious stare on the bold Long Knife. "Take this," he said, and handed the remaining broth to James with icy calm. "Stay well back."

Leaving the bewildered child, Wicomechee advanced on the pair, his voice a hiss. "You dare make love to my woman?"

Charity lurched, gasping, in Rob's hold. He broke off his kiss, though not his grip on her, and shot an unrepentant look at Wicomechee. "Charity was promised to me by her guardian. Until you stole her."

Wicomechee only just held back a feral cry. "Her guardian lies dead. You wish to join him?"

"Mechee—no." Charity struggled to pull away from Rob.

"Will you hide behind her, Long Knife? Let go of my wife."

Rob freed Charity and sprang to his feet. "She should be mine, damn you, Wicomechee!"

He'd surely kill this foolish man before he drew another breath.

Charity seized Wicomechee's arm as if to restrain him. "Don't—please."

He could tear free from a grizzly the way he felt, but stayed his hand with the calm that comes before a storm. "Have you the strength to take her from me, Rob Buchanan?"

The Long Knife halted, his mouth hanging open as he considered his challenge. "You mean fight only you?"

He gave the barest nod.

"Fine. Let's fight it out," Rob agreed.

Like a panther, Wicomechee waited for the right moment to tear into his adversary.

Charity lifted her white face to his, liquid eyes pleading. "No. He hasn't a chance."

Rob crossed both arms over his chest and cast her an indignant look. "I've a chance, Charity, if they don't all pile on me."

Wicomechee burned him with a scornful glance and swept one hand at the other braves. "I do not require their aid to deal with you."

"Do you intend making this a fair fight? I am unarmed."

"Waupee will hold my weapons." Wicomechee pried Charity from his arm and thrust her at Muga. "Wait there, Red Bird." The big warrior gripped her shoulder in obvious confusion.

His English brother pushed through curious onlookers. "What in the world?"

Wicomechee took the musket from his shoulder, the knife and tomahawk from his waist and handed them to him. "I will teach this Long Knife to keep his hands and lips from my woman."

Waupee rounded on the defiant captive. "Rob—you idiot. You actually kissed her?"

He faced him unashamedly. "She was entrusted to me by John McLeod. I've more right to her than Wicomechee does."

"Well, I'm standing beside one incensed warrior who doesn't agree. Confound it, Buchanan. How many times do I have to save your ass?"

Rob jutted out his jaw. "I did not request your aid."

"You would if you had any sense."

"I'm not afraid to fight him."

Waupee raked back his hair. "You should be. Oh, hell. Learn the hard way."

"Rob, offer Mechee an apology," Charity implored him.

He shook his head.

"No matter," Wicomechee said. "I will accept none,"

Waupee paced between them. "Don't be too hard on this rash pup, *NiSawsawh*. I promised his father and brother I'd look after him."

"I gave no such promise."

"Be reasonable. Outhowwa won't want you ripping him up."

"I'm no pup, Mister Dickson," Rob intruded. "Neither of us is armed, and we're about the same size. Why are you so certain I'll lose?"

"I've seen Wicomechee fight."

Charity reached out to him. "Mechee, listen to me."

He brushed her aside with scarcely a glance. What Rob had done was inexcusable, but she never should have allowed him the tiniest opening.

Waupee drew her back. "Come here James, Lily."

Braves stood aside, prepared to enjoy the clash. Charity waited in marked dread. "It's all my fault."

"Hardly. Buchanan asked for this," Waupee said.

And Wicomechee had had enough. She cried out as he drove his fist into Rob's jaw with the speed of a panther springing from the trees.

His head jerked back and he reeled, blood running down his chin.

Waupee gave a low whistle. "That was quite a wallop."

Shaking off the blow, Rob hurled himself at Wicomechee. The Long Knife was slightly shorter but stouter. Wicomechee dodged oncoming knuckles and punched his fist into Rob's gut.

Rob doubled over, and the braves cheered their own. Wicomechee didn't let them distract him, or allow his opponent a moment to recover. He slammed an upper cut to Rob's jaw then hammered his cheekbones with a series of clouts. The crack of bone hitting against bone resounded above the wind.

Charity clutched at Waupee. "Mechee's gonna kill him!"

"No—"

Rumbling like a rudely awakened bear, Rob straightened and charged. Wicomechee ducked his flying fist. He spun away then whirled back. Kicking out, he buried his moccasin in Rob's belly. Breath rushed from Rob's mouth and he tumbled to the ground where he lay gasping at his feet.

Wicomechee stared down at him. "If I had a knife you would lie dead."

"If I had one, so would you." Rob pushed up on

his elbows and staggered to his feet.

Once more Wicomechee drove his moccasin into Rob's middle and hurtled him to the ground. "You want more punishment?"

"Hell, yes," he grunted, and rose unsteadily.

Waupee shook his head. "He should have stayed down. But Rob's not a quitter. I'll give him that."

"Never has been," Charity added.

This time Rob evaded Wicomechee's fist and closed in, clutching his shoulders and grappling with him. Thrusting his foot behind Wicomechee's leg, he threw him off balance.

"Look at that! The fellow learns fast!" Waupee shouted.

Rob seized his momentary advantage and shoved Wicomechee backwards down to the ground. "Not so all-fired mighty as you think, eh!" he shouted, flinging himself at him.

His brawn landed atop Wicomechee with the weight of many stones. Air rushed out from him. Breathing hard, he battled back and forced the Long Knife to the side.

Over and over they rolled. Onlookers scattered as each wrestled to regain the upper hand. Rob ploughed his shoulder into Wicomechee's stomach then flipped him over to emerge on top. The Long Knife panted above him—unendurable.

"My brother is about to end this," Waupee predicted.

Straining every sinew, Wicomechee bucked his hips and threw off the offender. He grasped Rob and hurled him against the rock wall. Stunned, he sprawled on the ground as Wicomechee pinned his arms and straddled his legs. Rousing from his momentary stupor, he thrashed to dislodge him.

Chest heaving beneath his sodden shirt, Wicomechee bent over Rob and spilled black hair across his bloodied face. "You lose, Long Knife."

Rob ceased his futile struggle. "For now."

Wicomechee eyed him as he might a panther choosing whether to go for the throat first, or the head. "You still think to have my woman?"

Waupee rushed forward. "You have some nerve, Buchanan!"

Charity followed at his heels, her face stricken.

Rob ignored Waupee. His rebellious gaze targeted Wicomechee. "If I had won, would you let Charity go?"

"You lost."

"Answer me," Rob insisted.

"Never."

Rob spat a broken bit of tooth and a gobbet of blood just past Wicomechee's cheek. "Neither will I."

A disapproving rumble ran through the crowd. Wicomechee answered with cold rage. "Then I must take your life."

Rob met his fury with tight-lipped calm. "I can't prevent you."

"Dear God," Charity cried. "Have you lost all reason?"

Waupee shook his fist under the obstinate Long Knife's nose. "Damn it all, I'll whip you myself. Pound some sense into you."

"Before or after I kill him?" Wicomechee asked coolly.

Charity sank onto her knees. "Don't, Mechee. Please. I'll never forgive you."

Her pleas didn't soften the hardness inside him. "I'll not be led by a woman."

"I beg you not to do this."

He made no reply.

She slumped shaking to the ground, her head buried in her arms. Remorse pricked him, but still he said nothing.

"Don't take on so, Charity," Rob pleaded.

"I won't have your blood on my hands," she

choked out.

Wicomechee snorted. "The stain will be mine."

"'Tis because of me you're so angry with him."

Waupee knelt and patted her convulsing back. "*NiSawsawh*, you mustn't kill him. No matter how vexing he is."

"No?"

Charity lifted her head. "Mechee, for God's sake. Show some compassion."

"He would show none to me."

"Wicomechee," an authoritative voice summoned.

He turned his head to see Outhowwa pass through the hushed assembly. Rain streamed from his scalp lock and his clothes clung to his powerful form. His sharp eyes singled out the Long Knife still imprisoned beneath Wicomechee.

"I have no wish for your death, Rob Buchanan," the chief said. "You fought hard. Have much courage."

Rob scowled at him. "I'll not surrender this woman, Outhowwa. My heart is hers."

Wicomechee wanted to punch him again, but tensed as Outhowwa laid his hand on Charity's head. He held himself ready to spring to her defense if need be.

The chief spoke still to the obstinate Long Knife. "Speak to your foolish heart," he advised. "This woman is lost to you. Do you really wish to die for what is lost?"

Rob studied Outhowwa in sullen silence.

"It is easily done." He drew his knife and passed the leather-wrapped handle to Wicomechee. "In one stroke he will open your throat. If you wish."

Rob looked from the lethal blade in Wicomechee's hand to the wordless invitation he fired at him. He glared back through purplish, fast-swelling eyes, but shook his head.

Outhowwa extended his palm, and Wicomechee handed him the knife. "Pursue her no more. I will not speak for you again. Bind him, Wicomechee." With that, Outhowwa walked away.

The excitement concluded, the onlookers returned to skinning rabbits and plucking the rust-brown turkey taken in the day's hunt.

Muga led the wide-eyed children back to their card game, Weshe beside them.

Chaka said nothing as he strode off. Plainly, if he couldn't have Charity, this soon-to-be white brother wasn't about to claim her.

Only Posetha and Waupee remained, and Charity sagged on the ground.

Waupee held out Wicomechee's knife and tomahawk. His musket stood propped against the stone wall. "Take these. I'll bind him. You see to Charity."

Wicomechee rose from his glowering contender and reclaimed his weapons. Charity blinked up at him with glistening eyes, but he was stern. "You have much to answer for, Red Bird. I told you to stay from this Long Knife."

She got shakily to her feet. "Rob asked me for broth."

"You gave him far more."

"I never meant to."

He slung the tomahawk at his side and sheathed his knife. "What must I do with such a disobedient faithless woman?"

She winced at the hard term. "How can you call me that?"

"She's not to blame." Rob sat up. "I coaxed her near."

"Yet she went. And stayed."

"I held her fast. How was she to pull free?"

"Damn foolish. You're fortunate to live." Waupee took a length of cord from his pouch and knelt beside

Rob.

"None of this was Charity's doing," Rob insisted.

"Why did she not cry out? Were there not many to aid her?" Wicomechee asked pointedly.

"I didn't want him to be punished," Charity argued.

"For this, you let him kiss your lips?"

"Not her fault," Rob argued in rising desperation. "I begged her for one kiss."

Waupee seized his wrists. "One too many."

"How much more would you allow this Long Knife before you risk his punishment?" Wicomechee demanded.

Rob jerked from Waupee. "Punish me! Not her."

"Gladly," Waupee agreed, fighting to reclaim his hold.

Wicomechee shook his head. "It is enough punishment for you to know you can do nothing, Rob Buchanan. I will do as I like with my wife."

"Damn you to hell, Wicomechee!" he roared, elbowing Waupee in the stomach. He shoved him aside and sprang up.

Posetha lunged at Rob, toppling him to the ground. He forced him over and twisted both arms behind his back. "Shall I bind your mouth? Will you also curse Outhowwa?"

Waupee scrambled to his feet, rubbing under his ribs. "Knock me around again and by heaven, I'll—"

"Colin!" Emma cried. "What's happening?"

He tossed the cord to Posetha. "See to it this hothead sits here and cools his heels," he said through gritted teeth and strode toward the shaken woman.

Wicomechee grasped Charity's shoulder. "We will speak."

She wrenched away with surprising force. Leaving her blanket in his hand, she spun around and darted between two warriors and out from under the rocky shelter.

"Wait!" he shouted after her.

Heedless of him, she flew into the storm-tossed trees.

Chapter Fourteen

Charity refused to heed Wicomechee's hoarse call. It would take him an instant to grab his musket—a weapon he was never without—and chase after her. And in that instant, she intended to put as much distance between them as possible. She hadn't the faintest notion where she was going, just away from his anger.

Wind-swept droplets stung her face, but she'd have run into far worse weather. Rivulets flowed down over the rocks along the ridge and gurgled across her path. She splashed through the streams, soaking her newly acquired moccasins well up to her ankles. Wet leaves threw her off balance, and she hurled down onto her knees in a soggy pile.

"Red Bird!"

Oh, God. He was closing in on her.

She got to her feet and dashed ahead. Showery boughs slapped her face and briars snagged her skirts. Leaving yet more fabric behind, she tore free and sped around a curve in the misty trail. A downed chestnut limb loomed ahead, blocking her way. She sprang over the massive branch and landed in a lake of a puddle on the other side. Cold water swooshed up to her knees and spewed in her face.

Gasping, she scrambled to take off again. Just as quickly, her feet flew out from beneath her and she sprawled backwards into the yawning puddle. "Ooooh—"

The frigid water soaked her cloak and seeped through to the clothes beneath. *Stupid*, she berated herself, the icy draught bringing her back to her senses.

Again, she'd given into her impulsive nature. Running would only make Wicomechee angrier, if that were possible. There was nothing for it but to turn around and face him.

She must've been out of her mind to think he could ever love her as much as his late wife, Mequana. And Charity even yearned to be cherished above his lost first love. The most she could hope was that he wouldn't punish her too badly.

Frightened, chilled to the marrow, she struggled over the branch and started back up the trail she'd just flown down.

Wicomechee emerged in the gloom and sprinted up to her. "Are you crazy? You could be lost among the trees, or fall." He swept his hand at the trail and the steep drop to one side.

She hadn't even noticed the hazard in all the mist. "I'm sorry. I—" dissolving into fresh tears, she crumbled in a heap on the rain-drenched earth.

He knelt and spoke more gently. "Why did you fly from me? Did you fear I would punish you as I did Rob Buchanan?"

"There'd be little left," she squeezed from her throat.

"I said I will never strike you."

She shook in the pelting rain. "But you're furious."

"Yes."

She lifted streaming eyes and squinted at the mix of exasperation and tenderness in his gaze. "What will you do?"

"Get you to cover."

He closed his arm around her waist, helped her up, and guided her toward camp. They hadn't backtracked far when he detoured from the path and took an alternate route through the shrouded woods.

She wondered briefly where he was going, but was too enveloped in misery to really care.

Rainy whiteness obscured all but the nearest trunks. How he could find his way through this fog was beyond her. As if directed by instinct, he led her between the dripping leaves and lifted her over mini streams gushing through the woods. Her feet couldn't be any wetter, but she welcomed the chivalry he showed her in spite of the ire she knew had to be very much alive. She trembled uncontrollably by the time he stopped before what appeared to be the entrance to a cave.

Stooping under the wet stone, he disappeared from sight.

She had an aversion to caves but at least it was shelter. Ducking her head beneath the darkened rock, she followed. What was this—were her senses confused?

Rather than the mustiness of dank stone and moldering leaves, the tantalizing scent of roast game and the cheery crackle of a campfire greeted her. Anticipating a black hole, she gazed around the limestone chamber in wonder. Light bounced off the walls and the fire created a glowing circle.

It was as though they were expected. A plucked pheasant sizzled over the orange flames. A blanket had been spread next to the fire, and another tucked nearby. The spiciness of sassafras wafted from a small pot; a cup waited in readiness.

She spoke through chattering teeth. "You did all this?"

"For you."

Smoke rose to the murky ceiling and back toward an unseen alcove. Vast chambers might lie beyond this first room, but he'd made it snug for a cave. Remorse stabbed at her. "I had no idea—and now—I've spoiled everything."

The lines at his mouth eased. "Perhaps not all."

"Forgive me."

"Warm first. Speak later." He untied her drenched cloak and spread it to dry. "You must also remove your clothes."

She tugged at her bodice with numb fingers and fumbled the laces. He laid his musket down, slipped off his powderhorn and shot pouch. His vest joined the pile. He unbelted his sash, along with his pouch, knife, and tomahawk, and took off his shirt, adding these to the cave floor. Moisture glistening over his bare chest, he turned to her.

He quickly unlaced her bodice and pulled it from her then untied her petticoats. They fell around her ankles. Covered in goosebumps, she stepped from the mud-splattered cloth and stood trembling in her shift. The damp cascade of her hair lent her no warmth.

"Poor Red Bird. So cold you are."

He laid the bedraggled garments near the fire and swiveled back to her. He bent to unknot the ties that kept her high-top moccasins in place—the moccasins he'd helped her fashion. She stood awkwardly on one foot then the other as he pulled the wet deerskin from her and peeled off her disheveled stockings. She clutched at him for balance and warmth.

"Lift your arms," he said. "I will remove your shift."

"I'll be utterly bare."

"I have a blanket for you."

She lifted her arms hesitantly and stood as he stripped her clinging underdress. Surely she must be the most immoral woman on earth. Torn between what to shield first, she crossed both arms over her breasts. "I've never been naked in front of a man before."

"Good." He tossed her shift beside the other clothes.

"But I don't think 'tis decent."

"It would be far worse if this were common for you," he said with a smile, his eyes playing over her like twin flames.

She flushed hotly. "Why do you get to keep your breechclout while I've nothing?"

His smile broadened. "You wish it off?"

"I didn't mean—I—never mind."

She broke off as he scooped her up in his arms and bore her a few steps. The smooth slippage of their rain-slicked skin made her embarrassed squirming a disturbingly delightful sensation. He laid her down on the blanket. She snatched at the extra cloth.

"Don't cover all. I will warm you," he said.

"But you can see everything."

"Close your eyes. You will not know what I see." He slid beneath the blanket and turned onto his side facing her.

She squeezed her lids together, finding it easier not to be a witness. "I'm a muddy mess."

"No. Only beautiful."

He held her to him. The muscles and heat of his chest pressed against hers was distracting, to say the least. "Oh—I've never felt anything quite like this."

"You will feel more still."

He slipped his fingers over her shoulders and her back, grazing her shoulder blades. She arched her back involuntarily as he trailed along her spine, following the rounded curve of her lower back to circle his hands softly down the slope of her chilled bottom. "Everywhere you are cold."

She nuzzled her face against his cheek. "My nose is like an icicle."

"What of your mouth?"

He lowered his lips and settled them over hers...kindling an inner fire that flamed up in her like an oven. Her trembling lessened as he lingered at her mouth.

"Warmer now?" he whispered.

"Oh, yes."

"Good. We will speak," he said with sudden firmness. "This time you cannot fly from me."

She opened her eyes to the censure remaining in his. "How can you kiss me that way if you're still angry?"

"You lie bare in my arms. I wish only to love you, yet I must scold." He traced a finger around her mouth. "I will not share these lips with Rob Buchanan."

"I did not know Rob would kiss me the way he did. I asked him to kiss only my cheek."

"You think he would do this with your fair mouth before him?"

"Rob isn't like Chaka."

Wicomechee shook his head as if he couldn't believe her naiveté. "Do you not see how much desire Rob has for you?"

"I wish he didn't."

"Are you certain you bear him none in return? You wept, begged me to spare his life."

"Out of friendship only. I—love you—" she stammered. "I told Rob this."

The disapproval in Wicomechee's scrutiny softened a little more and he wound a tendril of her hair around his finger. "Rob would not hear you?"

"He refused to and said he will take me from you."

"How?"

"With the aid of an army under the command of Colonel Bouquet."

Wicomechee tensed and the mildness in his face vanished.

A shadow grew in her mind. "You know of this?"

"That army is one reason Outhowwa attacked in

your valley, to lure the soldiers away from our villages."

"And if they're not lured away, and the Colonel forces his terms?"

Wicomechee said without hesitation, "I will hide you."

"What if you can't? What if they take me from you? I'd rather die."

He grew somber, and for a long moment his eyes alone spoke for him. "Live, Red Bird. I will take you back."

"I never want to leave you, Mechee."

He considered her in bemusement. "Yet you ran from me only a short while ago."

"I was afraid," she whispered.

His breath warmed her ear. "Do you fear me now?"

"A little. Sometimes you are like a wild animal."

"I am *meshepeshe*, the panther, who moves through the trees on silent feet so no one knows...until he howls."

She looked into his face and followed every strong line. At times, his dark eyes were very like an enraged panther's, and ever watchful.

He firmed his jaw. "No man will take you from me."

"I pray you're right. Rob says I will forget you and learn to love him."

"Never." Wicomechee caught her close, crushing her against him. "You belong to me. Not Rob Buchanan."

****

Charity sucked in her breath, and Wicomechee lightened his near fierce hold. "Do not fear me, sweet one."

He bore possessive lips down on hers. Again, he was the panther, but with a far different purpose now, a panther claiming his mate. She did not yet realize, but she was about to learn. His throbbing groin ached to teach her.

Her lips parted at his urging, and she opened to his tongue. He touched hers, lightly at first, and she touched back in sweet uncertainty, and then he thrust into her mouth with a swelling intensity she was helpless to equal. Fresh goosebumps sprang up in answer to the heat he felt washing through her.

She was breathless when he drew back enough to allow her to speak. "I'm much warmer now."

"You shall be warmer still." He pressed his mouth over the tempting curve of her neck. "Your soft skin shall bear my mark. Not Rob Buchanan's."

The mantle of her hair shone and whispered against his skin as his lips quested downward. He slid one palm in a long stroke along her smooth side, like a supple young willow, and her wonderfully curved hip. Finally...he cupped his other hand around her mounded breast, circling its plump tip with the barest touch of his tongue. She gasped as he closed his lips around the nipple to suckle it. He didn't spare her a single sensation, but moved hungrily between her breasts.

She squirmed under the powerful emotion he sent through her and laid her hands on his shoulders, as if that might steady her. "I think you will do far more than warm me."

He blew softly on a taut nipple flushed deep rose. "Did I say I would do only that?"

Her breasts rose and fell beneath his seductive mouth. "No. But I'm not certain about all of this."

"I am." He'd never been more aware of every inch of his fevered skin, or of the aching need to plunge inside her.

The fire bathed her in orange-gold light as he glided caressing hands and lips over her womanly beauty. Any last reserve of resistance she still had seemed to dissolve...the fair spirit of the trees bound by love with the panther. What a coming together this would be, wind and fire. She seemed spellbound by him, intoxicated. Where he led, she followed, with less assurance than he, yet with tender passion.

Her seeking lips discovered his neck and she slid her fingers through his hair, over his shoulders and chest, stopping at his abdomen. She wasn't bold enough to explore any further down, but she slipped her hand over his hip, not as curved as hers, and his thigh.

"Mechee," she summoned in a breathy whisper. "You are so different from me."

"More than you know. Have you ever looked on the whole of a man?"

"Once, by accident when Craig was bathing."

He almost pitied her ignorance. She was in for a shock. Smiling slightly, he rose up on his knees above her and jerked away his breechclout, leaving only the narrow thong that had held it in place.

She gaped at the spectacular difference between them. "Your—" she stumbled, at a loss for words. "Oh my."

Laughter nearly escaped him. "I am not always as you see me now."

"I thought not," she managed, her eyes asking the unspoken question.

"I must be this way to enter you."

The wonder in her stare increased. "Good heavens. You can't actually mean to put all that inside me?"

He hid a grin behind his hand. "Where else?"

"It's not possible," she argued.

"I will show you."

"Oh, no." She scooted away from him and scrambled to her feet. Conscious again of her nakedness, she turned to the side in a useless attempt to shield herself from him. Once more, she tried to cover her glorious body with her hands.

He remained as he was. No need to alarm her anymore than she already was, better to lure her back. Feigning casualness, he gave a languid stretch and lay down with his head propped on one elbow. "Where will you go?"

She darted her gaze around the cave.

"Do you think to hide from me?" he asked.

"Not in here."

He swept his admiring gaze the length of her. "Will you run out into the night as you are?"

She reached down and snatched at the blanket. "Stop looking at me!"

He held onto the cover. "You stand before me."

Her eyes continually returned to his full-blown manhood. "Maybe you need a bigger woman?"

A chuckle rumbled up from his chest and it was all he could do not to howl.

"Mechee. I'm serious."

"I know."

Her face betrayed the workings of her mind as she snatched at ideas and blurted them out. "Couldn't you just go on touching me as you were?"

"You like that?"

She colored the pink that washed the sky at dusk. "Very much."

"You will like more than this. Come," he coaxed.

She chewed her lip and remained maddeningly out of reach.

If he weren't half crazed with need, he would enjoy her appealing quandary. As it was, he lay in mounting impatience. "Charity, must I chase you through the cave?"

She glanced at the surrounding stone flickering in the shadowed light. With a shake of her head, she dropped cautiously down onto the blanket and back into his waiting arms. He drew her soft curves against him. She trembled from her lovely head to her bare pink toes.

"You shake as if waiting for torture," he chided.

"I can't help it."

"Calm down."

He trailed his hand over her flat stomach and down between her shapely legs. She stiffened as he slid his fingers where no man's had ever ventured before...slipping lightly over her moist skin, between tempting folds, and her as yet untouched bud.

Squirming at the new sensation, she said, "Mechee—"

"Hush...I'll not harm you."

"Do you promise?"

"Yes."

"Rob promised to let me go after a kiss," she confided shakily.

Her innocence was astonishing. "He lied."

"What of you?"

"I tell you now. I will never let you go." He ran his fingers over the tumbled lengths of her hair glowing like red coals in the light. "I will make you *niwah*, my wife."

"*Niwah*," she repeated. "I like this sound. Am I not already yours?"

"Not fully. I am determined to let no man part us. But I must guard you well. You fly without thinking."

"I will be more careful. I swear it."

He covered her vow with his lips, coaxing her to silence while he gently explored within her. She was smaller than he would've liked and she tensed at first, but slowly relaxed as he expanded her with the rhythmic motion of his fingers.

Her reluctance at his seeming invasion diminished at the all-consuming desire he felt pulsing through her in the hammered beat of her heart. There was no part of her that did not seem to thrill at his touch and he pressed his advantage until she ground against his hand, wanting more.

She broke from his mouth. "What are you doing to me?"

Laughing softly, he buried his face in her quivering neck. He understood what she did not, the need that now possessed her for him and all he had to give. And yet, she seemed to have some inherent knowing of why he was made as he was. She gripped his shoulders as he moved over her, pulling his hard maleness down on her as he nudged her legs apart.

With an intensity that sprang from that primal place deep inside, he said, "You shall have my child."

Whether she understood what he was about to do or not, he'd held himself back long enough. Wrapping her in his arms, he eased his manhood inside her oiled warmth with a groan of profound pleasure.

Charity startled as though at a sudden sting. "Stop!" she cried, twisting beneath him in a struggle to free herself.

He held her down, his bliss at odds with her pain. "I cannot. This you must bear to fully join us."

Tears sprang into her entreating eyes. "You said you wouldn't hurt me."

"I regret to. You are small, tight. The pain will ease," he soothed, and penetrated her more deeply.

She gave an even sharper cry and dug her fingernails into his shoulders as he embedded his shaft in her rich wealth. This was where he'd longed to be from the first and he thrillingly repeated this most compelling of all movements.

"Enough," she pleaded.

He kissed her damp cheeks and rigid neck. "Not yet. Move with me."

"How? I only want to escape."

"Try. It will go better for you."

She took a shuddering breath and slowly released it. With clear misgiving, she rocked her hips up and down, back and forth, in rhythm with his. He was fully inside her, then partially out, and thrusting in again, like a strange wonderful dance. Yes, he'd done this dance before, but not with the same exhilaration and marvel that this exquisite creature was at last his. If he remained knitted to her like this forever, it wouldn't be long enough.

To his relief, the tension in her face and body faded away and he found her urging him back inside her. This time the moan she loosed was uttered in delight not pain.

"You can bear this torture?" he whispered.

She closed her arms around his neck and sought his lips. "Just."

Chapter Fifteen

After three stormy days the afternoon sun shone brightly. "Finished," Charity said to the small dog, her sole companion, and straightened from the river bank. Her newly washed hair dripped to her waist and she wore only her damp shift and moccasins. The clean laundry she'd spread over naked shrubs made the bushes appear as though they'd sprouted dripping linens rather than leaves.

Gazing at the turbulent waterway, she was struck again by how splendid the *Kenahway* looked glinting in the light. It plunged like a living beast between the ridges jutting high above it, as unlike the river rippling beside the meadow back home as a panther from a kitten.

No meadow spread here. Poplar trees strung along the edge of the water vied for room with sycamores and underbrush. The yellow blooms covering naked witch hazel made an unlikely spot of color along the rough path worn by countless wild animals and sometimes wilder men.

Few settlers came this way now. Many fled their remote homesteads during the recent Indian Wars. Only the very brave or the foolhardy would bring their families out here now to scratch a living from the narrow valleys and hollows tucked among these rugged mountains.

Wet and shivering, Charity searched out a large flat stone farther along the bank and stretched out lengthwise on its sun-warmed surface. Weshe curled on the patchy grass beside her. How good the heated rock and wash of gold light felt to her goose-pimply skin.

"We'll head back in a bit," she promised herself and the small dog.

If Wicomechee returned from hunting while she tarried here, Emma would send him down from their camp, just a stone's throw away up the side of the ridge...and he'd slip beside Charity. She smiled, envisioning what would follow. Wrapped in happy thoughts of him, she dozed like a cat in a sunbeam.

Growling broke through her drowsy stupor. She roused at the beagle's insistence, but heard only the roaring water. Had the warmth lured a snake from its den—worse, a bear?

She sat up guardedly. "What is it, Weshe?"

Seeing nothing out of place, she swiveled her head and stiffened. A small group of men were approaching with laden pack ponies. Bends in the trail and the river's roar must have concealed the newcomers from her watchful companion until they were only about thirty yards away. She'd never expected to meet anyone out here, let alone white men. Were they trappers? Beaver, mink, foxes, and deer abounded along the river. Would the strangers pass on by harmlessly? They lay between her and the path back to camp.

Weshe growled more insistently and the fur rose on his hackles. Charity's flesh prickled in warning. The men's rough appearance alone didn't fully account for her mounting dread. Frontiersmen often dressed this way. A crudeness in their demeanor, something indefinable that reminded her of Neville Paxton, sent alarm coursing through her. The biggest man even resembled Paxton, with long dark hair and an unkempt beard. But this fellow was far larger—a giant.

"Is the wench real or a spirit?" one man called out.

"Been terrible long since I've seen such a lass.

211

What a find, spirit or no," said another.

Terror engulfed her in a paralyzing tide. She must flee, but as in the cave with Chaka, her body would not respond.

The giant stroked his bushy beard. "The lass is real enough, and someone's been fool enough to leave her for me."

The others hooted. "You'll share her with your friends won't you, Reed?"

"I make no promise."

At last, Charity found her voice. "Mechee! Colin!" she shrieked. Colin was up grooming the horses—not far away.

"Who're you calling, lass? Think they can hear you?" the giant taunted.

Like a friend turned murderous traitor, the surging river had become her enemy. Jerked fully to life, she jumped off the stone and fled like the deer Wicomechee had compared her to. Unhindered by cumbersome skirts, she dodged the largest rocks and sprang over others, leaping from stone to stone, Weshe at her side. This rough ground was worse than the riverbank back home, but her moccasins barely touched down.

"Give it up, gal! We're on your tail!" a male voice shouted from behind her.

Summoning every last ounce of speed, she bounded forward even faster. With luck, she'd spurt well ahead of the men and find a place to hide then sneak back to camp after they'd gone on. A sharp stitch ate at her side and pains stabbed her burning chest as she raced through stands of dock and mullein. Nettles stung her bare legs above the moccasins like bees.

Scouting ahead, she saw her way blocked by a jumble of brown boulders and granite slabs. She skirted the landslide and skidded to a stop before a thorny patch of brambles. There was nothing for it but to go higher up the gravelly bank—but that route was barred too. Grape vines and thick brush brought her to a halt. She pushed and clawed to get past, fingernails breaking, palms scratched and bleeding. Without an ax or tomahawk to chop her way through, she had no hope of an outlet.

Her pursuers would flush her from cover and run her down like a hunted animal. Or trap her where she was. Half-running, half-sliding, she raced back down to the river. A man with a long, brown braid down his back was almost on her. Not far behind him came the giant. Either she must climb the treacherous slide, be torn to ribbons by the brambles, or—a towering sycamore stood within reach.

Breathless from flight and terror, she darted to its white mottled trunk and leapt up. Weshe whimpered, circling the trunk, as she caught the lowest branch and pulled herself up into the tree. She flung one leg over the branch, scrambled to gain her footing and stood. Immediately, she reached her arms toward the next. Midway up the tree she glanced down at the two men stopping at the base of the trunk. Chests heaving, they leered up at her.

"You a bear cub?" the big man called, and then gestured at his lean, shorter companion. "Go after the wench, Jack. I'm not much of one for climbing trees."

Fear choked her as the man called Jack hoisted himself up into the tree and climbed up the branches, his braid swinging behind him. "Give it up, gal! I can go high as you!"

Only one choice remained. Shaking so hard she could scarcely crawl, Charity climbed out onto the limb that extended over the water. Below her, leaves, sticks, and fallen branches swirled by in the foaming brew.

"Stay back!" she shouted at him.

"Easy," Jack cautioned. "You don't want to fall. Come now," he coaxed, easing onto her perch. "I'll not harm you."

"Stop! I'll jump!"

"You're crazy!"

"I can swim!" she shouted over her shoulder.

"Not in that you can't. You jump, you die."

A sense of unreality washed over her. "Then I die." If she didn't give herself time to think, just let go—

"You don't want to go and do a fool thing like that!" the giant shouted up at her. "I'll treat you right."

"And I surely will." Jack edged farther out the branch.

"Mechee!" Sobbing his name, she swung herself over the limb and clung to it, her feet kicking in the air. "Touch me and I'm letting go!"

Jack froze. "Steady, now. Don't waste yourself. Would this Mechee want you dead?"

"You want him to find your body dashed against the rocks?" the giant called.

Wicomechee's eyes appeared in Charity's mind weighted with inexpressible sadness. *Live, Red Bird. I will take you back.* His assurance came to her as though she'd heard him speaking in her ear. She owed him the chance to try.

Arms shaking with exhaustion, she appealed to the man crouching above her. "Help me! I can't hold on much longer!"

"Thought you'd see sense."

Jack scooted nearer. Gripping the branch with his legs, he bent down and seized her arms. The next thing she knew, he pulled her up onto the limb and into his grasp. Dazed, trembling, she collapsed against him.

"There, there, Jack'll see to you," he crooned, and towed her back to the trunk, leaning against its support. "Hey, don't I get a thank you?"

He was out of mind if he thought she'd offer him one.

"I just saved your life, sweetheart." Gripping her chin with rough fingers, he forced her face up. Lust lit his beady black eyes as his thin lips swarmed over hers. The sour odor of whiskey and sweat offended her only slightly less than Paxton had. At least Paxton hadn't kissed her.

She shuddered, enduring Jack's ardor while fighting through a haze of mind-numbing panic. What would Wicomechee have her do? For once, she must think before acting.

"Hand the girl down!" the giant shouted.

Jack ran callused fingers over her cheek. "Half a shake, Reed. She's the prettiest thing I ever saw."

This horror couldn't be happening. Charity thought she'd be ill or faint as Jack's demanding lips clamped back over hers. At least his vile mouth kept her near camp. The longer she remained where she was, the better her chance of rescue, she reminded herself.

"Get down here! She ain't out here alone!" Reed balled.

Jack paused long enough to peer down at the exasperated man pacing below them. "Give me your word I get a piece of her before I hand her over."

Reed pulled his beard. "What you gonna do if I say no? Sit in that damn tree until her man shows up and shoots you?"

"Come on, Reed. You and me go way back."

"You can have her after me," Reed said gruffly.

"What'll be left? Ain't you better suited to a cow?"

"Cheeky bastard! I'll cut your pecker off!"

One of the men left with the pack horses dashed up to the fuming giant. "What in blazes are you two waiting on?"

215

"Jack's up there," Reed grunted, pointing.

The newcomer shielded his eyes against the sun and squinted up at them. "Girl holding you prisoner, Jack?"

"Reed'll kill me if I come down."

"Hell, Reed. Let the man down afore we got trouble."

"Hain't I been after him to shift his ass—now, Jack!"

If Jack did as he ordered, they'd leave just as fast. "Don't, Jack," Charity urged. "I'd rather stay with you."

"Right grateful to me after all, eh?" he gloated.

"Jack!" Reed bellowed.

"Better do as the old bull says," he grumbled, and lifted her to the branch below. He climbed beside her and she had no choice other than to let him lower her down. "Here you go," he muttered, handing her to Reed. "Remember our bargain."

Reed closed massive arms around her. "After what you pulled, you'll be lucky to get anything."

His stench was as repulsive as Jack's and there was far more of him. Her fear ratcheted up ten-fold and she fought to pull free and touch her feet to the ground. "I can walk!"

Reed's hard brown eyes met hers. "And run. I seen you."

She realized with a sick weight in her gut that Reed wasn't the fool Jack was. If he hauled her away, she'd have no chance to flee. Wicomechee wouldn't be able to fire a shot without the risk of striking her. Weshe barked madly as she twisted in his unyielding hold. "Let me go!"

"You think that's what I been waiting around for?" Reed flung her over his shoulder and started back the way he'd come. The other two men fell in behind him, Jack glowering with resentment.

"Get your hands off me!" she cried, kicking at

Reed's girth, encased in a coarse brown shirt. She beat her fists on his back as his colossal buckskin-wrapped legs quickly covered the stony ground.

"Fight away." He tucked his unwelcome arm more snugly around her scantily clad bottom. "Suits me just fine."

Reed's jarring stride swung Charity in full view of Jack's sullen gaze, like a belligerent crow's. "No fair going after all the good parts while I'm back here," he griped.

"I'll hold the girl any way I damn well please."

Weshe ran alongside Reed, baying and nipping his heels. With a scrabbling jump, he leapt up and bit into his knee.

"Get off, you bugger!" Reed yelled, kicking out an enormous booted foot. He caught the dog in the side and flung him out of the way. Weshe yelped and scrambled up. Dashing back and forth, he baited Reed as he had the bear, dodging his kicks. "Can't have the yapping beast following us."

Charity swung her head as Reed took a pistol from inside the breast of his shirt where the overlapping cloth formed a pouch. "No!" she screamed, knocking at his hand.

The smoky shot tore past the dog, grazing his side, and sent him yelping off up the river. Tears blinded her. At least Weshe had escaped. Maybe he'd bring Wicomechee.

"Now who's the idiot?" Jack demanded. "If anyone's around, they'll hear that and come high-tailing after us."

Charity thrashed in Reed's meaty grip. "And track you down! You're all good as dead!"

He rounded on her. "Knock my arm again, and so help me, you'll regret it." He shoved a rude hand under her shift and parted her thighs in warning. "Quiet down or I take you now."

Jack bristled. "Thought you were in an all-fired

hurry to get out of here?"

She seized her opening. "Stop him, Jack. I want you."

"Told you I should be the first one with her, Reed!"

"Like hell." Reed strode over the track beside the river.

His fingers rode horribly near her unprotected thighs. If she stirred up a fight between them, she might escape in the confusion. "Don't you want me for yourself, Jack?"

"Not much chance of that."

She tried another tactic. "Reed's hurting me!"

Jack dashed forward and grasped his burly arm. "What're ya' doing to her?"

"Nothing. Yet."

"Get your hand out from under her shift!"

"I'm barely touching her."

"Yeah? Why's she taking on so?"

Reed shifted Charity in his arms. His flinty eyes scrutinized her. "What game are you playing?"

"No game. Jack, help—"

"Call to him one more time, and by heaven, I will hurt you," Reed growled.

Jack charged in front of him. "Why? 'Cause she fancies me?"

"Don't be a damn fool. One taste of those soft lips and you've lost what little sense you had. Gone off your head like a crazed cockerel."

Fists clenched, Jack danced back and forth. "Set her down. I'll show you a fighting cock."

"Challenging me are you, you strutting little bantam?"

"For her? Damn right."

The other men circled them. "You ain't got a rat's chance, Jack," one said. "Let Reed be. He'll whup your ass."

Reed fixed his shrewd gaze on Charity. "I surely

will. But a fight would slow us. Give your man time to find you before dark. And I'd have to put you down, so you can run."

His perception shook her and she stared at him mutely.

"Clever," he grunted.

Jack's face reddened. He drew back his hand to strike her. "You bitch. Playing us off against each other."

Reed threw out a big hand and blocked the intended blow. "No one touches her without my leave. You got that?"

Jack's lips curled down, but he gave a sullen nod.

"All you men clear on this?" Reed demanded, and the other five nodded. "Still want me to put you down, little girl?"

She turned away from his smirk. *God, send Mechee.*

****

The orange sun hung low in the west and cast its final rays through the darkening woods. Only then did the men stop in a clearing to make camp. Night was almost upon her, Charity realized in dismay. She'd been in Reed's grasp for several hideous hours. Though he'd said little, his straying hands left her in no doubt of his unspeakable intentions.

Water splashed over stones not far from where she was, probably just over that dip beyond the hemlocks. If she reached the stream, she could soon lose herself among the evergreens, and then double back toward camp. How else was she to escape? She'd seen no sign of Wicomechee or Colin and feared they hadn't caught up yet. And when they did, there were seven men to route. And one was a giant.

Reed finally loosed his loathsome hold and

219

lowered her to the grass. "May I have a drink?" she asked.

"Nice try. Won't work."

She met his lewd grin. "Are you denying me water? Even your animals drink."

"Please me first then drink all you want."

Jack glared at her with squinty eyes. "Bitch owes me."

"Bitch ain't the word I'd use for this beauty."

"She didn't trick you."

"No," Reed snorted, "and she won't. You'll get your share, but you treat her right or you'll answer to me."

Outrage flashed in Charity like fire set to dry kindling. They spoke of her as if she were no more than a chicken to be divided among them. "What sort of woman do you think I am!" she shouted up at Reed.

He grinned. "The best sort."

"Do you fear no punishment for your vile crimes?"

"The closest fort is days back through these mountains. Or are you dragging me into court?" he snickered.

"What of God? Do you not fear him?"

"Save your preaching for Jack. He likes a good sermon."

Jack and the others had tethered the horses and were removing their packs. "I'd like to give you a bloody sermon, Reed," Jack sniped at him. "And a good hiding to go with it."

"Shut your mouth, or I'll give you one," Reed hushed him. "Leave me be. The lot of you."

Six pairs of eyes narrowed at him like malevolent bulls.

Ignoring them, he caught Charity back up. She beat on his chest, shoulders, anything in reach, even boxed his ear as he carried her across the clearing.

"You can't do this!"

"How do you aim to stop me?" He cast his musket aside and laid her down in a grassy spot surrounded on three sides by boulders. "Don't need them looking on," he muttered.

This was his notion of privacy, she realized, and sprang to her feet. "I don't belong to you!"

He grasped her shoulders and threw her down onto the ground. The impact knocked the wind from her. "Mechee will track us—" she gasped out, scrambling to roll away.

Reed forced her onto her back and pinned her arms over her head. "Your man's a natural born fool bringing you here."

"He'll kill you, just as he did Paxton!"

"Neville Paxton? That useless son of a bitch. I should thank him for doing us a favor, just before I return it."

"No!" she shrieked, fearing just that.

She thrashed beneath Reed as he climbed on her. Even without bringing his weight fully down, his massive size threatened to crush her. If his organ were as big as he was, he'd tear her apart. "Get off me!"

A volley of musket fire burst around them in smoky fury.

"Shit!" Reed hissed in her ear against the guttural cries of the wounded. He rolled to the side of her, grabbed up his musket, and crouched behind the largest stone.

Here was the moment Charity had longed for— her chance to flee. She leapt to her feet, but hesitated, and scanned the clearing. One man writhed on the ground, a second lay still. Blood pooled around them. The others scattered for cover. She scanned the trees. Two familiar heads peered around a broad oak, their muskets aimed at the scrambling figures. She glanced at Reed's slitted-eyes. He'd caught sight of her rescuers too.

"Goddamned warriors." He raised his musket and aimed the barrel at the dearest head in the world.

But Wicomechee's keen gaze was on Jack. He fired and hurled him screaming to the ground. Jack flopped fitfully, then nothing. Reed cocked the trigger.

Heedless of her own safety, Charity flew at the giant and shoved the heavy barrel up with her hands. The musket discharged harmlessly over her husband's head.

Reed whipped around. "Indian-loving bitch!"

He swung his hand and cracked her across the cheek. She felt the stinging blow as she reeled backwards—but only for an instant. Blinding pain shot through her head as she collided with the stone and crumbled at its base.

She breathed out a single word. "Mechee." And darkness closed in.

****

With a howl of deepest anguish and blackest rage, Wicomechee flung down his musket and grabbed his tomahawk. Before the big Long Knife could reload, he sprang at him.

Clenching his own tomahawk, the giant rushed to meet him. Brown eyes burned above his broad nose and black beard. "I'll send you to hell, you Shawnee bastard!"

"Hell waits for you," Wicomechee growled, circling him with the intensity of a panther eyeing its prey. He ducked the razor-sharp edge. Reed might be far larger, but his reflexes weren't as fast. One slip on Wicomechee's part could prove fatal and he was desperate to get to Charity. Forcing himself to concentrate, he watched for an opening.

Again, he dodged the razor-sharp blade and whirled around. With a slicing blow, he cut his tomahawk into Reed's shoulder and rendered that arm far less powerful.

Reed bellowed, his arm awash with blood. Wicomechee wanted to sever the hand that had dealt the blow to Charity. So still she lay. Her silence called to him unbearably.

Again, he tore his mind from her and circled his wounded adversary. He closed in, tomahawk raised.

Reed's meaty fist shot out and caught him on the jaw. Ears ringing, his chin throbbing, Wicomechee staggered back. He shook off the blow and jumped aside as Reed's blade stung across his chest, slashing his shirt and grazing his skin.

"Not fast enough, old man," Wicomechee snarled.

Blood trailed warmth down his chest, but the demon Long Knife was far more stained. Wicomechee kicked out and hurled Reed back a few stumbling steps. Seizing the opportunity, he struck his bad arm again.

Reed screamed, dropping the tomahawk with useless fingers. But he showed no intention of awaiting his death when one good hand remained.

With the wrath of an injured grizzly, he charged and grasped Wicomechee by the throat. Fingers like saplings tightened around his neck. The mountainous bulk forced him back toward the ground. He struck wildly at Reed's back. The blade didn't cut in deeply enough to finish him. Struggling under the crushing weight, gasping for air, he went down.

Reed bent over him, eyes lit with hate. "Got you now, you bloody savage," he panted. "You killed my friends. I'm gonna choke the life out of you, Mechee. That's your name, ain't it? You're the Mechee she cried for."

Reed's sneer blurred in a red haze and Wicomechee envisioned Charity's tearful eyes seeking him, her mouth crying his name. Would she wake to find him dead and Reed hovered over her?

"Stupid bitch," Reed ground out.

The foul word fueled a surge of rage in Wicomechee that flooded new strength through him. He glimpsed the shock in Reed's tight face as he threw him off and scrambled to his feet. "Red Bird is all that's good! All that's sweet!"

He could have lifted the giant over his head and tossed him down a ravine. Instead, he struck her abductor with his fists and drove him back—ever back. He drew his knife. And lunged, thrusting it up between the stunned man's ribs. "Die with her name in your ears. Red Bird. My wife."

A choking grunt rushed from the giant and he slumped forward with a rasping gurgle. His inert body pressed heavily against Wicomechee. He shoved Reed off and he thumped to the ground. Red with blood, breathing raggedly, he staggered to Charity.

She lay where she'd fallen beside the treacherous stone. She could be fast asleep but for the unnatural way she was positioned, her body tucked up, face so white, except for the ugly purplish-red mark on her forehead and the welt on her cheek. Terror unlike anything he'd ever known seared him. He could battle a hundred men and not feel as weak as he did now.

He knelt and pressed trembling fingers to her throat. He found her pulse. Not strong. Blackest dread gripped him as he touched crimson-stained fingers to the evil bruise on her forehead. This injury wasn't one he possessed the knowledge to cure. He doubted even the wisest medicine man did. She lay beyond the reach of any healing root or plant.

Wrenching grief tore through him. Reed might as well have plunged the knife into his heart. With a cry from his innermost depths, Wicomechee gathered her in his arms. "Don't leave me, Red Bird. I am with you and will not leave you."

He sagged back against the stone cradling Charity to him.

Time lost all meaning. He had no idea how long he remained like that...minutes or hours. He only knew that all color and joy had gone from his world. Revenge brought him no peace. All that mattered now was the faintly beating heart of the woman he clutched. And he dared not let go. If he did, she would surely fly away. Somehow, he must will her to stay.

His will was strong. "Stay with me, Red Bird. Stay with me." Hot tears slipped down his cheeks and over her chilled face. Again and again, he entreated her and kissed her cool cheeks.

Dusk cloaked the trees when Posetha walked through the clearing and stopped before Wicomechee. He regarded him through his tears. Posetha's gaze dipped to Charity.

"I left none alive," he said, his voice weighted with pain.

Wicomechee nodded. It made no difference now.

"Red Bird, she lives?"

"Just." Wicomechee waved at the body of the man who had caused this black despair. "Get the big Long Knife from my sight."

Posetha grasped Reed by the ankles and dragged his grisly bulk behind the hemlocks. He hauled the other corpses across the grass to join him, each one swallowed up by the shadows. Wicomechee hugged Charity to his heart as Posetha built a fire. Then his friend took two blankets from the packs and held one out to Wicomechee.

He carefully wrapped Charity in the woolen cloth. "She dislikes the cold," he said dully.

Posetha draped another blanket around Wicomechee's shoulders, and sat beside him. Neither of them spoke. The wind whispered in the trees. The first stars appeared overhead. More came out until the whole sky glittered with lights—lights Charity should've shared with him. Her excited voice did not rise at the blazing streak that arched across the sky. The lonely brilliance seared Wicomechee's soul.

Distant wolves howled at the great moon rising through leafless branches. One full moon circle had passed since Wicomechee first took Charity captive. In that time she'd come to mean all to him. He softly kissed her cold face. "Do not fear the wolf, Red Bird. Posetha has made a fire."

"Perhaps she knows it burns," Posetha offered.

"Who can say?"

Night wore on, as did their sorrowful vigil. Wicomechee reached under the blanket and clasped her limp fingers. She should have squeezed his in return. He remembered the first time she'd pressed her uncertain lips to his and tears flowed unrestrainedly. He hadn't thought she'd find the courage to kiss him, but she had, and he thought of that blissful night only a few days ago when she'd joined herself to him. Each precious memory twisted the knife more deeply into his tortured heart until he groaned in anguish.

"I gave my promise to protect her. Yet she saved my life. I failed her."

Posetha clasped his shoulder. "We could not strike any sooner. You saw how closely the Long Knife held her."

Bitter rage seethed in Wicomechee's despair. "And how he touched her, my sweet wife. I should have fallen, not her."

"Red Bird's love for you is great, Wicomechee. She would not want to weep over you. Would you wish this pain on her?"

"Never. The big Long Knife swore to send me to hell. He has succeeded. Am I not in torment?"

"She breathes still," Posetha reasoned.

"So faint is that breath. How can I help her?" Wicomechee pressed his cheek to Charity's cold skin. Never had he felt so desperate. "She grows more chilled. I am losing her. If she flies I will swiftly follow."

"No. You, alone, carry the blood of your grandfather. If you take your life, will not his heart be torn from him?"

"As mine will be if I must live without her."

"Are you not my dearest friend and brother to Waupee? How can we bear to lose you? Be strong," Posetha pleaded.

An owl hooted overhead. He and Posetha sucked in their breath and stared at each other. Firelight bared Posetha's dismay, his face a reflection of the icy horror that had laid hold of Wicomechee.

As if in response to this dark omen, Charity uttered one barely audible word. "Craig."

Wicomechee gripped her. "No. Do not fly to Craig, Red Bird. Come back to me. Charity—" Choking on her name, he turned to his friend. "I must pray. Have you tobacco?"

"Take all." Posetha spilled the fragrant leaves from his pouch.

Wicomechee snatched up the sacred leaves and cast them into the fire. The pungent tobacco mixed with the wood smoke. He followed the ascending smoke through tear-blurred eyes. "*Manito,* hear me. Do not take my wife. Spare her life. Was it not you who gave Red Bird into my hands?"

Sobs overwhelmed him and he could not speak. But he would not let her go. He'd never let go. Posetha closed his arm around his shoulder and wept with him.

Again the owl hooted. Wicomechee lifted his head and saw great snowy wings sail across the sky silhouetted against the yellow moon. Had the spirit of his precious wife flown with this ghostly bird?

"Does she yet live?" Posetha whispered.

In dread of what he would find, Wicomechee pressed his fingers to Charity's neck. A faint, but detectable pulse still beat beneath his trembling hand. He shifted his fingers to her chest and felt the slight rise and fall of her breathing. "She lives," he said, in unspeakable relief.

Posetha gulped in air as though he'd just pushed his head above water. "I feared she was gone."

"She is weak, yet with me still." Wicomechee poured his will into drawing her ever nearer.

Bright constellations arched across the clear sky and set below the horizon. New ones appeared in their place as they kept watch. Wicomechee brushed the hair from Charity's neck and felt again for her pulse. "She grows stronger. Listen," he whispered with excitement.

Posetha bent his head near her chest and waited. "I hear her breathing! Is she still so cold?"

"Yes. Yet not so much as before."

"I will build up the fire."

The low flames crackled to life with the kindling Posetha fed them. The orange glow shone against the gray edging out the blackness as predawn light silvered the woods. Charity stirred, an almost imperceptible shifting, but Wicomechee was attuned to her every move.

"Come to me, Red Bird," he urged with his very soul.

She turned her head slightly, as though in response.

"Come Charity."

A faint moan escaped her lips.

"I am here. I wait for you, Red Bird."

And then, with unspeakable joy, he heard her whisper his name. "Mechee."

Posetha clapped him on the back. "She is

returning to you."

Streaks of rose tinged the eastern sky in the beginnings of a glorious dawn.

"With the sun."

Chapter Sixteen

Five days later

Clouds the color of lifeless coals overhung the ridges. Raw breezes blew under Charity's skirts and flapped her cloak and the blanket she clutched around her. The cold wind chased rust-brown leaves and heaped them into crannies among the trees like squirrels' nests. If only she could tuck down into a snug burrow to escape this bone-chilling damp. She longed for a cheery blaze and an end to this interminable day, but the end wasn't in sight.

After her horrific ordeal, Wicomechee and Colin both thought it best to try and catch up with Outhowwa's party, there being more safety in numbers. Failing that, they wanted to reach the village as soon as possible. Rather than allowing her time for an extended recovery, they'd spared two days and pressed on. This day was the worst since her injury.

She stood on the creek bank as the two men waded out into the brown torrent. Wicomechee staggered in the flow swiftly rising to his waist. "Too deep! Cross further ahead!"

Colin stopped behind him and waved the others back. Muga and Posetha turned away from the swollen stream and led the string of pack ponies taken from the trappers back up the bank. The blanketed heads of both children bobbed above the docile piebald, one of Muga's charges.

The two men slogged from the water, climbed between the moss-edged stones, and paused in front of the quiet gelding.

Emma sat atop the big horse clutching Mary Elizabeth in the folds of her blanket. Her face, partially hidden by the crimson cloak, creased in concern as she gazed down at them.

"You're soaked through, and 'tis such a raw day."

Puddles collected at their feet, but Wicomechee shrugged.

Colin stomped his moccasins to shake off the excess moisture. "Don't fret, sweetheart. We've suffered worse."

Wicomechee arched an eyebrow at him and teasing touched his eyes. "When was this?" Colin smiled wryly.

It was beyond Charity to understand how they could joke when she was so wretched and they were far wetter.

Emma shook her head at them and shifted her focus to Charity. "You look all in. Want to ride with me again?"

"That jostling bothers my head. I'll stay with Mechee."

"This pace is too harsh for her, Colin," Emma protested.

"I wish we could stop, but we can't make camp here."

Wicomechee nodded. "We must find another place to ford."

"No use standing here freezing our you know whats off." Colin took the reins and started over the trail after Muga and Posetha.

Wicomechee and Charity fell in behind, and it was all she could do to put one foot in front of the other. He closed his hand around her arm and helped her along the outcropping that blocked access to the water. Weshe followed, better mended from his wound, it seemed, than she.

A red-tailed hawk shrilled overhead and flapped from a tall chestnut, partly veiled in the haze. White-capped sparrows fled its talons, darting into the heavy boughs of a spruce. The evergreen stood out among the barren branches covering the ridge, witness of winter's inevitable approach.

Aunt Mary had said she wanted Charity wed before snow flew. It seemed the iron-willed woman had gotten her wish, though not at all as she would have wanted. If only her aunt could know Wicomechee—but, no. It was hopeless. Charity was cut off from her people and home, and couldn't join the past with the present. Her uncertain future lay with this man whose strong arms lifted her over the limb blocking the trail.

On and on the line of stones persisted, and the narrowing path forced her to walk behind Wicomechee. Laurel hedged them in from the right; the rocks prevented any outlet to their left. Fixing her gaze on his newly acquired deerskin coat, she followed him like a beacon, his back the focus of this bitter trek. But the stones seemed determined to outlast her limited reserves. She heard water tumbling beyond the wall. Perhaps the stream was fordable now. How to know?

The path wore on, dipping and rising again, strewn with obstacles of all sizes. No opening emerged in the unyielding barrier. She stumbled over a log, lurching down onto her knees, and slumped on the hard trail. "Mechee!"

Weshe licked her hand while Wicomechee squeezed between the damp stone and returned to her. "Come. We will soon find a place to cross."

It wouldn't matter if only a few yards remained. There wasn't a step left in her. She cried weakly. "I can't."

He knelt and closed his arms around her. "Reach deep inside. Find strength."

She pressed her face against his coat, inhaling his unique scent mingled with wood smoke and the cold forest. "You march me like a soldier."

"Not soldier. Shawnee warrior."

"What difference? Both are tireless."

He cupped her icy cheek. "All men tire."

"Not like me. You don't."

"I have no injury. Go just a little further."

"No. Let me stay here."

"We will find a better place to camp." He stood and pulled her to her feet. "*Ouishi cattoui*, be strong."

Her unsteady legs threatened to give out.

"I will help you."

"How? The trail's too tight."

He stepped ahead of her and reached an arm behind his back. "Take my hand."

She grasped his fingers like a lifeline. They made slow progression. A woodpecker hammered at the dead oak looming above them like an enormous corpse. Wicomechee turned and lifted her over a chunk from the decaying giant. Retaking her hand, he walked on.

Above the wind and water she heard a man shout something in Shawnee. It sounded like Muga. "What did he say?"

"Stones are soon gone. We can cross now."

"Thank heavens!"

Wicomechee helped her beyond the last of the rocky wall then half-led, half-carried her to the bank. She leaned against him, her chest heaving. Posetha was midstream with three ponies. Brown water rushed by just below his waist, lower on Muga waded a few yards behind him. Legs tucked up, the children clung to their pony while Colin sloshed behind them leading Stuart.

"I will carry you over," Wicomechee said to Charity.

"What of Weshe? He might be swept away."

"You hold him. I hold you—"

A chilling shriek, like a woman's tortured scream, shattered the late afternoon gloom.

"*Meshepeshe*," Wicomechee hissed. "Panther."

Her heart lurched, and Weshe growled.

Many settlers had seen the ravages these devil cats made on their livestock. Some had lost children to its powerful teeth and claws. The horses whinnied sharply. Empowered by the rush of fear, Charity stood without swaying as they scanned the dimly-lit trees on the opposite bank.

Again, the terrifying scream rent the air.

The pack ponies went wild. Posetha fought to control his charges, but they tore free in a mad scramble up the bank. Muga snatched up the children and just kept them from toppling into the current. His panicked ponies thrashed to shore.

Stuart snorted and tossed his head, but stayed as he was. Emma clung to his mane with one hand and her tiny infant with the other. "Will he throw us?" she cried.

Colin didn't even glance at the gelding. His focus, like Wicomechee's, was on the hazy trees across the stream. "No, darling. Stuart's steady as they come."

Charity wasn't so sure. "If he tosses Emma, she could lose the baby in this rough water. Nor can she swim."

"Waupee's horse has much courage—there," Wicomechee pointed. A large, black panther crouched on a high branch ready to spring on the ponies. "I despise to kill him. But I must." He leveled his musket.

Charity grasped his arm. "Stuart may bolt if you fire."

Before Wicomechee could speak or knock her hand aside, Colin snatched his musket from his shoulder and fired.

The explosion discharged near Stuart's head, but he adhered to his training as the feline menace plunged to the ground. Charity sucked in her breath. Wicomechee stared slack-jawed at the fallen panther then at his English brother.

****

Feet stretched out before the fire to dry his sodden moccasins, Wicomechee sat with his friends and James. How good to be in jovial company with the promise of a decent meal before him. The gloom of the day had lifted and the night was cold, but not bitter. Stars shone amid the clearing clouds.

He looked past the gathering where Charity slumbered with Emma and Lily beside her. This mountainous trek in late autumn was hard on the women, Charity so recently injured, and Emma not fully recovered from the birth.

He slanted his eyes at Waupee and the swaddled infant tucked against his shoulder. How tenderly he held his tiny adopted daughter. Wicomechee would give almost anything for a child of his own, but he'd said nothing more to Charity after her initial alarm. Longing for family was as strong in him as the will to live, especially after his father had abandoned him and his mother died...but he didn't want to dwell on that and buried the aching pain deep inside where it belonged.

He glanced down at James sitting between him and Posetha as he roasted a skinned squirrel on a stick. The pleasure in the child's face bespoke his part in its demise. Wicomechee smiled at the boy. "You will grow to be a great warrior."

James beamed. "Like you, Muga, and Posetha?"

"What about me?" Waupee prompted.

"You are Uncle Papa. Not a warrior," James explained.

Wicomechee laid his hand on his brother's arm.

"Waupee is also a warrior. We taught him. We will teach you."

"Papa wanted me to be a farmer, but being a warrior is heaps better. Will it take me long to learn?"

"Many years. There is much to know."

"Uncle Papa killed that panther good. Did you teach him to shoot?"

Wicomechee studied Waupee. "Not so well as this."

"A lucky shot," Waupee said.

"No. That shot took much skill."

Posetha regarded the adopted Englishman. "Why do you not share in the hunting?"

"I have," Waupee argued.

"Not for many weeks."

Waupee shifted his gaze to the women, an underlying anxiety in his good humor. "I'd rather see to the horses."

"Uncle Papa is real good with horses," James said.

Wicomechee rested his hand on the child's blond curls. "Yes. Yet there is more reason why Waupee does not hunt." It came to him in a flash. "You fear to leave your wife."

"After Chaka nearly scalped Emma and went after Charity, I felt uneasy being any distance away," Waupee admitted.

Wicomechee flung up his hands. "I also feel this."

Waupee met his exasperation with a half smile. "Someone must guard the women."

"A task I would gladly share."

Posetha grinned. "I also."

"Oh, no. Find your own woman," Waupee tossed back.

James snorted. "What do you all want women for anyway? They're a bunch of trouble and don't make hardly no sense."

Waupee chuckled. "In about ten years you will understand why we trouble with these puzzling creatures."

James brushed his assurance aside to reason with Posetha. "You are much better off without a woman. They like things clean. You'll have to take baths," he warned.

Posetha was unmoved. "I bathe in the river."

"But you can't have no fun with women around."

"I think I could have much fun with a woman." Lips twitching, Posetha glanced around as if searching the trees. "Where must I seek for one?"

"Well," James's said, conceding defeat in the face of Posetha's obstinacy. "I don't usually see them in the woods. They like cabins. You got any?"

Wicomechee closed an arm around the boy. "A *wikon* is like a small cabin. We have many in the village, also women."

James eyed Posetha as though he'd missed the obvious. "Look there, then."

Waupee chuckled. "The lad is right. What about a village girl? Nialinwe's not hard on the eyes."

"Beautiful," Posetha agreed. "Yet Nialinwe prefers Wicomechee. She waits for him."

Wicomechee gave his loose-tongued friend a look.

Waupee's smile broadened. "Now that my brother has a wife, perhaps she will have you."

Posetha turned quizzical eyes to Wicomechee. "Perhaps she has already had Wicomechee. I saw his lips on hers the night before we left the village."

Waupee chuckled. "I missed all of that."

Wicomechee lifted one shoulder and let it drop. "Nialinwe has a very willing mouth. Was I to refuse her?"

"I wouldn't have," Waupee admitted. "But tell us, did you find more than her mouth willing?"

"I searched no further."

"Are you certain? There was a lot of dancing and drinking that night."

Wicomechee had summoned all his willpower to put the tempting beauty from him before he erred. "You had more rum than me, Waupee. I tasted only Nialinwe's lips."

James glanced up. "Why did you do that?"

"Never mind," Waupee said. "I hope your memory serves you well, *NiSawsawh*, or we may return to find the young woman with child and an irate father awaiting you."

Wicomechee envisioned her scarred father. "I took care not to anger Wabete. He has the temper of a grizzly bear."

"And he's built like an ox." Waupee patted Muga's shoulder. "Like Muga."

Posetha shot Wicomechee a teasing smile. "Nialinwe will have much anger to see you with another."

"No doubt she hopes you will wed her," Waupee added.

Wicomechee rolled his eyes. "I gave her no promise. Her lips are sweet, but her tongue is bitter."

"Who knows what she told Wabete you did. I hope we don't find him breathing fire, demanding you take a second wife."

Wicomechee saw Charity startle beneath her blanket. She must have awakened earlier and been listening to them. She sat up bristling like an outraged cat and firing volleys at him with her eyes.

He'd done nothing to deserve such wrath and calmly faced her ire. "You are awake, Red Bird."

"Very much awake, *Wyshetche*."

He ignored her frosty tone. "How do you find your head?"

"Much clearer. And my hearing is perfect," she

added.

Posetha and Waupee exchanged mirthful glances. James peered in Charity's direction. "I saw her like that when I hid a snake in her bed. She chased me around the meadow."

Wicomechee stifled a grin. "Did she catch you?"

"Yep. Made me take the snake out and Papa gave me a whipping. I didn't do it no more."

"A wise choice."

"She looks even madder now," James observed. "I don't think she likes you tasting that Nialinwe's lips."

Waupee and Posetha laughed, even Muga grinned, but Wicomechee kept a straight face. "No. Eat your squirrel. The meat is ready now."

James happily withdrew his skewered game to blow on it. Wicomechee stood, stretched casually, and dipped a cupful of steaming liquid from a small pot near the fire. He walked the few steps to Charity and extended the cup. The spicy fragrance promised the pleasantness of sassafras, but she didn't reach out her hand. Rather, she regarded him with a chill in her eyes, darting them to the cup, then back to him.

He concealed his amusement at her effort to refuse what was clearly so tempting. "I made the tea for you," he coaxed.

She accepted the cup and sipped in brooding silence. Her stomach growled audibly.

"You are also hungry, are you not?"

She gave a grudging nod. He pivoted back to the fire, dished up a heaping bowl of cornmeal heavily seasoned with bacon, and returned. She reached out for his offering, but he kept a hold on the food. "We will eat together, *Niwah*."

She tilted her chin. "I prefer to eat alone."

He ignored her rebuff and sat on the opposite side from where Emma and Lily still slept. Letting the savory aroma waft under her nose, he dipped the wooden spoon into the bowl and held it to her closed mouth.

Her nose twitched and she swallowed despite her ire. "I can feed myself."

"Ah, but would you give me any?" He passed the spoon back and forth between them, though more often to her. The contents of the bowl vanished. "I have a gift for you."

Her expression was an endearing blend of annoyance and curiosity as he took rose-blushed crabapples from his pouch. "I found *meshemeenake* hidden under the leaves. Cold makes them good." He lifted the seductive fruit to her mouth.

She succumbed to his enticement and took a bite, then another and another. He wiped at the juice running down her chin, relieved to see her eating so well and looking refreshed from her sleep. "Is it sweet?" he asked.

She bit again and swallowed. "Very."

"Like you."

Her eyes lit up. "Not like me. I'm far too vexed."

"Why is this?" he asked in mock innocence.

"You know very well. I'll not have some shameless girl and her bad-tempered father making demands on my husband."

He almost smiled at her vehemence.

"The very notion of taking more than one wife is perfectly heathen."

"My people have been called this."

"For good reason. If you ever take another wife, I'll—"

"What?" he challenged, both fascinated and entertained.

"Slit her throat."

Low whistles escaped their appreciative listeners.

Wicomechee surveyed her in amazement. "You?

My gentle Red Bird who says her God desires mercy?"

"I'll not be asking His permission."

He secretly gloried in Charity's vehemence. "Ah. I must hide her from you."

She hurled the apple core at him. "You're so provoking!"

He chuckled amid surrounding laughter. "Come, then. Show me one wife is enough."

She crossed her arms over her chest. "Not until you promise never to take another."

"No?"

"Absolutely not."

As enjoyable as this was he couldn't tolerate such defiance. He firmed his tone. "Come with me, *Niwah*."

If she'd had the ears of a horse, she would have flattened them against her head.

"You refuse your husband?"

"Until I have his vow."

Waupee hooted. "That's the way. Stand up to him, gal."

She'd have difficulty standing up to anything if she were swept off her feet, and loosed a squeal as Wicomechee sprang up, scooping her with him.

"Put me back down!" She pushed against his chest.

He caught her wrists in his hand. "You're my wife and—"

"I'll not be *one* of your wives."

Waupee threw back his head. "She's got you there."

Emma sat up sleepily. "What in the world is going on?"

"They're having a bit of a disagreement," Waupee said.

Charity appealed to him. "Make Mechee let me go."

"And spoil all the fun?"

Charity tried Posetha next. "Help me."

Smiling, he also declined. And Weshe didn't bother to bark. Apparently, he also thought it a good joke.

James came to her defense in between bites of his squirrel. "Don't hurt her none, Wicomechee."

He grabbed up their blankets. "Do not fear, little one. Red Bird and I will speak."

Waupee chuckled. "Certainly. *Speak* all you like."

"Mechee, so help me—"

"Shhhh..." Enough fuss over nothing.

The stars spilled silvery light through the stand of pale-barked sycamores as he bore Charity away from their amused onlookers toward the outline of a tall hemlock.

She balked. "I'm not going under that tree with you."

He countered by thrusting her beneath its boughs on a blanket. She rolled over and sat up. He caught her as she scrambled and gently, but firmly forced her onto her back. She displayed a great deal of vigor for one so recently exhausted. "Must I hold you down?" he asked, and pulled the other blanket over them like a cocoon.

"Not fair, Mechee."

"Why is this?" He pinned both arms over her head with one hand, while untying her cloak with his other.

"You think to have me whenever you please."

He bent over her, swollen with need. "I have not had you for days."

"I'm injured."

"If you have strength to battle me, you have strength for love."

"That doesn't give you the right to me now."

"Has not your husband this right?"

He strayed to her bodice, unlacing the front, and slipped his hand inside beneath her shift. Hunger pulsed through him as he cupped her cold round breasts. Her nipples firmed and goosebumps ran over her, but she seemed bent on resisting him.

"Do you care nothing for my anger?"

"Your anger is without cause." He buried his lips in her perfect neck, pressing them over her chilled skin. A gasp accompanied the tremor he felt running through her.

"Then give me your promise," she demanded.

He nibbled the soft curve where her neck met her shoulder. "What promise is this?"

"Oh! You're the most—"

He silenced her protesting lips with his mouth, eliciting more shivers and not just from the chill. Exasperation alone wasn't sufficient to repress her desire and she returned the heated pressure on her mouth. Lightly at first, like clouds whispering across the moon, then with the force of a shooting star, she leaned upward and drew his mouth to hers. Violent need pulsed though him and left him breathing like a runner.

With great exertion, she broke away. "Enough."

He hadn't begun to have enough. "Do you surrender?"

"I shouldn't."

"Shouldn't?" Still restraining her arms, he lowered his head and pressed his lips over her breasts, closing his mouth around a taut nipple.

He sensed her trying to calm her panting breath and lie unresponsive as he teased her breasts in slow suckles, but she gasped and arched into his mouth.

"You must refuse me with less desire," he whispered, and freed her wrists.

She encircled her arms around his neck. "You make it very difficult."

"Unless I take a second wife."

She nearly convulsed beneath him. "Mechee—"

"How can you think I would do this?"

"You had a wife before me, a woman you loved very much."

"Yes. *One* wife," he emphasized.

"I fear some circumstance may force you to wed another."

"No one can force me to do this," he assured her.

"No matter what?"

"No matter what. Few warriors have more than one. You are enough for any man."

"Even if Nialinwe's father threatens to beat you?"

"I will take the beating, not the daughter."

"If he does beat you, Mechee, I'll throw myself on you."

He chuckled. "I prefer you to do this now."

****

Fear engulfed Charity, as impenetrable as the blackest night. Soldiers—nameless, faceless men—grasped her and tore her away from Wicomechee. Helpless against the masculine tide, she reached out, sobbing his name.

Wicomechee leveled his musket. But there were too many for him to fight. Long barrels pointed at him. More terrible than fiery demons, an explosion ripped into his chest, hurtling him onto the grass beside a large stone. "God! No!"

Gentle arms shook her. "Wake, Red Bird. You dream."

Heart bursting inside her chest, she opened her eyes. Stars glittered through breaks in the evergreen boughs. No army threatened them. Yet.

"Calm down, sweet one. I am here."

She panted out, "Don't let the soldiers take me away."

He enfolded her in his muscular warmth. "I will not."

The horrific image of him falling to the ground filled her mind. "You can't fight an army. You'll be killed."

"No man can. If they come, I will hide you."

A warning tolled in her head like a church bell. "What if you can't? We mustn't return to the village."

"Where would you have us go?" he asked gently.

"Nowhere. Remain here."

"These mountains are harsh in winter. We do not know for certain what this Colonel Bouquet will do."

"I do. My dream told me."

He sighed and ran his fingers over her hair. "Men have taken you from me. I have no surprise you dreamed this."

"But it was so real. You must listen to me."

"I hear you. But another voice calls, my grandfather, Eyes of the Wolf. We must go to him."

"Oh, Mechee, I'm so afraid—of living with Shawnee, of being taken away by the English."

"Both? There is much you fear."

"I just want a safe place where we can be together."

"My grandfather, *Nimesoomtha*, will know what to do. Eyes of the Wolf has the sight. More than your warnings."

"He can see into the future?"

"Yes. *Manito*, or God if you wish this name, gave him this way of knowing."

She listened in wonder. "The gift of prophecy."

"Perhaps, I know not. Before I left the village, *Nimesoomtha* told me I would find great treasure."

"What could he mean? Settlers have little of value."

"It is you he spoke of, Red Bird. For you I would give my life. Is there greater treasure than this?"

"Nothing. Did he say more to you?"

"Never does he speak more than we need know."

"I need to know more."

"Believe in him as I do. We cannot refuse his call."

Urgency welled in Charity to cling to Wicomechee, to savor their time together. "Love me, *Wyshetche*. Make me forget my fears and think only of you."

Chapter Seventeen

Four days later

Wicomechee sniffed the acrid scent of burning wood. Smoke curling from behind the trees snaked up into the blue sky. He was out in front today and stopped. The whole party halted along the trail. The horses snorted, pawing the earth.

Charity craned her neck to see beyond him. "A campfire?"

He shook his head and held a finger to his lips. "Something far larger," he whispered. "Stay here."

Leaving her, he stole into the trees. As expected, Waupee soon appeared at his side and they slipped through the lichen-encrusted trunks. Muga and Posetha would guard the women, children, and horses, ready in an instant if needed.

A twig snapping behind them alerted Wicomechee to Charity's presence. He saw that Waupee also knew she had disobeyed and followed. But to turn and rebuke her might alert whoever was ahead. Would she never learn?

Annoyed, he continued his silent approach and beheld the smoldering remains of a cabin, the first he'd seen since his final sight of her guardian's log home. Charity would think of this and be saddened. He did not wish this on her. He and Waupee exchanged glances then crept nearer the smoking ruin.

Purple-berried pokeweed and spikes of gray mullein rose around the charred timbers. Unlike other homesteads, only the barest patch of forest had been cleared and the stumps left sticking above the earth like raw thumbs. The outline of split-rail was absent, as were the sheep and garden it might have enclosed, and there were no outbuildings. Whoever built this had been in a hurry to erect shelter before winter.

The structure leaned drunkenly under the weight of smoldering timbers and appeared as if it might topple in upon itself at any moment. He and Waupee paused just beyond the scorched threshold and looked inside the burned-out interior. Smoky light slanted through gaps in the roof and lent some illumination. Rough-hewn chairs lay overturned on the earthen floor and the slab of wood that had served as a table was thrown down. No foodstuff or anything of value remained.

"It's been ransacked," Waupee said.

Wicomechee sensed Charity edging nearer. He glanced around at her and frowned. "Can you not wait where I say?"

"I'm behind you," she reasoned in a whisper.

"You are as curious as a fox kit."

She strained to see past him. "Whose place was this?"

"Trapper's." Who else?

Her eyes filled with alarm. "Are they gone?"

"They cannot live here now," he assured her.

"Not without considerable repair." Waupee turned from the blackened doorway and stepped over smoking rubble. "I'll take a look around back." He veered off behind the partially collapsed cabin.

"Mechee," she whispered. "Can I take a peek inside?"

"If I say no, will you obey me?"

She nodded, and he grudgingly waved her beside him.

Keeping her cloak and blanket well up, she lifted her moccasins over the debris and peered into the murky room.

"*NiSawsawh*! You'll want to see this," Waupee called.

Wicomechee swiveled and sprang over the debris. Charity did the same, dashing after him behind the cabin. He saw at a glance why Waupee summoned him. "No, Red Bird," he warned.

Too late. She recoiled from the lifeless figure of a man sprawled by the woodpile, the scalp torn from his bloody head.

With a strangled cry, she staggered back and stumbled over the outstretched arm of a second man partly concealed beneath the collapsed portion of the roof.

"Dear God—" she gasped, reeling into Wicomechee.

He gathered her in a shielding embrace. "I told you to wait with Muga."

She hid her face in his coat. "I just wanted to see."

"Now you have."

"More than you wanted to, poor girl. Sorry. I should have warned you sooner," Waupee said.

Wicomechee had. "She must learn to heed me."

Waupee squatted beside the fallen men for a closer look. "These two haven't been dead long. Perhaps only a day."

Wicomechee nodded. "No buzzards. Or wolves."

"Who killed them?" Charity gulped.

"Outhowwa's party," Wicomechee concluded. "We are not far behind."

Waupee straightened and leaned on his musket. "Not nearly as much as I'd have thought. If we continue at this pace, we may overtake them. I wonder why Outhowwa slowed?"

"Injury perhaps. Or hunting. We've taken little time to hunt since gaining the supplies," Wicomechee pointed out.

"And we've pushed the women and children harder than I liked—" Waupee broke off in mid-sentence. "Are you all right, little sister? You've gone white as a ghost."

She shuddered. "Why did they have to die?"

"Do not waste your pity on these men," Wicomechee chided. "This is Shawnee land. They have no right here."

"Even so, it's no sight for ladies. Do you feel faint?" Colin asked.

"I'd prefer swooning to what I feel like." Pulling from Wicomechee, she bent over, groaning with the swell of what appeared to be acute nausea.

Concern displaced his exasperation. "Are you ill?"

"I feel dreadful." She clasped a hand over her mouth and lurched back through the growth at the front of the cabin.

He hastened beside her. "Because of the men?"

She doubled over. "Oh, I want to die."

Wicomechee reached for her.

"Don't hold me now!" Grasping a sapling for support, she heaved the contents of her stomach onto the ground.

He laid his hand on her shoulder. "Poor Red Bird."

She groped for a handkerchief from beneath her cloak and shakily wiped her mouth. "I want to go to the river."

Waupee spoke from behind them. "We could all do with a break. I'll tell the others."

"Can you walk?" Wicomechee asked gently.

"Yes. Just let me lean on you."

Under his support, she staggered past a thicket. Maroon leaves blew among the brown drifts beneath their feet as they trod over the bluff and arrived on the bank of the *Spaylaywitheepi*, the Ohio River. Inhaling the fresh water-scented air, she knelt and wet her handkerchief.

Wicomechee kept a hand on her shoulder while she sponged her face and cupped the cold liquid to her lips. "Not too much. You will make yourself ill again."

He helped her up. Bright afternoon sunlight glinted off the rushing water, but she shivered in the wind. He drew her down to sit with him on a stone and opened his coat, wrapping it around her. She sagged against him, hugging his warmth.

He let her rest a moment before speaking. "Better now?"

"Yes. Still a bit queasy though."

"I regret you saw the men."

"I've seen worse. I'm not certain why this upset me so."

Emma handed Mary Elizabeth to Waupee and stooped to drink. "It surely would have turned my stomach."

"Not me!" James declared, swooping past them like a bird.

Lily hugged Waupee's leg. "Why were the men kilt?"

"They were foolish men who do not belong here."

Her wide eyes sought his face. "Do we?"

"Yes, little darling."

The child's blue gaze shifted to Charity. "Did the scary bad men make you sick?"

She glanced around. "More sick. I wasn't right to begin with."

Emma dried her hands on her skirt. "You were ill before?"

"Not ill exactly. Just off the past few days, mostly in the morning. Maybe it's something I ate."

Emma regarded her closely and Waupee looked on as Wicomechee absorbed this life altering revelation. "Why did you not tell me?"

"It wasn't so bad until today. I still might have

251

managed if..." she trailed off, seeing several pairs of eyes on her. "What is it?"

Waupee offered no reply. Rather, he smiled encouragingly and snagged James around the waist then took Lily's hand. "Come on. Let's leave them alone for a bit."

Emma grew brisk. "I really ought to feed this baby. Over there by that pine, out of the wind."

James squirmed in Waupee's grasp as he hauled him away. "I don't see why I got to go too."

Charity observed their departure in confusion. "Mary Elizabeth is sound asleep. Why are they in such a rush?"

Wicomechee did not answer at once, but thought how to best explain the rhythms of life to his volatile young wife. "Do you remember when you wished upon the star?"

Now, she seemed completely taken aback. "The night after we gave each other our pledge. You made no wish."

"Because I have you and you will give me all I wish for."

She lifted her gaze to his. "Why speak of this now?"

He trailed his thumb over her cheek, wanting to enfold her in a wave of tenderness while fearing to overwhelm her. "I think you carry my child."

Her mouth fell open, but no words came out.

He smiled slightly. "So surprised you look."

She gaped at him in shock, a shock she gave voice to the instant she found her tongue. "Wherever did you get such a notion?"

Had no one told her anything? "You are past the time for your monthly flow, are you not?"

"No—yes. A little."

"When a woman is past this time and ill in the way you are, often—"

She clapped her hand over his mouth. "Don't say

it. I couldn't possibly be—what you said. I'm just getting used to having a husband. Don't you see? This can't happen now. Haven't I said?"

Part of him pitied her, while the other wanted to laugh. "That makes little difference."

Had she the energy, she probably would have paced in circles. "We haven't even reached your village. I haven't met your grandfather. What will he think if I arrive—" she broke off. Withdrawing her fingers, she covered her face. "Oh, God."

"Charity, *Nimesoomtha* will be happy, as I am."

She stared at him through her fingers. "Are you really?"

"Oh, yes." From deep in his soul.

Her hands slipped to her sides and she slumped in his arms. He imagined her trying to grasp the likelihood that a tiny life had begun within her.

"Does it always happen so quickly?" she asked.

"No. Sometimes many moons, even years pass."

She pulled back slightly to search his face. "Why couldn't I have had years? I'm not ready to be a mother." She balled her hands together and brought them against his chest. "What have you done to me?"

He covered her fists and brought them to his lips. "No more than you allowed, or invited." A flush spread over her cheeks with the knowing in her eyes.

"Do not be ashamed. So sweet you are."

"Being with you is so—pleasant," she faltered. "I couldn't resist."

He couldn't repress a chuckle. "Good."

She collapsed back against him. "How am I to manage a baby? I barely remember my own mother."

"I see you with Emma's little one. You will do well."

"I can give Mary Elizabeth back when she cries. I'll have to keep this one."

He laughed. "I will help you. Many will."

"You had better. And what of this journey? It was hard enough before. Now—"

"The village is not far," he soothed. "Soon you will lie on soft furs in *Nimesoomtha's wickon.*"

"But I feel awful."

"This will pass."

"When?"

"I am not certain."

"One thing I am certain of. You can no longer march me like a warrior, *Wyshetche.*"

The sobering thought occurred to him as well.

Chapter Eighteen

The respite passed too quickly. The next morning, Colin lifted Charity up onto Stuart and settled her behind Emma's swaddled figure. "Ready or not, we're away."

"Not," they chorused.

He offered them a rueful smile. "Someday, ladies, I promise you life will be easier."

This was definitely not going to be that day. The mist that had crept in fully declared itself. Heavy haze clung to the trees and hugged the trail. Mile after mile, the chill fog gave the landscape a ghostly appearance. Rocks and trees emerged through the cloudy soup and quickly disappeared, swallowed up again. And the woods were still. All sensible creatures must have sought shelter, except for the human ones.

"At least it's not horribly windy," Emma muttered.

Apart from that, Charity found little to be thankful for. The horses plodded on and on through the fog with nothing to distract her from her misery. Huddled against Emma, she listened to the endless fall of their hooves. Beyond this monotonous tread, the *Spayleywitheepi* tumbled, hidden from sight.

A cold, hasty lunch and equally cold drizzle added to her misery and her queasiness returned. Despite her increasing discomfort, or perhaps because of it, her eyes refused to stay open. It occurred to her that she should alert someone to her drowsiness, but this thought blurred, as did the hazy outline of the trees.

For her, the gloom ceased to exist. In its place, a snug room took shape with a stone hearth and warm fire. Chunks of kindling were piled in the corner and a table set with shining pewter plates. A roast goose engulfed the platter beneath it and a plate of corncakes stood ready. A plump matron stood by the hearth, stirring a pot of strew.

The woman turned and waved her near. "Come, my girl, and get yourself warm."

"Aunt Mary?"

She held out a steaming cup of tea. "Aye. Drink, lass. 'Twill settle your stomach."

Charity reached gratefully for the cup. "You're not angry with me?"

"Nay, lass. Just fretted nigh unto death over you."

Charity stepped toward her, but Aunt Mary fell away.

"Watch it, gal!" a man rapped as strong arms caught her.

"Uncle John?"

"You really are gone, little sister."

She opened her eyes in bewilderment and gazed into Colin's worried face.

"Do you have any notion how close you came to taking a tumble?" he asked.

"I should have realized she'd fallen asleep," Emma said from atop Stuart.

"No harm done, darling."

"But if she'd fallen. It doesn't bear thinking about."

"I don't dare put her up there again. We'd better stop and make camp." He ran his eyes over the dreary landscape. "Not much shelter here."

"Give her to me, *NiSawsawh*."

Charity hadn't noticed Wicomechee walk back to them. He took her from Colin and held her to him. "What would I do if you fell? You could lose the little one—break your neck."

Neither of these possibilities had crossed her mind. As for the baby she carried, it meant little more than the source of her present misery. "I'm sorry."

He said nothing more and followed the others. The deepening gloom reflected his dark mood. "I heard you speak the name of your guardian."

"I dreamed Aunt Mary was calling me to a lovely fire, offering me a cup of tea. I wanted the tea," she sniffed.

"I will build you a fire, make you tea. Do you not think I can care for you?" Hurt welled in his words.

"I know you can, Mechee. But I feel so awful, and Aunt Mary is the closest I've come to having a mother."

"Do you wish to return to this woman?"

A ragged sob disrupted further speech.

"Don't weep," he pleaded. "I regret my words."

"I can't—stop." All-consuming misery accounted for her weepy state more than anything he'd said.

Upraised voices from up ahead broke through his efforts to console her. She tensed, fearing some new danger. "What's happening?"

"Muga says Outhowwa's party is near. He sees campfires."

Her relief at this announcement brought the calm that had eluded him. But what about Rob?

****

Flames from the nearby campfire bathed Charity's chilled body like a balm as the rain beat down beyond the broad half-cave carved into the earth and stone along the river bluff. Some of Outhowwa's party had gone on to the village, but a hearty assembly sat around the main fire pit, while she lay beside the cozy blaze at the other end like a rabbit tucked in its burrow. If her stomach would allow her respite, she'd do more than just drift beneath the surface of consciousness.

"Drink this."

She roused at Wicomechee's coming, but it seemed more effort than it was worth to sit up. He lifted her against him and she sipped the ginseng, praying the tea would aid, not offend her volatile condition.

"Tonight we eat corn mush and the rest of the bacon. None want to hunt when they can cook from supplies," he said.

She made a face. "I'd rather have roast pheasant and new-made bread."

Emma spoke up. "Wouldn't we all?"

Colin chuckled. "How about a plump stewed chicken, meat pastries, and apples dumplings? And don't forget the brandy."

A memory surfaced in Charity's weary mind. "It was all there, in the grand house in my dream."

"That's why we call them dreams, darling."

Wicomechee nuzzled her cheek. "Tomorrow, I kill you a fat rabbit to cook. We will all eat well." He turned his head toward Colin. "Have you finished tending the horses?"

"Not yet. I left Muga hard at it."

"Leave Posetha with the women. I will help you."

"And boast to Outhowwa about the giant you felled," Colin teased. Wicomechee smiled faintly, and Colin stood, bending his head beneath the low stone. "I'll just bring the women some food first."

Emma laid the bundled baby across her lap. "What about James and Lily?"

"They're telling anyone who will listen of our adventures and eating scraps the men toss them. Outhowwa is waiting to hear more of your battle with the trappers, *NiSawsawh*."

"We will speak."

"How badly wounded was Chaka?" Charity

asked, surprised that she cared.

"He gave his leg quite a whack while chopping wood—feels foolish about it, but he's mending." Colin bent and pressed a kiss to Emma's fingertips, then walked off into the smoky shadows beyond their circle of light.

Wicomechee slid from beside Charity. "When I return, I wish to find you have eaten." He stooped under the rock shelter. "I leave Red Bird in your care," he said to Emma.

Charity flopped back down the instant he vanished. "Oh no, I expect some cooperation from you, my girl," Emma chided.

"Good heavens. You sound just like your mother."

"Suppose I do. Here comes Colin with food, up with you now."

He handed Emma two bowls. "Who are you ordering about?"

"Charity. Wicomechee left me in charge."

"I didn't realize you had the makings of a colonel."

Charity dragged back up. "She gets it from Aunt Mary."

"I can readily envision Mary McLeod marching everyone at attention. Remember, my dearest, the best officers have a streak of mercy."

"I'll be firm, but gentle," Emma agreed.

"I can't imagine you otherwise," he smiled, and turned away, ducking beneath the stone.

Emma's tender gaze followed him into the foggy drizzle. "God forgive me, I love that man more than my life."

"I trust God will pardon us both." Anything else Charity might have said remained unspoken. Rob Buchanan was making his way toward their campfire. Her queasy stomach knotted and she gripped Emma's arm. "Look who's coming."

Emma muttered, "Just what we need right now."

Charity watched like hunted prey as Rob nodded at Emma, and slid into the spot Wicomechee had left empty. He exuded a passionate intensity she didn't feel equal to.

"It's been ages since I last saw you, Charity. I feared for your life."

"I'm sorry you suffered. Our party fell behind, took us days to catch back up."

His eyes drank her in. "What's wrong? Are you ill?"

She touched her forehead. "I was injured here," she said, hoping this would content him. "I suffer weakness."

"That explains your arrival in Wicomechee's arms."

"He cares well for me."

Rob's mouth tightened. "I'd hardly expect him to leave his wife lying along a trail. I suppose you are by now?"

She looked away from his displeasure as though from a striking snake, and watched the misting rain. "Yes."

"Have you utterly forgotten who he is, what he is?"

"When Mechee holds me, I think only of his love."

"I could do the same if I had the chance," Rob argued.

"It's not that simple. I can't just forget one husband and take another."

"In time I could persuade you to think differently."

"Mechee's not going to let you try."

"He can hardly oppose an army."

She almost choked at his blatant threat. "You don't know for certain that Colonel Bouquet will prevail."

"I'll bet he already has."

"Enough, Rob. I'll not have you upsetting her," Emma scolded. "You aren't even supposed to be together anyway."

Charity eyed her usually mild cousin in surprise.

Even Rob seemed impressed by Emma's newfound authority. "Bold words for you, Ma'am."

"I shall be bolder still if you don't behave."

A faint smile eased the tension at his mouth. "I shall be a perfect gentleman. Pray continue with your meal."

"Charity can't possibly eat with you staring at her."

He raised his hands in a conciliatory gesture and averted his head. "Thank you, sir," Emma said with chilly formality.

Charity forced down a small portion then set the bowl aside. "I'll finish it later, Emma."

"That's not enough to keep Lily going, let alone you."

"I'll be fortunate to keep this down." Trying to ignore Rob, she wrapped in her blanket and lay down, but, like a disturbed spirit, there was no escaping his brooding presence.

He bent over her. "You're truly ill. From your injury?"

She was loath to answer. "Not only that."

Anger radiated from him. "Never mind. I can guess what ails you. Wicomechee's gotten you with child, hasn't he?"

She kept her eyes from his recrimination but made no denial.

"Works fast. The bastard."

She sucked in her breath as if Rob had driven his fist into her stomach, too breathless to immediately reply.

Not Emma. "I understand you're upset, but to speak so. 'Tisn't fit language for Christians."

"Let me remind you good *Christians* that this marriage isn't valid."

Charity got out, "In the eyes of God, it is."

"Perhaps. I'll not speak for the Almighty."

"Humble of you, I'm sure," Emma said.

Rob ignored her sarcasm. "Their union has no validity in the eyes of the civilized world."

Emma cut him short. "We've heard more than enough."

"Not quite. The child she carries is a bastard as well."

At that rude utterance the tiny life within Charity took on a great deal more significance than she'd previously accorded it. Pushing up on one elbow, she stared Rob in his baleful eyes. "Don't you dare call my baby that horrid name!"

"Can't take the truth?"

"Whose truth?" Posetha demanded. "Not Shawnee truth."

Charity hadn't noticed him rise from the circle of warriors nearest them until he stood glaring down at Rob.

"Stay away from the wife of Wicomechee, Rob Buchanan."

Rob set his jaw in sullen lines as he eyed Posetha. "You wish more punishment?" the warrior invited.

"Please, Rob, do as he says," Charity pleaded.

"Fine." He scooted a short distance away.

Posetha touched her shoulder. "His words cannot harm you."

"'Tisn't only his words I fear."

"Have courage. I am near if you have need of me."

Through her blurred vision she watched Posetha return to his appreciative listeners and the tales he was regaling them with. Seeing Posetha distracted, the dogged young man inched his way nearer to her. "Rob, you mustn't," she entreated him.

"Will you summon your guard dog or let me speak?"

"Careful, Rob," Emma warned. "You will have Posetha back over here in a flash."

Rob regarded Charity with fierce yearning in his gaze. "I think of you all the time. Your face is always in my mind. I'll not give up until you're my wife."

"You still want me, knowing I carry Mechee's child?"

"This delicate state didn't deter a certain Englishman from taking the wife of another. Did it, Mrs. Estell?"

"That was entirely different," Emma argued.

"How?"

She eyed him coldly. "I don't owe you an explanation."

"Afraid it won't hold up?"

"Who made you judge over us?"

"Your mother would gladly appoint me to make the pair of you see sense."

Emma thrust the sleeping baby at Charity and drew herself up like an enraged dog. "I am a grown woman. You'll not tell me what Mama would want." Swinging her hand, she slapped Rob across the face with a resounding smack.

Charity's jaw dropped.

He fingered his reddened cheek in amazement. "We've known each other since childhood. You never struck anyone."

"About time I did, you pompous, overbearing—bastard!"

Charity sputtered, "Emma. You never ever swear."

"No, she does not," Wicomechee agreed from the mist.

263

Colin took shape and dodged the stone ceiling. "Someone must have been extremely provoking."

Posetha pointed an accusing finger at Rob. "Outhowwa's captive distressed the wife of Wicomechee."

****

Wicomechee stalked just behind his brother.

"You did leave Emma in charge, did you not, *NiSawsawh?*" Waupee asked, a hard edge to his flippant remark.

The despised Long Knife must have a death wish. One he would gladly oblige. He was aware of Charity's stricken face, but stopped before Rob and fixed on him with the intensity of a panther ready to spring. "We will *speak.*"

The Long Knife stood warily.

Waupee stayed Wicomechee's arm with his hand. "One moment, Emma called him out first. Will you fight him, darling, or shall I?"

Mary Elizabeth wailed. "Please be serious." Emma lifted the baby and slipped a hand beneath her blanket to her bodice.

"Quite right, most awkward to fight while nursing an infant. Wouldn't you agree, Rob?" Waupee asked, that steel in his voice still underlying his light manner.

Rob shifted his eyes between them. "Who does that leave me to deal with Dickson, you or Wicomechee?"

"Both. You insulted both of us, did you not?" Wicomechee flung back.

The cocky Long Knife didn't even attempt an apology.

Emma nestled the infant beneath her wrap. "I'd rather fight him myself than see the two of you tear into him."

"With a baby at your breast?" Waupee inquired coolly. "Come along Rob, the three of us will have a little talk."

"Wait, Mechee, big brother."

Charity would interfere. She got shakily to her feet then staggered and clasped a hand to her head. "I feel so giddy." With a moan, she swayed, sagging toward Rob.

Wicomechee looked on in outraged disbelief as Rob caught Charity and lifted her in his arms. "Poor girl."

Fire inflamed him. "Take your hands from my wife."

"Hold on, Wicomechee. She's swooned."

"This is your doing."

"Mine? I'm not the one who got her with child."

Only the dread he felt for Charity kept him from felling the Long Knife where he stood. "You cause her distress she has not the strength to bear. Can you not see her weakness?"

The indignation in Rob's eyes lessened and concern took its place. "Is it the child alone? She spoke of an injury."

Charity lay unmoving as Wicomechee took her from him and hugged his precious burden. "The injury almost claimed her life. Now she is ill with my child. I fear for her," he admitted. "The journey is too hard."

Rob's solemn gaze followed Charity. "I didn't realize. She was always so strong, so fast."

The reminder pierced Wicomechee. "No more. She needs food, rest. Why can you not stay from her?"

"I've loved Charity for so long. And just when her guardian agreed to our marriage, you stole her away."

"She never wanted you, Rob Buchanan. When I first took her captive she told me she feared to wed you."

"I could have gotten her past that and won her

265

love. I still could," Rob said, longing in his face and voice.

"Can a heart be taken, like a horse? Even horses remember their masters. A man cannot force a woman's heart as he can her body."

"I know that," Rob conceded. "All I'm saying is I could win Charity's love if I had the chance."

"Her heart is mine. She seeks my love in return. Not yours. When she wakes with fear, she holds to me, not to you. Her tears wet my shirt, not yours. When she is glad I hear her laughter. For me she sings." Wicomechee smoothed her chilled cheek. "If this English colonel aids you in taking her from me, she will fly from you in death."

Horror touched his eyes. "Death? Surely not."

"She has done this once," Posetha said. "When Wicomechee called to her, she returned to him."

Rob stared at him. "You mean to say Charity was dying and he summoned her back?"

"Already her spirit was lifting into the night sky."

Rob gave a low whistle. "I don't know what to say."

"How about, forgive me, Wicomechee. I've made an ass of myself?" Waupee said. "Include a promise never to trouble Charity again. Then maybe, just maybe, he will let you live."

Rob heaved a sigh and the knowledge that he had lost her forever shaped his expression. "I couldn't bear to cause her such grief I endangered her life. I give you my word, Wicomechee. I will trouble Charity no more."

"It is good you speak this, for I will not allow you to."

"Take good care of her, as I swear I would have done. And now, if you no longer wish to strike me down, I will return to Outhowwa's campfire."

"Hold on a minute, Buchanan," Waupee

summoned. "Your insult to my lady, and consequently to me, still remains."

"I apologize for my poor behavior, Emma. Please forgive me," Rob said with far more humility than he had before.

"I already have."

"You are fortunate to find her so forbearing, else I would be honor bound to demand satisfaction," Waupee said.

"I'm as grateful as a miserable wretch can be, sir."

"Oh, go on. Take that long face back to Outhowwa."

"That'll cheer me up no end," Rob muttered, his voice trailing off with his muffled tread.

Waupee nudged Charity's arm. "You can come to now, little sister. He's gone."

She opened her eyes. "How did you know I was faking?"

Waupee smiled. "The way you angled that swoon toward Rob. You're quite the actress."

She looked up at Wicomechee. "Did you also know?"

He gently reproached her. "Yes. Though not so soon as Waupee. I feared much for you."

"I'm sorry, but I couldn't have the pair of you lighting into Rob. Do you think he noticed?"

"No. You are too clever." And weaker than Wicomechee cared to contemplate. She might have pretended that swoon, but it could easily have been real. It would take all his strength to preserve her.

Chapter Nineteen

Charity stared from atop Stuart at the dozens of bark-covered lodges spreading along the banks of the Scioto River. Smoke rising from the openings in their roofs drifted up into the cold blue sky. What she'd expected the village to be like she couldn't have said, but so many lodges overwhelmed her. "I'd no idea the village would be so big, like a city."

Emma's blond head nodded in front of her. "We've never been to an English city, let alone one filled with Indians."

Colin grinned. "This is one of the larger villages I'll grant you, but nowhere near the scale of Philadelphia. Just imagine how impressed you'd both be with London." He reached his arms up to help them down. "Come on, ladies."

Emma clung to Mary Elizabeth with one hand and the big gelding with her other. "Wait. I feel safer up here."

"On Stuart?"

If she'd asserted her love of horses above all creatures, Colin couldn't have looked more surprised.

"He's become a faithful friend. I'd rather view the villagers from—" she shrank against Charity as a crowd in colorful blankets surged toward them. "Lord preserve us."

Wicomechee studied them in bemusement. "Do you also wish to remain on the horse, Red Bird?"

Charity was weary beyond words, but fear jarred her to wakefulness as she stared at the throng. "For a little."

"This is foolish."

Colin shrugged. "I see no need to pull them off yet."

"As any warrior could do if he intended them harm," Wicomechee pointed out.

Any remaining argument went unspoken as the noisy tide of men, women, and children engulfed them. The two men were caught up in the welcoming swell and swept away.

"Colin! Wicomechee!" Emma called, apparently having reconsidered her impulsive request, but the preoccupied men were hailing friends and didn't seem to notice her.

"We'll be all right." Charity felt anything other than the assurance she'd offered as warriors already returned from raids, and men too old for war, converged on the new arrivals. Sharp eyes swept the women on Stuart with an appreciative glint or with no apparent interest at all, but without malice. "I think none wish to harm us."

"Colin and Wicomechee are paying little mind if they did," Emma said.

Despite her uneasiness, Charity was intrigued. "Look at the women."

Their shining eyes and expressive faces made a lively contrast to the more restrained warriors she'd journeyed with. The feminine welcome elicited smiles from the home comers. Long black hair flew as strong arms swung laughing women up into their embrace. Lustrous braids and cascading torrents adorned with ribbons and silver brooches made Charity feel plain by comparison, as did the clothing she glimpsed beneath their blankets. Colorful beads embellished solid-colored shirts or those made from bold checks and prints and a rainbow of ribbons decorated swirling skirts.

Children ran through the crowd, their excitement amicably born by the adults. Curious little boys inspected the women before resuming their high-spirited flight. "They remind me of James." He bounded into view with Weshe, not the least bit intimidated. "How unafraid he seems, so unlike poor Lily."

"James knows he's to remain with us. I hate having to surrender Lily, and Colin feels wretched about it," Emma said.

Charity had last seen Lily clinging to Muga who'd been given the sad task of transferring her to Wacuchathi. "What can we do? As captor, Wacuchathi has the right to adopt her."

"At least if his wife is eager for a girl to replace their lost daughter, they will treat her kindly," Emma said.

"Look. Those must be Posetha's parents."

A pleasant-faced woman with Posetha's smile rushed up and wrapped her arms around him. Behind her, an older warrior approached with more dignity, his finely chiseled features reminiscent of Posetha's. He laid a hand on his shoulder.

Emma pointed through the crowd. "Look at your husband."

Charity's attention flashed to the cluster of females gathering around Wicomechee and Colin. One young beauty lifted her arms around Wicomechee's neck, her lips at his ear. He shook his head at her apparent invitation, gesturing toward Charity. Still, she held to him, her black eyes appraising Charity with resentment, a sentiment she heartily returned. "That's Nialinwe, I'll wager. Her boldness is beyond belief."

"Mama would have plenty to say about such unladylike behavior."

Centuries of Scottish temper melded with English determination fired Charity's blood. "I could say a great deal myself. If Mechee doesn't pry her off, I will."

"For pity's sake, you can't just jerk her away."

"She's not much bigger than I am."

"Calm yourself," Emma attempted.

Calm was the last thing Charity felt. "Now she's weeping against him. I'm getting down."

"Don't dismount unaided. You could be injured. Think of the baby, dearest."

Charity had forgotten everything but wrenching Nialinwe from her husband. She hesitated and glanced around. A familiar figure caught her eye. "Chaka!" He turned, his dark brows arching inquisitively. "Will you help us down?"

Emma tensed. "Have you lost all reason?"

"He won't harm us."

Chaka left a young woman and two small children. He walked to them, limping slightly from the injury to his leg. A teasing smile hovered at his lips. "Where is your husband?"

"In the arms of another."

"Ah. What do you think to do?"

"Tear Nialinwe from him."

His smile broadened. "Nialinwe has the temper of—" he paused as though searching for the right word. "She-bear."

"There. You see. Have a bit of sense," Emma pleaded.

Lips pressed together, Charity scrutinized the young woman shaking against Wicomechee and his effort to console her. "That girl can do her weeping elsewhere."

Chaka shrugged broad shoulders and lifted Charity from the horse, holding her an instant longer than necessary before setting her down. "Have care, pretty one."

Emma hugged Mary Elizabeth as Chaka lifted her to the ground. "Waupee is fortunate in such a wife," he said.

Emma looked at him dazedly. "You wished my

271

death."

"No more." Leaving them, he rejoined the waiting woman. A shy smile lit her eyes as he closed his arms around her and slipped his fingers through long hair spilling to her knees.

"That must be his wife," Charity said. Chaka perched a giggling girl of about three on his shoulder, caught up a chubby toddler, and disappeared into the throng. "I never imagined he could be like this. Thank heavens he didn't bring me home as a second wife. She seems very fond of him."

"And he of her, though I doubt he'll ever be faithful."

"No. But Mechee promised to be." Charity glared at the spot where he'd been standing. "Emma, he's gone."

She swiveled her head. "Colin and James are missing as well. Likely Wicomechee's with them. I see Muga. Take hold of Stuart and let's go to him."

Charity grasped the bridle. "Come on, boy. Looks like we'll have to fend for ourselves."

"I'm certain our men have a good reason for leaving us to be escorted by a horse," Emma muttered.

"Mechee's reason had better not be Nialinwe."

A thinning crowd parted to let them pass, though Charity sensed the villagers tracking their every move. "Why does Muga still have Lily? He should have made the exchange by now." The frightened child clung to him; not only that, but Muga spoke in earnest tones with Wacuchathi while a distraught woman, whom Charity assumed must be that brave's wife, wept.

"Muga!" Charity called uncertainly. The men turned angry faces toward her, an expression she'd never seen in Muga.

He waved them over. Wacuchathi gestured at Lily. "Take girl."

"*Nilaweh?*" Charity asked in confusion, using the Shawnee she'd learned for 'us.'

He nodded, and his wife cried even harder. He spoke in her ear, eliciting a watery smile, and they walked away.

Relieved at this turn of events, Lily stopped crying and nestled against Muga. He took Stuart's reins and motioned for the women to follow. "*Wetemeloh,*" he said shortly.

"What's happening?" Emma asked as they fell in behind.

"For some reason they no longer want Lily. I've no idea why. Muga says to go with him," Charity explained.

"I'm glad you understand their strange tongue."

"Only in part and not when they speak rapidly."

"'Tis far more than I know."

"Mechee's a good teacher." In many ways. Charity badly wanted him with her. Mauve and gray blended with rose across the western sky as the saffron ball dipped below the tree line. "It'll be dark soon. Where can they be?"

"I can't imagine, but I'm certain neither abandoned us."

It seemed dishearteningly as if they had, and so strange to be wandering among bark-covered lodges rather than gathered by a campfire. Charity even felt wistful for the trail. This village overwhelmed her weary senses. Dizziness washed over her and the rows of *wickon*s lost their distinction.

"I don't feel well."

Emma circled a free arm around her. "Quick, lean on me."

Colin called from behind them as Charity slumped against her cousin and closed her eyes. His voice was muffled at first, then clearer. "Emma! I've been searching for you."

"And we've been looking for you. Help me with

Charity."

He caught her up in his arms. "Poor girl. I'm terribly sorry to be so long. Wicomechee and I were greeting friends."

"We saw one *friend* weeping against him," Emma said.

Colin whistled under his breath. "Nialinwe was fit to be tied when she heard about Charity. Your coming wasn't greeted with much enthusiasm by several of the young women either."

"I doubted they were there solely to welcome Wicomechee," Emma said sagely. "Where is he?"

"With his grandfather. After a brief hello, I came back for you both, but you'd gone on."

Their conversation grew faint. Charity was only vaguely aware of Colin stooping to enter a dwelling. He laid her down before a fire. The warmth enveloped her as she drifted away.

Like a melody growing nearer and more distinct, the sounds and voices around Charity gradually penetrated her awareness. Opening her eyes, she stared at the interior of a snug lodge. Elk and deer skins covered the walls.

She turned her head and counted four platform beds covered with skins, and blankets. She didn't lie on one of these. Rather, she found herself on a thick bearskin in the center of the room near a cozy fire, startled to find the heavily lined face of an elderly woman peering down at her.

The woman bent to smooth her hair with aged fingers. "*Pocoon sisqui.*"

She'd compared her hair to blood-red leaves. "*Megwich,*" Charity said, assuming she intended it as a compliment.

The old woman smiled, showing two black spaces where her front teeth were missing. Turning her attention to the fire, she stirred the stew in an iron kettle with a wooden ladle.

The meaty fragrance would have been welcome had Charity's stomach not felt distinctly unsettled. Wishing for lighter fare, she surveyed the iron and copper pots, woven baskets and cutlery stored in the cupboard. Knives, spoons, cups and bowls lined one shelf, most carved from wood, though some pewter pieces shone in the firelight. These supplies were every bit as adequate as Aunt Mary's had been.

Apparently satisfied with her dinner preparations, the woman dipped a cupful of steaming liquid from the clay pot resting by the fire. Then she slid a sturdy arm beneath Charity's shoulders and raised her head. A pungent herbal fragrance assailed her.

"*Olame ne tagh queloge,*" she protested, declaring she was too sick.

"*Shiskewapo ouisah chobeka,*" the elderly woman countered, insisting the tea was good medicine.

"*Naga. Puckechey,*" Charity argued, telling her to go.

Wicomechee stepped beside the determined woman. "*Megwich*, Apekonit." He knelt and took the cup.

With a good-natured shrug, Apekonit left him to it. A smile hovered at his lips as he set the brew aside. "You defend yourself well in Shawnee, Red Bird."

Though vastly relieved to see him, Charity reproached him. "Most fortunate, as you left me to fend for myself."

"You told me you wished to remain on the horse."

"Not that long. Not while you consorted with Nialinwe."

"I was not. She consorted with me."

"I didn't see you trying very hard to escape."

"I tried."

"You should have tried harder—"

"Enough, Penashe Pocoun," an authoritative voice interceded, speaking her Shawnee name.

Any further outcry stilled in Charity's throat as she gazed up at the tall straight figure of an older warrior. His piercing black eyes seemed to search her very soul. She instinctively knew who he was. "Eyes of the Wolf?"

He nodded and the silver cones hanging from his ears bobbed slightly. "You may speak my English name."

"Would you speak mine?"

"If you wish."

She was both afraid and fascinated.

Wicomechee's grandfather knelt beside them. Gray hair fell loosely to his shoulders, the same hue as the silver brooch fastened at the ruffled neck of his green-striped shirt. Like the trader she'd once met, the ornate shirt even had ruffles at the cuffs and was fastened with pewter buttons.

A red breechclout extended below the thigh-length shirt, its fringed edge sewn with white beads. Creamy Elkskin leggings decorated with beads and dyed quills encased his long legs and embellished moccasins shod his feet. In him was blended the distinct garb of a warrior with the regal bearing of a duke, and something more. Here was a far-seeing mystic. She saw the knowledge in his eyes, and also his disapproval.

"My grandson brings a wife of much beauty with too swift a tongue. Do you always speak to him in this way?"

Charity squirmed under his rebuke. "When I'm vexed."

"Are you often vexed?"

Wicomechee drew her into his arms. "*Niwah* is not well and easily distressed, *Nimesoomtha*. The fault is mine. I regret I left her too long on the horse."

She retreated against him. "I'm sorry I spoke as I did."

Eyes of the Wolf was stern. "You must have greater respect for your husband."

Wicomechee spoke in her defense. "She has much."

"Her tongue speaks too freely. She must have more care."

Charity reached out her hand to the intimidating warrior. "I will try, *Nimesoomtha*."

The severity in his face lessened and he took her fingers in his warm grasp. "Your heart is good, *Neetanetha*, my daughter. Do not speak with such haste."

"I did not mean to."

"I see this."

She sensed wisdom, like a spring, welling deep inside him. "What else do you see?"

"Love for the other fills each of you. Shall I tell you of the child you carry?"

"Yes, please."

"In the heat moon you will give birth to a son. His eyes will be colored like the leaves. Your eyes, Red Bird."

She looked expectantly at Wicomechee. "You will like that, won't you?"

He nodded, seemingly intent on his grandfather. "Tell of the child."

"He will be handsome, strong, clever. All you wish for."

She sensed something left unspoken, a somberness hinting in the older man's creased features.

"Will all be well, *Nimesoomtha*?" Wicomechee asked.

"The boy will live, grow to be a man."

Uncertainty clouded her husband's face, as

though, he, too, had the same unsettled impression. "What of Red Bird?"

"Her life is in your hands, Wicomechee. I cannot say what you will do."

Charity couldn't fathom what Eyes of the Wolf meant, but she didn't like the grim sense accompanying his revelation.

Wicomechee clutched her to him. "I saved Red Bird's life, more times than one. Never would I harm her."

"I know." Yet the fathomless eyes held clear warning.

"You see the love I bear her. For her I would die."

Eyes of the Wolf laid a weathered hand on his grandson's shoulder. "For her you must live. Though perhaps not as you would wish."

"What do you mean?"

The inscrutable gaze fixed on Charity. "Your wife has some knowing of what I speak. Do you not, Red Bird?"

The familiar prickle traveled her spine. "You will be tested somehow, Mechee."

Eyes of the Wolf gave a slight nod. "In a small way you have the sight, *Neetanetha*."

"Yet she knows no more than this. Tell me of the test," Wicomechee pleaded.

"I cannot."

"Cannot, or will not?" Groaning his frustration, Wicomechee buried his face in her hair. "How am I to fight an enemy I cannot see, one I have no knowledge of?"

"You know him well," Eyes of the Wolf said.

Wicomechee lifted his eyes to his grandfather. "How?"

"The enemy lies within you."

Chapter Twenty

Wicomechee sat before the fire in the lodge holding Charity as though it might be their final hour. Resolve filled him, and frustration. He wished his grandfather would speak plainly, but Eyes of the Wolf was as he was and Wicomechee could not change him. He glanced up as Waupee lifted the skin at the *wickon's* opening and walked inside.

"I've seen to Stuart and had plenty of help tending the pack ponies."

Charity raised her head from Wicomechee's shoulder. "What of James?"

The child darted in behind Waupee. "Here I am!"

"Easy, lad. You'll collide with something, or someone."

Wicomechee shook his head at the little boy's seemingly inexhaustible supply of energy. "Where did you find him?"

"With Posetha. His mama was feeding him like a stray dog. I left Weshe begging for scraps."

Emma snuggled the baby against her shoulder and patted her back. Lily sat beside Emma, her blue eyes trusting, not filled with the fear Wicomechee had witnessed earlier.

"You should have left James as well," Emma quipped.

Waupee smiled. "I didn't think it right to inflict him on them quite so soon, though he would have stayed."

Eyes of the Wolf laid his hand on the boy's fair head. "Have you no fear, small one?"

"No sir. I'm gonna be a warrior. They're never afraid."

"Not true. Only a foolish man is without fear."

"Warriors are always brave," James argued.

"Courage and fear walk the same path."

Finding this insight beyond him, James scurried to the simmering stew. "Can we eat now, Uncle Papa?"

"How have you any room left in that stomach?"

"Children are always hungry," Eyes of the Wolf said, his gaze lingering on Waupee's little band. "The boy calls you father. The girl also."

"I remind Lily of her father."

"What of this fair wife you brought and the little one?"

"Emma was never my wife," Waupee admitted. "I took her from another man, now dead. The infant is his."

"Now you speak the truth."

"You knew I lied about her?"

"Also of your love for this woman."

"From the first. I begged her to wed me, but she was afraid," Waupee explained.

"And now, she is yours?"

Warmth touched Waupee's eyes. "She gave me her pledge."

A smile flickered at his grandfather's mouth. "So, you have a wife not yet taken and three little ones not your own."

Waupee smiled wryly. "True. But I will take her and her daughter shall be mine. The children also, if I'm able to hold on to these I love." Worry overshadowed the affection in Waupee's face, the same anxiety that afflicted Wicomechee.

"What are my brother and I to do, *Nimesoomtha*?"

His grandfather didn't reply at once, but stood staring into the flames. A sense of expectancy settled over the room. Even James grew quiet and Lily looked questioningly at the solemn assembly. Charity hardly seemed to breathe, and Wicomechee had the sense that Emma and Waupee did the same. His own breath was tight in his throat.

Still, Eyes of the Wolf did not speak. The wind whistled beyond the lodge's fur-draped walls. Wood popped in the fire and he roused as if drawn from a distant place. He looked at Charity. "You know of a prince called Charles Stuart?"

His question took Wicomechee totally by surprise.

She answered in perplexity. "The Scots call him Bonnie Prince Charlie. He wished to be king, but he lost the war."

Eyes of the Wolf nodded. "Waupee admires him much."

"Better him than George the Third who now sits on the throne," Waupee said.

Eyes of the Wolf spoke quietly. "One day, you will be rid of King George. Did Waupee tell you he named his horse for this Stuart prince?"

"No. Though it makes sense now," Charity said. "Did you fight for Charles Stuart, Colin?"

"I was too young. My older brother Harry went to Scotland to fight for the prince's cause."

Emma lifted startled eyes. "You never spoke of a brother. Was he killed?"

Bitter lines edged Waupee's mouth. "Injured. Harry survived that bloody defeat at Culloden Moor, but supporters of Charles Stuart were vigorously pursued. He fled to France. Now both my father's sons are fugitives."

The sadness in Waupee was reflected in Eyes of the Wolf. "Like this Stuart prince, my people are defeated by the English. Colonel Bouquet's hand is heavy against us."

Now Wicomechee understood why he spoke as

he did. "What will happen, *Nimesoomtha?*"

His knowing gaze touched each one, and came to rest on Wicomechee. "I cannot speak all the Great Spirit has shown to me. Yet I will tell you this. One is coming soon who has the power to aid you, if you agree to his terms."

Wicomechee stiffened. "Are these terms harsh?"

"You may find them so."

****

Wicomechee smoothed Charity's moist cheeks in an effort to soothe her even as he grappled with his grandfather's baffling prediction. He was ready with all his heart to fight, but *Nimesoomtha* had said this was not the way. Battling for control over debilitating turmoil, he offered the bowl of stew to Charity. She must be prevailed upon to eat.

"Tears will not feed you, Red Bird. Would you have me wed to a shadow?"

"Will I still find myself your wife tomorrow?"

"Do not fear so. Soldiers have not come this far west."

"The English colonel will not send his men to trouble us this night. Have hope, *Neetanetha*," Eyes of the Wolf said.

At his assurance, she wiped her eyes and studied the steaming bowl in Wicomechee's hand. "I'm too ill to eat."

He held a spoonful to her lips. "It will settle your stomach."

She swallowed reluctantly and slowly ate all that he gave her, even sipping the tea she'd refused. Gradually, her discomfort seemed to ease, though he kept his triumph to himself. Unlike her, the others were downing second portions.

Eyes of the Wolf looked on as they devoured the meal. "You have many mouths to feed, Waupee."

Wicomechee agreed. "He is content to let me feed them."

Waupee lifted his hand in protest. "I tended the horses. They carried much on our journey."

Eyes of the Wolf smiled faintly, his eyes thoughtful. "This liking for horses will serve you well."

"How so?"

"In the time to come."

Waupee shot him a look of frustration. "Again you speak only in part. Why will you not tell us more?"

"You are not yet ready. Shall I tell you a story?"

"The whole story?" Waupee pressed.

"All that has been."

James brightened. "The grandfather man will tell us a story, Lily."

She paused, a spoonful midway to her mouth. "Whose?"

"A good question, small one. I will tell Wicomechee's."

Wicomechee surveyed his grandfather guardedly. "Of what will you speak, *Nimesoomtha*?"

"Your name."

His clenched his fingers as the old ache asserted itself.

Eyes of the Wolf was resolute. "It is time."

Charity seemed puzzled. "Why does this trouble you so?"

Wicomechee made no answer. All eyes targeted him with a mixture of curiosity and sympathy. Only Eyes of the Wolf's perceptive gaze held understanding, but he, too, was silent.

"Why won't you say?" Charity entreated him.

He sighed, anticipating the questions his reply would prompt. "Wicomechee is not the name chosen for me at birth."

"Why did it change?"

"Something happened." He wanted to stop with this.

"What was your first name?" she pressed.

"I was called Kitate, the otter, favored by my people as a bearer of good fortune. Only ill came of it."

She considered. "What does Wicomechee mean?"

"His father left him."

Her limited grasp of the language hadn't prepared her for this shocking disclosure. "Who changed your name?"

"*Neegah*, my mother, before she died."

"How odd, sad." Charity turned bewildered eyes to his grandfather. "Pain fills him, *Nimesoomtha*."

The older warrior took a small wooden pipe from his buckskin pouch and lit it in the fire. "Much pain lies in Wicomechee's past. Mine also."

"And in mine," she said.

"I see this."

"Why speak of the past? Perhaps 'tis better left alone."

Eyes of the Wolf shook his silver head. "Wicomechee's past is in his future, and yours, Red Bird. Waupee's also is woven together with my grandson's."

"How?" Waupee asked.

"The same thread runs through you both."

"Again you speak in riddles," Waupee argued.

"Perhaps. Yet it is Wicomechee's story I tell now." Eyes of the Wolf drew on his pipe and sent a smoke ring drifting overhead. Another ring ascended. His eyes again targeted Wicomechee. "What do you remember of your father?"

Wicomechee's gut was taut and he looked away. "I have no wish to speak of *Notha*."

"Look at me, Wicomechee."

Reluctantly, he met his grandfather's long-sighted gaze. "You have thoughts of your father. Speak these."

"*Notha* was a big man," Wicomechee said

gruffly.

Eyes of the Wolf wasn't to be put off. "All men are large to a child. Yet you are right. You remember more?"

Memories tore at him, more than he could bear to speak.

Charity closed her fingers over his clenched hand. "Please, Mechee. I also wish to hear."

He forced himself to answer her. "*Notha* held me in his arms and spoke of places I do not know and people I have never seen. He wished to show me."

Eyes of the Wolf looked at him sharply. "You remember this? You told me you remembered little."

"When I found Red Bird, memories returned to me, like secrets." He lifted the auburn lengths of her hair and let them fall. "*Notha*'s hair was this same color."

Charity stared at him. "Your father was English?"

"Yes."

"An Englishman won your mother from Outhowwa?"

He smiled faintly. "Did I not say Outhowwa has no liking for red hair?"

Waupee's jaw dropped. "You might tell a fellow, *NiSawsawh*. I had no notion your father was English."

"When I was little, I only thought he was my father."

More smoke rings floated over the stunned gathering. "Wicomechee's father became Shawnee. I took him into my *wickon*, give him the Shawnee name, Scootekitehi. Do you know meaning of this word?" Eyes of the Wolf asked Charity.

"Fireheart."

"Good. You learn quickly. Scootekitehi was one with the Shawnee, yet he returned to the English."

"Why did he leave?" she asked.

"To understand this you must know more of Scootekitehi. When I first found him in the mountains, he was weak, lost. I cared for him, fed him so he had strength to travel to our village. My sweet Netathwe aided me with his care, yet soon I saw it was not as a sister he wished my daughter."

Resentment flared up in Wicomechee and a red haze seemed to float before his eyes. "Better if he had."

"Then I would not have you. And your mother wanted only Scootekitehi as her husband. What do you remember of her?"

A softer emotion tugged at him. "Her hands were gentle, her face beautiful, and sad. Always I remember her sadness."

"Yet she knew joy with Scootekitehi before the sorrow."

"I remember not the joy," he said flatly.

"Then you forget much. Scootekitehi had desire only for *Netathwe*, and she would have no other husband. I told him he must learn to hunt, to fight, before I would give my consent."

"*Notha* must have done so," Wicomechee muttered.

"He did well. Great was his joy to take *Netathwe* to wife and sleep no longer apart. Your birth soon followed in the harvest moon. In you, Scootekitehi also had much joy."

"For a time, perhaps. *Notha* abandoned me."

"He had no wish to. After *Netathwe's* death, Scootekitehi begged me to let him take you with him. I refused."

"Why must he go from us?"

"He suffered such pain he could live here no longer."

"So, he left his son to seek happiness with his people."

"He knew you were in good hands," Charity

reasoned. "If he couldn't bear to stay, he had no choice but to leave you."

Wicomechee gritted his teeth and shook his head.

"How did you feel when Red Bird lay near death?" Eyes of the Wolf persisted.

Wicomechee took a deep breath, slowly releasing it. "I have no words to speak my pain."

"How are you different from your father?"

"*Notha* wronged me. He wronged *Neegah*."

"How did he wrong her?"

"He caused her much grief."

"Mechee, you said your mother changed your name to Wicomechee, yet she was already dead when your father left you," Charity reasoned.

"*Notha* left many times before that final parting."

Eyes of the Wolf tapped his pipe. "Scootekitehi could not forget he was English. One day he said, "*Notha*, I love you. I love Netathwe and Kitate, but I long to see my father. He has no other son. I must go to him, yet I will return.'"

"You agreed to this?" Charity pressed.

"I would not bind him to prevent this journey. When Scootekitehi returned, the face of my daughter was only glad, his face also. He had much happiness to hold his small son again. He spoke his wish for another child as fine as you, Wicomechee, yet Netathwe carried no more for many moons."

"How was *Neegah* to conceive with her husband forever gone to the English?" Wicomechee demanded.

"When Scootekitehi was with *Netathwe*, he loved her well. I heard them in the night. Your mother was content until the time he was gone so long from her."

Wicomechee punched his fist down onto the bearskin beneath them. Fur muffled his anger, but

Charity startled beside him. "How can I forget my mother holding to me, weeping her eyes red with fear *Notha* will come no more? He caused her death."

Eyes of the Wolf shook his head. "Sickness struck the village hard that winter. Netathwe fell ill. The child she carried came too soon. Weakness took them both."

"Grief first weakened *Neegah*. Her heart was broken."

"Yet Scootekitehi had no wish for this. When he came again, I learned sickness prevented his return sooner. Grief weighed him so heavily I feared he also would die. You gave him much comfort, Wicomechee."

"Still he left."

His grandfather looked at him sadly. "You never again spoke of your father."

"*Notha* is dead to me."

Waupee bent toward him, his blue eyes lit with fire. "Confound it, *NiSawsawh*, your father was heartbroken. I don't know as it makes any difference after all these years, but I think you ought to forgive him."

"You do?"

Waupee gripped his shoulders. "Damn right. I didn't know the cause of your brooding, but now that I do, I've half a mind to pound some sense into you."

"Is this a fight you think to win?" Wicomechee challenged.

"If I use all the moves you taught me, I'd say I stand a pretty good chance."

Wicómechee smiled slightly as he glanced down at Charity, her face pressed to his chest. "We've a woman between us."

She looked up at him with great liquid eyes. "I'm deeply sorry for all you've suffered, Mechee, but Waupee is right. You are being stubborn."

"This, from you?"

"Just because I'm stubborn, doesn't mean I can't see it."

"What will you do to alter me?"

"Pound you myself."

"You haven't the strength."

"I'll move aside and let big brother convince you."

Wicomechee clasped her to him. "Stay, sweet one. I prefer your scolding to his punishment."

"Then bury your anger."

"It is not so simple. Yet I tell you this." Huskiness thickened his voice. "I much loved my father."

"I know, or you would not love me."

Chapter Twenty-One

Wicomechee stood beside his bed and watched Charity stir drowsily under the nest of skins and blankets. She'd bathed last night in his grandfather's brass tub and fallen asleep without her clothes. She sighed, the murmured exhalation of a contented woman. The subtle sound further aroused him. His groin was ready, aching, for her. It had been too long.

He whispered in her ear, "Red Bird."

She quivered, blinking shadowed lids, and then squeezed her eyes shut as though deeply asleep.

Little minx. Did she think to fool him? He smiled and slipped his fingers over her hair. "Of what do you dream? Me? My thoughts are all for you."

A smile touched her lips and a tremor passed through her.

"So sweet you are in my arms when I love you. Never have I known such joy," he said.

The word seemed to catch her. "Never?"

He couldn't resist a chuckle. "Open your eyes, or do you prefer to pretend sleep?"

She looked up at him with endearing warmth. Reaching out her hand, she curled her fingers at his cheek. "Did you speak the truth when you said never?"

He entwined his fingers with hers. "I always speak the truth."

"Except when you tease," she reminded him.

"I did not tease."

"Then you meant it?"

"All. More. I love you beyond any."

The piercingly sweet light in her eyes shot through him.

She sat up, the blanket slipping down over her creamy shoulders, and closed her arms around his neck, enveloping him in whispered softness.

"'Tis the best gift you could give me."

He held her to him. "I have another."

Her curiosity aroused, she asked, "What?"

"First, eat." He took the steaming cup Apekonit held out. "Drink, before you feel ill."

Charity sipped the minty tea as he sat beside her. He handed her a chunk of corn bread. "Eat also."

She nibbled a corner then took a bite. "Very good."

"Apekonit will be pleased you like her bread."

Charity smiled her appreciation at the older woman who sat holding Mary Elizabeth. She nodded in response. "Where did Apekonit go last night?"

"To the *wickon* of her sister. She comes to cook and wash for *Nimesoomtha*."

"She has many mouths to feed with our coming."

"This makes her happy, especially the little one. Apekonit will have much joy to help with the care of our son."

"Will we be here then?"

He tensed, but answered evenly. "The army will come and go. By summer we will have returned."

"From where?" she asked.

He put her off. "Eat first. Speak later."

"Mechee, what are you not telling me?"

"We will walk to the river, speak there."

Charity ate in silence, and he let his gaze wander the lodge. Emma sat near the fire combing out Lily's hair. Eyes of the Wolf sat with them speaking quietly. Waupee was out seeing to his horse and had taken James with him. But it wasn't only the absence of childish exuberance that accounted for the sense of peace in this room. It went beyond simple quiet. Inner calm flowed out from Eyes of the Wolf, like ripples on a pond, encompassing all within his circle.

Charity's final swallow of bread needed more tea to help it past the lump that seemed to have formed in her throat. She blinked at the moisture in her eyes. "I do like it here."

"Did I not say you would?"

"Yes. And now, I must dress. Where are my clothes?"

"I have new garments for you, Red Bird."

She brightened and the glow in her face pleased him. "What? Where?"

"Close your eyes and lift your arms."

"But my blanket will fall. I'm still bare."

Wicomechee wished he were too and that they were in this lodge alone.

"I will not look on you," Eyes of the Wolf assured her.

She raised her arms and the blanket slid down the curves of her breasts while he pulled the intricately designed shirt over her head. He reveled in the feel of soft cloth slipping over her smooth skin. Rows of red, blue, and gold beads shone like tiny gems in the light. "Look now, Red Bird."

She stared down at her new shirt in wonder.

"This belonged to *Neegah,* my mother." He opened his hand in near reverence to reveal the round silver brooch, its edges scalloped and a circle of hearts engraved in the center.

Charity was speechless as he fastened the pin to the fabric at her neck. "You also need the skirt." He held out the blue folds of wool ringed with red and gold ribbons.

She stepped mutely from the bed into the waiting cloth. Like the shirt, it was made of the finest fabric. Wicomechee drew the ties at her waist and knotted a blue woven sash worked with white beads around her middle. He knelt to help her pull on elkskin leggings decorated with red and green quills and tied the blue garters just below her knees.

Holding to him for support, she pushed one foot and the other into fur-lined moccasins embellished with dyed quills. His mother had spent hours by the fire plying her needle. And he remembered his father giving her the cloth, beads, ribbons, and brooch. It was right that Charity should have them now.

She gazed into Wicomechee's tender approval. "I've never seen anything so beautiful."

"*Neegah* would be glad for you to have her clothes. *Nimesoomtha* thought to give you these."

"He did?" She flew from Wicomechee to Eyes of the Wolf and flung her arms around his neck. "*Megwich.*"

He gathered her close in return. "Your heart is good, like my Netathwe. Go now. Wicomechee waits for you."

Wicomechee lifted his coat from one of the poles serving as rafters and pulled it on. Charity wrapped in a scarlet blanket and followed him out beneath the buffalo skin.

How was he to tell her what they must do?

****

Gold light spilled from a clear sky over the many lodges. Wicomechee took Charity's arm as they walked through the village, greeted warmly by everyone they passed. He nodded or lifted his hand, but did not stop to talk. Seemingly intent on inner purpose, he led her from the collection of *wickons* through trees to the Scioto. He walked farther along its bank, stopping beside a large flat stone. Shrubs shielded one side of the rock, and brown grasses grew around it.

"This stone is like my favorite place where you first saw me," she said.

He laid his musket across the wide surface. "I thought this then. When I was a child, I came here many times."

He climbed up on the stone and helped her beside him. She sensed his need to speak, also his aversion to whatever it was he had to say. If only they could remain like this, suspended in time, but like the river, time flowed on.

He pressed his lips to her head. "Red Bird, you are the sun to me. How can I live without the light of your face?"

She felt ill. "Dear God. Will you have to?"

"I refuse to give you up."

"What's happened?"

"Before Colonel Bouquet will discuss terms of peace, he demands every captive be taken to Fort Pitt. There he holds Chief Black Snake and Black Hoof hostage, Delaware chiefs also. These he will not release until he is satisfied."

Charity's stomach tightened into a sick knot. "And if some of the captives do not wish to be returned?"

"Many do not. This makes no difference. Unless they are hidden away, they must go back. His soldiers will search. Each hour we delay puts us in danger of detection."

"Then we must away. Now." She started to scramble from the stone, but he held her back.

"*Nimesoomtha* says we must stay for this day."

"Why?"

"I think he waits for someone."

"The mystery man. Did he speak his name?"

"No. I fear to know it."

"So do I. What does Waupee say?"

"The same as I do, we must flee, yet he will not defy *Nimesoomtha*."

"Surely, Eyes of the Wolf would not place us all at risk?" Still, anxiety heaved in her like a stream overflowing its banks. "Tomorrow—do we leave tomorrow?"

"I cannot say."

Another thought occurred to her, one that had eluded her in the mad urge for flight. "Where will we go?"

"Back to the mountains."

She shrank at these tidings and the grim lines at his mouth. "Is there nowhere else?"

"I do not know how far the English will search, but they will not go there. It is a good place to hide."

"And die. To be forced on a long journey to such a bitter place with winter soon upon us. I'll never survive."

He gripped her tightly. "You will. *Nimesoomtha* taught me to build shelter, to hunt with my bow when powder and shot are gone. I know how to live in these mountains in winter."

Mountains in winter. The very words kindled dread. "How many hungry panthers and wolves await us, I wonder?"

"I have powder and shot from the supplies taken for any that threaten. Waupee has skill to help me hunt."

"He is coming with us?"

"Yes. He cannot return to the English and his wife will not leave him."

"What of the children?"

"We will take the baby. The others must return to their people. We cannot care for so many."

Charity took a shuddering breath. "It's so unfair."

"The English do not concern themselves with what is fair."

"No. But to leave *Nimesoomtha* and venture on this harsh journey seems unbearable."

"How else may we remain together? For me, will you bear this?"

Despite her mounting hopelessness, she nodded. "I prefer to die with you, than live without your love."

"Do not speak of death. You will live, Red Bird," he said, his voice rough with emotion. He clutched her to him and closed urgent lips over hers.

Sensing the desperation behind his passion, she returned his near-fierce kiss. His hands slipped through her hair, under her blanket, and up her sides. He covered her breasts and released her mouth, pressing his lips over her neck. "I know a place I hid as a child," he whispered, pointing to a hemlock with low sweeping branches. "We will go there, where none can see us."

Maybe they could hide there forever.

He leaped down from the stone. "Come."

A month ago she would have jumped as he'd done, even raced him to the tree. Not now. She hadn't the strength.

Sad knowing touched his eyes. "I will help you."

She reached for him and closed her arms around his neck. Sunlight streamed over them as he lifted her and stood with her in his embrace. His hungry lips returned to hers. If only she could melt into him and truly be one.

"Put the girl down and back away!" a man barked.

Charity's heart nearly stopped before a wild hammering set in.

Soldiers wearing the scarlet uniforms of British regulars and others dressed in the hunting shirts of frontiersmen burst through the trees. A clean-shaven young man with gold braid trimming his red coat led some two dozen men. "I am Captain Dawson acting on Colonel Bouquet's orders. Unhand the girl!"

Every muscle in Wicomechee was coiled, but his face revealed only cold rage. "*Memequiluh*," he said, and stood her on her feet. "*Te qui.*"

She understood his directive to run to the tree, but numb with dread she hesitated.

He gave her a shove.

Panic lent her the speed that weakness had taken and she flew toward the hemlock. She could soon lose herself beyond its branches.

"After her!" the officer ordered.

"Any man who gives chase, dies!" Wicomechee called in turn. "Will you fall first, captain?"

She knew what her husband threatened them with and what he sheltered behind. The large stone lay between her and the pursuing soldiers. But there were too many. An image flashed in her mind of him hurtling to the ground shot through the chest. Dear God—her dream.

"Don't fire, Mechee!" Spinning around, she raced back toward him.

"No, Red Bird."

"They'll kill you!" She ran to him in a burst of speed borne of sheer adrenalin.

Anguish filled his eyes. He lowered his musket and caught her to him. She held to him in horror as the men stalked nearer, their faces angry, barrels pointed at them.

"Step away, Miss," the captain ordered.

"No. I want to stay with him."

"We have orders to return all captives."

"Your orders be damned and you with them!" Wicomechee shouted.

The musket barrels were only ten yards away. "Seize her! If this bastard resists, shoot him."

"Shoot us both and have done with your torment!" Charity flung back.

With the guttural groan of an injured wolf, Wicomechee pried her from him. "You will not die.

Nor the child."

Tears blurred his precious face. "Don't fight them," she pleaded. "Find some way to get me back."

He nodded.

Though she couldn't imagine how he'd recover her, she had no choice but to walk away, each hated step taking her toward the waiting captain. She stopped before the young officer and glared at him with streaming eyes. "Call my husband a bastard again, Captain, and by heaven you'll answer to me."

Astonishment displaced the annoyance in his arched gaze, and something else—admiration. "No, Ma'am. I won't."

"I'll say you won't, Captain Dawson! And any man who fires on that warrior will die by my hand," a man warned.

Charity was too stunned to move. Beyond the captain, she saw a tall gentleman emerge through the trees.

He rounded on the officer. "You've made a mess of this."

"My apologies, Mister Ramsey."

The newcomer strode into full view and bore down on them. He wielded authority, yet he wasn't a soldier. His clothes befit a wealthy gentleman, from the brown tricorn hat trimmed in gold braid, to the brown wool coat with double capes extending over his broad shoulders. Fine breeches of the same hue hugged his long legs above black riding boots.

"I told you not to get ahead of me, Dawson. Look what you've done," he scolded.

"This woman is a captive, sir."

"Have you forgotten the whole point of my coming?"

"No, sir. You seek to recover your son."

"Whom we have just learned has a fair wife with hair like fire. Her, perhaps?"

"That warrior—" Captain Dawson faltered. "Is

your son?"

"What did you expect, a young man in evening dress? His mother was Shawnee, for God's sake."

This sudden turn of events nearly sent Charity toppling to the ground. As it was, she felt her knees giving way.

"Look to the lady, Captain!"

He sprang to her side, closing his arm around her middle. The gentleman swept through the parting soldiers. "You've frightened her nearly to death. Give her into my care."

Charity was promptly transferred to her new protector, who lifted her as if she weighed nothing. She stared up into a strong face that bore an undeniable resemblance to Wicomechee's. The red hair her husband had remembered so well was beginning to gray and worn tied back with a black ribbon.

"Don't let them take me away, sir," she pleaded weakly.

His blue-gray eyes softened at her appeal. "Calm yourself, my dear. Everything will be all right." Vexation charged his expression again as he returned his attention to the officer. "Go on, Dawson. See if you can keep out of trouble while I speak with this lady and my son."

"I dare not leave you alone, Mister Ramsey."

"I don't require your blasted protection!"

"The savage is armed, sir."

Mister Ramsey fixed the captain with a look reminiscent of Wicomechee's at his most provoked. "If anyone uses that unfortunate term in my presence again I will call that man out. Do I make myself clear?"

Chapter Twenty-Two

Somewhere deep inside him, Wicomechee had known his father would come, though not when. Perhaps he'd inherited a bit of the sight. Whatever it was, this sixth sense hadn't prepared him for the churning emotion tearing through him. This was no time to lose his wits. He struggled to think as he stood staring at the man who now held Charity. Gone were the warrior clothes he remembered. Mister Ramsey, as Wicomechee had heard the newcomer called, was pure English.

"Leave us, Captain. I don't want to see your face again until I seek you out!" the forceful man ordered.

"Yes, sir. Just going." Without any further protest, the detachment of soldiers rapidly retraced their steps.

Their deference was impressive and might prove useful, but it wasn't lost on Wicomechee that it was his father who'd brought them. If he had that power, he would shoot each one.

"Bloody nuisance, the lot of them," Mister Ramsey muttered, but did not seem inclined to fire on them. He paused and spoke more gently to Charity. "Forgive me, dear lady. I forget myself. I'm Hugh Ramsey, and you are clearly overwrought. We best get some brandy into you. Steady your nerves." Still holding her, he walked toward Wicomechee.

He sensed his father's hesitancy as he paused before him, likely an altogether unusual state for this commanding man.

"Hello, Kitate. Do you remember me?"

Wicomechee studied him narrowly. "I remember

you, *Notha*. Not as you are now. Will you give me my wife?"

"Certainly, if you sit and speak with me," the shrewd man bargained.

"Sit," Wicomechee said tersely, and scaled the stone.

The man once known as Scootekitehi surrendered Charity and climbed beside him.

Wicomechee wrapped her in his arms. "Calm, sweet one. You shake so."

Hugh Ramsey reached into his coat and took out a silver flask. "I deeply regret her alarm. If that captain had done as I said, he wouldn't have arrived before me. I was delayed in the village greeting old friends."

"*Shawnee* friends?" Wicomechee emphasized.

"I still have them." Mister Ramsey unscrewed the cap and extended the flask. "Give your wife a little brandy."

Wicomechee accepted his offering and held the flask to her lips. "Drink, *Niwah*."

She sipped while holding to him as though she feared being wrenched from his grasp. "I have you now and will not let you go," he assured her, desperately glad she was restored to his arms. His tender demeanor altered abruptly as he eyed his father. "Why did you bring soldiers to us, *Notha*?"

"Colonel Bouquet insisted I have an escort. I much preferred to come alone."

"You know this colonel?"

"He's a friend."

"With such a *friend* you have no need of enemies."

"Do not scorn the attachment. Without Colonel Bouquet's written permission, I could not enter Shawnee land to seek for you. He has vowed to keep all settlers, and anyone else lacking official approval, east of the Alleghenies."

"If the Colonel is successful in this, we will thank him," Wicomechee conceded grudgingly. "Yet only for this. He would cut our hearts from us."

"I know. Still, Colonel Bouquet isn't a monster. He's an honorable man who simply cannot believe any captives would prefer to remain with their adopted families."

"Does he think if he allows them to choose they will stay with us only from fear?"

"I see her love for you."

Wicomechee gave Charity a final swallow and returned the flask. He scrutinized his father, a scrutiny Mister Ramsey fully returned. "So, *Notha*, you have come. Why now?"

"Years of war prevented me from returning sooner."

"Before that?"

"My father counseled me to leave you to Eyes of the Wolf and not to confuse you with a father who could not stay." A sigh escaped him and yearning welled in his blue-gray eyes. "When I saw you last you were a small boy. Now you're a man, fine in every way. You're so like your mother, Kitate."

"I am called Wicomechee," he reminded him coldly.

"I refuse to call you that. I had no wish to leave you."

"Yet you did."

"And lived to regret it, beyond all description. Only I haven't had the opportunity to tell you until now."

Wicomechee weighed his explanation.

"Will you hear me?" Mister Ramsey pressed, as if detecting a chink in his anger.

The force of his father's personality mingled with his own longing gave Wicomechee pause. "I will hear you."

"Thank you," he said with an expression

Wicomechee never expected, humble gratitude. "Those first months after leaving the village, I barely knew where I was, hardly ate or slept. In time my grief for Netathwe lessened and I grew stronger. Yet always I longed for the company of my small son."

Wicomechee voiced the question that had eaten at him. "Why could you not stay with us?"

"A visit I could bear, but to remain...memories of your mother would have been too painful. And I don't belong here. Though for her sake I tried to bridge the two worlds."

"You were often gone."

"Yes, and I missed you both terribly when I was."

"What were you doing?"

"Learning to run my father's estate. As his only son, I owed him that. There was much to learn and seemingly endless matters to see to. It's a large holding."

"I have no knowledge of what you speak," he said shortly, not inclined to hear about the white world that had stolen his father from him.

"No. Though I did once try to explain."

"I remember."

"I think you remember quite a lot."

Wicomechee gave him a look. "Yes. Much."

"Hear me out. I decided long ago that your grandfather was wrong, that we should know each other. Please, Kitate, forgive me for not coming sooner. I beg you."

Plainly, this proud man wasn't above humbling himself, but Wicomechee wasn't easily dissuaded from his anger. Not after all these years. Saying nothing, he set his jaw.

Charity came to life. "For God's sake, Mechee. Forgive him."

"You do not understand, Red Bird."

Sparks fired in her green eyes. "I understand

you have a father who loves you, sitting by your side. What do you think I'd give to see mine again?"

"Your father did not abandon you."

"He did, by dying in that battle."

"Now you are being foolish."

She cupped his face in her hands and looked him straight in his eyes. "No, I'm not. You are, and I won't have it."

His father followed her with keen interest and not a little bemusement. "What will you do to remedy matters?"

"Tell the truth, if he will not."

Wicomechee rebuked her. "This is not your affair."

Ignoring his resistance, she turned to his father. "Mechee loves you, sir. He said so."

A smile hovered at his lips. "Did he indeed?"

"Yes. Only he won't admit it." She grasped Wicomechee by the shoulders as Waupee had done and tried to shake him. "Tell the truth, Mechee—"

His father chuckled. "She really is something, this Red Bird of yours."

"Is she not?" Wicomechee pulled her arms away and pinned them to her sides. "Stop. You tire yourself."

"I will not rest until you speak your heart."

She'd trapped him into confession. "It is true, *Notha*. I loved you much."

Tears swam in his father's eyes. "Perhaps you still do?"

"Perhaps."

The Englishman extended his hand.

Slowly, Wicomechee clasped it.

Exerting the power of his muscular frame, his father pulled him close and enfolded both him and Charity in an embrace. When it had lightened, equal moisture blurred Wicomechee's eyes.

"Thank you, sweet Red Bird, for pressing Kitate

to this admission."

"You are very welcome, sir." Her voice quavered.

"I know so little about you. What is your English name?"

"Charity Edmondson. The last name matters not. I'm without any living family."

"Then I will think on the first. It suits you well."

"Why is this?" Wicomechee asked.

"Charity means mercy which she clearly has in abundance."

A strange sensation came over him...another sort of knowing. "Why did you not tell me, Red Bird?"

"You never asked. Does it matter?"

"This is a sign, as is *Notha's* coming." He scrutinized his father. "For you to see this in her is more reason why I must hear you and request your aid."

Notha seemed moved, as though he realized what it had cost him to make this admission. "You have all I can give."

Wicomechee kept his voice low. "How am I to escape the soldiers with my wife?"

"Even if I help you slip past them, where will you flee?"

"To the mountains until all the army has left our land."

"That won't be before spring. The Colonel intends to round up captives wintering with Shawnee families in hunting camps. Is Charity strong enough for the journey you propose?"

"Red Bird is weak from injury and ill with my child."

"Eyes of the Wolf says I carry a son," Charity told him.

Mister Ramsey touched her cheek. "I'm delighted to think of having a grandson, and yet..." Gravity dimmed the anticipation in his face. "You

305

put her at great risk, Kitate. A wintry trek into the mountains may further weaken her."

He wanted to pound the stone. "What am I to do? I will not let the soldiers take her."

His father said calmly, "Return with me. Both of you."

Wicomechee's mouth fell open. "Are you mad? I am not to flee from the English, but go to them?"

"Allow me to explain—"

Wicomechee shook his head. No explanation was possible.

His father gripped his shoulders, making far more of an impression than Charity had. "Do you wish for my fate, Kitate? A son without his mother. Unspeakable grief."

He flinched. "I prefer death to losing Red Bird."

"So did I. But like me you are strong. Death does not come for the wishing."

"Mechee, come what may, give me your word you will care for our son. Never leave this child," Charity entreated.

Her plea seared him, and anguish welled in his father's eyes. Steeling himself, he said, "Tell me your plan, *Notha*."

"Thank God. The aid I offer doesn't lie in the kind of escape you long for, but I can do much to help you. Journey with me to my estate and remain as long as you need. I can gain any necessary permission from Colonel Bouquet."

Wicomechee couldn't believe his ears. "Do I hear rightly? You would take a warrior to the English?"

"Are you not my blood and half English? I will take you under my protection."

"You can assure this?"

His father's eyes glinted dangerously. "Just let any man dare to threaten my son. He will swiftly come to regret it."

Wicomechee answered with a fleeting smile.

"Still, you are a warrior, *Notha*."

"Always. Give us some precious time together, Kitate. We've been robbed of so much. Learn of this other world while your sweet wife grows strong."

Hope warmed Charity's eyes like the sun's bright rays. "You wish for this?" Wicomechee asked her.

"Yes. He offers us refuge. I must still undertake a journey but not such an arduous one—"

"Not nearly," his father broke in eagerly. "We will go by horseback until the roads improve. At that point I'll hire a coach for Charity. I am a wealthy man, Kitate. She will lack for nothing and have the best of care."

He felt as if he were being sucked down into a black pit. "Yet to leave my people—even for a time." His voice broke.

"You will learn much and might even discover some aspects of English life to your liking," his father reasoned.

Pain beyond description engulfed him. "I am not English. Would you make me so?"

Charity grasped his hand. "Don't despair, Mechee. It's only for awhile."

They both waited, eyes pleading, for some concession from him. But Wicomechee's agony remained and he could not speak.

An expression of sad weariness lined his father's face. "Will you allow me to take Charity to preserve her life?"

The request gnawed at Wicomechee like ravenous rats, but he gave a nod.

Charity shuddered in his arms. "Please, sir. I can't go without Mechee."

He patted her shoulder. "It will be all right, Charity. I will care for you like my own daughter, and smuggle you back to him when conditions are safe."

"That will not be for months. I couldn't bear to be without him for so long."

Wicomechee steeled himself as if to the worst torture. "The time will pass. *Notha* will return you to me."

Charity was like a wildly flapping bird. "No. If you do not come your father will bury me after I birth your son."

His resolve crumbled and he crushed her to him. "Do not speak this. How can I go to the English? Ask anything else."

"Don't you see? My life is in your hands just as Eyes of The Wolf said. 'Tis the test."

Air escaped Wicomechee as though he'd been forcefully struck and he reeled in realization.

"What is she speaking of, Kitate?" his father pressed.

"To keep Red Bird's life, I must be tested. Not by an enemy I can fight, but something I must do."

"Then for God's sake do it, or you'll suffer as I have."

"I see the terms now, Notha. *Nimesoomtha* said I would find them harsh. I must also go with you."

Charity wept against him. "Thank you, Mechee."

"Enough tears, Red Bird. For you, I will do anything."

Chapter Twenty-Three

"There is another who needs your aid, *Notha*. One called Waupee."

Wicomechee's words broke through the unreality enveloping Charity. "Oh yes. And my cousin Emma."

"Emma would be the young beauty I glimpsed in the *wickon* of Eyes of the Wolf?" Mister Ramsey asked.

Charity nodded excitedly. "She would."

"Fortunately my escorts haven't seen her yet. I assume Waupee is Kitate's adopted brother? Eyes of the Wolf spoke of this captive."

Wicomechee was earnest. "We also are blood brothers."

"Colin, I mean Waupee, is like a brother to me too," Charity confided.

"Colin?" Mister Ramsey echoed. "What is his full name?"

She weighed his response as she replied, "Colin Dickson."

"Good Lord. Who would have thought he'd end up here?" Mister Ramsey mused, speaking as much to himself as to them. He rubbed his clean-shaven chin with long fingers, similar to his son's. "Life is indeed strange."

Wicomechee observed his father's every movement. "Do you know of him?"

"I very well may."

"Will you not say?"

"Patience, Kitate. First, I must meet this renegade. Where is Waupee now?"

"With *Nimesoomtha*, or the horses. Unless the

soldiers have taken him," Wicomechee added gravely.

"Not when I was with them. We had better go and see. I suspect this fellow is the sort to kick up quite a fight."

"I also, *Notha.* They cannot take him. The English seek his life."

Hugh Ramsey grasped his son's arm. "No more talk of fighting. We will find some other way."

Charity fervently prayed so. "Can you aid him?"

"If this young man is who I suspect he is, I can be of considerable help."

"Colin's in a great deal of trouble, sir."

Mister Ramsey received this information without surprise. "I'm acquainted with his difficulties, up to a point, anyway."

Wicomechee stared slack-jawed, and Charity wasn't certain of the man's sanity. "How is that possible?"

"You will learn soon enough."

Though normally adept at concealing his emotions, Wicomechee looked as stunned as she felt.

His father leapt down from the stone and beckoned to him. "Don't just sit there gawping, Kitate. Let's go find this wild brother of yours." He smiled reassuringly and held out his arms to Charity. "Let me help you down, my dear."

She swiftly found herself on her feet. "Thank you, sir."

"Sir sounds too formal. You can hardly call me Hugh, and Mister Ramsey is little better than sir. How about Papa?"

She brightened. "I've needed a father."

"I'd be delighted to stand in." He pulled her arm through his. "You will allow me to escort your fair wife?"

Wicomechee gave a nod and slipped his musket over his shoulder. He walked behind them as his father strode through the trees with her by his side. The sun shone overhead in a blue sky. The day that had seemed so black was lit with hope.

"Fine weather for late fall," Mister Ramsey said.

"Yes," she agreed, but her surroundings held little clarity. She almost expected to wake any moment and find herself back on the trail.

"Your hair is lovely in the light, Charity. So pretty, flowing to your waist."

"Outhowwa didn't think so."

Her escort smiled wryly. "No, he wouldn't."

"Mechee saved me from his anger."

"Unleashed it on you, did he? I'm sorry." His father reached behind him and pulled Wicomechee up beside them. "I know I left a great deal unfinished and my coming is a great shock. But I'm overjoyed to have found you both and promise to smooth your way, beginning with these soldiers."

Charity counted fifteen men in a clearing outside the village. Some groomed horses, others sat near a campfire playing at cards. One stirred the contents of a pot hung over the flames. Thankfully, she saw no trace of Colin among them.

Wicomechee fingered his musket. "I am used to firing on soldiers. I think I can fell two before they return fire."

"No doubt." His father pointed at a broad oak. "And if you take cover behind that tree, you could pick off another, maybe more. I've heard of your skills, Kitate. However, your chiefs have requested terms of peace. Firing at these men will not further that aim. You must begin to see the English as something other than your enemy."

"This is difficult. We have warred for years."

"Yet your wife, and father, and brother are all English."

Wicomechee considered, though in a slightly dour way. "I will have thought for your words,

Notha."

Captain Dawson looked up at their approach and hastened to them. Evidently anxious to make amends, he nodded politely and waited for Hugh Ramsey to speak. "My son and his wife will accompany us to Fort Pitt, Captain. After conferring briefly with Colonel Bouquet, we will continue to my estate."

The young officer glanced at Wicomechee in marked surprise. Likely he expected the warrior would refuse, at the very least. "I'm pleased you have found them so agreeable. When do you wish to proceed, sir?"

"On the morrow. Not too early. This sweet lady is easily wearied and I will not have her overtired."

Captain Dawson's eyes lingered on Charity. "We have nothing pressing us save the weather. The colonel's orders, apart from accompanying you, are to return all captives."

"My son has informed me of several more lodging with his grandfather. I will explain matters to them, but anticipate no resistance in meeting the colonel's demands."

"Again, I am pleased by these tidings." The captain singled out one man in the assembly. "Chief Outhowwa has relinquished a Rob Buchanan, who tells us few captives remain in this village. Most have departed for the Fort."

So, Rob hadn't given them away. Charity spotted him among the soldiers wearing frontiersman garb, and looking more relaxed than she'd seen him in ages. She waved at him. "Rob!"

He sprang up and hastened to where they stood, his questioning gaze passing between Charity and her companions.

Wicomechee gave a short nod and made gruff introduction "My father, Hugh Ramsey."

Rob gaped at the Englishman.

"*Notha*, this is Rob Buchanan, a man who very much wishes to have my wife."

His father smiled at his bluntness. "As will others, Kitate, but the lady is spoken for," he said pointedly.

The color heightened Captain Dawson's cheeks and he slanted his gaze away from Charity.

"I am pleased to make your acquaintance, Mister Buchanan," Hugh Ramsey continued. "No doubt we shall see more of each other on our journey to the Fort. Now if you will excuse us, we must be on our way." With a slight bow, he turned and drew Charity away with him.

She glanced back over her shoulder. "Mechee and I are going to stay with his father!"

Rob still hadn't uttered a word.

****

Cheerful voices called to the adopted Englishman as Hugh Ramsey lingered outside the *wickon*. Charity ducked under the buffalo hide and followed Wicomechee inside. Colin looked up from the small group clustered around Eyes of the Wolf, his expression bleak.

"I hear your father's come, *NiSawsawh*. And a detachment of soldiers."

Wicomechee slid in to sit beside him. "*Notha* is the one *Nimesoomtha* said would aid us. He wishes to take Red Bird and me to stay with him, for a time."

The incredulity in Colin's expression lessened his gloom. "Is the man insane?"

"I thought so." Wicomechee caught Charity's hand and pulled her down into his lap. "*Notha* insists he can do this."

"Wait until you meet Mechee's Papa, big brother. You will like him."

"I've always had a fondness for eccentrics. Ah well, at least we can all be together for my hanging."

313

"Oh, Colin—don't speak so." Lips quivering, Emma buried her face in her hands.

"What's a hanging?" Lily asked, trying to shove James from Colin's lap.

The little boy pushed her down onto the bear skin. "It's when they tie a rope around your neck and—"

"Never mind," Colin said. "And stop that tussling." He dodged the children and circled his arm around Emma. "Sorry, darling. I shouldn't have been so blunt."

Wicomechee lifted his hand to her back. "Do not fear so. *Notha* will aid us, also you."

Eyes of the Wolf asked, "Did I not tell you this?"

"Yes," Colin agreed, "but I'm wanted for murder."

"Mechee's father knows all about you," Charity said.

"How on earth—" Colin began, breaking off as the flap lifted and Hugh Ramsey entered, bringing a sense of vitality into the somber gathering.

Eyes of the Wolf rose. "Welcome, *Niquithe*, my son. Remove your hat and coat. Sit with us. These wait for you."

Colin was too encumbered by the children to rise, but he appraised the newcomer. "I'm told you know of me, sir?"

Hugh Ramsey returned Colin's close regard. "Your name, certainly. I find it highly unlikely another would bear the same. And I see before me the very image of my father in his youth. His portrait hangs in my hall."

Charity had never seen Colin at such a loss for words.

"He was also your mother's father," Mister Ramsey said. "My dear sister, Sara."

Comprehension flashed in Colin's widened gaze. "Uncle Hugh?"

"The same."

"Good God. Emma, he's the uncle I tried to reach." Putting James and Lily aside, Colin got to his feet. "I don't believe it. How in the world—"

His uncle caught him in a hearty embrace and choked off his outpouring. He pounded Colin's back, and then held him at arms length for another look. "I'd give you a scolding if I wasn't so relieved. I've heard a bit about your doings, and gather you've all been through a great deal together."

"That we have, Uncle, and you shall hear our adventures in time. But first, you must meet my darling Emma."

"Gladly." Mister Ramsey motioned for Emma to remain as she was. "Please, don't get up, dear lady."

Colin rejoined her and patted the space beside him. "Come sit between son and nephew."

An even more incredible relationship occurred to Charity. "Good heavens. That makes you cousins."

Colin clapped Wicomechee on the back. "I always felt there was more between us."

Wicomechee thumped him in return. "We are much alike."

"You both have quite a temper," Charity said.

"They came by that honestly." Hugh Ramsey hung his coat from a pole. The tailored cloth made a marked contrast with the buckskins. His expensive hat followed. "I haven't always been known for my cool head. Temper runs in the family." He settled between the young men.

"You have need of a cool head now. Many lives depend on you," Eyes of the Wolf reminded him.

"I know, *Notha*, and am deeply grateful for the second chance I've been given."

"You will do well, *Niquithe*."

"After all this time, you still believe in me?"

"I knew you would return." He swept his hand at the circle. "Your place at the fire has been waiting for you."

"So it has. As long as I have breath I will come. If only Netathwe could have known."

"She has peace now."

Hugh Ramsey embraced the older warrior. "I hope so."

"She loved you to the end, *Notha*. She said."

He swiveled his head at his son. "You were with her?"

"She spoke your name in my ear. Her final words."

"You never told me this," Eyes of the Wolf chided him.

"I could not."

His father's moist gaze met Wicomechee's. "Thank you for telling me. I never stopped loving her or you. I can't undo the past, but by heaven I shall deal with the present."

Wiping at his eyes, he turned his attention to Colin. "You've collected quite a family, I see." He touched Emma's cheek. "And you, dear lady, have my sympathy for all you've been forced to endure. Despite everything, I perceive that you are also devoted to my nephew?"

"I am."

"Then I will lay no fault upon him." Hugh Ramsey smiled. "Are all of these accompanying us to my estate?"

Colin held up his hand. "Wait, am I?"

"Of course."

"But how? I'm told you know of my circumstances?"

"I do. Your father wrote me at length."

"I also wrote to you, Uncle."

"I never received that letter."

"I'll wager I know who did."

A gleam lit Hugh Ramsey's eyes. "Oliver Montgomery. He will trouble you no more. There's nothing like pointing your sword at a man's gullet to gain his cooperation."

"You called that dandy out?"

"He chose swords. I'm even deadlier with pistols."

Wicomechee grinned. "*Notha* defended you well, *NiSawsawh*."

"So it would seem. What of Oliver's vindictive brother? Did you sail to London and deal with Lord Montgomery?"

"No need. It seems he had similar inclinations as his vile son. An outraged husband put an end to him."

"I'm delighted to hear there's some justice in this world, but what of the charges?" Colin pressed.

"With Lord Montgomery dead and buried, one of the seconds at your duel came forward and cleared your name."

"So, I'm a free man?"

"If we keep your part in the battle of Bushy Run to ourselves. And one or two other matters."

Emma clapped a hand to her mouth and burst into tears. "Thank you, Uncle," Colin said huskily. "I expect we'll have to watch our backs. Oliver will attempt to get even."

"He's rather humiliated for that just now, finding the air in France more to his liking at present."

"Big on dueling, the French. Perhaps he will annoy someone less forgiving than you."

"I preferred to let him live with his embarrassment. Your father will be overjoyed to hear of your recovery."

"Poor man. How is my sister Rachel?"

"Happily wed. The couple resides on his estate. You best not tell them how you came by your wife when you write."

"Speaking of wives, why did the family never

learn of yours? I knew you'd spent time in the frontier, but had no idea you could be the Englishman Eyes of the Wolf spoke of."

"My father insisted I keep this secret. But he's gone now. I'm not ashamed I had a Shawnee wife. Netathwe was all that is good." He clasped Wicomechee's arm. "And I'm so proud of you, Kitate. It is high time word went out."

****

Charity sat with her new father by the fire. How different this humble lodge must be from the elegant house on his estate. "Do you have Christmas parties, Papa?"

He took her fingers in his. "Yes, lovely affairs."

"I think I visited your house in a dream. People were feasting and dancing. Mechee was there."

"So he shall be. And I promise you we shall have dancing. Caroline adores it."

Wicomechee bent down and poked up the fire with a stick. "Your wife?"

"Yes. I married again, years after Netathwe died. Caroline's a gracious woman. I told her about your mother, Kitate, and you. She knows I'm here."

"Has this woman given you children, *Notha*?"

He shook his head. "A great disappointment to us both."

Charity squeezed his hand. "Your family has swelled overnight. Will your wife mind you returning with so many?"

"Caroline will adore having more people about the house. I'm so often out traveling the estate. She grows lonely."

Emma tucked Mary Elizabeth into her basket. "I'm accustomed to Colin making a fuss over horses."

"Good. I've many mounts for him to tend to."

"He will need the distraction, Uncle. Colin will find it very difficult to leave these people."

"Who knows better than I what he faces? Still,

he has you and the children, and the company of his brother."

Emma sat beside Hugh Ramsey. "I hope 'tis enough."

"When he lies in bed at night with you beside him, he will be content, as will you, Kitate."

Wicomechee knelt and wrapped his arms around Charity. "Always then I will be content, and never would I be if she lay in the arms of another." His mouth tightened in the manner Charity knew well. "I do not like the way this captain looks at her, *Notha*. It is good I am coming with you."

"I hope you aren't going to attack him."

"Mechee, you must behave on this journey," Charity said.

"And at my home," his father added. "I can't have you starting a war with the neighbors."

"If your son doesn't, your nephew may," Emma warned.

"I shall have my hands full, I see."

Wicomechee shrugged. "Your neighbors would do well not to provoke us."

"I shall certainly caution them, though it's likely to give old lady Patterson a start."

"We will not challenge her, *Notha*," he smiled.

"I am relieved to hear it. That's one less for me to trouble with."

Charity wasn't convinced. "Promise me you will be on your very best behavior, Mechee."

"I will promise only my love." He stood, pulling her up with him. "You have rested. We will seek my brother. You wish to come, *Notha*?"

He nodded at Emma and Lily. "Thank you, no. I will remain with these fair ladies."

"As you like." He took Charity's hand, and ushered her from the snug room and out past rows of bark covered lodges.

"Not so fast," she pleaded.

He slowed. "Forgive me. I forgot."

"Someday I will race you again."

"Like the deer," he said.

The sun was an orange ball slipping behind the trees. "I can't believe we've been here so short a time. I hate to go."

"You did not wish to come."

"Maybe it will be the same for you at your father's."

He shook his head. "I am Shawnee. Never will I forget. This is where I belong."

"We will return, Mechee."

"I fear you will become accustomed to English life and wish to stay."

"I will go where my husband takes me."

"In the planting moon, we will return here."

"I shall be swollen with child by then, *Wyshetche*."

He smiled through the pain in his eyes. "I will find a big horse to carry you."

They walked on through the blue twilight and saw Colin in the grassy enclosure with the horses. James was perched on Stuart's back, while he rubbed the gelding down. He waved as they approached. Dusk didn't fully conceal his troubled eyes.

"I'm nearly finished here. I've bid farewell to Muga and Posetha, even Outhowwa. I never thought I'd be doing that."

James was glum. "I wanted to be a warrior."

"So did I, lad."

"If I can't be one, I want to live with you, Uncle Papa."

Colin lifted the little boy from Stuart and hugged him before standing him on the ground. "We've been all through this, James. You can visit us, but your mama needs you."

"Mama don't let me have no fun."

"She's staying with your Uncle Robin now. You like him," Charity coaxed.

"I like Uncle Papa and Wicomechee better. It's not fair Lily gets to live with them and the new grandfather."

"Leaving here won't be easy for any of us. Wait until you discover the joy of breeches, *NiSawsawh*," Colin said.

Charity slipped her fingers under Stuart's mane to warm them. "It can't be all that bad."

"One gets used to it, as you will to corsets."

"Not those. I hated stays."

"All proper ladies wear them, little sister."

"I don't know the first thing about being a proper lady."

A smile lightened Wicomechee's expression. He leaned against the docile horse. "Wear what you like. I shall."

"Oh, no," Colin said. "Your father's not going to allow us to go about dressed as we are now. Charity will have to put Netathwe's creation aside and you must adjust to breeches. I refuse to touch a wig. Riding boots aren't bad, though."

"Perhaps I could abide boots." Wicomechee's tone held little joy at the prospect.

"Boots would be fine," James offered.

Wicomechee tousled his hair. "You shall have a pair."

Stars appeared overhead and the night air grew chill. "We should return to the *wickon*," Colin said, but neither man made a move. Sensing their desire to linger, Charity snuggled against Wicomechee as bright stars filled the cold night.

Eyes of the Wolf appeared in the blackness with the stealth of the animal he was named for. He stood with them, gazing up into the sky. "Tomorrow you go from me."

Colin sighed. "As you knew we would."

"My heart is heavy to see you go, yet you must."

"This is much to bear, *Nimesoomtha*," Wicomechee said.

"Yet, you must learn of English ways. These people will only increase in our land. To better understand them is useful for you and your people when you return."

"For Red Bird, for you, I will do this."

"Good. Is there fear also in you, Waupee?"

"Now that the time has come, I am almost afraid to return to that life," Colin admitted.

"Hold fast to the courage I saw in your eyes the day I took you captive. Remember your Shawnee brothers."

"I swear to you, before God, my hand will never be lifted against my brothers if our people war again."

"I am glad you speak this, for they will. *Ouishi catoui*. Be strong."

Author's Note

Wicomechee, the hero in *RED BIRD'S SONG*, was a Shawnee warrior who lived early in the nineteenth century. The Moffetts, an early Valley family to whom I'm related, include a reference to him in their genealogy. His father, John Moffett, was captured by the Shawnee at the age of eight and adopted into the tribe. It is said that John was a boyhood companion to the great chief Tecumseh. Forced to return to his English family as the result of Wayne's treaty (1794), John, then a young man, ran back to the Indians and wed a Shawnee woman. For years he tried to live in two worlds, eventually opting for the white one.

Sometime after John Moffett's removal from the tribe, a Moffett niece stopped at a trading post along the Mississippi and was eagerly examined by an elderly Shawnee woman who exclaimed, "Moffett, Moffett, you are Moffett!"

It seems she recognized the family resemblance, still evident in the Moffetts to this day. A conversation was struck between both women. John Moffett's abandoned Shawnee wife related her bereavement at his leaving, and the name of her son, Wicomechee, which means, 'his father left him.'

Historian Joseph A. Waddell records this account in *The Annals of Augusta County*. The attack at the opening of *RED BIRD'S SONG* is also based on an attack that occurred to my Shenandoah Valley ancestors and is recorded by Waddell.

Historian Waddell also notes that during the Black Hawk Wars Wicomechee recovered the captive daughters of a Dr. Hull and brought them safely into camp, which reminds me of Hawkeye in ***The Last of the Mohicans***.

A few words from the author...

I am a member of RWA®, Virginia Romance Writers, For The Heart Romance Writers, and Celtic Hearts Romance Writers. My work has finaled in a number of chapter contests, including the 2007 Golden Pen. I am also a 2008 Golden Heart Finalist in the Historical Category.

I am married to my high school sweetheart and live on a farm in the heart of the Shenandoah Valley of Virginia with children and multiple animals. The beauty of the valley is an inspiration, as are my roots, which go well back into Virginia's history.

My fascination with the colonial frontier and the Shawnee Indians is an early and abiding one. My English and Scot-Irish ancestors had interactions with this tribe, including family members taken captive. Intrigued with all things Celtic, much of my writing features the Scot-Irish who settled the valley and spread into the mountains and the Carolinas. This absorption with early America also extends to the high drama of the Revolution and ancestors who fought and loved on both sides of that sweeping conflict.

Moreover, I am ever intrigued by ghost stories, and Virginia has more tales than any other state. I find myself asking if the folk who've gone before us are truly gone, or do some still have unfinished business in this realm? And what of the young lovers whose time was tragically cut short, do they somehow find a way? Love conquers all, so I answer 'yes.'

Visit Beth at www.bethtrissel.com